I0772381

SERVANT
OF THE
LOST POWER

Published by Winterset Books
www.kaykenyon.com
Hardcover ISBN: 9798988401117

Published in the United States of America

Cover by Deranged Doctor Design

Visit www.kaykenyon.com and join the author's newsletter for a free short story and find out about new releases and reader perks.

Don't miss the first two books in this series, *The Girl Who Fell Into Myth* and *Stranger in the Twisted Realm,* available in print and ebook at most online booksellers.

Also by Kay Kenyon

Watch for book four, *Keeper of the Mythos Gate*, the conclusion of
The Arisen Worlds quartet: *The dark machines are on
the march. In their path, a lone girl awaits.*

Fantasy Novels

THE ARISEN WORLDS QUARTET

The Girl Who Fell Into Myth, Book 1

Stranger in the Twisted Realm, Book 2

Servant of the Lost Power, Book 3

STAND ALONE FANTASY

A Thousand Perfect Things

Queen of the Deep

THE DARK TALENTS TRILOGY

At the Table of Wolves, Book 1

Serpent in the Heather, Book 2

Nest of the Monarch, Book 3

Science Fiction Novels

The Seeds of Time

Tropic of Creation

Rift

Maximum Ice

The Braided World

THE ENTIRE AND THE ROSE QUARTET

Bright of the Sky, Book 1

A World Too Near, Book 2

City Without End, Book 3

Prince of Storms, Book 4

Collections

Dystopia: Seven Dark and Hopeful Tales

Worlds Near and Far

SERVANT OF THE LOST POWER

BOOK THREE OF THE ARISEN WORLDS

KAY KENYON

WINTERSET BOOKS

The Nine Powers

Foreknowing
Manifesting
Creatures
Warding
Healing
Verdure
Aligns
Elements
Primal Roots

PART I
THE SORCERER'S CAGE

Chapter One

Her carriage thundered down a road in the endless forest. Black and dripping, the trees on either side formed a long tunnel, where occasionally a branch thrust out like an arm as though trying to escape the cage of the woods.

Nashavety was leaving Drogeliv, that half-mad house that had sheltered her for the past three months as she recovered her powers. She would miss the old mansion that had welcomed her in her infirmity, took inspiration from her transformation, and became her dark companion.

But Drogeliv had always been a temporary refuge. Now she headed to the Volkish capital of Hapsigen where she would at last receive her due. Prince Albrecht himself would sweep down from the grand steps and welcome her to Rothsvund Palace.

He had better.

Sofiyana, she thought. *Wake up, my darling. Things are about to change. All that I promised you is about to happen.*

The girl had done well. Though young and undisciplined, with unfortunate, disheveled hair that sprang into ringlets at the slightest excuse, she had ingratiated herself into the ranks of power. She stood as Raven Fell Hall's *fajatim*, one of the five leaders who could appoint or dismiss the head of the realm. No doubt this had Princip Anastyna twisting in her bedsheets at night, sweating from her lovely pores at the thought of when the *fajatim* would depose her. *Not yet, Sofiyana. Not yet, you restless, grasping child. You do* nothing *without my command.*

The coach swayed heavily as the driver drove the team of horses into a curve. The boxes and trunks tied to the roof made the carriage tip precariously at high speed. She hoped that the cage perched on top was securely roped in place.

A whiff of mold threaded into her nostrils. Only three hours on the forest road and already a blackish fur was growing upon the coach windowsill nearest her. Some of her powers had an unpleasant aspect. Mold sprouting near her, loss of weight, strands of hair darting like snakes. It was worth it.

Somehow, whether she wore a glove on her maimed left hand or not, flecks of mildew marked everything she touched. Power resided in the small finger of the left hand. It was why Nashavety had been forced to cut it off. What Princip Anastyna did not understand was that it could grow back. If somewhat unnaturally. The mold, after all. What had things come to? Once she had been a loyal *fajatim* to the old princip, Lisbetha. She had held the respect of Osta Kiya. Then Anastyna was princip, and the woman wished for the realm to *open*. Accepting foreigners, and everything that implied. She gazed at her gloved left hand. *You see what you have wrought, Anastyna.*

Nashavety reached into the basket at her side and removed a small mirror framed in human bone. A parting gift from Drogeliv. The glass, badly cracked, but Drogeliv meant well. And she would not have wanted an intact mirror. Numinasi did not hold with mirrors. But this cracked one, it had proved useful. Through it, she could reach out to the amber ring. Useful indeed.

Now, fresh challenges. Today she would enter a place with military hierarchies and naive ambitions, where she must take charge of things. Prince Albrecht needed her close guidance and strength.

He had lost much in his confrontation with the mundat, the girl of Earth. In the crossings as he pursued her, she had knifed him in the groin. He had held her by the neck, but she sank to her knees. He pulled her up, and as she rose, she had a blade in her hand, and it did its wicked job. Who would have thought the creature had so much venom in her! And then, how could his arm have been stuck in the very walls? How could the fabric of the crossings imprison him like some bog sucking an unwary animal into its depths? Had the girl of the mundat acquired, in her renegade way, a new power, a second one— likely elemental power—that had come to her only lately or that she had made bold to use only in her desperate struggle with Albrecht?

He survived the blood loss, but he would never lie with a woman again. He was understandably bitter about this. Maddened with revenge might be a better description. But he had lived, that was the main thing, or all her plans might have faltered.

She brought her concentration to the Raven Fell *fajatim*. Sofiyana received her orders through the amber ring. It had always been a rather good ring, and with the help of the bone mirror, it was now half of the conduit between the two of them.

Holding the bone mirror, she began to conjure her minion at Osta Kiya.

But as she sank into her power, a guttural moan issued from the baggage atop the coach.

Silence! Nashavety wordlessly commanded. In answer, the moan rose into a howl. Well, it was awake. She took that for a sign that now was not a good time for a chat with Ringlets.

She rested her head against the back of the bench seat. Sleep called to her, nudged on by the gloaming dark of the road tunneling through the tall, ancient trees. She could not tell the hour, for though Volkia used clocks, she still could not bear to be near timepieces. As she rested, she contemplated her growing strength. Her recovery had been long, but at last she could walk unaided, and her headaches had merci- fully vanished. The dark arts had taken their toll on her frame and her appetite, but she had fought her way to renewed life. Anastyna had banished her from Numinat at Yevliesza's bidding, but Nashavety was stronger than ever, and ready to destroy Yevliesza and her ilk: Anastyna, Valenty, Rusadka, and Valenty's henchman, Urik. Even underlings would not escape her special rituals. The boy, too, whatever his name was. And the insufferable *satvars* who had taken Yevliesza in. She would see them suffer. With that pleasant thought, she allowed herself to sleep.

She awoke when the carriage came to a halt. The coachman knew better than to stop in the middle of Breminger Forest. Who knew what beasts might lurk here? Men's voices mixed with the stomping of horses, and when she craned her neck out the coach window, she saw that a unit of soldiers had arrived. Among them, Prince Albrecht, swinging stiffly off an enormous horse, a movement that probably caused him considerable pain.

"Lady Nashavety," he said, when he greeted her at the coach window. "May I join you for the approach to Hapsigen?"

"Ah, my prince. With pleasure."

His men on horseback arrayed themselves around the carriage. When Albrecht hoisted himself inside and took the seat opposite her, he tapped the coach roof with his cane, and the group got underway. Already he was taking control, of course he was. He was born to the role, and thought he still had all its prerogatives.

"How do you fare?" Nashavety asked as he placed his cane on the floor.

"Well enough." His direct look made clear it was all he would say.

As the forest thinned, peasant hovels appeared here and there with sodden fields keeping the forest at bay. The woods held on in patches, now more frequently giving way to small holdings coming awake in the tardy spring thaw.

"I am glad to see you looking so well," Albrecht said.

Nashavety allowed herself a flattered smile. She was thin as a fence post, with outsized nose and mouth crowded into the wedge of her face, and with locks of hair that tended to escape her bun and snap as though upset. But what else could Albrecht say? The less attention to her physical presentation, the better. Her long black dress with its wide skirt and close bodice hid many faults. Her style of dress was the only thing she brought with her from Numinat, the realm that betrayed her long service but was still her beloved land.

"I have been eager to join you in Hapsigen, my lord. It is time for me to relinquish the woods and walk free."

He had no answer to that. By his expression as he gazed at her, he was perhaps reconsidering whether he wanted her to leave the woods.

He should have thought of that before he sent her the coach.

"Madam, I must apologize for my troops' failure to capture the man who defiled your household. When we take Numinat, he will have a suitable punishment."

Valenty. He had evaded the Volkish manhunt. The boy he came to rescue was home safe now, a victory she could scarcely abide. Ah yes, Pyvel, they called him. Yevliesza's minion. "The man invaded my house and killed two of my guards. A dishonor to Volkia. And to me."

"Patience, madam. Soon, he will have cause to wish we had hanged him."

As the carriage and its escort thundered down the road, Albrecht revealed his plans for the annexing of Numinat. The snow was gone, or almost. Troops had been forming at Rorrs Gate and of course Volkia commanded the crossings. It was time to invade through Lowgate, destroy the garrison, and push on to Osta Kiya. Their machines could smash through every defense, and into the breach would come the Volkish thousands.

After Osta Kiya, the next conquest would be Zolvina, where Yevliesza was known to be hiding; it had been *satvars* who brazenly effected her escape, and their *satvary* where she took refuge.

He informed her of all this as though she was an officer under his command, and she tolerated it, for it was to her purpose to know his thoughts and mood. As he spoke, he became more affable and voluble, a man at ease in his domain.

Nashavety stored away the information of troop numbers and stockpiles of the enlivened implements of war which she must direct to their best use. Through Albrecht. She had no need for the credit. Just the power. Volkia would take Numinat, yes. But only to remake its leadership and bring it back to Numinasi traditions. It had become weak and dilute, straying from its fierce origins and ways. Nashavety would never be Volkish. But she would use their strength to save Numinat from itself.

They entered the city, the largest habitation she had ever seen. It was a proud capital, vast and impressive and under obvious control. She approved of it at once, even the orange haze hanging over the city from the forges. She was done with hiding in the forest. Here, her mind could expand, her heart find nourishment.

As they debarked from their conveyance in the palace courtyard, Albrecht ordered his men to gently lower the cage from its perch on the coach roof. The soldiers draped blankets over the cage for secrecy. Although now the occupant had seen Hapsigen, the city streets and its inhabitants. That might have been a mistake.

As the men unfastened the ropes and struggled to bring down the cage, a deep groaning came from inside.

"Take it to the underway," Nashavety snapped at the soldiers. "Its place is prepared?"

Albrecht hastened to answer. "As you wished, lady."

Having wrestled the cage to the ground, several soldiers made off with it, looking worried that their burden might escape.

In the growing dusk, a few palace windows lit up. Nashavety looked up at the frontage wall, comparing its smaller size with the great Osta Kiya. It almost made her homesick.

"Albrecht," she said. "I enjoyed our conversation in the coach. It is pleasing to me that you have drawn up such thorough plans for taking Osta Kiya."

His eyes narrowed, as though waiting for her to add an unwelcome suggestion.

She would oblige him. "We will take Numinat, of course, that is beyond doubt. But—I must insist—not yet. Osta Kiya, where I lived most of my life, is far too strong." He took in a breath to put her in her place, but she rushed to finish. "I have a better plan."

His face turned stony, his blue-eyed gaze signaling quiet outrage. The dear boy. "I have a different invasion in mind, my prince. And I believe you will approve it. In fact, I think you will take the greatest pleasure in my idea." She was in Hapsigen now. Time for him to understand how things were going to be.

In his displeasure, he sent a jab of creature power at her. He enjoyed the same affinity that she did, creature power, but he was not a noble practitioner. When she deflected this with ease, she saw his flicker of surprise. And fear.

"Albrecht, my prince," she said to reassure him. "Together we are stronger than any who have come before us. You will rise in power, and quickly."

For a time. And then it would be her turn.

Chapter Two

The sun warmed Yevliesza's back as she carried another heavy stone to the garden wall. The ground was still frozen, though the snow had receded in this corner of the *satvary*.

She had been working all afternoon on the wall repair when Dreiza came with a slice of warm, buttered bread and urged her to rest.

Dreiza glanced at the narrow flagstone path marking—for those without align power— where they traveled across the courtyard and through the garden wall. "Why not use the align to carry rocks? It would ease the task."

Sweating from her labors, Yevliesza had cast off her cloak. "I have to get strong." She would need to be when she figured out what came next. The next thing with the new power that had come to her, that might save the Mythos from the nightmare that awaited.

It had been six weeks since she came to the Zolvina *satvary*. She still thought in weeks, even after so long in Numinat. A habit, or a holding on to the old ways. At the *satvary* she was too idle, without any duties, urged to rest by too many. The *satvars* treated her as though she needed healing when what she really needed was something to do.

She thanked Dreiza for the bread and took a bite of the fragrant slice, hungrier than she had realized. Dreiza, despite everything, was unfailingly kind.

Her friend handed her a napkin for her greasy fingers.

"Please don't wait on me like this," Yevliesza said. "You must have other things to do."

"It seems I cannot help myself. And the Devi Ilsat asked me to come."

The High Mother often employed Dreiza as an intermediary, since Yevliesza's good opinion of the elder *satvar* had lasted only a few days after she had first arrived. After she learned how her new power had come to her, the power over the crossings.

The High Mother had admitted that she had arranged for it. She and her inner circle, the *satvadeya.* They had implored the First Ones to bestow root power on someone who could be objective, beholden to no monarch or narrow loyalty. So that the Mythos realms might be spared from the poisons of dark machines. Machines now in the hands of the Volkish.

Against all odds, the power came into *her.*

Now Dreiza was a member of that inner circle, but she hadn't been when the . . . interference had taken place. So, a friend, a supporter. But one who also served the Devi Ilsat.

"I came to tell you something," Dreiza said. "If you will come with me."

Yevliesza shoved the bread in her pocket and picked up another of the fallen stones, a heavy one that taxed both her arms and her thighs.

"Leave the rocks for now?"

Lugging the stone over to the wall, Yevliesza adjusted its position, finally getting it securely wedged in. She was enjoying repairing the stone wall. Getting the rocks in the exact right place was an entirely satisfying job.

Finished with placing the stone, she went with Dreiza.

From the roof of the domicile, she and Dreiza looked over the compound with its courtyard and numin pool and, beyond, the fallow planting field and the greenshed and several out-buildings housing their tools and supplies. A high stone wall surrounded the courtyard, and on its walkway all through the early spring Yevliesza had paced, grateful for a place to gather herself and face her future. But it was only physical work that brought her peace.

Dreiza turned to face the valley where the hillsides were beginning to thaw, creating streams that cut crevasses into the snow. At night the snow acquired a skin of ice and, on sunny days like this, the valley shone with a cold fire.

"We have a gifted manifester," Dreiza said, still gazing outward. "She took a hike into those hills in one of her guises and discovered something interesting."

Yevliesza joined her at the perimeter half wall.

"We are being watched." Her gaze was fixed on a saddle of rock. "Seven men have set up camp behind that ridge."

Yevliesza squinted at the jagged ridge. "Maybe they're travelers pausing on their journey?"

"After four days they would have moved on." She turned to Yevliesza. "Therefore, the High Mother sent Dyura out to investigate."

She and Yevliesza shared a look. Then, Dreiza said what they both knew: "If they meant well, they would ask for succor here on their way through the mountains."

Yevliesza looked at the snowy ridge, now seeing it as a threat. There were disadvantages in being in such a remote place. "They've come for me, haven't they."

Dreiza didn't respond. She had been training as a *satvar* and had become less inclined to *fill the air with words*, as she put it. Yevliesza admired her calmness. It was a good example to her and one of the reasons she had chosen the *satvary* as a refuge.

"They're unwilling to violate a sanctuary. And waiting for me to come out."

"It is possible. So the High Mother asks that you do not leave the confines of the compound walls."

This new threat plunged Yevliesza's thoughts into the usual morass, the fog-laden dilemma of having a Mythos-altering power. One which would be coveted by saints and sinners, the well-meaning and the unscrupulous—if one could even tell them apart.

Did she owe Numinat her allegiance, to use her influence over the crossings for Anastyna's war plans? Could the Mythos even survive major physical changes in the crossings? And who was she, at twenty-one years old, to alter the fabric of the world? She *would* do something. She had decided to stop hiding. But she feared for the fragile kingdoms —all of them, not just Numinat. She needed a specific plan.

"They could be Volkish," Yevliesza murmured. "Or maybe from Osta Kiya."

Dreiza frowned. "The palace? Would Anastyna try to bring you back unwilling? I do not see it."

She was probably right. And besides, Valenty would never allow her to be taken by force. But if he came to Yevliesza's aid he would lose the princip's trust. She knew that. They both knew it. It was a barrier, or would become one, between them. In the Mythos, she had found a place and a partner. A place that her old house in Barlow County, USA could never be. A lover she could never have imagined. Those things might not be possible now, now that she held the key to larger, infinitely larger, things.

"I doubt that the princip would force you to go home," Dreiza said. "She has nothing to gain by doing so. She does not know who you are."

No, Anastyna did not. Valenty had promised not to divulge that. But the princip had already exploited her. "She gave me to Albrecht."

Dreiza's face took on a look of concern, tinged with the sort of pity that Yevliesza couldn't stand. Pity, even though Yevliesza had never revealed what really happened to her in captivity: Albrecht's ultimatum, to come to his bed in exchange for allowing Valenty to escape from Volkia.

"She gave me to Albrecht," Yevliesza said again. "Gave me to him in trade for the son of a noble—"

"Yevliesza," Dreiza interrupted, trying to cool the hot resentment.

"*In trade* because he was the son of a *fajatim*, and she needed to shore up her power. She sent Valenty off on a mission so that no one could help me. I told her that the Volkish were known to me, known from the mundat, that they were vicious and ruthless, but she sent me anyway."

That thin excuse of needing to apologize. Which Albrecht never cared about in the first place.

"He interrogated me, threatened me, and in the end, beat me. I was afraid every day. So I don't trust Anastyna, not for a moment."

Dreiza sighed. "After all that has happened, I do not trust her, either." She added, "At least you struck back at him."

"But he isn't dead, is he." There had been no word of Albrecht's death, though every day she hoped for it. Her knife in his groin. Albrecht's arm imprisoned in the wall.

"No," Dreiza answered. "We think he survived."

A flash of sun off the ice made Yevliesza squint, as another thought loomed. "I think those men can watch the approach to the *satvary*, can't they? And Valenty is coming to see me." A spike of worry. "He'll leave Osta Kiya tomorrow."

Dreiza frowned, looking at the snowfield in front of the compound. Yevliesza always wondered if she still had strong feelings for Valenty. But any sense of competition between them had long since abated.

"He will travel with an escort, though," Dreiza said.

In the frozen breeze, Yevliesza hugged her wool cape closer. Those men behind the hill might not wait forever. Whoever had sent them—Nashavety's harsh face flashed into her mind—could decide that their prey was not going to leave. Then they would come for her, *satvary* or not. It was time to leave. The only question was, how?

Chapter Three

The great palace of Osta Kiya had not yet thawed from winter's grip. The great stones of its walls still held the deep ice of the season, though the courtyard grasses were greening.

A snowy breath swept down Valenty's path as he walked the hallway leading past the royal quarters. Everywhere, people gathered in small knots to discuss the news of the war, Anastyna's War, as some called it. He nodded to women dressed in furs and velvet, stopped to greet courtiers and friends, all the while with a slightly perplexed aspect, as though he could not quite grasp what all the fuss was about.

Such deception was the cloak he always wore. Much good it would do him now, now that Nashavety knew him for an agent. If Nashavety knew, then Sofiyana surely knew, as well as all her minions. Strange that not so long ago Sofiyana had been a minion herself. No longer. *Fajatim* now. One who could summon him to attend her at Raven Fell Hall.

He glimpsed Andrik on a balcony overlooking the doors to the royal apartments. He kept watch on comings and goings. Andrik, who knew the name of every high person, and many low. Valenty's man for these fifteen years, and chief among his spies. Needful spies.

Anastyna refused to believe she was at risk. She had sent an army of seven thousand to Lowgate a tenday ago, and no one could gainsay it, not openly. Well. The five great halls could take her down, the *fajatim* could, but it had not been done for four hundred years. More likely she would lose the silver torc by mischance. An accident. Or a weak heart, aided by a powder, oil, or concoction.

He feared for her. She was young, had worn the torc only six years, and had youth's impulsiveness. But, as well, a shrewd grasp of politics. Usually.

He passed a group of women deep in conversation. Elivasa stood with them, wearing her I-love-gossip face, and laughing at a jest. She met his eyes for a moment and ducked her chin in acknowledgment, managing to blush, as though he were a lover. He gave her his best self-satisfied smile, and the other women took all this in.

Elivasa's full figure and dimpled face belied her true skills. No one guessed that besides a merry humor and charismatic charm, she wore a knife fitted in her boot and ran a team of watchful servants in the great houses. Even Valenty did not know their names.

In the arena of the lower city, he had Grigeni, his Keeper of Books. There the habitations and byways clung to the sides of the great rock outcropping of which the vast palace was the crown. Grigeni had risen from the low city and was welcome among its folk, whose smithies, tanneries, butcher-yards, and tallow shops made possible the daily life of Osta Kiya. Many there did not approve of the war. They reasoned that Osta Kiya was eternally safe on its granite perch. Let Volkia do its worst, for why should Numinat lose its sons and daughters to foreign conflicts?

In all these places, Valenty had an ear. And with the princip herself, he had her warm attention, her often critical need, and a backway to consultations—through a narrow, hidden path within the castle walls that gave her quick access to the intelligence that Valenty's web of spies had culled.

At the courtyard in front of Raven Fell, he paused. Here, the frontage was three stories high, bearing decorative balconies and glazed windows. It was a lesser place with Nashavety gone, she who had been the natural leader of the four other *fajatim*. He feared the new *fajatim* was in touch with the old one. And if so, Sofiyana knew what he was.

He felt the ways and customs of Numinat unraveling. When a twenty-five-year-old could lead a great hall; when Volkish agents walked among them; when people dared to defy the princip. For example, the woman he loved refusing to tell the princip of her powerful affinity. The thought bulked large in his mind. His allegiance to the princip was no longer total. He walked a careful line. By the Deep, he did. While trying not to name it treason.

As he approached Raven Fell's elaborate main door, he imagined that the dark stench of Nashavety's sorcery still clung to the place.

⁂

Sofiyana sat at the broad desk that filled one end of the office of the *fajatim* of Raven Fell. She felt too small for it. It was as long as a tall man and almost as wide, but Nashavety had never seemed small sitting behind it.

Before her, on a sheet of velum was a list of things to discuss with Valenty. She had been practicing what to say and how to say it, but she kept forgetting some of the topics: *the helpful exchange in Volkia; Y in satvary to avoid princip; Valenty to bring Y back.*

The jump in her status—from minor noble to great lady of Raven Fell Hall—had been dizzying. She missed Nashavety. Her wisdom. Her confidence. Added to that pressure, keeping everyone in their place. Servants. But more to the point, the *fajatim*. It had taken a full tenday before she had them under control, and the effort was ongoing. Every day she made that effort, remembering them one at a time, and worse, when they met as a body, when the labor of controlling them became arduous. Her left hand was beginning to show an ugly indentation in her palm from grasping the ring in her pocket and clenching it as though to squeeze out more of Nashavety's vigor.

It was perhaps no wonder that she was starting to forget things.

After a discreet knock, her steward, Daraliska, entered to announce Lord Valenty and usher him in.

"My lord," Sofiyana said, rising to greet him. She felt her smile wobble. *Remember who you are.*

"Lady Sofiyana." He did not smile but kept a blank look, as though she were a stone wall.

She waved him to the chair in front of the desk and seated herself, regarding him across its expanse, adopting her own blank look. "Thank you for coming, my lord. My schedule. My duties. Perhaps you have more hours in your day."

He waited for her to go on, refusing to respond to her little gibe. So that was how he would play it. No longer the superficial courtier, but the unapologetic deceiver. Anastyna's spy. He knew that he could no longer pretend, at least with her. She glanced at her notes.

"I asked you to come in order to speak of Yevliesza. We of the *fajatim* know that she is in your special regard." *That she is your concubine.* "We are grateful that she undertook her errand for the exchange of Oxanna's son. The *fajatim* especially asked me to convey this to you."

"I had nothing to do with that exchange."

"We do understand this. The princip sent her. We also understand that she is staying for a time at the Zolvina *satvary.*" *What was the next point? Ah.* "By doing so, she avoids giving a report on Volkia. That is most unusual. As her special friend, do you know why?"

"The princip asked the same of me, and I told her my opinion."

"What *is* your opinion?"

Valenty frowned slightly. "I take it that the princip has not shared this with you." He shrugged. "It is not of larger concern. You can rest easy that it is a personal matter."

Sofiyana nodded pleasantly, feeling like slapping him, but keeping her temper. It is what Nashavety would have done, *The larger goal, the larger goal.* Which was to coax Yevliesza to leave the *satvars'* compound.

"As she is normally under your close regard, Lord Valenty, when you visit her, please suggest that she return to Osta Kiya. She was in the Volkish capital for twenty-six days, and the *fajatim* are eager to hear her impressions."

"Twenty-six, was it?"

"Or thereabouts."

"I was reviewing the boundary forts at the time, so I cannot say one way or another."

Lying. He was in Volkia. Attacked Nashavety in her refuge. He might have killed her. He took the servant Pyvel, killing several guards. She wanted to sneer at his perfidy. Wanted badly to expose Anastyna for sending him to kill a woman who had been pardoned. She wanted to crawl across the desk and strike him. Oh, how she wanted to. But she would restrain herself. Perhaps even at this moment Nashavety knew what she was enduring with this palace fop. Her mentor had said, *I will always be watching you.* The thought buoyed her.

Valenty had begun to look restless. How long had the silence stretched between them?

He rose from his chair. "If I visit Zolvina, I will let her know your concerns, Lady Sofiyana."

She hardly heard him, as she scanned her notes, trying to make sense of them.

He was waiting for any last remark from her. To her relief, she grasped one. "Remember that the *fajatim* are eager to know what Yevliesza saw or learned in Volkia. Yevliesza must come here to report." And when she set out, she would never arrive. Instead, delivered to Nashavety. Why Nashavety wanted her, she did not know, but Sofiyana had instructed her men to watch and wait for Yevliesza to leave the compound. Then take her.

"We will bear that in mind, my lady," Valenty said. Saying *we*, as though he spoke for Yevliesza. As though he was above Sofiyana. Someday soon he would regret this rudeness.

When Valenty left, Sofiyana was drenched in sweat. She looked at her notes. Absently rubbing her hand, her ring finger, she thought that she had made her three points.

But after concentrating so hard and, with the effort to appear calm, she could not remember.

THE SMOKE FROM THE COOKFIRES OF FIFTEEN THOUSAND SOLDIERS darkened the Volkish plain. A great shed had been constructed across the road from the camp, housing for the devices of iron. Inside, some already stood in readiness, ready for the elemental energy that would awaken them.

On the embankment at Rorrs Gate, Albrecht watched as another battalion came around the curve of the hillside, the thudding of their boots bringing a rhythmic drumming to his ears. He stood with his officers looking down on the ramp descending to the great door of the crossings, his mind on the battle to come. But in this familiar place he also thought of the struggle just passed. The one with the spy of Numinat, the witch-girl.

Once the new operation began, it would take precise planning to move the troops into position. There could be no effective defense again such a force, with his soldiers plentifully supplied and weaponed, and especially with iron cladders and volley guns. It would be immensely satisfying to observe their performance in battle.

But his mood went dark as he remembered. This crossing was the place he had come to that night, having ridden his horse like the very devil to seize the fugitives, and finding them already having passed through, already gone. His captive's betrayal. Her cunning pretenses.

His stomach roiled when he thought of how she had outwitted him, how he had let her slip away. And in the company of a noble of the realm, Duke Tanfred. One whom no one would question, one who had turned on his country, defied his sovereign, and given his allegiance to a scrawny creature who had come to the palace and spread venom throughout, in brazen actions and intimate moments.

And that moment in the tunnel. The blindingly clear, inescapable imagery that visited him like a howl in the wilds of his mind. How the wall impossibly formed over his arm. She knelt at his feet. Then, rising, rising with a knife . . .

He staggered. An arm reached for him lest he topple onto the ramp.

Albrecht jerked away.

"Pardon, Commandant!" the battle marshal said. "I thought you might fall."

Albrecht nodded to him, angry, but on guard lest he seem out of control.

He forced his thoughts to the future when he would find Yevliesza. His imagination soothed him, a foretaste. Lord Valenty, her secret lover, would be made to watch. And then, he would take her life. But not too soon.

He knew what the officers lined up on the embankment were thinking. Was he still weak from his injury? The injury that a woman had delivered to him, that was rumored to affect his virility. A woman who had been his whore. Some of them no doubt despised him.

But since Lady Nashavety had come to Rothsvund Palace, his command staff had begun to treat him with more deference. Though she maintained a quiet, assured manner, they could read the fierceness in her, and it frightened them. No doubt they were impressed that such a woman served him. A woman, some of them knew, who kept in a special holding cell in the dungeon a deviant being, quietly vicious. Quiet most times. The lady had made herself a conduit for unnatural power, he knew that, but to bring a creature of darkness into Rothsvund Palace. It was unnerving. All this he overlooked because of her special gifts. How she had divined a process to fuel his war machines. The profound tactical advantages. The terror they would bring to a battle.

He needed her. And she needed his army for her revenge on Numinat. But it might well become an uneasy alliance.

Marshal Reinhart had come late to the group and now joined him, the officers giving way for him, exchanging salutes. They looked at Reinhart with respect. He had come up through the ranks, and was now Albrecht's highest-ranking officer, controlling intelligence. Nor could anyone say that his rank was purchased or inherited. The men liked that he was not born to privilege, and they liked his power and that he did not hesitate to use it.

It galled him to remember that Reinhart had warned him about the girl. He had never come under the witch-girl's spell.

Reinhart saluted. "Commandant."

"Marshal," Albrecht said. "The third battalion is finally here. We have assembled the greatest army ever seen."

"But you must bring them to battle."

"Yes. That we shall do." They were ready. More than ready. "The invasion of Nubiah. A blow for which the enemy will be entirely unprepared."

Reinhart smirked, an expression he should avoid, as it made his face with its small mustache twitch like a rodent. "It will. No one will expect it. There is no declaration of war, but it is not, strictly speaking, necessary."

"And our planned advance against Nubiah is known in Numinat?"

"I have made sure of that."

"And its timing? This is known by Princip Anastyna?"

"Yes, my prince. Our people in Osta Kiya have confirmed it."

Excellent. All as planned. It was Nashavety's scheme, this surprise action. She should have been a soldier.

Chapter Four

In the army camp outside Lowgate garrison, Rusadka approached the *harjat* leader's tent, its pennant of black and yellow snapping in the wind. Urik's tent. Not as imposing as Commander Staniv's across the field but grand enough. She hoped to learn if orders had come.

Rumors flew through the camp: they would be sent to Alfan Sih; they would attack Volkia; they would languish here through the spring and summer waiting for the enemy to pour out of the gate. Rusadka had spent eight years preparing herself to fight, five of them as an elite fighter, a *harjat*, and while she longed for action, she had learned to wait. Since Anastyna had declared war on Volkia, she had little doubt that they would fight. Where and when—that was for higher ranks to know.

Her immediate question was more basic: Why, as a fourth-order *harjat*, was she summoned to Urik's tent at all?

As she approached, the guard outside made eye contact, giving her permission to enter. She ducked through. Urik was sitting at a makeshift table, and two ranking warriors stood next to him, deep in conversation. Second and third rank, by their wristbands.

Urik ignored her while he finished speaking to one of the men, who soon left the tent without acknowledging her. She had time to observe Urik in his hardened leather tunic over breeches, and under the tunic, a padded shirt bearing a gold-and-black band on the sleeve denoting his rank as chief of the *harjat* contingent. His boiled-leather helmet hung from a tent pole.

The other man was Yisandr, similarly dressed, and tall and fierce though he had been gray-haired as long as Rusadka had known of him.

"Fourth Rank Rusadka," Urik said at last, regarding her with a piercing gaze.

"Sir."

"How do you find our troops and the camp?" He sat back and waited for her assessment.

She had to say something. "Our units are in order. Rested from the march from Osta Kiya."

"And the troops from the polities?"

"Less so, sir. They are not hardened yet." In fact, some of them looked like little more than farmers with pikes. "Some of them are bedraggled, but their lords are drilling them."

"The mood?"

"Confident, sir. Eager for glory."

Urik raised an eyebrow. "And you?"

"Confident."

"Not eager for glory?"

"I will take what I can get, sir."

He digested that, then glanced at Yisandr. The warrior gave a small nod.

Rising, Urik said, "We will walk." He headed for the door and motioned for her to follow him out of the tent. Yisandr came behind. Rusadka wondered what they could want with her, but it was not her place to ask.

It had been dry for two weeks, and now as they walked, their boots kicked up dust, adding to the gritty air stirred by the thousands of soldiers and their wagons.

Urik, she noted, wore his hair clipped short these days, whereas Yisandr wore his long hair in a knot at the back of his neck like most *harjat*. Like she did. Short hair was unusual. Why had he cut it? Also unusual: that Urik commanded the *harjat* forces here at Lowgate. He was first rank, but not the most senior. Clearly, he had come into favor.

When they left behind the last group of cookfires, they faced the plains and the indistinct butte in the distance. Nearby a line of trees followed the path of a dried-up stream. To one side in the distance, the Numin Mountains crouched, the far mountains where Yevliesza had taken refuge. At Zolvina. The thought flared hot in her gut. Yevliesza needed a refuge because Volkia had battered her, had nearly killed her. So Duke Tanfred had informed her, the man without whom Yevliesza would likely not have escaped. After his debriefing the Volkish noble had left to find a more conducive exile in a men's *satvary*. He was a man of religious faith. His priest, Father Ludving, at his side. She wondered how they would fare at a Numinat *satvary*.

Urik gestured into the open country. "What do you see, Rusadka?"

She brought her attention to the vast plain: the occasional far-off butte and the line of trees close by. Though the channel of the streambed was out of sight, she sensed there a ribbon of power carving into the land.

"An align, sir."

Urik flattened his lips, seemingly pleased. "Yes. And how would we use the align if we were brought to battle here?"

At Osta Kiya, Rusadka had graduated from the arcana of aligns. If fact, she had won first position, and had given much thought to aligns as a force in war. "Those who have aligns will have an advantage standing upon one."

"And those who do not have aligns?" Yisandr asked.

"For them, it is just a streambed, sir."

Urik turned to her. "That is why you will lead the army's aligners in the gully if we fight here. If we do, that gully is our fallback, and you and two hundred aligners will form a wall."

"And hold it," Yisandr added.

That line would see a hard fight, Rusadka thought in satisfaction, and she would be in the center of it. Her face impassive, she responded, "Yes sir. In case of a fall back to the gully, make a wall of power." In her mind's eye she imagined the fight. She was eager for it.

Yisandr led them into the ravine, and they walked it. Snow still clung to the side of the dried bed sheltered from the sun.

"It follows the streambed?" Urik asked.

"Here it does, sir. At the bow up there"—she pointed to a spot where the gully bent out of sight—"it continues toward the butte."

Urik squinted at the formation as though he could see the align pointing to it. In a soft voice he said, "Our foreknowers believe the Volkish have some manner of hidden advantage."

"The machines we hear rumors of?" Rusadka asked.

"They are not rumors. They empower metal battle wagons and projectile shields." His lips curled. "Among other things."

Yisandr joined in. "Our warders are tasked with conjuring barriers to these implements. And our elementalists will attempt to negate their propulsion." He noted her confusion. "The battle machines are empowered by Volkish elementalists."

Rusadka had heard of these implements from Duke Tanfred. Fear of them had spread quickly through the city-palace.

"What can aligners in the gully do against such things?"

"You will observe these things during the fight. Test whether aligns drain or empower these weapons. I depend upon you to report whether aligns have any effect on the dark machines."

So her unit of aligners would serve as a testing ground. Whether they held the position or not, they would learn something. Not as valiant a role as she had been hoping.

As they walked back into camp, Urik asked, "How did you find the align arcana? Useful?"

"Interesting, sir. The training and the triad itself."

Urik glanced at her. "A *harjat,* a future *fajatim,* and Yevliesza of House Valenty. Interesting indeed. I will have to hear sometime what you made of Lady Sofiyana."

"That is quickly done, sir. She was, and may still be, committed to Lady Nashavety, beyond loyalty to friend or kingdom."

Urik traded a look with Yisandr. "A brief rendition, Fourth Rank Rusadka."

She knew it was not her place to say, but she finished with, "Sir, the woman walks hollow."

THE NEXT MORNING, RUSADKA ROSE EARLY TO WALK THE ALIGN IN THE gully. She followed it in both directions, noting the physical features, the deadfall, the boulders, and the bright swath of align that met her eyes and her inner perception. The narrow confines called for close fighting and a determination to hold position. Her detachment would drill on these things tomorrow. She felt the pull of water beneath her boots. A cold flow in the ground, she imagined, although of course it was the align, full of the Deep, like the veins of her body. She was acutely aware of align energy coming into her left hand; it was why all align soldiers trained to use a sword in either hand. Being left-handed helped. It was what had inspired her to take military service.

In camp again, she passed near the stables, noting a magnificent bay horse led from the field by a young man. It was too fine a horse for someone that young, wearing the cross-belt of a low ranker.

The youngster looked at her. Pyvel, it was. He noticed her, nodding an acknowledgement of her rank. Rusadka knew he had joined the army now that he had fourteen years.

"Pyvel," she said, approaching. He had a bruise the size of an orange beneath his left eye.

He petted the side of the horse's face. "I joined up, ma'am," he said unnecessarily.

"Yes. And you have an opponent. Right-handed, it seems."

He nodded unhappily. "If we had used knives, I would have won." Her silence pushed him to add, "He insulted Lord Valenty."

"To his face?"

"To my face. Because I served in his House."

The youngster hero-worshiped the man. She had to admit she was curious why. "What did he say?"

"That my lord had relations with many partners. Not all of them with two legs."

She smirked. "You upheld his honor." Although the man brought contempt upon himself. "What sort of man is Lord Valenty, then?"

Seeing that Rusadka was not impressed by the depth of the insult to Valenty, Pyvel's eyes flashed. "He is loyal and fair. I could not have had a better master! He was at Yevliesza's side at the trial when everyone thought she had committed treason. He is brave. Afraid of nothing!"

"Fears nothing?"

"Yes," he murmured, perhaps aware that he had pressed his opinion too hard.

"How do you know? Maybe you are making him into something he is not."

"I just know," he said, setting his jaw. Pyvel had changed; she remembered him as a youngster who talked much and listened little, but now he seemed older, surer of himself.

"Ma'am, do you have news about Mistress Yevliesza?"

"Visiting Lady Dreiza," Rusadka said. Most people seemed to know she was at Zolvina.

"Why, though? Why does she not come home?"

Rusadka narrowed her eyes at the boy's innocence. *Because this cannot be home to her.* Numinat had only begrudgingly adopted Yevliesza. It left a bitter well in Rusadka's heart, that Yevliesza was so poorly done by. A woman she had admired from the beginning. Whose welfare she would fight for, though it should be Valenty who did. She shrugged off these thoughts. "Maybe she will go for a *satvar*."

He looked stricken.

"Whose horse is this?" Rusadka asked to change the subject. It was a noble animal, clearly belonging to a high ranker.

"Commander Staniv's. I work for him. Mostly with his horse, though. Valenty spoke for me, and I got to be here, like a reward."

"Well, you must watch that you do not forfeit your position. Never fight in anger."

"Does not anger make you strong?"

"No. It makes you stupid."

The horse nudged him, eager for the stable. Pyvel took a better grip on the reins. "I should bring her to her feed. Thank you for talking to me, ma'am."

Rusadka watched him lead the commander's horse to the stables. Was she so taciturn she must be thanked for conversation? And she also wondered, *reward for what?*

Chapter Five

Raking snow from the numin pool, Yevliesza watched as an elderly *satvar*—they were *all* elderly—worked the pool from the other side. She envied the *satvar's* contentment but couldn't share it. Valenty had been due to arrive the evening before, and still had not come, so raking frozen leaves could hardly occupy her mind.

The numin pool was sacred to many Numinasi, and all *satvars*. The numin pool, when it wasn't frozen, reflected whatever was above it, even with a wind-rippled surface. The *satvars* said the numin pool was like our minds, sometimes observing clearly and sometimes less so. It was the symbol of wisdom and how equanimity brings us to clarity. As an emblem of the mind and heart, reflecting the world, it was apt. But tending it against stray snowflakes was taking things a bit too far.

The tines of her rake made little scratches on the ice. "A light touch, my daughter," the *satvar* said. Yevliesza nodded to her and made a decent pass at the frozen surface.

Then the *satvar* was looking toward the entrance gate. Yevliesza turned. Valenty stood in the middle of the courtyard. She quelled the urge to run to him. Everyone would be looking, from the compound walls, from the domicile windows.

Unhurried, she went to him. "Valenty," she said, looking at him with fresh eyes, longing ones.

He made a small bow, his mouth quirking in an ironic smile. He gazed at her, catching up. The lost days, while she had been in Zolvina. Nearly two months. "I have missed you."

He looked weary, and perhaps it wasn't just from travel. She took his arm, "Come, my lord, and have something to eat in the kitchen."

"Can we not be alone for a time?"

"Alone . . . in what sense?"

He put his arm around her shoulder as they walked to the domicile entrance. "In every sense."

She laughed. "Of course not. This is a *satvary*." She opened the door for him, and when they passed through, he took her hand, demanding that much, even if the sisters might stare. His grip was strong and gentle at the same time, taking her total awareness.

⚜

ONCE VALENTY WAS SETTLED IN THE SMALL GUEST LODGE, HE PAID AN obligatory visit to the Devi Ilsat, and gave her news of Osta Kiya, none of it good. The High Mother took it all in, frowning at *Anastyna's War* —as though the princip were the aggressor, she murmured—and asked after the welfare of those she knew personally, and their children, and grandchildren, all of which he recounted.

He felt the peace of the *satvary* and the comfort of its whitewashed walls. "You are fortunate to be far away from the concerns of court."

The Devi Ilsat smiled. "Oh, we are closer to it than you know, my son. Have you spoken with Yevliesza at any length?"

"Not yet."

"Ah. Then you have not heard about the camp of miscreants in the hills." She told him when they had arrived, and how they had tried not to show themselves.

He was alarmed to hear this and immediately thought them a threat to Yevliesza. "How many, do you know?"

"Seven were in camp when we counted."

The men likely had qualms about forcing entry into a *satvary* and were waiting for Yevliesza to leave the compound. They might be attempting an abduction because someone—Nashavety, perhaps—had guessed about her capabilities. An ugly thought. Or Prince Albrecht might want her to pay for injuring him during their fight in the crossings. If they were Numinasi soldiers, how could they act without the princip ordering the arrest? Which she would never do. He thought about Sofiyana as the new *fajatim* of Raven Fell and began to think her a traitor. One directed by Nashavety.

"I want to bring Yevliesza back to Osta Kiya, High Mother," he said. The fortress would be her protection. *He* would be. She needed it more than she would admit, and more, far more, than the Devi Ilsat knew.

"You think they have come for her." She nodded. "You may be right. But you have only one man in attendance. It would bring her into more danger by exposing her now. This is the best place for her, Lord Valenty."

"And if the men out there grow impatient?"

"We have survived here for five hundred years without such desecration. No one would come into the *satvary* and take one of our people."

He hoped she was right. In any case, seven was too many for him and his escort of one.

"I could stay here until my man goes to Osta Kiya and returns with soldiers to clear the hills." And his own presence in the compound might discourage the watchers from making a move.

"We have no need of soldiers, my son."

"We are at war."

"Then they will come or not. But our ways continue." Her pleasant expression was a shield, her words gentle as granite. This was her domain, by the eight hells. He bowed his head in concurrence.

As he left, he could not see a way through this. Even if he stayed, what could one man do against seven, if the men tired of waiting and brought swords into the compound?

When he emerged from the domicile, Yevliesza was waiting for him in the courtyard.

"Rusadka has sent you a gift," he told her. "I asked a *satvar* to put it in your room."

Her face lit up with pleasure, and it made him happy to see her smile. "How *is* Rusadka?"

"Sent to Lowgate with our main force. Pyvel is there too, groom to the Commander."

Her voice turned wistful. "He's gone for a soldier, then."

"Always what he wished to do."

"Couldn't you talk him out of it?"

Valenty paused. "I got him his position." He was prepared for her reaction, but it still hurt him to know he had disappointed her. "He is a young man now, or will be soon."

"I know. But he seems so young to me." She sighed. "I suppose Rusadka is happy to be facing the enemy?"

"We do not cross paths." The *harjat* warrior held him in low esteem. "But this is what she has trained years for."

"God, I know that, too."

He knew how much her thoughts must be on the war and put his arm around her shoulder. She drew close to him, allowing herself some comfort.

He glanced up at the walkway on the compound's wall. "Who is the young woman?"

"Oh, that's Kassalya. The sisters have taken her in because she's gone nearly mad with her power of foreknowing. A harsh gift."

"Harsher than yours?" he said, trying for lightness.

That got a smile from her, as she dryly said, "I would be glad to trade with her." She led him down to the fallow gardens with its flag-stone paths. When they were far enough from the domicile, she went into his arms and he held her against him, brushing his hand against her head with her short hair, part of the disguise for her escape from the palace in Hapsigen. He wanted to protect her, and he hated that he might not be able to.

When they resumed walking, the subject of Anastyna hovered.

Finally, she asked how his conversation had gone with the princip, the one about sending her to Volkia.

"Anastyna knows my displeasure," Valenty said. Anastyna was well aware of how badly Yevliesza's mission had gone. "Well, maybe not the depth of my displeasure," he admitted. "She *is* the princip. But she told me that she regrets having allowed Volkia to deceive her about their intentions."

"Regrets? She said *regrets?*" Yevliesza said with a dismissive smile.

"Little enough, but yes." They walked in silence, their mood darker. "Yevliesza," he began. "We know Volkia will come. Pyvel is at Lowgate. Rusadka has gone. They may need your help." He didn't say it aloud, but: her root power. "I know it is a hard choice. All choices are bad. But you are Numinasi, and we are in peril."

She shook her head, not wanting to hear. "But it was a mistake. My power coming to me. It was a mistake. It never should have been me. They wanted a warrior, a leader. Instead, they got me."

It was a strange thing to say. "Who is *they?* Who wanted a warrior?"

She did not answer right away. Then: "Valenty. There's something you don't know. Something I learned when I came here."

He waited, sensing the gravity of what she was about to say.

"The *satvadeya.* The High Mother and her close circle. They knew what Volkia's intentions were, knew how the entire Mythos was in danger. From machines, how they could poison the Deep, the source of magic." She frowned. "I know I'm not supposed to use that word."

He knew that the Deep powers—what Yevliesza called magic— were disrupted by machines. Machines driven by elemental powers, as they feared the Volkish had, could shake the foundations of the Mythos.

Yevliesza went on. "That girl you saw on the wall, she told the *satvadeya* what might be coming. And they called upon the First Ones to bring the lost power to someone."

"The *satvadeya.*" It was too much to believe. "Yevliesza, this cannot have happened. You are wrong."

"I wish I was. God, I wish I was. But the High Mother told me. She *told* me. It was her doing. Her and the *satvars*."

He tried to reorient to this new information. The Devi Ilsat had told her what the *satvadeya* had done. So this is why the High Mother asked him if he had spoken to Yevliesza. The missing piece.

Yevliesza gave a wan smile. "I know. Why would they choose me? The High Mother told me they wanted someone impartial, without commitment to any kingdom. Someone who wouldn't let the power be used for bad aims. And they got me, when I was struck by lightning, or the dactyl was. That was the delivery system. Then the burns turned into markings. Markings of the primal root power."

He had seen those. That night in the tent on the plains when she had escaped from Volkia. The urge was now stronger than ever to get her away from here. Away from the *satvary* and its schemes.

They had walked to the far end of the formal garden, where a tool shed was nested in a grove of saplings. They sat on the shed steps, and he brought her under his cape, close to his side. "Let me take you away from here."

"To where?"

She would not go to Osta Kiya, he knew that, but he asked anyway. No. No, she would not come under Anastyna's control.

"When the time comes," Yevliesza said, "I'll decide what to do. How to do it. When I do, I won't be under anyone's power, so help me, I won't."

He pulled back to look at her. Not being under anyone's power . . . What had the Volkish done to her? Had she told him everything? "Was there something else that occurred in Hapsigen?"

She looked away from him. "I told you I saw the war machines. I saw men dying of having their elemental power drained. I also saw that Volkia had decent people. Brave people. Like Duke Tanfred and Father Ludving. And this one soldier, Lieutenant Martel, he led me to see how people died of having their elemental power drained. He died for it."

He gripped her hand. It pained him to think of all that she had been through. And he, being in Volkia at that time, and having no idea, thinking she was safe in Osta Kiya.

She was shaking her head, weighed down by the burden she carried. "I'm afraid of what I have to do."

"Anyone would be," he said, knowing it was even more true for her, so young and without any kind of military training.

"I'm afraid that any wrong move I make will hurt the Mythos. Maybe destabilize the crossings. And there's no one I can trust."

That cut him. "You think I will tell Anastyna?"

"No, you swore you wouldn't. But I think it will come between you and Anastyna. Eventually you'll have to choose between us. And it's not just because you serve her, but because you love Numinat."

"Not more than I love you," he said.

She pulled away from him as she stood up. "You can't say that."

He rose, harshly grabbing her arm. "By the Nine, I *can* say it. I will never betray you."

"Say it again."

"I will never betray you. Never." He pulled her into his arms and kissed her, hard and long. She held tightly to him, and his embrace almost lifted her off the ground. Her body pressing hard against him, melding with him, even through their clothes.

"Take me," she whispered to him.

They were locked together, and in another moment the shed planking was at her back. She lifted her skirts as he pressed her against the wall.

"Please," she harshly whispered. "Now."

They fumbled with their clothes, the ones that got in their way, and she straddled his hips. He entered her, lost in the desire for her, desperate to have her, carried off by a wild and painful necessity. Everything else retreated, except her. She owned him; he possessed her. He heard her cries, it was the only sound, and then he lost even that.

THAT EVENING IN HER CELL, YEVLIESZA FOUND RUSADKA'S PRESENT sitting on her bed.

She had forgotten that Rusadka had sent something with Valenty, and now her friend's gift was reminding her of a woman she cared for so much.

The present was heavy, its wrapping tied with thick string. Stripping it all away, she looked down at a pair of sturdy ankle-high boots. New boots, and finely crafted. This pair looked like they could carry her far and over difficult terrain. Rusadka had given Yevliesza boots once before, but those were left behind in Osta Kiya. These were finer and sturdier. She rubbed her fingers over the new leather, smiling to herself. Rusadka thought that there was little that could not be accomplished as long as one had a good pair of boots. Maybe she was right.

As she sat on the bed, she thought of Valenty, and how they had clung to each other in the garden. Despite their hunger for each other, she thought it might be better if he didn't visit her again. Not until they saw a way forward, a way to have each other. Sometimes she imagined them going away together, leaving all the affairs of state behind. She imagined a small village; an orchard to tend; children and friends . . . It might be unrealistic, but the idea kept coming into view, full grown: a life. A simple one, but her own.

Chapter Six

Sofiyana woke in the middle of the night. The fire in the grate, though fallen to embers, shed a gloaming light in the great bedchamber. She was not used to sleeping in such a large room, a space that could contain so much more than her bed and herself. It had, after all, contained Nashavety.

As she sat up, she snagged the amber ring on the covers. She untangled it, noticing that the stone was pulsing with heat. The large stone—as thick as her finger and almost as long—glowed like a misshapen, hot moon.

The warmth of the stone seemed at first to be from her own body. But it was too warm for that. Somehow, the fire in the stone must come from Nashavety. She longed for the contact, to hear Lady Nashavety's voice.

A movement caught her attention. In the corner of the room, an indistinct form, a lighter shade of gray than the room. It resolved into a thin figure in a long dress. She knew who it was.

"My . . . my lady," Sofiyana whispered, startled and afraid. Childhood fears of ghosts and demons threaded into her mind.

She laid her hand on the ring, hoping to bring the visitation into clearer form. "Are you there, my lady?"

From the corner came a voice that seemed to fill her ears. "Yes, dear one. And I grow strong."

"Then I am happy."

"Yes, be happy. Soon you will see in the world the evidence of my strength. You will hear Numinat cry out in anguish."

The idea troubled her. "But you have taught me that we must protect Numinat. Have you not?"

"To a degree." The stick-like shadow paused. "To the degree that I allow. But Numinat must suffer before it can prosper." Her voice plunged into a guttural pitch. "But do not question me, child. It is not your place."

Sofiyana cowered at the change in tone. And now the figure advanced toward her. "You are my weapon and my will. I point the way, not you, though you may be *fajatim* of Raven Fell."

As the stick-form came closer, Sofiyana saw how ravaged her mistress was, how the bones of her face protruded sharply, how her jaw had lengthened, how the fingers of her right hand—for her left hand was gloved—were scarcely more than bones with a drape of skin. Surely, she could not really look like this in the flesh. It was only a sending, that by its nature must distort the true form. She hoped Nashavety's essence did not approach the bed any closer.

"Tell me of the mundat girl. I am waiting to receive her. I have a prince who is also waiting."

Sofiyana had worked hard on this matter, but she had not accomplished all that she had hoped. "She is under watch, my lady. Close watch." Yevliesza was her adversary and had been from the time they had met in arcana. Yevliesza had risen in Osta Kiya rather than sank as she she deserved, and it blackened Sofiyana's thoughts.

"When she emerges from the place," Sofiyana said, "we will take her."

"Will? *Will?* Why do you delay?"

Sofiyana's words stuck in her throat. It would be a dangerous thing to order her men to invade the *satvary*. She had no authority. It would all be exposed. The *fajatim* might wake up from their forced calm and condemn her. She had thought that she had done well by sending men

—ruthless, experienced men—to lie in wait. But Nashavety was not pleased.

"It is well that they watch," Nashavety said, coming closer. As she approached, she brought a whiff of rot. Sofiyana pressed back on the bed. "However, they must enter the place, since the mundat will not come out."

"But it is a *satvary*, my lady. My men would not like it."

Nashavety's voice went guttural and over-rich, as if coming from a much larger being. "They must set their superstitions aside and take her."

Suddenly her aunt's form was standing at the foot of the bed. Alarmingly, strands of her hair lifted and coiled. Pushed back against the pillows, Sofiyana could retreat no farther. "I . . . I will tell them. Yes. To take her."

"If they wish to live, they will do so." Nashavety's lips did not exactly fit with her words. "I see blood dripping from their hands. A little blood does no harm. But bring her to me alive."

But Yevliesza needed to die. She was ruinous to Numinat and to Sofiyana's own happiness. Which did not matter—her own happiness did not—and yet she would not be content until the woman was brought low. Low and dead. "After all, would it not be best to kill her? I think it would be best."

"Do not think so large, my little *fajatim*. That part is mine. Bring her out alive. And give me possession of her."

"Yes, my lady." It was the only answer she dared give.

"My prince must have his time with the mundat. And we have more to do, much more. Next, it is the princip. That one, if it please you, we will kill." Again, her voice fell into an impossibly deep rumble. "What think you, the walk out the Tower door, or a knife in her stomach?"

Sofiyana whispered, "I do not know, my lady."

"No, child. You do not." Nashavety's form faded, and then melded into the shadows.

Sofiyana stared at the corner until she was sure the apparition was gone.

After a few moments she noticed that the amber ring that had been resting upon her thigh had singed a hole in her nightgown. Underneath, she felt a welt rising on her skin.

◈

A TEMPORARY VILLAGE HAD SPRUNG UP AROUND THE LOWGATE ARMY encampment. There were three taverns, a goods store, a shack with pallets and sex partners on offer, and a *numiner's* post for transmitting earnings home—the tallies recorded, and then sendings in a mirror.

Rusadka entered one of the taverns, tired from maneuvers on the gully align, but not yet ready to sleep. She found room at a table with several of her fellow aligners, most of them already drunk, but that was for the best since conversation was not her strong point.

They greeted her with loud hails, and gibes about her new duty, for no one in the ranks could be lifted above the rest without getting raucously and mostly good-naturedly vilified.

"Drinks for the table, ma'am?" Gandrey, the least drunk among them, suggested.

Rusadka smirked and waved at the serving boy, ordering drinks all around.

"No!" Gandrey protested. He waved at the server. "Boy, tell 'em we want t' other one, Lideka. She can fill our cups!"

The boy scurried off to bring a buxom young woman who already served too many tables, but had a merry way about her, laughing her way through the crowd. "What will y' be havin', you good soldiers? More brew?"

Rusadka said, "Wine. Two pitchers. These boys never had a decent drink in their lives."

Hoots, and a few cheers, greeted this pronouncement.

Lideka gave her an impudent look. "You got a full purse, then, Fourth Rank, do you?"

"Full enough. Wine, if you please." She tossed a coin that Lideka plucked out of the air and dropped down her low-cut smock to general appreciation around the table.

As the serving-woman left, Gandrey said, "For 'nother coin you could take your joy of her, Rusadka! By 'er looks she could handle you and not spill a drop from the pitcher!"

"I 'ud pay plenty to see that," someone shouted.

"You always do," Rusadka threw back, "since no woman would take you for free."

That sparked a round of loud, stinging comments, and someone gave Rusadka a half-full cup of ale as reward.

When Lideka returned with two pitchers of wine, she made a point of bending low over the table to pour each man's drink, and Rusadka's, which put the table in a fine mood, and toasts ensued to Lideka, Rusadka, and the pallets at the whorehouse.

"Question is," Rusadka shouted out over the revelry, "why they charge you lot twice as much for what the rest of us get cheap. Must be because you do not hold with soap."

"What is soap?" someone threw back.

Gandrey raised a toast to nothing in particular, and she joined in, draining her cup and pouring herself another.

The lads were having a good time, and they should. It would be their last night of drinking for a while. That afternoon Urik had told her that Volkia had invaded Nubiah.

Urik had said that Anastyna would not countenance it. So they would be sent to fight at Nubiah's side. She remembered a large, handsome man, the envoy from Nubiah, who had spent some months in Osta Kiya. Anastyna's lover, everyone knew. And Numinat had close trading ties with Nubiah. Now the two realms shared an enemy.

Rusadka's unit would not have to hold the line in the gully. They would take battle against the Volkish army on the plains of Nubiah.

Her doubts, when she allowed herself to have them, came from the fact that Numinat had never fought a pitched battle. Numinat had never raided another realm, much less pressed through the crossings with a full army. Since the Volkish were already in Nubiah, they had the advantage of the restriction point at the gates. Numinat forces would have to push through fast, in overwhelming force. The first unit into the breach would take heavy losses.

Once through, the main army would have to quickly judge the battle positions and deploy effectively.

Plenty of glory for all, she thought darkly, pushing aside her cup.

She nodded at Lideka as she left the tavern. The woman had spirit but sharing a pallet for the evening held little interest now. Tomorrow would be Rusadka's first battle.

⚜

A KNOCK AT YEVLIESZA'S DOOR. SHE ROUSED HERSELF, NOTING BY the dark window that it was well before the first bell.

When she opened the door, she found the High Mother standing there. She stood aside and gestured to the room's only chair.

As the High Mother took a seat, Yevliesza pulled on heavy socks and her wool shawl. "You are up early, High Mother."

"So the day begins," the old *satvar* replied.

Yevliesza waited to hear what brought the woman to her cell.

"How did you enjoy Valenty's visit?"

"I would have liked him to stay longer."

"You are sad that he has gone, then," the High Mother said in a flat tone as though she had never been in love.

"I'm not if he can come back."

The *satvar* did not respond. Male visitors would not often be allowed, though.

Valenty would be coming to see *her*, and she was not a *satvar*.

"My daughter, I am considering an idea."

Instantly Yevliesza was on her guard. Some of the High Mother's ideas were bad ones. And she was powerful enough that most of them were carried out, no matter who paid the price.

"I have been thinking that it is time for you to take arcana training. Training in your second power."

Startled, Yevliesza replied, "Arcana? But we can't have a triad. I'm the only one." A new thought arose. "Aren't I?"

"Oh, yes, you undoubtedly are. However, it does not have to be three, does it?"

"How would *I* know?" Yevliesza blurted. "And who could lead it? You?"

"Oh dear me, that would never do. No, I have someone in mind."

"Someone with primal root power?" Despite her reservations about the Devi Ilsat, she felt a surge of hope. Someone to guide her, someone who knew about root power.

The High Mother pursed her lips. "Not exactly. But, no matter, it could be done, for the individual has great experience with matters like this."

But *arcana*. How could it be an arcana?

The *satvar* noted the expression on her face. "The one I have in mind is a seer. A very good one, I assure you. It is a bit of a journey, but not overlong. The teacher lives in the Agarvesky Forest."

"Someone who will convince me to accept my power," Yevliesza skeptically said.

"To accept *yourself*. And show you how, which I am afraid this *satvary* cannot adequately do."

Yevliesza murmured, "You said I could stay here as long as I needed."

"But not as long as you would like."

Just a day or two ago she had been thinking that it was time to leave. But now that the possibility lay before her, she hesitated. There was the band of men lurking in the hills. . . .

Yevliesza rose, going to the window. The sky, as dark as tar. Maybe she needed to go. But how could this teacher know about root power? How could anyone guide her as to the right actions?

"How fragile is the Mythos?" she asked as she gazed out. When the *satvar* didn't answer, she turned to face her. "How fragile?"

"Well. More so than the land you come from. More than the origin world, certainly." She took a deep breath. "I cannot say how much. But yes, it is fragile. Remember, the First Ones found their magic waning as machines became the way of the old world. Yes, they were reviled, but that was not the only reason they fled. They could not accept becoming lesser beings, shadows of their vital selves, surging with the Deep. They fled for their very spirits. Because machines of the kind that transform the workings of the world are inimical to all the beings of the Mythos as well as the very ground under our feet. That is the threat. That is the *Volkish* threat. Not the alteration of the crossings."

Yevliesza listened hard. The High Mother's message was a shaft of light in the darkness. "But you don't know for sure."

"Why would the First Ones send you that power if they thought it would destroy us?"

The High Mother had made that point before. But now another thought came to Yevliesza. "What if the First Ones are not . . . well-meaning?"

The *satvar* joined her at the window. "They are well-meaning because they are still present. Only the good live on, my dear."

"And bad people?" Yevliesza could think of two or three people who she hoped didn't live on.

"Their life force dissolves with their body."

Yevliesza's hand rested on the deep reveal of the windowsill, and the High Mother brought her own hand to rest upon hers. She went on. "All spirits are good beings, but their connection to the living fades with time. When we asked the First Ones for help, they responded, perhaps because our world was in danger. We could not be sure they would speak to us, of course."

Yevliesza wanted to believe her, but she felt skeptical. Still, the High Mother's hand on hers was emanating a warm comfort. She felt herself relax and come into this moment at the window in a peaceful way.

She jerked her hand away. "Stop that!"

The High Mother sighed, hands now at her side. "The healing touch. My gift seeks out the wounded."

"Is that what I am, wounded?" Albrecht did not own her. She had escaped him, thrust a knife into his crotch. Justice was done. She had not let any of the *satvars* with the power of healing administer to her. A *satvar*-style peace was not what she needed. Maybe wounds and anger were the fires to light her way.

"Are you wounded?" the High Mother mused. "Only you can say."

Yevliesza watched the sky as the stars began to dissolve like bright souls who lived for a time and then faded.

At the door the High Mother turned back to Yevliesza for a moment. "The seer's name is Ishtov." Then she left, softly closing the door behind her.

Chapter Seven

Pyvel brought Fleet Wind, the commander's tall, dun-colored horse, from the stables to the command tent where Staniv stood with his officers. Before dawn on the plain outside Lowgate, the army was assembling, and in a little while the commander would rally his fighting force for the battle to come.

Staniv, in battle dress, red tunic with white trim over light chain mail and black trousers tucked into boots. The red and white for Osta Kiya, the royal colors. No horses would enter the crossings until the army had broken through into Nubiah, but Staniv would be mounted on his horse this morning so he could speak to the soldiers and be seen by all.

As he took the horse's reins, Staniv glanced at Pyvel. "You will join my field messengers today. They will carry word between the officers of needs and conditions, especially in Nubiah."

Pyvel swallowed his surprise at this good fortune. "Yes, sir!"

Staniv glanced at one of his officers. "That man will tell you your job." He mounted Fleet Wind and gave Pyvel a nod. Startled by the prospect of his new role in actual battle, Pyvel forgot to nod back.

He wanted to hear Staniv's speech to the army, but the man he had pointed out was approaching. He introduced Pyvel to two boys about his own age. One was dark and wiry. Alaric, he was called. The other, Borstov, was stocky and round-faced with hair so curly it formed a helmet on his head. They both eyed him warily.

The officer handed him a padded jacket like the other boys wore. It was heavy, with banded strips of metal sown into it. As the four of them walked toward the fort where the doors were thrown open, Pyvel shrugged into his new jacket. The added warmth was welcome as a cold, light rain began to fall.

"Put these on." The soldier handed each of them a snug-fitting leather cap painted with a white ring, the emblem of the princip with her torc. "The white makes you easy to find if anyone has a message for the commander." He handed out pouches on long straps. "If the message is written, put it in your pouch."

Each of them would be attached to a specific unit, and Pyvel would attend the second contingent in the line of the march, the outland unit belonging to Prince Othmar, lord of Dorodna Polity. Pyvel wanted to ask more questions about his role, but the officer was already walking away.

The boys waited nervously for their respective units to pass through the courtyard. Today, Pyvel told himself, he would see Nubiah and a great battle. Undercutting his happiness was uncertainty of how he would perform in the fight.

Pyvel had seen Borstov and Alaric in camp and thought they had been with the army a while. Longer than him. But even if they knew more about fighting, they had never been to Volkia. They had never seen the demon Nashavety up close, or trekked through Volkish forests and villages with the *harjat* chief Urik and Lord Valenty.

He had not exactly distinguished himself. In fact, he had been Nashavety's prisoner. But his two mates did not know that. No one did, because the princip had decided that Pyvel's story would remain unknown. Valenty's mission had been secret, and therefore Pyvel's captivity and escape must be secret.

Borstov, the bigger of the other two boys, said, "I go with the first unit. The elite force that makes the breach at the gate." He tried to look proud, but his expression betrayed him.

"An honor," Pyvel said, envious.

Alaric smirked. "If you fall into a faint at the gate, I will pick you up on my way through."

Borstov grinned, giving his shoulder a push. "Try not to lose your breakfast."

They heard a great roar from the plain outside the fort. And then another.

"We have nine thousand out there," Borstov said. "It will take a quarter day to get through the crossings."

"What if the Volkish come at us in the crossings?"

"If they do, we kill them," Borstov said.

Alaric shook his head. "Their troops are all massed in Nubiah. I heard sixteen thousand."

Pyvel wanted to see that. Wanted to see the *harjat* slicing through the ranks of common Volkish fighters. "They do not have sixteen thousand. They have to hold Alfan Sih and Norslad. I heard twelve thousand."

"We will soon find out," Borstov said. He turned to watch his contingent marching four abreast toward the fort. "Here they come."

◈

Rusadka and her fellow *harjat* under Urik were attached to Prince Othmar's forces. After the first fighters swarmed the gate at Nubiah, the *harjat* would reinforce the spearhead and make sure the breach held. She had no special role, only a fighter with sword and shield. Her shield was small, not even as long as her arm, but it was solid, of strong fir and metal, with a central grip that allowed her to maneuver in close fighting.

She had watched as men hauled the great battering ram down the stairs into the crossing. It took ten men to carry it, a great length of poplar with a blunt end of iron. No gateway door could withstand it for long.

In line with three of her fellow *harjat*, she descended the gateway stairs, and was soon enveloped by the crossings' soft glow and its strong and yeasty smell. They maneuvered around the Volkish barriers that had been erected as the first defense against invasion. All empty of soldiers now. As were the crossings.

Their spies knew that Volkia had pulled every soldier possible into the assault on Nubiah, and she dearly hoped they were dying now at the hands of the fierce Nubiah warriors.

Behind Rusadka's contingent of *harjat*, the thousands of the army marched. They came briskly down the stairs and then moved forward as quickly as possible to keep the line of march moving. Ahead, the sounds of the marching, and now, behind, as well. It was a fast march. Soon they would mass in front of the gate at Nubiah.

Except for the rhythmic footfalls of the fighting force, all was quiet. They moved in silence, the spears of the peasants vertical, the swords of the higher ranks held at their sides, shields in place or hanging from belts. Already Rusadka was sweating from the weight of her weapons and her reinforced jacket. At a turn in the corridor, she looked back to see Urik and his guards. Yisandr too, his expression neutral, which on him looked daunting. She thought her own expression was the same. She was prepared to fight and relished it with cold resolve. Last night, a little fear. But now with battle near, she wanted only to engage.

They passed a strange feature. Rusadka had only been in the crossings twice before, but she had never noticed a tall sheet of metal embedded in the walls. In fact, how could something be embedded there, with the walls of such an unyielding material? As they passed, she noticed the sheet—almost as high as she was tall—had two holes the size of her fist. One of Othmar's men saw it, too. "They made themselves at home when they held the crossings. That is over now."

The *harjat* next to her, Midyur, was a foreknower. Staniv had never countenanced foreknowing as a fighting resource. Such gifts, he felt, were wrong as often as right, and he wanted no guessing from people who discerned the threads of time. Midyur knew to keep his mouth shut about what the future showed, but he muttered to her, "They know we are coming. They relish it. I see them awaiting us."

"As we relish meeting them," Rusadka cast back.

This main path, the great tunnel connecting Numinat, Volkia, Alfan Sih, and Nubiah, shuddered with marching. The sound reverberated, filling the air until it seemed no room remained for more. By now, Rusadka guessed, they had a thousand fighters behind them. Ahead, the gate of Nubiah, the one called Okavezi.

Pyvel walked twenty steps behind Prince Othmar, where banners in blue and green proclaimed his polity. He wished he had been given a knife or a club to fight with if it came to that. Instead, his hand rested on the pouch hanging across his chest, and he gripped it hard even if it was empty.

Before they descended into the crossings, one of the nobles with Prince Othmar had pointed Pyvel out to the leader, and Othmar looked at him for a moment, his expression hard. But at least Othmar knew who he was. The one who would take a message. If it was verbal, he hoped he could remember it. Borstov and Alaric had never been in the crossing before, but Pyvel had. When he had been abducted from Numinat and then, many days later, with Urik and Valenty, slipping through the cordon of Volkish to return home.

After what seemed like a full day in the crossings, the long, snaking line of the march came to a halt as word was passed down the line for a break. Water skins came out, but few sat down to rest. One figure moved, coming quickly toward them from further up the line. It was Borstov. He dug in his pouch, producing a folded paper that he handed to Othmar. Borstov waited to bring back an answer, and Pyvel moved closer, in case he was needed.

He heard the words "metal shield," and then one of Othmar's men beckoned Pyvel to his side, giving him the missive and telling him to reach the third contingent and get the message into Prince Vyrador's hands. Pyvel thrust it into his bag and hurried back along the tunnel, taking a moment to look for Borstov, but the other boy was already threading his way forward to his group.

THEY HAD ENTERED THE CROSSINGS SHORTLY AFTER DAWN, AND NOW Rusadka judged the sun was well across the day. Outside. Here, in the perpetual twilight of the tunnels, it was impossible to judge.

The Volkish had abandoned the crossings, saving the fight for open battle where their superior numbers could be deployed. The close confines and the thudding of feet combined to cast a pall on the journey. Murmurs sped through the ranks that it was unnatural, that they would arrive in Nubiah depleted, their sword arms weakened by the quiet and the lull of the twilight. Leaders moved among the troops, offering encouragement and urging readiness.

Noise in the distance erupted. Shouts and the sound of metal on metal. The first contingent had reached the gate. Yisandr held up his arm, holding the main force back. He shouted Rusadka's name, and when she ran forward, he told her to go forward and report back what was happening. She dashed past the marchers who were already slowing as the bottleneck ahead held them back.

Distant screams grew louder as she pushed through the first unit. Rushing into the cavern in front of Okavezi Gate, she saw two large man-like creatures with skin and muscles of iron. They stood shoulder to shoulder, barring the way, and had thrown aside the battering ram. One of them lurched forward and swung its great metal arms into the press of attackers. The iron creatures could not be alive, but they were. That, or a man inside the metal skin gave them motion and life. The horror of the sight stopped her as she stared at the monstrosities.

The huge gate behind them was shut, an impossible obstacle. A pile of bodies lay before the metal men. Seeing nothing that she could do, she turned and rushed back to report.

As she did, she heard several loud noises ahead of her. They sounded like hammers striking metal, impossibly loud hammers.

Pyvel had seen Borstov several times, bringing messages to Othmar. Pyvel was now at the side of the lord, taking Borstov's notes back to the next contingent, sometimes seeing Alaric, his eyes wide with excitement as he in turn took notes back down the line.

One of Othmar's leaders put a hand on Pyvel's shoulder to get his attention amid the growing din. He bent down to give him a verbal message. "Two iron cladders guard the gate. Send warders forward."

Iron cladders? He did not know what those were, but by the expression on the man's face, it was bad.

As he ran, shouts and the sound of combat filled the air. From side tunnels uniformed soldiers—Volkish soldiers—poured through. So there were some still here. But the army was prepared and met them, weapons raised. Pyvel paused as he came upon a skirmish where swords and maces swung through the air. With a knot in his stomach, he crouched down and, keeping to the side of the tunnel, rushed through. In the melee, he took a fall as one of the combatants rammed into him, sending him sprawling. He crawled out of the knot of fighters and ran on, looking for the leaders who Alaric reported to.

Down the stretch of the tunnel, he saw more Volkish soldiers rushing from side corridors, storming into the army's ranks. The fighting was desperate and close, with the superior numbers of the Numinasi unable to maneuver into position to engage. Pyvel now had a new message to deliver: the Volkish were here, here in numbers. They had hidden in the side tunnels.

He spied an important-looking noble of the polities and gave him two messages, about warders and the tunnels. The man said, "We know, boy. Go back to your unit."

He ran. The fighting was so crowded that no one noticed he was making his way forward. He saw a man with a sword through his neck, and another with his arm gone. Bleeding hard, the soldier held the stump at his shoulder. Another man, lying on his back, his hand at the neck of a Volkish soldier who sat on him, trying to drive a knife into his chest. The enemy fighter pushed with great strength until the knife pierced the man's chest.

When Pyvel got to his unit, a scene of carnage met him. Scores of men lay in bloody heaps. The metal doors spat projectiles, catching those who went past. The doors were shields with holes in them to allow the iron pellets to hurtle out. He watched, horrified, as a stream of iron pellets mowed Othmar down.

Pyvel looked for one of Othmar's ranking soldiers, but he found no one. Up ahead he heard the distant sound of iron pellets spitting. To get forward he would have to crawl along the tunnel floor right next to the door. He wiped blood out of his eyes and approached the door, crouching low to stay out of the range of fire. He did not know if he was bleeding or had merely been in the rain of blood, but he went to his hands and knees and crawled by the door. The hail of pellets was deafening. In the middle of the tunnel, men died and died.

❧

RUSADKA RECRUITED FOUR STRONG *HARJAT* AND RAN WITH THEM TO the closest metal sheet, one of those spitting balls of iron.

Once there, she set the men to digging the metal out with their swords, even as it continued to eject iron balls in pulses. The men lunged their swords into the gaps between the shield and the wall, and wrenched.

One of her crew fell as a Volkish soldier skewered him from behind. Rusadka dispatched the lone soldier and took the place of the *harjat* who fell with a mortal wound. With a last heave, the metal sheet fell to the ground, and Rusadka plunged in to find two soldiers feeding pellets into the pipes. In the small cavity, her sword worked havoc.

Without pause, she waved her team onward to the next door.

❧

PYVEL SAT AGAINST THE CROSSING WALL. HE STARED AT THE movement of soldiers of both sides as they swarmed to and fro. He could hear nothing. The princip's soldiers moved silently as though they were already dead and no longer had voices.

Borstov lay in his arms. Before Borstov's eyes closed for the last time, Pyvel tried to tell him that it was all right, but he could not hear his own voice, and he was not sure that he believed it, anyway. There were too many dead for it to be all right. They had never made it to Nubiah. He had never done anything to help except bear messages that did no one any good. In the deep silence, there was still vicious fighting. Despite this, Pyvel thought he could easily fall asleep. Or maybe he was dead because he hurt everywhere. He closed his eyes.

Pyvel woke when someone put a hand on his shoulder.

A *harjat* looked down on him. He said something to him.

Urik's uniform was soaked in blood, but he was standing, so that was a good sign.

Urik hauled him to his feet. A few *harjat* were with him. One of them put a sword in Pyvel's hand, and they walked down the tunnel, in which direction, Pyvel could not tell. They passed by bodies and fallen weapons. All silent. He was holding a heavy sword, wondering where he had gotten it. Tears were stinging his eyes. Furiously, he wiped them away with his forearm, deciding to kill the first Volkish soldier he saw.

Urik's men flanked him, and once fought off a short-lived attack. Pyvel swung and swung, but there was so much blood he could not tell if he had caused any. Someone put a hand on his shoulder when he was about to kill a dead man. They resumed their trek through the dead.

As they walked, he began to hear things, muffled, but unmistakable. They were not shouts or the clang of swords. They were the cries and groans of the wounded. He wondered if they would be in the crossings forever. They would walk forever with their fellow dead, looking for a way out.

But Borstov could have told them. There was no way out.

ALBRECHT WALKED THROUGH THE CROWDED TUNNELS SURVEYING THE aftermath, the disposition of bodies, the manner of the deaths. The Numinat wounded had been taken to the door at Lowgate where the garrison was welcome to them. The Volkish casualties had already been taken to Rorrs, arriving to a hero's welcome. It had been a glorious battle, a crushing victory.

Albrecht only wished it had been his idea.

But it had been Nashavety's plan. Take them in the crossings when they believed the Volkish were in Nubiah. Let our spies say that Nubiah is to be the next conquest, that we had drawn our forces from the crossings to supplant our invasion force. Then, when retreat was impossible, pick them off from the side tunnels. With a little help from the volley guns, those astonishing, elemental-driven shooters.

Even though the honor was Nashavety's, it was a deeply satisfying moment, to strike at Numinat with so little cost. To send a message to Anastyna: *Oppose us at your peril.*

And to the witch-girl: *I am coming for you.*

He and his officers passed the area where he had caught up with her the night of her escape. It was a darkling bruise in his memory, that moment when he had her by the neck and she had a knife in her hand. It was over now—but never over. Perhaps when Yevliesza emerged from Zolvina it would be over. If not, then when they took the kingdom of Numinat. His only decision then would be how long to keep her alive, and the spy Valenty, her lover. They would watch each other suffer, but for how long, he had not yet decided.

"This one is still alive, Commandant."

His lieutenant was kneeling by a Numinasi with a head wound. The officer put his hand on his knife scabbard, waiting for Albrecht's nod. The wounded man looked up at Albrecht and his officers, the hope gone from his eyes, face impassive as he waited for the end.

"Have him brought to Lowgate," Albrecht snapped.

Honor demanded it.

Chapter Eight

Nashavety smelled the blood before she saw it. Turning the corner in the Rothsvund Palace dungeon, she found the jailer, viscera trailing from his ripped body. In a few steps more she saw that her creature had escaped its cell. Having dug a hole under the iron bars of the door.

She swung around, looking for the *strigoi*. It had not fed on the jailer, so its appetite would not yet be curbed. Was she in danger? She thought not. She commanded it with her creature affinity; it would not attack her. Rushing up the stairs, she found a soldier and demanded that a unit search the dungeon.

They soon found the tunnel that the creature used to escape to the outside. The *strigoi* was only the size of a four-year-old child, even with its thick, leathery wings, so a small tunnel was all it needed.

Now she had a dangerous predator loose in the city.

"Madam," a captain said, as he strode up to her. "The beast has been seen in the Church of All Graces."

Thank the First Ones. "Bring the cage on a wagon and meet me there."

"As you wish. I will bring soldiers."

"No soldiers." They would overreact. It was not for nothing that she kept the *strigoi* out of sight in the dungeon. It did not have a pleasant aspect. She took some comfort in the fact that it was uglier than she was.

"Madam, it has killed a priest and several churchgoers. We need soldiers."

"You will summon no one." As punishment for his arrogant attitude, she said, "Drive the wagon yourself."

Marshal Reinhart was striding toward her down the hallway, out of uniform, awakened as he was in the middle of the night. He looked haggard, having waited outside Rorrs Gate through the long night until the battle of the crossings was won.

"Lady Nashavety," he said. "I am at your service." He made a stiff bow, a small protocol that he always afforded her. She smiled at him. He was vile and unscrupulous, qualities she wished Albrecht had.

"Come to church with me, sir."

❧

THE CHURCH SANCTUARY LOOKED NORMAL ENOUGH WHEN THEY PEERED in from the main doors, but when they approached the altar, they saw the bodies, blood pooling beside them. The priest lay on the floor, vestments ripped as well as his throat. Some of the parishioners were even more badly used, the ones that had fought back. A head had rolled against the wall under the stained-glass window, looking like it had sprouted there.

"Just one *strigoi* did all this?" Reinhart asked in some awe.

"Yes, just one." She had to learn to control the thing better, because there were a lot more of them back in Drogeliv. "It will obey me, but first we have to find it."

"It flies. It could be anywhere in the city by now."

"Follow me." She hurried back down the main aisle of the church, thankful that the creature had chosen nighttime for its rampage or there would be panic in the city.

Outside, she scanned the skies. Clouds glowed from the light of the industrial forges. The captain was waiting in the wagon.

"Anything?" she asked him.

"Look!" he cried, pointing in the direction of the river. A dark, fat shape flapping in the distance.

Nashavety and Reinhart joined him on the bench seat as he whipped the horses into a gallop. Snow still lined the road in great banks where details of workers had shoveled it. Dirty snow, almost black from the floating ashes of the furnaces. Ahead in the frozen, slumbering city the *strigoi* hunted. Silently, she called to it. *Come to me. Your drinking is done. We will warm your bowl of blood from this time forward. Come to me.*

As they passed a great edifice with a dome and spire, Reinhart pointed up. There, the *strigoi* crouched on top of the dome.

Nashavety bid the captain stop the wagon. The *strigoi* saw them and plunged from its perch, great wings spread, the naked body hanging below, gristled arms and legs dangling.

Nashavety loved to watch them fly. They looked ungainly, but what they lacked in beauty, they made up for in intelligence. In fact, legend had it that they had been human once, and in learning to feed on blood, they also learned to love the taste of fear. Though it was not clear which hunger drove them, one or the other had deformed them. But they had a strange power. They could understand human thoughts. At Drogeliv, over time the *strigoi* had found her, attracted by the thoughts that emanated from her. They came close to the mansion just to be near her, often tucked beside each other, against the house or in the woods, brown wings pulled over their bodies like giant beetles.

Reinhart walked toward the domed building, sword in hand.

Before Nashavety could warn Reinhart not to be the only moving thing in the street, the *strigoi* appeared in the nearest alleyway and raced toward Reinhart. Its bald skull stretched forward on its neck, mouth opening to show pointed gray teeth. Reinhart bolted.

Stop, strigoi, *stop,* Nashavety cried out in her thoughts. *You cannot have him, he is mine.*

Reinhart had run to the portico of the closest building, bracing his back against the door, holding his sword in readiness. The *strigoi* stopped some distance away, observing him, and then moved toward him, one boney leg stepping forward, and then another, as it moved its head from side to side, smelling him, not listening to its mistress.

Come to me! Now come to me!

From the wagon, the army captain rushed forward, heading for the creature. In another instant, the *strigoi* pivoted from Reinhart and jumped on the captain, ripping at his face with long claws. The man fell on his back, writhing. The *strigoi* folded its leathery wings over its prey.

Nashavety heard sucking noises from beneath the wings. It was too late to save him.

Reinhart came forward for a closer look. She had to admit he was no coward.

Nashavety turned to him. "I regret that it pursued you, Marshal. I did call to it. But," she said with a shrug. "You ran."

Reinhart watched as the creature finished its meal and stood. Satiated, it swayed on its feet, the lids of its eyes half closed.

"It is splendid," Reinhart whispered, staring at the creature. "Simply splendid."

Nashavety watched the *strigoi's* slow progress to the wagon where the cage sat with the door open. *Get in the cage. Or I will pull your wings off.*

As it shuffled toward the wagon, she added, *You splendid thing.*

❦

ALBRECHT MET THEM ON THE MAIN STEPS OF THE PALACE. HE HAD JUST arrived from Rorrs Gate, and had managed, after the long ride, to look handsome and commanding in his brocaded and medaled uniform.

He came down to join them at the wagon. "Your creature got loose," he said casually, daring to enjoy the trouble she had been through.

But Nashavety felt content with the evening, having avoided a disastrous event that could have inflamed the city against her. "Yes. The *strigoi* was ill-behaved. But only seven died. Unfortunately, your captain was among them."

He frowned. "I thought you said it obeys you." Not waiting for her response, he went to the wagon and inspected the *strigoi*, now crouched down on the cage floor, its face nestled against the sturdy wooden bars.

Nashavety followed him. "It was upset with its food. I will remedy that."

Albrecht held onto one of the bars, peering closely at the *strigoi*.

Uttering a soft moan, the creature cocked its head and stared at Albrecht. Its tongue darted out and licked the prince's hand.

As Albrecht yanked his hand back, the *strigoi* got onto its knees and placed its forehead on the floor.

"By God," Reinhart said as he joined the prince at the wagon, looking at the monster which appeared to be prostrating itself. "What is this?"

In amusement, Nashavety watched Albrecht receive the homage. "It seems, my prince, that you have found your *sympat*."

Chapter Nine

Behind the *satvary* compound, Yevliesza scrambled up the steep path, hard to see in its icy bed. Ashka, among the strongest of the *satvars*, led the way, making tracks for Yevliesza to step in. She carried a large coil of string over one shoulder.

Kassalya had run off and they had to bring her back.

In Zolvina's isolation there was nowhere to go. And yet there was everywhere. She could have gone into the wilds of the Numin Mountains in any direction, but the sisters suspected she had gone to the caves.

Kassalya's companion for the day had been Mitasha, one of the *satvadeya*, who should have known better than to leave Kassalya by herself, especially as she had been in a distressed state. Mitasha had left her alone for only a few minutes, but when she returned, the girl was gone. It had taken them too long to discover the tracks in the snow and now Yevliesza and Ashka pushed hard to follow her. Lagging behind was Dreiza, who knew Kassalya best, but she had been nursing blisters on her feet and could not keep up. Dreiza had asked Yevliesza to help because many of the girl's prophetic visions were entangled with Yevliesza, and she hoped this might prove helpful in getting the girl to emerge from hiding.

At a ledge high in the hills above the compound, Ashka turned into the maw of a cave opening.

Yevliesza paused, looking in the direction of the ridge where men kept watch on the compound. Here above the *satvary*, she and Ashka were hidden from the ridge by a shoulder of the hillside. So the watchers didn't know they were outside the walls. She followed Ashka into the cave.

Manifesting a glimmer of light, Ashka took the end of the coiled string she carried, and secured it around a fallen boulder. As they set out, she fed out the string, saying, "The cave system is deep, with many turns."

From the large cavern they had entered, the cave narrowed until they had to step sideways to pass. "It widens, do not fear," Ashka said. Everyone was wary of the caves, with yawning gaps in its floor, the twisted routes, and caverns of ice.

Yevliesza feared that Kassalya would do herself harm. Had the future become intolerable to know? Or were the visions poisoning her peace of mind, no matter what their content? Kassalya had come to the *satvary* to find peace. As Yevliesza had found out, sometimes that didn't work.

The narrow canyon bulged wide again, and they had a choice of directions. "Shall we call out to her? Or wait for Dreiza?" Yevliesza asked.

"You call out."

Yevliesza did so, but there was no answer. "How did she find her way in this place?"

"Perhaps she brought a lantern." Ashka knelt and inspected the cave floor. "This way," she said, turning to the left. Ahead, a long rocky gallery hugged the wall. Below, a vast depression, lost in darkness. The halo that Ashka projected from her left hand brightened their path but could not penetrate the abysmal depths at their side.

As they walked, Yevliesza allowed herself to wonder if the power of foreknowing should have come to her instead of aligns. Primal roots and foreknowing would have been a potent combination, relieving her of uncertainty about what to do next. If the resulting visions were unfailingly true . . . but they were not. So there lay the problem of seeing the future.

"Kassalya!" she called out. "It's Yevliesza."

The gallery descended steeply, and soon they entered a tall canyon of stone. Ashka was unwinding her braided string, leaving a trail along the ground. The cave warmed, and rivulets of water streamed down the walls.

A noise from behind. They turned to find Dreiza limping down the slope. She had brought skins of water, and they all drank, feeling better for it.

Yevliesza pulled the strap of a water skin around her shoulder. "Why did Kassalya run away?"

Dreiza shook her head. "Beyond the usual? Beyond that she can barely endure the light of day? I know not." She looked down the tunnel. "But I do know where she is."

"Where?"

"At the black lake."

Ashka frowned. "How far in?"

"Farther," Dreiza said, setting off down the steep path. Yevliesza remembered that Dreiza also had foreknowing. Perhaps she used that now, foreseeing where Kassalya was.

They emerged from the narrow pathway into a small cavern with swords of melted stone hanging from the ceiling. It was the end of the braided string.

Dreiza stopped. "One of us stays here. If we become lost, whoever stays behind can guide us by voice."

"I must go on with my light," Ashka said.

"And you must stay, Yevliesza," Dreiza said. "I am best with Kassalya."

Dreiza was an important *satvar* now, but Yevliesza wasn't sworn to obey. "This time, it's me." The two women looked at her skeptically. "I think I'm wrapped up in some of the worst futures she sees. Maybe, in a way, she and I are in this together. Let me go on, Dreiza."

Finally Dreiza nodded and without further discussion, Ashka and Yevliesza set out again.

After what was likely about an hour, but which seemed much longer in the cavernous dark, they came upon an ink-black pool some thirty yards wide. Its depth might be six inches or sixty feet. As they stood there, its surface threw back glints from the women's halo of light.

Yevliesza looked up at the vaulted ceiling far above. A shelf protruded some forty feet above the pool. There she spied a huddled shape sitting close to the edge.

"Kassalya," Yevliesza called out. "It's me. Yevliesza."

No answer came. But at least she was sitting, not standing.

"Go away."

Encircling the lake was a narrow cuff of stone. Yevliesza nodded Ashka to light the way, and they walked the narrow path toward the ledge. There were rocks jutting out from the wall that could be used to climb up. But the best thing was for Kassalya to come down. If they went up the girl might be driven to jump. Yevliesza didn't know if it was a worse fate for the pool to be shallow or deep. But she mustn't goad her.

Again they heard, "Go away."

Yevliesza looked up to where she sat. "I think if you tell it, you can release it."

"Ah, that never works."

"It does if it's me." She was at the point of a great decision; she could feel it in this black wilderness. "You can help me, Kassalya. Because I have the ninth power, and I mean to use it."

Kassalya rose and stood precariously on the edge of the shelf.

"Please step back from the edge," Yevliesza said, keeping her voice calm.

To her relief, the girl did. "But you do not use that power," she said.

That was true. So far, she had done little except spy out the Volkish weapons and their power source. And try to kill Prince Albrecht. But she had known since her captivity in Volkia that she *would* use it, somehow.

"People died two days ago," came Kassalya's voice. "Thousands died. Blood from swords and dark machines. In the crossings. The dead, oh, the dead! And those who wished they were! Limbs gone. Faces. You cannot know what I see."

As Kassalya stared at the black pool, a moan came from her throat, like an animal's cry. "And worse to come."

The words sent a cold shudder through Yevliesza.

A drop of water from the ceiling plunked onto the glossy face of the pool. Then silence again, as ripples of light expanded across the surface.

"I'm done waiting," Yevliesza said with new conviction. Her voice seemed to fill the cavern. "I'm done."

"Then come up." Kassalya looked down at her, but what did the girl see? A weakling? A savior? "If you can bear to see, come up."

Yevliesza gave her cape to Ashka and turned to the rock face. She placed her hands on a protruding stone within reach and climbed, finding purchases for her feet and hands, the same as Kassalya must have done.

At the top, she saw that Kassalya had seated herself near the shelf's edge.

"Come back further," Yevliesza said.

"No." Kassalya pointed down. "Look at the lake."

Yevliesza sat beside her.

The girl didn't look at her but gazed downward. Ashka's manifesting light polished the near side of the pool with a scrim of silver. Yevliesza wondered if the pool had some significance to her, and that was why she had come there. "What is this pool?"

"It is my mind. Can you not see things?"

"No. Tell me."

Kassalya whispered, "I am afraid that if I speak the words, then everything comes dragging up out of the water."

It was a mad thought. But in the darkness, Yevliesza could almost imagine things emerging from the pool, lugging chains and sorrow behind.

"That won't happen. When you speak the words, I will have the truth. Finally. And you can release it. Let me keep it for you." She hardly knew what she was saying. But she thought she knew what Kassalya saw. It was what Earth had already endured from twisted myths. Now they were coming here. She had known that for months. Against all of that, what were her personal hopes, her longed-for refuge in Numinat, the man—both gentle and strong—who loved her, and the simple life of growing in wisdom as she aged?

She had better say it before she lost her courage. "I'm ready, Kassalya."

They sat in the quiet for a few minutes. The air seemed to fill with distant ringing.

Finally, Kassalya pointed at the half-dark water. "They are coming. See them? The soldiers? So many, so many." Kassalya grabbed Yevliesza's arm, her fingers digging into her flesh. "Do you see? And not just in the gray uniforms, there are our people, too. They walk in their ranks, a great army swollen with men forced to serve."

Yevliesza imagined them. In the vast emptiness the blackness felt alive with soldiers. They herded the people of Alfan Sih, Nubiah, the Jade Pavilion, Norslad, Arabet, many colors of people, enslaved to do battle. And to suffer and die in vast prisons.

Kassalya pointed to the black side of the lake. "Oh, there . . . see."

"Tell me."

"A stranger wearing the Numinat torc of rule. Her hair is wrong, it is not Anastyna. People falling from the Tower."

Her nails dug into Yevliesza's skin. The pain helped Yevliesza bear the vision, which now seemed almost real.

"And then the torc gleaming from the throat of a demon-creature. Oh, see the thin, hungry woman with a glove on one hand? Do you?"

Yevliesza had to scrape the words from her throat. "I see her." Imagined she did. No demon from the underworld, it was Nashavety, in all her living evil.

"The machines, oh, the metal things!" Kassalya moaned. "The grass dies before they even roll or walk over. The land hates them, the aligns hate them."

"What? What of the aligns?"

Kassalya's voice went to whisper. "They die. See how they fade? The brilliant spirit of the land, gone gray."

The light below vanished. Ashka was growing tired and dropped her manifesting light, plunging the cave into darkness.

"All the Nine recede. They leak out of some people; they flee from some. Receding. Dying."

Yevliesza looked into the blackness. All the powers were gone. Then the vision came to her: the Mist Walls ceasing to move. And then they moved again. This time in the wrong direction.

Kassalya was still speaking. But her voice had become Yevliesza's own knowing. One by one things vanished into nothingness, like the great desert of interstellar space, or space beyond the stars.

It was the future beyond which Kassalya could not see because it was not there.

Chapter Ten

Rusadka knelt by the side of the wounded *harjat.* Three days had passed since the battle of the crossings, that awful defeat when creatures made of iron flung soldiers into bloody heaps, and iron balls spat from shields embedded in the tunnel walls.

Midyur lay on a pallet in an atrium where the lightly wounded—those who had been able to return from the crossings—were recuperating. A dozen healers circulated among the patients or helped them walk outside in the nearby courtyard.

"I knew they lay in wait for us," Midyur said, as a healer re-dressed his shoulder wound. "I knew."

Rusadka shook her head. "You thought they waited in Nubiah. I thought the same." But, instead, an ambush. A massacre. The battle still raged in memory. The sound of it, echoing in the tunnels. The smell of blood and excrement.

"How many dead?" Midyur asked.

"Still counting." It was nearly eighteen hundred, but she spared him that number. Among that number, thirty-three *harjat,* a catastrophe for their order. And some of the survivors back at Lowgate would not rise from their pallets.

Rusadka left him and made her way to others that she knew. She saw Urik approaching and formally nodded to him.

"Rusadka," he said, scowling as he stopped in front of her. A red scar down the side of his face puckered his skin.

"Sir." She was ashamed that she bore no visible scars, although her thigh and hip were purple from a deflected sword strike. "May I ask how Yisandr is?" He remained at Lowgate.

"He has died."

As she had feared. "A sore loss to us. May his family know peace."

Urik cocked his head toward the door, and she followed him from the room. "Your bravery in the battle has become known to me. One of the last acts of Commander Staniv was to approve your elevation to third rank."

"Thank you, sir." The honor barely registering in her sober mood. "But last acts? The commander fell in the battle?"

"The princip stripped him of leadership." Urik's harsh expression —perhaps his permanent one, given the ugly scar—showed his displeasure.

Anastyna was placing the blame on the army, but it was she who had ordered the attack, she who believed the intelligence that Volkish had invaded Nubiah. Now, blaming Staniv.

Rusadka saw that Urik's people were waiting for him. "Sir, I wish to commend the messenger Pyvel for his steadfastness in the fight. He handled himself well." Rusadka felt she had to look out for the boy. Yevliesza would want that.

"That has been noted. He is on leave to recover. With Lord Valenty. The new commander will choose his own groom."

Urik raised an eyebrow since she obviously was not finished with the topic.

"He deserves a good posting, sir. Lord Valenty has not much to teach him."

A pause as the *harjat* chief considered her. "Lord Valenty has *everything* to teach him."

That surprised her. "I regret if I spoke out of turn."

"What is your concern with the boy?"

"His former mistress, Yevliesza, is known to me. She favors him."

Urik regarded her with a flat stare. "*I* favor him."

"Yes sir."

He left to join his men in the hallway.

She had not made a good impression. But she could not have guessed that one of the highest ranking among the *harjat* held a high opinion about both Valenty and Pyvel. Obviously, a story lay here. Obviously, too, she had misjudged some things. It left her mystified and a little unsettled.

❦

VALENTY USED A TORCH TO LIGHT HIS PATH. THE WALLS ON EITHER side of the passage were dark and thick, like the deep roots of the towering rock outcrop upon which the castle sat. This secret passageway was so remote from light or access that not even a spider could have ever found its way inside. The strange silence of the place always cleared his mind of everything except fundamentals.

The disaster at the crossings. The danger to Anastyna. The losses growing every day as the wounded at Lowgate died. Anastyna must use great caution now.

She waited for him in the little aerie with the single lancet window. She had been pacing when he came through the door that, with a careful push, swung wide on its pivot.

He nodded to her. "My lady."

"You have heard what they are calling it?" Her silver torc glinted in the light of the candles lit in the wall niche. "Anastyna's Travesty."

As long as it was not Anastyna's Demise. "Yes, I have heard."

Her eyes flashed. "So you agree?"

Her *sympat* falcon perched on the windowsill, keeping its distance for now. Anastyna's pale cheeks flared bright with anger.

"I do not agree. But I am afraid, My Lady Princip. I am afraid for you."

She would not listen to that. "How could your sources not have seen underneath the false Nubiah invasion?"

To be fair, it had not been his sources, but Anastyna's own favorite courtiers. Vulnerable to the planted intelligence.

"Deception is an art of war, often successful. But it is bitter to lose because of it." A cold silence hung in the chamber. The falcon watched him as though he were prey. "My lady, the *fajatim* may move against you."

Her face hardened. "They would not." She was delicate in stature, but he did not mistake her for weak. "And could not. I have Oxanna's esteem, and Red Wind Hall."

She certainly should have Oxanna, after saving the *fajatim's* son from Volkish imprisonment. If the princip had two *fajatim* on her side, Sofiyana did not have the four votes to depose her.

"The mood is changing," he went on. "People are listening more intently to those who opposed the war."

"And so?"

"I would have you guarded more closely. If the *fajatim* do not depose you, they may employ other means to strike at you." He saw her incredulity. "Sofiyana may try. If she does, it will be Nashavety's hand that wields the knife, no matter who makes the attack. Bring your household guard close, I beg you. Let it be said that we guard against Volkish assassination."

She held out her leather-cuffed wrist to the falcon, and it flew to her. The *sympat,* her raptor weapon. She stroked its feathered throat. "You have built this fear up so high, Valenty, it must fall of its own height. And I will not be intimidated. I will not. As for the *fajatim*, it is within their right to remove the torc from my neck." She noted his expression. "You do not agree?"

"One of them is under foreign control. And perhaps more." They could not assume it was only Sofiyana.

"We do not know that." Anastyna sighed. "Valenty, they will not depose me simply because of the war. The war is my right to declare, even to lose. It would be unlawful to remove me."

If they cared about the law. Perhaps he was wrong, had let the swirling sentiments and rumors unbalance his thinking. And yet . . .

Sofiyana was under sorcerous control. Anastyna had heard his reports but could not believe herself in danger.

Anastyna went on. "We will lose some battles, but we must fight. Volkia can bring the Mythos to ruin. Not just by conquering the realms. By *destroying* them." She drew herself up, looking outraged enough to do the fighting herself. "These dark machines they have. The kingdoms of the Mythos cannot hold if the Deep withers and dies. We must fight."

A shiver spread over him at her words. By the Nine, this was the woman to lead Numinat to the fight. It was impossible to imagine Anastyna's losing the torc. And unthinkable who might then wear it.

YEVLIESZA, ASHKA, AND DREIZA LED KASSALYA OUT OF THE DARK caverns, Ashka's manifesting light showing the way. As Yevliesza held Kassalya's hand, the girl squeezed back in a determined grip. Perhaps her visions were now less terrorizing.

Formations of dripping stone emerged from the darkness like sentinels. The glow cast by Ashka made for an eerie, almost mystical progress through the labyrinth of stone, but Yevliesza's thoughts were far away. She was in the greatest hurry now that she had decided to take a stride forward. She didn't know how to stop the Volkish, but she could see the first steps. The freeing part was that she no longer *had* to see beyond that. She was ready to leave.

They came to the place where Ashka had dropped the end of the twine. The *satvar* stooped to take it in hand and rolled it up as they walked.

In the hour she had spent with Kassalya on the ledge, she had learned of the visions, visions of a world controlled by Volkia, visions of the world come undone. Kassalya's burden was that she saw only the dark things. And that was a clue to Yevliesza's own future. Because Kassalya did not see Yevliesza ruining the world. No visions of the crossings coming apart, at least not by Yevliesza's hand. The right thing still *could* happen.

She had seen the worst future. Nothing that she did could be worse.

When they emerged from the cave, a freezing rain pelted them. The High Mother was there with a few sisters. They took Kassalya into their embrace, draping a cloak around her.

Yevliesza looked up at the sky, letting the sleet fall on her face.

The Devi Ilsat waited until Yevliesza finally looked at her. "My daughter," she said.

Yevliesza answered. "I'm ready to leave."

"Where will you go?"

"The Agarvesky Forest." Someone put a cape around her shoulders. "Is it far?"

The old *satvar* smiled, the skin crinkling around her eyes. "Four days, my daughter. And," she said brightly, "we have found you a horse."

PART II
THE DOOR IN THE FOREST

Chapter Eleven

It had been snowing all night. As Yevliesza stood at the back gate of the *satvary*, the snowflakes glinted in the moonlight like softly falling stars. It was the month of April—what in the Numinat they called the fourth month. The idea of snow in April seemed strange to her, but of course she was high in the mountains.

Although the snowfall had been subsiding throughout the early morning hours, the *satvars* assured her that the day would be a good one for traveling.

Dreiza was at her side, fussing with the straps on her backpack, saying, "Do not worry about the watchers. They are not able to see this side of the compound."

"I know." A cloud passed over the half moon, looking like a drifting figure of a woman in a long gown.

"They would not expect you to leave in the dark and in a snowfall. And they will not think you would head farther into the mountains rather than out of them."

"Yes, Dreiza." Her friend was reassuring herself. But Yevliesza didn't need encouragement. She was eager to meet this teacher called Ishtov, ready to find her strengths.

"Remember that the horse will be at Handre's farmstead in the first broad valley."

"Yes. Handre's stone house in the first valley." They had been over all this. She quirked a smile at Dreiza, trying to soothe her agitation. "So, if you found a horse, did you know I was going to leave?"

Dreiza faced Yevliesza. "We were not sure, of course. But prepared."

Yevliesza could not be surprised. The High Mother was seldom caught off guard.

"You have a supply of food, but if you are delayed, Handre will replenish your kit. The horse will forage, you need not be concerned about him." At Yevliesza's ironic look, Dreiza sighed. "I am fussing."

"Why does the High Mother call it an arcana?" The strange word Numinasi used for training in the control of powers. An arcana always had three students. "There aren't three of us. And the seer doesn't have my power, so how is it any kind of arcana?"

"Yes, well. The Devi Ilsat did not mean it would *be* an arcana. Only that it would be *like* one."

Yevliesza felt a smile tug at her lips. Dreiza was fitting well into the life of renunciation. She did public relations for the Devi Ilsat.

After so much uncertainty about what to do, now that she was at the *satvary's* back gate, she was impatient to be on her way. But she wasn't sure what to say next. *Pray for me* came to mind, but *satvars* did not pray. Numinasi did not.

"It'll be dangerous," Yevliesza said, finally admitting she was scared. She looked in the direction she was going to take. "The wilderness of the mountains."

Dreiza swallowed hard. "The aligns will guide you."

It sounded a bit hollow. The two women embraced, holding each other for a moment.

Then Yevliesza was ready. She pushed the gate open and stepped into the rock-strewn snow. Her legs were wrapped in hides, the fur side against her wool trousers. The boots that Rusadka had given her were skillfully wrapped in an outer layer of leather. Her fur cape, crafted by the sisters, came only as far as her knees, allowing her freedom of movement through the deep snows.

She took a last look toward the ridge behind which the watchers camped. It was a half-mile away, invisible in the darkness. Seeing Dreiza wave, she raised her hand in reply, then turned and walked away from the domicile, making deep tracks. Footprints, she reminded herself, that would soon be obscured with this snowfall or another one.

In the moonlit night, she was in a white landscape without features, but she was acutely aware of the aligns that appeared to her as tendrils embedded in ice. Zolvina's best aligner had drilled her on the patterns she would see and how to discern the way through the mountain pass and not get sidetracked into dead-end canyons.

The vast sky began to lighten. As the night retreated, she saw more clearly the profound distance before her and gathered her resolve. But the aligns would be her guide. She was glad there was more than one; she could not mistake the pattern. It was almost like being in the cross-ings, where she had known, *known*, the map of the tunnels. But those close spaces had comforted her, and in this endless world of snow and forbidding peaks, she felt a stranger.

Her path down the mountainside soon brought her closer to a region of towering slopes divided by a valley. Here the snows would have been impenetrable, except that a route lay clear before her. The *satvars* had known of this gorge and sent their elementalists ahead to forge a path. They had directed snow to the sides all the way down to pack ice. She followed this ravine for a long time until she came to a rocky field where the sun had melted the ice.

Behind a nearly vertical pinnacle, the sun was rising, limning her side of the valley with a molten glow. In the distance, she spied a tree. It stood alone, like a wayfarer who had paused on the journey. Her first guidepost.

BY EARLY AFTERNOON, SHE WAS EXHAUSTED, HER LEGS BURNING FROM exertion. She pushed on to her first stopping point, a small hut used by travelers. It had everything she needed: a charcoal stove with kindling, blankets on a raised cot. She carefully unwrapped her fire-making materials and when a little warmth filled the room, she removed her cape and unwrapped her legs and boots. She ate a meal from her pack and then lay down on the bed, pulling the blankets over her and sliding quickly to sleep.

The next day she descended into a region of sparse, twisted trees. Traversing a steep hillside, she followed an animal path. Among the trees she had the unwelcome notion that she was not alone. Snow cats might live at this elevation, but she was more afraid of people.

She quickened her pace, thinking she heard distant voices. But she didn't trust her ears. The wilderness here was so quiet that her own thoughts seemed to take up residence all around her, speaking, remembering, murmuring.

Tracking her would be easy in the snow. She didn't think the watchers could have seen her leave the sanctuary, because they likely would have overtaken her by now. But if they found her footprints outside the *satvary* walls only this morning, and if they traveled fast, they might be close. Once these thoughts alighted, she could think of little else.

She decided to hide for an hour or two and see if anyone followed her. When she saw a place to leave the trail next to a talus slope, she gathered up a fallen fir bough and tramped back up the trail twenty feet or so. Then, walking backward, she raked the path clear of her footprints. She climbed up the hillside, her destination an upright slab of rock among a cluster of them. Once there, she was hidden, but could still look down on the path. Resting, she ate from her rations and watched for movement.

Nothing. She rested her head against the wall of stone for a moment.

Startled, she came awake. How could she have let herself sleep? She turned to survey the path below. Nothing stirred. In the valley, a cold fog had crept in. The mountain peaks were gone; the pale sun curtained off. How long had she slept? What if anyone tracking her had gone past this location, following the animal path? That would mean she might come upon them from behind. She tried to banish her dismay. She had no choice but to go on.

On the path again, she walked carefully, trying to keep her tread quiet. Rounding a curve on the hill, she saw a man. Stopping, Yevliesza darted a look around for others, heart leaping in her chest, body primed to fight.

The man hadn't noticed her and was still resting at the foot an enormous evergreen tree.

But the man wasn't resting. He was dead. She approached the body. A horrid gash in the man's neck. Blood had formed a red icicle hanging down his side. The fur on his winter cap blew sideways in the wind. He wore good quality winter clothes, his knife fallen at his side. She took it, shoving it into her belt.

At a twist in the path, she found another body and then spotted two more that lay on the downhill slope. Four men bloodied and dead. They had followed her, going past her when she had left the trail and inadvertently fallen asleep. Who were they? But of course, sent by Nashavety. She was more powerful than ever, after her stay in the dark mansion that Valenty had described. Her dark fingers reached even here in the mountain wastes.

But then who or what attacked these men?

She left the scene of death, hurrying down the side of the hill, all stealth forgotten.

A soft knock at Valenty's door announced Elivasa's arrival. As he opened the door, she went into a flirtatious curtsy. He pulled her up and took her into his arms with a lingering kiss. Spinning her around to the door jamb, he pressed her against it, moving his hands over her ample chest.

The performance complete, they entered his bedroom, closing the door behind them.

"You are lusty tonight," Elivasa said, grinning and adjusting her dress.

"Perhaps you could cry out in ecstasy," he suggested.

"I think the seduction should take longer."

"Then laugh in delight?"

"Oh, my lord!" she loudly cooed.

He went to the fire to adjust the logs with a poker, and she joined him there, warming her hands.

They knew that someone had inserted a spy in the household. Without Dreiza to oversee the servants, Valenty had failed to identify the new cook's helper as a minion of the enemy. He was not sure which enemy, but guessed it was Sofiyana. He had decided to leave the servant in place. The boy would learn exactly what Valenty wished him to.

Elivasa turned serious. "You remember Nashavety's ring?"

"Of course. Sofiyana wears it when she sleeps." He had summoned Elivasa to discuss the protection of Anastyna—the clandestine steps they were taking to shore up her security—but apparently Elivasa had something else on her mind.

"Well, she speaks to it. My girl saw her doing so last night, when Sofiyana did not realize that she had left the door open."

"She is besotted with Nashavety. Her mind is unseated if she talks to the ring."

"Not just that. It talks back."

He stared at her.

"My girl was sure of it. She could not hear the conversation, but there were two voices, and one was coming from the ring."

He stalked away from the hearth. "By the Nine," he muttered. "By the hellish Nine, she is taking orders from the demon." He thought again of how he might have killed Nashavety at her hideaway in the Breminger Forest. He killed her bodyguards, and she was to be next, but instead he freed Pyvel and took him home. Urik had disapproved of the decision. Maybe he had been right.

"Dark arts," Elivasa said. "How else to speak between the realms?"

Sofiyana would forfeit her life for this. Nashavety was known to have gone over to the Volkish. So for Sofiyana, it was treason. But they had no proof. "The girl's testimony would not be enough," Valenty had to admit.

Now seated on the divan, Elivasa reached down to her ankle and adjusted the knife strapped there, an unconscious movement that betrayed the drift of her thoughts. "What are they planning?"

Valenty was now sure that the men camped outside Zolvina were Sofiyana's men. Sofiyana was not going to bring her back to Osta Kiya. She was going to give Yevliesza to the demon. His impulse was to ride up to the *satvary* with an escort and bring Yevliesza to safety. But he had already tried to persuade her; she would not come.

"Let it be known to the princip," Elivasa said.

"Yes. But she can do nothing without proof."

Elivasa bit her lip. "The real question is, besides taking Yevliesza, what else do they have planned?"

He ran his hand through his hair. "I should have killed her. And I let her go."

Elivasa had heard the story. "Her soldiers were in the hall, hurrying to her side. The only thing you would have accomplished would be to die at their hands."

"Worth it," he muttered.

"By the great almighty Deep," Elivasa scoffed. "Would you break my heart? Get me a cup of wine." She waved him to the sideboard. "And bring the pitcher."

He did. Then they worked into the night on the contingency plan. The one that would save Osta Kiya if Sofiyana wanted the torc.

⚜

ALBRECHT GAZED AT THE BURNING LOGS IN THE FIREPLACE. THE dinner with his command staff had been long, capping off a day of planning. They finally left, except for Marshal Reinhart and now, Nashavety, who had joined them from her room.

His mind spun with troop assignments and movement; reports on occupied Alfan Sih and Norslad, intelligence on Numinat, the next front. His senior staff were pushing hard to exploit the victory in the crossings and the fall of Anastyna. They were right to do so. Volkia was rising.

Yet he felt sobered. His old friend Lothric had died. His master at arms, the man who had taught him swordsmanship. He missed him, though he had been prepared to say goodbye for months. When Nashavety had first instructed Albrecht in how to exploit his soldiers' elemental powers, Lothric was the first to use his own elemental gifts to drive machines of war. And paid dearly for it. Men died in war, but some losses were personal.

Marshal Reinhart, sitting in the opposite chair, noted Albrecht's mood. "There is something, my prince?"

"No. My thoughts go wide, gazing at the fire."

Nashavety, ever in black, hunched forward in her chair. "How wide?"

"To strategy," he lied. He did not like it when she looked at him that keenly with those intense violet eyes. As though she saw things in him or wanted to. She was his central ally, but he did not trust her. What did she really want? Numinat, of course. She would be queen of Numinat. But was that enough? Obviously, she could not hope to rule Volkia.

She deferred to him less and less, but she had no taste for trappings. Her first quarters in Rothsvund Palace had been those occupied by the girl they both hated. But Nashavety disliked the suite and wanted rooms so small they seemed like caves. She kept the curtains closed and seldom emerged from her suite. When she walked the halls, he saw how uneasily his men watched her. She did not look well. Unnaturally thin, her face too long, her left hand shrunken and gloved, and her piercing gaze hard to meet.

He rose to refill his wine, but a knock at the door interrupted. An adjutant came in and in a lowered voice told him that the guards were encountering a disturbance on the roof.

"Disturbance?" Albrecht snapped.

"Birds, Commandant. Large ones. They look dangerous."

"Attacking?"

"No. Bunching."

Whatever that meant. He turned to Reinhart. "To the roof." He tilted his head toward the door, and Reinhart got to his feet at once. They strode down the hallway, with Albrecht acquiring a few soldiers along the way.

Once through the roof access door, the blind night met them. The moon was occluded, and no torches lit the scene of milling guards.

The senior guard came to his side. "Sir, there are four creatures that flew over us a few moments ago. Broad wings. We could not identify them when they landed. So far, they are occupying that corner." He pointed to the far end of the roof.

From behind, Nashavety's voice: "*Strigoi.*" She was pushing through the clutch of people, coming to Albrecht's side. "Do not be concerned, they have come to see me."

Something about her easy assessment annoyed him. "If they are *strigoi*, I rather think they have come to see *me*."

He and Reinhart moved across the roof, Reinhart with sword drawn. He had seen *strigoi*. Up close.

Albrecht saw a lumpy pile before them, sometimes gently moving. As his eyes adjusted to the darkness, he could make out four separate bodies. Leathery wings were tucked close beside them, but he knew they possessed small humanoid bodies. Albrecht stepped forward, holding back a hand to signal Reinhart not to follow.

He approached the pile for a closer look. One of the beasts lifted a wing and looked out almost coyly at him. Pointed teeth expressed what might have been a smile or a grimace. They were not as ugly as he first had thought when he had seen one in the cage on the night of the church rampage. Maybe he was getting used to his *sympat*, Strigo. Sometimes its expressions looked almost imploring.

Gradually, the creatures pulled away from each other, more alert now, and waiting. He believed that these *strigoi* had come to be with their fellow-creature, his *sympat*. Nashavety had told him that they flocked together and huddled in sleep.

He turned to a soldier who had followed him to the corner. "Bring bowls of blood. They are hungry after their journey."

The soldier nodded. "It will be done, Commandant."

The man hesitated.

"And?"

"The roof guard, sir. If they are attacked by the animals."

"Dismiss the guard from the roof. Post them at windows, below."

Nashavety had come up to him. Sometimes, in her presence, he detected the faintest smell of mold. Did the woman never bathe? Before she could interfere, he went on. "And bring the *strigoi* in his cage up from the dungeon. He will be next to his kind."

Beside him, Nashavety's face tightened.

He sucked in a lungful of cold spring air, letting his gaze go out to the city. Hapsigen pulsed with a reddish glow. The furnaces ran through the night, birthing machines. The harbingers of what was to come.

As he looked back to the roof, the unwelcome image came to him of his hostage, she of Numinat, the cunning witch-girl, who had walked here. Walked with Duke Tanfred, planning lies, treachery, and murder. She might have killed him in that small tunnel in the crossings. She had killed part of him, but he pushed that thought away. In its place came the question, once again, of how it happened that his arm had sunk into the substance of the wall. His men had cut it away, freeing him, but how had it happened in the first place?

Afterward, they had pressed on the wall, and it was solid. But not for her. Did she have elemental power that she directed to the wall, and caused it to soften and then imprison him? One could not have more than two powers, and she was known to have aligns. If she was also an elementalist, what of the verdure power that she claimed the pattern on her back represented? And if the skin pattern was not about verdure power, then what could the branching pictures depict? It was a missing piece. It felt important but would not come into focus. He was tired, and ideas did not cohere.

When he glanced at the *strigoi*, now looking up at him like hungry dogs, he imagined feeding the girl to them. Let her be naked. Let her be covered by leathery wings and lose her life blood slowly.

"Sir," Reinhart said. "A good idea to leave the *strigoi* on the roof?" It was a suggestion, not a question.

Albrecht gave a silent laugh. He had heard from Reinhart how *strigoi* fought.

"The roof now has their special protection."

They would see any intruders as food. They *would* be food.

Chapter Twelve

In a broad valley dotted with evergreen trees, Yevliesza fought to put one foot in front of the other, legs protesting but obeying. A film of ice hugged her face like a mask. The end of day two had brought her into the foothills, an almost welcoming place after the harsh landscape of snow and ice.

The images of the slain men kept her company. Peering into the mist-shrouded trees, she remained watchful for others, but as the hours passed, it seemed less and less likely that anyone pursued her. This valley was the wide basin that the *satvars* had told her she would find. A single align guided her now, faint in the icy mist but distinct to her deep knowing. The direction to the farmstead.

Step down, swing forward, raise a leg, step down. She marveled that her legs still worked. But she was out of the deep snow, walking on frozen grass and mud, an easier path.

She sensed something in the sky. A large shape flew over the valley. A dactyl. And now, two of them. Above, they circled each other, then came together, so close they should have collided. They swept their wings over each other and then did so again as they spiraled through the air to repeat the dance. At last they disappeared over the far reaches of the forest. Perhaps they would mate, but one of them might also reject the other. Maybe they were testing each other, testing for strength, for resolve. For loyalty. If life was kind, they might accept each other, bear young, fight off dangers, and find what happiness dactyls were heir to. Not a given.

The sighting left her keenly aware of her separation from Valenty. A mountain range lay between them, and always, affairs of state. But on this side of the Numins, her thoughts had cleared. It was a wilderness, but a pristine one, devoid of people and their relentless designs. Except that Kassalya's vision reminded her that those designs still mattered.

She kept watch for the dactyls but didn't see them again. Also hidden behind the ranks of trees, the Mist Wall in the distance. The Mist Wall that her ally in Volkia, Duke Tanfred, had put so much hope in. The wall that revealed the landscape to come as its curtain receded, leaving the nascent land behind. Land that would become a geography of rock, soil, and growing things. If there was something to worship in the Mythos, maybe that was it.

A gray mass emerged not far ahead, looking like a lifeboat in a white ocean. It became a a stone building. Smaller outbuildings appeared. A split-rail fence.

Handre's farmstead.

❧

The horse was tall and sturdy. Against dappled gray flanks, the black mane and tail. Handsome in a sturdy way. Handre said that Mitri was no longer young but did not know it. As Yevliesza patted the animal's broad forehead, she took a moment to become lost in his deep and dark eyes. He calmly gazed back at her.

Handre had thick short hair and a long beard, his face almost lost in the bear-like visage. Short for a man, his eyes met her at her level. He said that the horse would go the distance— although what distance it would mean in the end Yevliesza didn't know—and he would be sorry to part with the animal, but he had been paid well. Coin was always welcome with the four boys and a girl and their mother to provide for.

Yevliesza was no horsewoman. She had ridden only a few times before, at Osta Kiya, but from the first she had loved it. Fortunately, Mitri came with a saddle, small but sturdy-looking. And, Handre proudly pointed out, with stirrups.

Thinking of the journey still to come, she asked Handre if there were any men likely to be on the road with violence in mind. He waved the idea away. No one would dare. It was a peaceful region.

He tipped his head toward the road. "There is nothing there, young mistress. Nothing but forest. On the other side of it, a few villages. A long journey to take by yourself."

He meant it as a question. She pretended she hadn't heard it. If anyone came looking for her, the less Handre knew the better.

"You are not from here," he went on. Obviously, she had come through the mountains and wasn't a local. If there *were* any locals besides Handre and his family.

"Maybe you go to see the *providez,*" he slyly said, pronouncing the word with an emphasis on *prov*. She had heard the High Mother use the word.

Providez meant seer, and so he had guessed her destination.

"I'm going to meet my husband." That was her stock answer to anyone suspicious of her. It would satisfy most people, since she was obviously young and alone and surely in need of a man.

"Are you now." Letting go of further questioning, he said, "Then my Mitri will take you there. But only if you let him run now and again, you understand."

Mitri's ears pricked up at this, and Yevliesza scratched between them. "He likes to run?" She thought she and this horse would get along.

At Handre's table, his wife dished up bowls of stew and, in her almost delirious hunger, Yevliesza wondered if there would be enough for eight of them. Well, she reasoned, the children were small.

The stew was the best meal of her life. She paced herself, being careful not to be the first to finish her bowl. When offered another ladleful, she said no, but with a knowing smile her hostess gave her a helping anyway. The children watched her, wide-eyed and quiet, as though she was an apparition and not just a weary traveler.

They let her sleep by the fireplace. She dreamed of speeding in her old Celica down the long highway to the village store, windows down, racing a tornado. Winning.

❦

MITRI WAS A GOOD HORSE, SURE-FOOTED ON THE BROAD PATH, AND NOT easily spooked even when the forest grew thick. The great Agarvesky. The wind in the trees played against the branches with a soft thudding sound, always in the background. It was a region of pine and fir and greens so deep they courted black. But even here aligns appeared, cracks of fire broken into dashes by tree trunks. She could see one of them high to one side; somewhere in the fog it must be traversing a hillside. To the other side of her, a closer one that she merely sensed since it lay in a gully. The aligns were skewed toward each other at the correct angle, forming an arrowhead shape that was the pattern leading to the dwelling of the seer.

But then she was not so sure. The fog had grown thick, and sometimes she could not even see the aligns. She held Mitri's reins lightly, trusting him to stay on the path, but if there were intersecting paths, they might easily divert onto the wrong one.

She didn't know how long she had been riding when she came upon someone sitting by an open fire in a clearing. Yevliesza drew up on the reins. It was a woman.

"Good day to you," Yevliesza said.

"And to you," the stranger said. She wore a cloak, the hood thrown back. Her long hair fell in two braids past her shoulders. A black horse was tethered to a log, its saddle of tooled leather and silver grommets suggesting that its owner was a wealthy woman.

"I have hot tea," the woman said amiably enough. Bending over the fire she pulled a small pot off the coals to pour the tea into two cups.

Yevliesza dismounted, leading Mitri into the small camp and securing his reins. In the back of her mind, she wondered why someone traveling alone would have two cups. But her attention focused on the woman's face: narrow, with lines around her eyes and mouth and some white in her hair; a friendly aspect, and seemingly at ease in these deserted woods.

They sat beside the fire. Yevliesza hoped that the woman was headed in her direction because she would welcome company. At the same time she was wary. How did this woman happen to be on a deserted road when there was so little reason for travel?

The tea was very pleasant, but Yevliesza was on her guard. In the silence, she felt obligated to offer her name. "I'm Liesa."

"And I am Ana."

Yevliesza noted that her cloak bore a finely crafted brooch as a closure. But if she was wealthy, why would she be traveling without so much as a servant? "Which direction are you going in?"

"Well, no one would be going into the mountains. Maybe hunters." She shrugged. "I am headed in your direction. We can travel together."

A pause before Yevliesza answered. But on this single pathway they would have to travel together, at least until their paths split.

Ana collected her things, and soon they were back on the trail. She didn't seem in a hurry to have conversation, but Yevliesza was. "What's your destination, if I can ask?"

Ana gave her a sharp glance. "I am going to see a teacher. A very wise man."

"Would that be Ishtov?"

"Aye. The same."

It lessened the coincidence of finding someone on this road, but not by much.

"So you, too?" Ana asked, a smile playing at her lips. When Yevliesza said that she was, Ana went on, "I can show you. I have very good directions. I think we might be there before nightfall."

Yevliesza watched Ana closely. "Do you know much about this person?"

"Everyone knows about the *providez*. But if you do not, why do you come here?" Ana softened the remark with a smile. "He has lived a long time and has never left the forest. So, being alone, he has grown wise. If he agrees to speak with me—and that is never assured—I hope to become wise as well."

As they rode, the sound of the wind in the trees pounded harder. Yevliesza could see the tops of the trees swaying, but down on the path it was strangely calm.

"What do you want from Ishtov?" Ana asked.

"I'm not sure. I don't exactly know."

"Do you not desire to be free from ignorance? To speak to the dead? To become an advanced being?"

If those were the things that Ishtov dispensed, Yevliesza thought she'd come here for nothing. "Maybe he'll know what I need."

Ana seemed to like that answer, and they fell into silence. When they came to a meadow, they stopped to let the horses forage, then rode on as the light drained away, first at the feet of the trees, and then farther up.

In heavy dusk, they came upon a small lake, and an encampment with five or six huts and lean-tos.

"And so we are here," Ana said.

The woman seemed confident. "I think you've been here before."

"That is true."

Yevliesza was on guard now. Ana had pretended to be a stranger with good directions. But she seemed to be familiar with the place. A spike of worry went through her. She was in the largest forest in Numinat, armed only with a knife, and with no allies within hundreds of miles. Why had that ever seemed like a good idea?

There was a small bonfire going and people were gathered around it to eat their dinners. Some of them now stood up and stared at them.

The two women dismounted. "Who are these people?" Yevliesza asked.

"They are hoping to speak to the *providez*." Ana shrugged. "A few of them have been here for weeks. At some point they give up and leave."

The thudding of the trees increased, and Yevliesza looked around to see if a storm was coming. If it was, the darkness concealed it.

"So they've come a long way, maybe days on foot, and he just turns them away?"

"Some people are not ready. Not ready to hear what she has to say."

"She?"

"I am Ishtov," her traveling companion said. She cocked her head, a small smile at the corner of her mouth. "I hope you are not too disappointed." She urged Yevliesza to follow her around the curve of the lake.

Ana was Ishtov? "The High Mother at the *satvary* told me that the *providez* was a man."

"Are you sure she said that? Or did she only call me Ishtov, and so you assumed it? Ishtov is what I go by. It can be dangerous for a woman alone in the woods. Bad men might take advantage." She didn't seem to be worried about that, though. "By the way, you can call me Isha." A smirk, as though sharing a joke. "I know it is hard to keep all this straight."

They came to a small cabin furred in moss, with snow still clinging to the side of the house away from the sun. Wood lay stacked in precision against the cabin, and on the roof, grass grew from the shakes in withered clumps.

Past the cottage, Isha led her to a small, three-sided shed for their mounts. They spent some time laying out oats and filling two wooden buckets with water from a cask.

Yevliesza was still trying to adjust to the idea that she had been traveling with the seer all this time. From their conversation on the trail, she was not impressed. Talking to the dead? Becoming an advanced being? She wanted to know why the seer came out to meet her. That and many other questions circled around her.

The simple cabin had only one room, with the walls timbered and not dressed. In contrast, Isha had a finely made table and nice if mismatched chairs.

Isha saw her looking at them. "People bring me things. I cannot stop them."

They removed their cloaks and leggings, and Isha laid a fire. As she pointed a finger, the wood leapt into flame.

"You are an elementalist," Yevliesza observed. Isha shrugged, smiling, and her face looked younger than before. Much younger.

Yevliesza added, "And a manifester." Isha had changed her appearance from a very convincing middle-aged woman. In her new look, she had high cheekbones in an unlined oval face, and violet eyes framed by black, arched eyebrows. She was a striking woman. Or appeared to be, at least for now.

"Is this your true form?"

"Good question. Some days even I am not sure." She went to planked shelves and began to bring food and dishes to the table. "I suppose you expected an old crone. Everyone does."

"How old *are* you?"

Isha paused, dish in hand. "So we are starting with easy questions." She sighed and laid the plate down. "I have thirty-four years. Perhaps you hoped for someone who has spent their whole life becoming wise. But you can do it in a day. All you have to do is stick your head out of the fog."

One day to enlightenment. *All righty, then.* Yevliesza was confused, tired, and annoyed.

Isha took a long, wicked knife from the scabbard on her belt and placed it next to a brick of cheese. She glanced up at Yevliesza and motioned her to take a seat. "Do not worry, it is clean."

Had Isha killed those men in the mountains? Impossible, but the idea jumped out at her.

Isha watched her for a few moments without expression. "Are you hungry or not?"

She was. In silence, they ate bread and cheese and toasted nuts. All the while, Yevliesza surreptitiously inspected the knife for blood.

Chapter Thirteen

Shortly before dawn Andrik and Grigeni waited in Valenty's bedchamber as he hurriedly dressed. He grabbed the clothes he had worn the day before from a pile on a chair and threw them on. Grigeni held out a cloak, and Valenty fastened it around his neck as they rushed to the door.

In the dark hallways of the city-palace, no one stirred. The news had not spread yet. On the Great Circle, the *fajatim* were assembling in a rite not seen in living memory. The deposing of the princip. Valenty wanted to go to Anastyna. His every instinct was to protect her, but he could not stop what was going to happen. Was she still asleep, or had the *fajatim* sent word that her reign would now be judged?

Grigeni whispered to him and Andrik, "The vote will be invalid. One of them has forfeit her station through sorcery." As Keeper of Books in Valenty's household, Grigeni knew the laws.

Andrik snorted. "You have proof?"

"Not yet," Grigeni admitted. "But could we not accuse Sofiyana? Put her role in doubt?"

Valenty's silence was enough to quash the idea. It would not work. His wool cloak felt heavy around his shoulders like a great burden of obligation. *Anastyna,* he thought. *Oh, My Lady Princip.*

That it had come to this. The woman who wanted to open Numinat to the outside, to all other realms, to the mundat itself. But along with openness came the need to defend other kingdoms, and suffer new ideas of relationship and change. Some could not accept that. Some hated it.

They found a balcony overlooking the central courtyard. In the predawn, they could make out three of the *fajatim* standing on the great circle. Two others were approaching. Each bore a long-stemmed nightbloom rose in her hand.

On a balcony to one side and above where the three men stood, Valenty saw Anastyna. She wore a silver gown that shone in the light of the room behind her. Unlike the fashion of high-collared dresses, the neckline was scooped to display the silver torc. But it had never been an ornament, only a chain that yoked her to the kingdom, in service until death. Or until she was no longer wanted.

Andrik saw him looking at the princip. "I am sorry, my lord."

They had watched over Anastyna as best they could. Valenty, Andrik, Grigeni, Elivasa and the network of informants and operatives sprinkled throughout Osta Kiya. And now they likely had failed.

Anastyna stood without moving. Michai, the Lord High Steward, stood behind her with the key.

"Why," Andrik muttered. "Why?"

"Because of the eighteen hundred who died," Valenty said. "And how they died. Because the princip sent them to stop the Volkish from conquering another realm."

Now Valenty was able to identify the faces of the *fajatim*. Oxanna of Iron River standing to the north, anchoring the circle. So she would vote first. The others spread out equidistant: Alya of Storm Hand, Vajalyna of Wild Hill—always Nashavety's ally—Ineska of Red Wind, and Sofiyana of Raven Fell.

By now every balcony was full, all the windows with dark shapes watching. The units of the army had gathered in the center of the courtyard to bear witness. It was bitter cold, as befitted the proceedings.

Then a movement from the Great Circle. Oxanna raised her hand and slowly lowered it to shoulder height. She dropped the nightbloom rose onto the ground. So much for gratitude to Anastyna for bringing her son home.

Vajalyna was next. The rose fell from her hand.

At least four of them had to throw down the rose. So even if they had been able to discredit Sofiyana, if the *fajatim* could muster four votes, the thing was done.

Alya's rose left her fingers next.

Ineska of Red Wind had usually been a supporter of Anastyna. She did not look at her princip but dropped the rose.

Four. Anastyna was deposed.

There was still Sofiyana's vote. She could be counted on to make it unanimous. And she did not disappoint. She threw her rose onto the grass. The roses would remain in the circle, withering, until the next princip was proclaimed.

Bitter moments. Valenty's chest was tight with anger and dismay.

Standing behind Anastyna, Lord Michai reached up to insert the key in the torc. Having done so, he gave the collar a half-turn to the second insertion point, and the torc fell into two halves. Anastyna took one of them in her hand and Michai the other. She turned to him and gave him the section she held. A great murmur went up from the thousands observing her final action as princip.

Anastyna put her hand on Michai's shoulder and gave him a small smile to steady him before leaving the balcony.

As Valenty and his lieutenants left the balcony, Pyvel stepped into their path.

"Lord Valenty!" Pyvel said, his face contorted in distress. "How could this happen?" He wore civilian clothes, on leave from military duties.

Valenty met Andrik's gaze, dismissing him and Grigeni. The halls were filling with people. "It is our custom, Pyvel." Said for the benefit of any who might overhear.

"But she could not have known about the ambush!" Pyvel should know better than to openly criticize the *fajatim*.

"It is their right to depose her if they think there is cause." Valenty saw how his words only increased Pyvel's rancor. "Some may disagree, but we have no say in it." He put his hand on Pyvel's shoulder and steered him away from a knot of courtiers.

When they were walking toward Valenty's apartments, he asked, "Are you at leave to do me a brief service?"

"Yes, my lord, if it helps!"

"Helps *what*, Pyvel?"

The boy paused. "Nothing, my lord."

"Then get you to the *harjat* courtyard and find Urik. Ask him to meet me on the Tower steps after dark."

Pyvel's eyes grew round.

"And see that you do not arouse curiosity. Do you understand?"

"Yes, sir!" Pyvel turned to go, but Valenty called him back.

"Do not hurry."

"Yes, sir."

"And from now on, if you wish to help, you have no opinion about what has happened. You do not know about matters of high personages."

By his expression, Pyvel understood that he was being given a chance. To do something, something more than deliver messages.

The boy had certain advantages. He was housed with the army, but at his rank, he was not under the same discipline as the soldiers. He could pass relatively unnoticed in the halls of the city-palace, and he would be considered too young to be a traitor.

Grigeni was waiting for him outside the door of his quarters. "She has been given quarters in the north wing," he said, keeping his voice low.

They had wasted no time in ushering her from the royal suite.

"Will you go to see her?"

"No, Grigeni. What is there to say to a woman who has lost the torc?"

As they entered his hall, Valenty said with some force, "Have you nothing to do except gossip? Arrange the books, then."

Grigeni nodded. *Arrange the books.* Finally, the code words. He knew what to do.

"My lord," Urik said. Moonlight ghosted through the Tower doors. In the shadowed top room of the Tower, he was barely visible, but Valenty knew who it was by his voice and bearing. He had not seen Urik more than once or twice since their mission to kill Nashavety.

"Urik," Valenty said in greeting. To remain unseen, he stayed well away from the three doors.

"I see you have the boy on the steps below, to warn of any approach," Urik said.

Valenty had Pyvel sitting a few turns of the circular stairway below. "I asked it of him."

Silence. Urik disapproved his bringing the boy into danger.

"These are perilous times," Valenty said.

"They are."

Though Urik was barely visible in the darkness, Valenty thought he could read the man's expressions. He had spent a month with Urik in the wilderness of Volkia, and a bond had been forged between them. Unspoken, but they had taken each other's measure.

"You remember the house in the forest, Urik?"

"I remember." It had been enlivened by Nashavety's sorcery.

"The demon is now at work in Osta Kiya." The stones of the tower made a faint clicking sound as they lost their warmth to the cold winds of night. "She has control of Sofiyana."

Silence met this statement. Valenty was going to have to do all the work in this conversation. "The *fajatim* may be punishing her for the disaster in the crossings. But there is more."

"More that you are sure of, or surmise?" Urik leaned against the wall, regarding him.

"I am sure of some of the pieces. Others . . . are my prediction. But here is my question for you. What if Sofiyana becomes princip? Will the army support her?"

"Yes."

A quick answer. "Even if she brings sorcery into our midst?"

"You have seen her engage in dark arts, my lord?"

"She has a ring. It speaks to her." The Tower room seemed to grow smaller, as though leaning in to listen. "My spy in Raven Fell has observed this."

"Who speaks to her?"

"It is not a far reach to know who speaks to her."

Urik's voice came from the shadows. "This would not persuade our warriors. They have not seen what I have seen." The house in the forest that had ensnared them, almost blocking their escape, Nashavety's creature control of the guards and servants, and even a wooden statue that nearly crippled Valenty.

"If not the regulars, what of the *harjat?* "

"They have not seen what I have seen," he repeated. "And even if the *harjat* believed it, there would still be the army."

From down the stairway, Pyvel's voice: "My lords, I heard something."

Urik, closer to the stairs, said, "I heard it, too. It was an owl. Back to your post." They heard Pyvel's retreating steps.

"He is not too young to be cast from the Tower, Valenty."

It was strange to hear Urik call him by his name. But they had looked death in the face together and were no longer lord and body-guard. They had walked into the Volkish stronghold together, in the crossings when they deceived the Volkish soldiers, when Urik cast a manifestation on him to resemble Marshal Reinhart. They never would have escaped without Urik. At least in this Tower they were equals.

"Pyvel chooses to join me," Valenty said.

"And you ask the same of me?" Urik asked.

"I do."

"Anastyna cannot be restored to the torc by you or me. Or the army." Only the *fajatim* chose a princip.

"No. That is finished. But I fear for Numinat if sorcery wears the torc."

"Nashavety is far away, Valenty."

He feared that he was losing Urik. He heard it in his voice, could have predicted it from what he knew of the man's loyalty and the traditions of the *harjat*. To serve the princip.

"She used to be far away, Urik. No longer."

"I will bear that in mind." He pulled away from the wall. "Valenty. Do not depend on my influence. I am not first among the *harjat*."

"I gather what support I can. And warn who I can."

"Then I am warned." Urik's voice went into a whisper. "Go safely, Valenty."

"And you."

As they descended the Tower steps, Valenty was keenly aware how much was at stake, and not only for Anastyna, but for Yevliesza. If Sofiyana became princip, the men keeping watch in the mountains would descend on the *satvary* and take her.

Chapter Fourteen

Yevliesza turned over again on her cot, waiting for the night to pass. Isha had given her the narrow bed under the window while her teacher slept in the overstuffed chair. The creaking of the old hut sounded like someone walking on the plank floor. It kept Yevliesza on edge, and she slept only fitfully.

Was Isha dependable, or even well-meaning? And how keen were her powers if the woman had killed the men who followed her? And here she was, bedded down in the seer's cabin.

She pulled the blanket more closely around her, as a new thought occurred. On the road Isha had been testing her. She wanted to know if Yevliesza had grand ideas about becoming enlightened or speaking with the dead or whatever most pilgrims wanted.

"Time for class."

Yevliesza gave a yip of alarm and sat up to face someone by her bed.

Isha crouched at her side. Yevliesza flopped back down on the pallet. "Middle of the night," she moaned. Isha didn't move. Finally Yevliesza sat up, fumbling for her boots. When she had laced them, she found that the seer's face blurred for a moment, and now she looked like a man.

"Please stop changing around," Yevliesza said. Her teacher wore a heavy belted robe that could be for a friar or a nun.

Isha sighed, but dropped the appearance of being a man. "You seem to take men more seriously."

"I do not."

"Your father more than your mother?"

"What are you talking about?"

"You were quite entangled with your father, I heard. Your mother, all but forgotten."

"Right, I did forget her. She died at my birth. And I wasn't entangled with my father, I had to care for him." She paced away, trying to control her temper.

A shrug. "Valenty more than Dreiza? Dreiza was the one who supported you from the first." As Yevliesza wound up to object, Isha went on. "You're more concerned with Prince Albrecht than Nashavety."

Yevliesza leaned her hands on the table that lay between them. Slowly, she said, "You don't have any idea about me and those people."

"All right." Isha pulled a cape from a hook by the door. "Bundle up. We will go out." She opened the door, letting in a blast of frigid air.

"*All right?* You're accusing me of things, and that's just all right?"

They faced each other as Yevliesza fastened her own cape.

"I am testing for cracks. A little anger is all right. A lot of anger will not work."

Yevliesza was thoroughly awake now. The insults and the cold air had done their job. Maybe that was part of the plan in this weird arcana.

Predawn was still hours away. Though the forest huddled near on three sides, on the fourth side was the lake, and over it, the stars smeared a path across the sky. What did Numinasi call the Milky Way? She had forgotten.

As they walked, Yevliesza said, "A group of men followed me in the mountains. Somebody killed them; I didn't see who." Isha did not break her stride, and Yevliesza went on. "Maybe a snow cat or a bear?"

Without turning around, Isha asked, "How many men?"

"Four. Do you know anything about that?"

"No."

Four men would be impossible for Isha to take on. But still, the woman had been waiting for her on the road. Maybe she had been following her for a long while, and when Yevliesza stopped at the farm, Isha went ahead and staked out a place where it would look like she was another pilgrim.

When they reached the edge of the lake, Isha led the way onto the water. It looked as though her cape trailed along behind her across the surface. But then it became clear that there was a narrow dirt causeway. Yevliesza followed her along it until they came to a small, treeless island. On the side farthest from the pilgrim camp, split logs surrounded a stone firepit. They took seats opposite each other. Class would apparently be conducted here.

"Albrecht is not the one," Isha began. "He is not the one to fear."

"I don't fear him." That was a lie, but she needed some things to be private.

"He took things from you. But Nashavety wants to take *everything*. It is important to be clear about this. It weakens you to not see things for what they are."

She went on. "Albrecht is ignorant. He has succumbed to pride and ambition. Common maladies, as common as horseflies."

"How about cruel and bloodthirsty?"

"As I said, ignorant."

"Are you saying I suffered merely from his ignorance?" Anger flared. It surprised her how often it was coming out against Isha.

Isha said softly, "So you did suffer."

Yevliesza wanted to deny it, but instead she became aware of a cold well of water in her chest. She didn't need this. She hadn't come here for this.

In the silence, the cold in her chest. She sank into it. Things lay submerged in that cold well. Losses. People who had left her, even if they couldn't help it. Her mother. Her father. People who had taken things from her. Sofiyana. Nashavety. Albrecht. But all that was in the past. Now she had friends, helpers, a man who loved her. It helped to remember that.

For a long time they sat around the dark fire pit. The thudding of the wind in the treetops was like the beating of a heart.

"I took my revenge," Yevliesza murmured, trotting out the thing that had been a satisfaction to her ever since she fled the Volkish capital. "I think I gelded him."

"That usually does not work."

"He can still use sex . . . as a weapon?"

"Those days are over for him. But revenge is what does not usually work. For anyone."

Yevliesza tossed out: "I don't think Albrecht is the problem I need to work on. I need to save the world, OK?"

Isha threw a pile of sticks into the firepit, and they erupted into flame. "Grab some of those branches behind you."

Yevliesza felt behind the log where she sat and found a few tree limbs that looked small enough to burn. She laid them over the kindling.

"We do not have to consider what Albrecht did. Or when your mother left you, or what Valenty will do. They are all the same things. We can start anywhere. Or, if you're in a hurry—and you should be—we will just do everything at once."

Yevliesza had no idea what the woman was talking about. As she gazed across the lake, the trees at the water's edge emerged from the darkness like a jagged fence. The sky had begun to lighten. In the distance there was an enormous mountain. A mountain . . . except it appeared to be moving back and forth like a curtain blowing in the wind.

It was the Mist Wall. It shuddered now and then, beyond the last trees of the forest. What she had mistaken for wind in the pines had been the Mist Wall quaking.

She was so startled that she rose and stared up at it. Only the top of it was visible, as the thick forest obscured the lower region. Looking at it made her cower, with its aspect of a looming tidal wave.

Isha glanced at the Mist Wall. "I chose this place thinking it would keep people away. You see how successful that has been." She looked back at the little encampment on the other side of the lake. "People come anyway."

But people everywhere suffered. Couldn't she offer some solace?

"Solace is for *satvars*, Yevliesza."

Yevliesza didn't think she had spoken her thought aloud. But in her present state of confusion—in dealing with Isha and finding the Mist Wall looming nearby—she couldn't say for sure.

Isha went on. "What you need is the truth."

"The truth," Yevliesza said. "That's what I came here for."

A small smile edged into Isha's face. "If you did, you are the very first."

❦

YEVLIESZA WAS SWIMMING IN THE LAKE. IT WAS CRAZY, BUT IT WAS her first assignment: Take a swim in the lake. Actually, she didn't know how to swim, but Isha had told her to strip and then go in past her shoulders and practice. She was splashing about but had little idea how to proceed.

"It's freezing in here!" she shouted at her teacher.

Isha was building up the fire in the pit. "What did you expect when there is still snow on the ground?"

She was in a lake in the mountains so early in the spring that it might as well be winter. If the swim was to shock her awake, it had worked. She was hyper-alert and submerged up to her neck, which left her looking across the lake at eye level. Under the surface lay a hidden geography as well as fish and the other creatures. She wondered if that was why she had to get into the lake. To understand there were things beneath the surface.

Or maybe it was just to toughen her up.

When her feet had become unfeeling blocks of ice, Isha came to the water's edge and held up a cloak for her.

Yevliesza emerged from the lake shaking, her skin bluish. The cloak absorbed some of the wetness but the air bit at her like a thousand ants. She went to the fire pit and dressed, but she was still shaking.

Isha steered her to the log that served as a bench for two and put her own cloak around both of them as they sat together. Her arm came around Yevliesza's waist, and Isha became a source of warmth as well as the fire.

The flame crackled and spit, leapt and flickered. Yevliesza's mind emptied and there was only the fire, the lake, the forest.

They sat for a long time. Yevliesza felt drowsy and let her head rest against Isha's shoulder. "So tired."

"Then sleep."

When she woke up neither of them had moved, and the sun was higher.

"Are you hungry?"

"Starving."

Isha went to the stones surrounding the fire, removing a metal pan with a small pie in it. A spoon came with it. Yevliesza broke the crust and found a fragrant gruel underneath, infused with honey. She ate quickly.

The swim and the sleep had renewed her and her doubts about Isha receded somewhat.

"I feel better," Yevliesza told her.

"Yes. You appear to have recently had a concussion." From the crossing when Albrecht had struck her as he flailed against the grip of the wall.

Isha went on. "It is gone now."

"You are a healer," Yevliesza guessed.

"You have needed one for some time."

Yevliesza put down the metal pan and spoon with a clatter. "You worked a healing on me." She tried to muster anger over Isha's unwanted ministrations. Succeeded. Though she *did* feel better. "The swim was a ruse so I would be cold!"

At this outburst, Isha narrowed her eyes. "The swim was a swim. Not everything is a plot, Yevliesza."

"A lot of things are plots. You might not know if you've never been to Osta Kiya."

Isha smiled at that. As they regarded each other, her teacher sobered. "You came here to be my student. So you will take my lessons."

That was fair. She had decided to come.

Isha went on. "And yes, I am a healer."

"You have manifesting and elements. And healing, too? Three powers?"

"We should get this out of the way," Isha said. "I have all the powers. To one degree or another."

That stopped her. "I never knew that was possible."

"Ah. You never knew." She sighed. "Well. I have taken a different perspective. One that does not have all those limitations."

"What does perspective have to do with it?"

"My dear. It is all about perspective."

A little disappointing to hear. She had come all this way, and now it was about perspective. Then the startling thought: "Do you have the ninth power?"

"I do not. All except that one."

Yevliesza tried to grasp who she was dealing with. "Are there others with many powers?"

"I cannot know. If there are, they are rare."

On the other side of the lake, people sat watching them. Waiting for their turn to cross the causeway with the seer and find wisdom, or pretend to. A fog crept over the lake. As Yevliesza looked to the Mist Wall, it faded from view.

"Isn't it dangerous to be so close to the Mist Wall?" Prince Tirhan had said so when she had entered Alfan Sih with him.

"Very."

"So you live here, hoping people will be afraid to come. And when they show up anyway, you refuse to help them."

"I do not refuse everyone." She looked back at the encampment of pilgrims on the lake shore. "A lot of these people believe their dead loved ones reside in the Mist Wall." She gave Yevliesza a can-you-believe-it stare. "They believe spirits reside there. Some kind of afterlife."

"Is that why they're here?"

"I'm afraid to ask. Some of them hold on to a local legend about that." She rose from the log seat and regarded her student. "But why I do not work with most people, here is the plain truth. Almost everyone who comes to me wants one thing or the other in their life to go away. This is opposite of what I offer."

"But you offer healing—"

"Not usually. Because any healer can offer that. You do not need to brave the Agarvesky Forest and emanations from the Mist Wall to get that. And it is not one of my strong powers. What I offer is harder to accept, and frankly most people do not want it."

"The truth." Yevliesza frowned. "But you said . . ." She was stuck on something else. "There are bad emanations from the Wall?"

"Of course. That's why there are only a handful of people here and not hundreds."

"You can die of it?"

Isha closed her eyes as though summoning patience. "No one died. They are afraid to come. Just like you."

"I'm here, aren't I!"

"Yes, you are. But you are filling the air with questions."

"Dreiza says that, too."

"Dreiza is wise."

And I am not, Yevliesza mentally supplied, realizing that she had at last learned something.

Chapter Fifteen

Rusadka limped to the edge of the practice yard, favoring her right leg, which bore a bruise from hip to knee. It was not much of a battle wound, and she would not shy away from her duties for so little.

A few *harjat* had mentioned the Tanner's Square feast to be held for those wounded at the battle of the crossings. A decent gesture from those in the lower city, an event that a few high nobles could easily have paid for, if they could take their minds from the fall of the princip and their worries about their standing under whoever next wore the torc. There were rumors of roast pig and the last of the fall stores of corn.

When she got to her room in the barracks, she found a folded note on her cot. *Come to the grove in the courtyard before evening meal if you value your friend's life.*

Her friend? Rusadka's thoughts darkened as she considered whether that meant Yevliesza. Was she not safe at Zolvina?

She changed out of the hardened leathers she had been wearing for sword practice and considered the note. *Her friend's life.* No one would defile a *satvary* by forcibly entering. Or would they? Change had come to Osta Kiya, and everything was off balance. She no longer even knew who the army commander would be, much less who might take a violent action against Yevliesza.

Strange, that the message was a note. If it was from a *harjat* or a regular, they could have spoken to her in person. And if not a soldier, it was still someone who knew she was now third rank and therefore had a private room where a note could be left.

Yevliesza in danger. By the eight hells, had she not *told* her to reveal her new power to Anastyna so that the princip could protect her? And now it was too late for Anastyna's protection. The torc was in the Lord High Steward's care until the *fajatim* elevated someone to the role.

Rusadka put her leather jacket back on and buckled her sword at her hip. She would go, but armed.

A COLD FOG HAD SETTLED ON OSTA KIYA. BUT RUSADKA NOTED THAT the stable area and nearby woods were not affected by the fog, making her wonder if an elemental practitioner had brought the weather to the great yard.

The lights of the palace were beginning to come on, the windows glowing like a thousand small fires, blurs in the mist.

The temperature had dropped, perhaps another ploy to keep people out of the courtyard. As she entered the trees, Rusadka pulled her knife from her belt. Several paths intersected in a clearing. There, a small bench sat upon an align, one of the aligns that cut through the courtyard.

The clearing was deserted. But as Rusadka scanned the trees, she saw a figure move.

"Speak, if you mean well," Rusadka said.

The figure did not respond, and Rusadka thrust her knife in her belt and drew her sword.

"I am unarmed." A woman's voice.

"Show your hands and step forward." The woman did so. She was dressed as a noble, in tight bodice and full skirts, wearing a shawl around her shoulders.

"Speak, then, ghost-woman."

"No ghost, Rusadka. I come to ask for help. You know that your friend is at Zolvina, but she is not safe there, not anymore."

"What has happened?"

"Power has shifted. The princip was brought down."

"That is no concern of mine." If this was about ambitions for the torc, Rusadka wanted nothing to do with it. It was one reason she had joined the military. To have a clear role, to be free of the palace intrigues, and to know her place.

"I will tell you the story you do not know. But you must come closer. In case I have been followed."

"First, who are you?"

"Leave that for now." A note of impatience. "Do you want to hear or not?"

Rusadka liked that. It was more real than being over-friendly. She walked closer to the stranger. Shorter than Rusadka. A round, pretty face but with a strength about her. Court dress, but standing like a fighter.

"I am listening."

"When Yevliesza was sent to Volkia, you remember that Lord Valenty had been sent to inspect the garrisons. A royal jaunt, everyone thought, except he went to Volkia to kill Nashavety. He failed."

Valenty sent into Volkia? It seemed unlikely. But if the claim was true, of course he would fail.

"Get on with it, woman."

"He had a choice when he found her. Kill her or save the youngster Pyvel, who had been kidnapped. Kidnapped to send a message to Anastyna that Nashavety could pluck whoever she wanted and force them to serve her."

"And he saved the boy single-handed? A pleasing story."

"Oh, it is a grand story. He did have help, but I cannot disclose who. By this other person's great gift of manifesting, Valenty passed in and out of Volkia by appearing to be a well-known Volkish officer. If they had been caught, the two of them would have hung as spies."

Rusadka detected the woman's loyalty to Valenty. It seemed everyone had a high opinion of the lord except her.

"He saved the boy's life. That is why Pyvel is devoted to him."

So her story was that Valenty was not a useless noble. He was a man of courage, and a spy for Anastyna. A lot to put together.

She tried to identify the woman. Her face was familiar. She almost had her name . . .

The woman went on, "Here is the part that affects you: Nashavety has grown her power back. By sorcery. She controls people by creature power. And she has devised a trespass use of elemental gifts to power battle machines. Those you have heard of. Those have killed your fellow warriors."

Nashavety. She had gone hollow, and worse than hollow. She had gone into diabolics.

"Does Yevliesza know all this? Does she know the real Valenty?"

"She was deceived at first, but he trusted her and told her who he is."

"And now you trust me?"

"Because we have a common purpose: to protect Yevliesza. If Sofiyana becomes princip, she will order Yevliesza taken from her refuge. And then to the Tower. Or make her a gift to Nashavety."

"They would never give the torc to someone so young."

"They might. If they are infected by sorcery. I know that Sofiyana is under creature power. She speaks to the amber ring, and it answers her."

Rusadka muttered, "Eight dark and wretched hells."

The woman chirped a laugh. "Indeed."

Drawing in a cooling breath, Rusadka felt an encroaching dread. She sheathed her sword and drew closer, lifting the woman's chin so she could look into her eyes. She *did* recognize her. "You are Elivasa." One of Valenty's bedmates.

Elivasa steadfastly met Rusadka's gaze. "Yes."

"Swear that these things are the truth."

"I swear it. But I think you know they are true."

Rusadka withdrew her hand from Elivasa's chin and turned away, walking a few paces. She faced Elivasa again. "What do you want from me?"

"Wait for outcomes. Then, if the worst comes to pass, help us."

Help us. The words hung in the air. She was on the brink of treason. At stake, her very honor. All the things she had sworn to do. Serve the princip of the realm; obey her orders; give her life if required.

And this woman, this Elivasa, who might be Valenty's lover, had assembled the evidence in a way that exonerated him. It did explain why Yevliesza could love him, there was that.

Elivasa murmured, "Why do you dislike Valenty so much?"

Rusadka felt her mouth twist. He pretended to be a scoundrel, but he had done much for Yevliesza. Including seeking out the messenger whose testimony at her trial brought Yevliesza's acquittal. The messenger who had seen Nashavety's hand behind the storm and the lightning. But Valenty got something in return. Her love, her body . . .

"Maybe you are jealous," Elivasa said.

"Of Yevliesza?"

"Of Valenty."

Rusadka barely contained her anger. "That was the wrong thing to say." She turned away and left the grove, plowing her way into the fog, trying to pull it closed behind her.

Eight miserable hells. The woman was arrogant and annoying in the extreme.

Chapter Sixteen

Pyvel made his way through the pathways of the lower city, the coins in his pocket jangling with every step, loud in his ears, but no one seemed to notice. His task was to distribute money, purses of coin for specific merchants. The first one was for Hyrador, at the ale house known as The Owl's Perch.

In the middle of the day, few customers were at the tables or warming themselves at the hearth.

He spied a serving woman funneling ale into pitchers, getting ready for the noon meal trade. "Please, miss, can I speak to Hyrador?" She pointed down a hallway, and Pyvel approached the man rolling barrels into the hall from the back door.

"Hyrador, sir?" Pyvel asked.

The man turned to him, sizing him up as he wiped his forehead with the back of his arm. "Ain't no sir, but I answer to Hyra," he said, looking down from a great height. His pant legs only came to his shins, and Pyvel wondered if he was still growing.

"My master wants to, or he feels like, that since there's a feast to be held—"

"Your master being?" he interrupted.

"Lord Valenty, I meant to say."

"Well, a feast means someone brings the food. Valenty's man —Grigeni was it?—was already here and asked for a roast pig, and things bein' what they are, I said I would think about it. And that is what I am doing."

"Yes, sir. But my master wants to show his support, so he sent me with some coin for a pig or two, if you have a mind to be a part of it." He dug in his pocket and retrieved one of the small leather bags.

Hyra took the proffered sack and noted its heft appreciatively. "That would go a ways toward a pig."

"Or two," Pyvel said.

"Might." Hyra put the sack of coins in his pocket. "I want to do my share, and I would have. But now it will be two pigs, my boy, and fat ones. Tell your master he can enjoy a cup of ale at the Perch any time, and no cost. You tell 'im that."

"I will, sir! I will, Hyra, and thank you."

"Maybe we will see you at the feast. A cup of ale for you, too!"

Pyvel ducked a bow, smiling about how the owner said he would be welcome to a cup of ale. Once out on the street that ran along the side of the hill, he looked down the steep drop, and wondered how many patrons of the Perch had fallen off from too much ale.

Turning into a set of stairs, he went down to the next level to find Mistress Vasha's bread ovens. The thought of food, and lots of it, made him sorry that this was a party he was going to miss.

For Valenty's mid-day meal in his chamber, Andrik brought a tray of boiled mutton and parsnips, as well as a fresh loaf of bread and an apple only a little wizened with age. Everything was to be done according to Valenty's habits.

Valenty looked at the tray without appetite. The excuse for Andrik to be there.

"Anastyna is out walking, under escort," his chief spy reported.

At last, a chance to see her. Valenty went to the wardrobe and grabbed his best velvet jacket. "Where is she?"

"Passing the Elemental Balcony."

He would have to hurry. Leaving his personal quarters, he quickly moved through the household corridors and into the palace proper. The halls of Osta Kiya were almost deserted, as though everyone was keeping to themselves, too bruised by events to carry on normally.

Valenty had not slept. He, Andrik, Grigeni, and Elivasa had briefly met to finalize their plans should the worst happen—that Sofiyana came to the torc. Or any other *fajatim* who might now be under sorcerous control. He had to persuade Anastyna to cooperate. Now that she was no longer princip, her cooperation might be easier to secure. But he could not be sure.

He shook off his weariness and strode into the main corridor leading to the north side of the palace, the location of her new quarters from which she would be coming.

Ahead, voices from one of the chambers drew his attention, and he stopped at the entrance. Anastyna was in the Waxing Moon Chamber, tracing the circle in the floor with her steps. With her were two noble-women as companions and, oddly, a member of the princip's guard. The guard, monitoring her.

"My lady," Valenty said from a deep bow.

"Oh, Valenty, no bowing, please. We are equals now."

"How do you fare, Lady Anastyna?" He had advised her for the last six years. She might think their relationship was different now, but to him, she would always be the princip.

"I am becoming accustomed to the north wing," she said with a wan smile. "One can see the Numin Mountains. They are still snow-covered."

He approached her and offered his arm. She took it, and they strolled to the tall, lancet windows overlooking the courtyard. The guard watched them, but they were only standing at a window, and he could not object.

"Have you everything you need, my lady? I can put my servants at your disposal."

"Thank you, my lord, but I do have servants, still."

She did not read his meaning. He pressed on. "You could send them to make sure you have all your personal belongings. Surely, with . . . events and the press of things, you have left things behind. Or I could escort you there. Maybe to retrieve things with sentimental value?" She had to get into the small room next to her bedchamber. From there, he could lead her through the hidden passage to safety.

Overhearing, one of the women, Paulia, said. "I would be happy to fetch anything, my lady."

Anastyna looked at her with icy indifference. If she thought that such familiarity was now acceptable, she had just learned that Anastyna still knew how to deliver a royal snub.

Anastyna whispered, "If Sofiyana is next, you must expose her."

Valenty laughed as though they were sharing a bit of gossip. He whispered back. "Get you to your sleeping chamber. All is ready."

"I will not run." She patted his arm and disengaged from him. "No more gossip, my lord. I am in no mood. For any of it."

By the Nine, she still did not see the danger. Sofiyana would never trust her. Anastyna was in grave danger.

"You can walk with us, if you will," Anastyna offered, as she rejoined her escorts.

It was maddening, but she acted as though she were taking a royal walk to chat with her subjects. In frustration, Valenty joined the group for their stroll.

Before they could leave the chamber, Michai appeared at the entrance. The Lord High Steward bowed his head of snowy hair, bending too low for her new status. "My lady," he said in a sonorous voice. In the princip's Audience Hall he had conducted many meetings with a voice that carried.

Behind him stood two guards.

"I have the duty to give you this decree, my lady." He brought forth a piece of vellum folded and tied with a violet ribbon, showing that it was from the *fajatim*.

"Lord Michai," she said gently, seeing his distress. "Tell me, what does it say?"

"It says . . . that is, the *fajatim* declare . . . that you are accused of treason."

Anastyna did not react. But by the stillness of her features, she was having difficulty believing what she had heard.

"If you please, Lord Michai. Read it to me."

He swallowed and by his expression, he would rather endure a beating than open the letter. He undid the tie and read:

"Anastyna, former princip and noble personage of Osta Kiya, is under arrest for the crime of treason in which she, by reason of personal gain, misdirected the Army of Numinat to Nubiah. This grave decree is solemnly made by the assembly of *fajatim* into whose hands has come a letter from the former envoy of Nubiah, Prince Chenua, who demands by her love of him, and by their many promises to each other, including for the defense of his realm, that she must hasten to his aid now that Volkish troops were in readiness to break through to his kingdom. This she did, without caution for the great loss of life that ensued. This she did, inspired by her amorous alliance in a foreign land."

And there it was. Sofiyana's plan. Not an assassination. A fall from the Tower.

Anastyna lifted her chin and said in a clear voice, "There is no such letter. I had no such agreement."

Oh, but there *was* a letter. No doubt Sofiyana had made sure of that.

"My lady," the Lord High Steward said. "The proceedings will discover the truth. I will conduct the trial with all my ability."

"Am I to come with you now?" Anastyna said, glancing at the two guards.

"Yes, my lady."

"May I stop in my sleeping quarters to take a personal keepsake with me?"

"I am sorry," Michai murmured.

"Anastyna," Valenty said. "You do have supporters." He spoke carefully, to be sure his words were not interpreted as defiance of the *fajatim*. "They will not abandon you."

He caught Michai's eye. "Who will preside over the trial?"

"Our new princip, my lord. The Lady Princip Sofiyana."

So it was done. The *fajatim* had voted, their hearts fouled with sorcery.

He asked Michai, "Where are you taking Lady Anastyna?"

"She will await trial in the nethers." With that, he gestured Anastyna in front of him, and she walked toward the guards who stood on both sides of her, each holding a wrist, as though they thought she would run from them. Did they not realize Anastyna *did not run?*

And so his plan was broken. Broken by a charge no one could have imagined. It was so much worse than the murder that Valenty had feared. They planned to take not only her life but, by accusing her of treason, would destroy her reputation, her legacy. A cold darkness twisted in his chest. As the feeling worked its way into daylight, he found it was a strong and crystalline anger.

Nashavety's revenge. She had waited nearly three months to bring Anastyna to the same place she had been: the Trespass Door in the great Tower.

Chapter Seventeen

In the hut, Yevliesza sat on the cot while Isha settled into the one comfy chair. The hearth fire kept the small room warm, and the snapping flames helped to mask the thudding of the Mist Wall, a sound she found hard to ignore.

"The first instruction," Isha said, "is that you do not repeat what you learn here." She paused to make sure she had Yevliesza's attention. "No one will believe you. Save your energy. You will learn things from me, but you are not ready to be a seer."

"I wouldn't try to be."

"Oh, it will come to you: A certain person needs saving. Another person needs to learn things. Maybe. But they will not thank you for it. Most of the time people just want their pain to go away. Quickly."

Yevliesza gave a small nod of agreement. But given Isha's dismissal of the pilgrims, she wondered, why *her*, then?

When she asked, Isha said, "Because you passed the test. Remember on the road how I asked what you wanted from the seer? I offered wisdom, speaking with the dead, and becoming a superior being. You said you did not know." Isha hiked her shoulders. "A good answer. You were not running from something or grasping at something."

"I did run, though." Trying to keep her old life, trying to fend off something bigger than she could contain.

"But you did not keep running. You came here. You are open." Isha shrugged. "More than most."

A howl came from the woods, and Yevliesza's head snapped up in surprise.

"Wild animals," Isha explained. And with a wry smile, "Would you expect any less of the Agarvesky?"

Isha had begun to smile more often. A welcome change from her first, abrupt manner. But still, her comments often threw Yevliesza off. She found that she had to pay strict attention.

Isha went on. "So I decided to invite you in. Otherwise, you would be out there with the other seekers." She tilted her head to the little camp of hopefuls. "Also, I knew all about you from the Devi Ilsat."

That surprised her. She had wondered how Isha knew her background and had assumed it was some kind of spiritual power. That's what she had expected of a *providez*.

"She sent me a letter. I suppose you were expecting magic. I *can* receive letters, you know." Isha rose and rummaged for something among the open shelves. "Not easily. But occasionally a messenger actually arrives." She came back with a fistful of pages. If this was the letter, it was a long one.

"I do not need it anymore, so you can feed it to the fire." She held out the sheaf of paper.

Yevliesza took them to the hearth. The High Mother's looping cursive filled the pages, and she caught a few words as she looked at the top page: *dactyl, Ansyl, origin world, bridge of the moon, House Valenty* . . . It was Yevliesza's story, and it seemed wrong to burn it, but she didn't want to appear attached to it. Into the fire it went. The pages curled and blackened.

"The part I do not know," Isha said, "is how you escaped from the Volkish palace."

Well, Isha didn't know what happened *in* the Volkish palace, either. Or, thinking about the cold swim and her time in the seer's embrace, maybe Isha did know.

"Tell me the story of your escape."

Yevliesza gave her the short version: The vine growing up to her window; Albrecht at church; the fog; the wilderness of brambles. The waiting carriage; the fear, the panic. And then the wolf. How it came to her, disappearing and returning. The wraith wolf. If that is what it was. How she and Tanfred had almost made it to the Numinat gate when they learned that Albrecht was on his way, and how she had turned back to put a stop to him. And how the crossings helped her, holding fast to his arm, imprisoning him.

After the story was done, Isha made no immediate comment, but stirred from her chair and clattered around the kitchen area until she came back with a plate of cookies. Lunch, Yevliesza assumed, and she reached for one.

"That explains it then," Isha said. "How the bad men died. It was the wolves." She smiled at Yevliesza's puzzled expression. "Your close creature, your *sympat,* brought a few pack members, and they took care of the threat."

So a wraith wolf *was* her *sympat*? A frisson of excitement darted through her.

"All right," Isha said. "Time for your walk." She took a cookie and munched on it. "You are going by yourself. A little forest walk. Do you good."

"Is this another test?"

"No, it is an assignment. Go and meet him."

"Meet who?"

"Your wraith wolf. I have seen him around. I thought he was interested in *me*. But it appears not." Cocking her head at the door, she said, "Go."

Yevliesza took her cloak from the hook by the door. "What do I do?"

"Make friends, my dear. And give him a name."

"Maybe he has his own name, and I should learn it."

Isha repeated slowly, "Give him a name."

"What about the emanations? What if I walk too close to the Mist Wall?"

Isha swallowed, and probed her teeth with her tongue. "I must admit that emanations do not exist. I keep the rumor going to protect my privacy, keep people away." She looked up and gave Yevliesza a bright smile. "So it is good to know it still works."

She waved her hand toward the door.

ABOVE THE TALL TREES OF THE CONIFER FOREST, THE SUN SHONE IN A blinding patchwork of blue, but at ground level, shadows prevailed. Yevliesza walked into the dense woods. She spied out a path not far in, a narrow one such as deer might follow from their dens to the lake. She expected bird sounds, but the woods were quiet except for rustling in the tree boughs and once, the chittering of a squirrel. It was still winter here, but it was retreating.

She knew the wolf—her wolf, she thought she could say—would find her or not, would come to her or not, all on its own. She hoped it would. Even though it might be in company of other wraith wolves, and they might not have the same connection with her as the one who had led her from Albrecht's palace. They were dangerous. They had killed those men in the mountains. She felt no remorse about that, only wariness of being in their presence.

But she wanted to find her wolf. If it was her *sympat*, it would prove something; prove that the lost power coming into her wasn't a mistake. Why it would be proof, she couldn't explain, but she wanted this *sympat,* this remarkable connection with the Mythos.

The trail wound far into the woods, down into gullies, over fallen and moss-covered logs, through patches of snow hiding from the sun like white-pelted creatures. Her senses filled with the heady scent of pine and snow and soil, wiping her mind clean of thoughts.

She came to a great fallen trunk of a tree and sat on it to rest. The sun pierced the forest understory in long, slanting ingots. Watching the play of light, she let her eyes follow the shafts into the shadowy distance, like bright sentinels guarding the forest.

A twig snapped behind her. When she turned, a wolf stood some ten feet away. Her breath went shallow as she watched the creature. It was the size of a large dog, but compact, with strong shoulders and legs. Its coat was coarse black, the underside a lighter shade. Green eyes regarded her in an alert, splendid face. It was wild, with no hint of friendliness, but also no fear. The wolf took a step closer.

Yevliesza felt frozen in place. She didn't think other wolves came with it, but she couldn't take her eyes off this one. It had come very close to her without making a sound until the twig snapped. But it might not have come from the woods. Maybe it had stepped through from the otherworld.

Was it aggressive to keep eye contact with it? She thought it might be. Closing her eyes, she remembered to breathe, but breathing was not easy, and she consciously filled her lungs and let her breath fall away. She wished she knew where the wolf was now, but she forced herself to keep her eyes closed.

Against her knees, the press of a flank. The scent of animal fur, filled with forest and snow. The near pass of a cool wet nose, not quite touching her wrist.

"Oh, Kiya," she said, knowing the wolf for her companion, and knowing its name.

With her eyes closed she took in more about her *sympat* than when she had been staring at it. Like all wild animals, it was an unknowable being, familiar in frame and movement, but utterly strange. It was also immortal. Wiser than she, in its own knowing, its own apprehension of the world, the many worlds. She felt humble and joyful at the same time, a collision of feelings that filled her with light.

When she opened her eyes, it was dusk. The wraith wolf was nestled against her feet. Yevliesza carefully shifted her feet a little, and the wolf stood. She wanted to touch its head, but she didn't think either of them were ready for that, and might never be.

She needed to use the remaining minutes of the day to return to the cabin, to find her way there. She didn't want to leave her wolf, but it was time to go. She left her perch on the log and started down the path, less obvious now in the falling light. The padding of feet behind her told her that Kiya was following. The name of the city-palace, Osta

Kiya, meant *castle of clouds*. She didn't know why the name came so easily. *Kiya* for cloud. But she knew it was right.

When Yevliesza entered the clearing where Isha's hut stood, she could no longer see Kiya. He was gone. And Kiya was a he, not an it.

The cabin's few glazed windows flickered with light, and she went inside.

Chapter Eighteen

I t was night in Hapsigen, but the sky glowed from the forges through a murk of smoke. Workers kept the iron-working fires stoked without pause, such that Nashavety wondered that the forges themselves did not melt.

Over the roar of the nearest forge mouth, Reinhart was explaining the process of clarifying base ores into workable iron. In the great pits, the very air seemed to catch fire, as pieces of slag erupted from the flames and fell like burning snow.

As the two of them continued the tour, men stepped out of Nashavety's way, more daunted by her than by Marshal Reinhart, who had a reputation for cruelty. A shirtless, sweating man stood to one side, leaning on his shovel. But beside him lay piles of coal in need of shoveling. The invasion of Numinat was coming, and he was resting?

Reinhart led her into a great free-standing building filled with the smell of oil and metal. Here, the war machines were warehoused, the various and wondrous machines.

Nashavety stopped to take in the vast assembly of iron shapes. They were inanimate now, but with elemental power, the power over adamantine materials, each iron weapon could be turned to killing.

It was she who had recognized the possible role of human-powered machines. Her breakthrough had come at Drogeliv, as she repaired the small finger of her hand and, in doing so, left common understandings behind. During her recovery, she had learned how to draw powers from her servants. She could extract powers, at least for a few moments, giving her not so much the specific powers she siphoned, but the strength of them, which she could then bring to bear on her dark arts.

That had given her the idea that Deep powers were malleable. And since elemental power was one of her affinities, she had practiced with its essence and eventually had Albrecht bring a sample machine to see if it might be driven by elemental power.

It could.

Within just a few months, the forges had been repurposed. And now, this army of iron.

It was true that unnatural machines were inimical to the Mythos. But these machines were not powered by offensive energy, as in the mundat, but by birthright powers, which were natural to the realms. And the Mythos could not be disturbed by that. Or, if it could, they would have to be judicious in their use. But what could be more natural than elemental power?

They passed an impressive row of cladders, each armored body supported by a pole, waiting for its driver. Nashavety passed close to one, its body looming unnaturally massive, its face shaped like a creature of nightmares. The hands were oversized, adept at grabbing and delivering sideway swipes that could smash skulls.

"The fingers can be activated to fire fragments of metal through their hollow cores," Reinhard explained.

She remembered the tales of the battle of the Nubiah crossing when Numinasi soldiers fled screaming from them.

"But," Reinhart went on, "they have a weakness that the rebels in Alfan Sih exploited. The eye slits. A well-aimed arrow can kill the operator inside. As well, once a cladder falls, the operator cannot by himself bring the casing to stand again." He shrugged. "But they have special value in causing panic in the field."

Panic. Shock. Despair. Such useful things for draining the heart, weakening the body.

Now they approached a formation of implements that looked like man-high metal shields, except that a tube projected from each. Looking at the backside of the shields, she could see a device for receiving bullets.

"A volley gun," Reinhart explained. "The shield component is lightweight, allowing two men to move it quickly for strategic advantage. One of these can hurl projectiles faster than the eye can see. Dozens mowed down within in the space of one breath." He added, "Stopping breaths," and laughed at his witticism.

"How many of these are ready?"

Reinhart glanced at the major who accompanied him.

"Three hundred and fifty-four, sir."

Nashavety asked, "And how many elementalists are trained to the weapons?

"Almost two hundred, madam," the major said, in a tone that seemed entirely too satisfied.

The weapons must be fueled. But if those trained in their use did not last long, they must train more. They had learned how soldiers became useless—depleted of their birthright power— during the takeover of Alfan Sih and Norslad.

In the far reaches of the hall lay the battle wagons. Flush-sided conveyances on four wide wheels and bristling with projectile tubes. Nashavety had seen other versions of them patrolling the streets of the capital. Common folk had a terror of them and with good cause.

As they retraced their steps through the warehouse and then the forges, she spied the same shirtless man still standing idle.

"Major," she said, turning to the officer accompanying them. "Why is this man not working?"

"Madam, even a man of Volkia must rest," he said indulgently.

"Have him approach the forge."

The major paused, but with a quick glance at Reinhart, ordered the man to take his shovel to the forge door.

Nashavety nodded approvingly. "Now throw him in."

Reinhart jerked a look at her, his eyes narrowing.

"Let him be an example," Nashavety said.

"Madam," Reinhart murmured. "The men must sometimes rest."

"He will have a long rest now. Do it."

Reinhart nodded to the major, who gave the order. As the miscreant went into the flames, the forge mouth vented an explosive burst of light.

Workers from the other forges stood gaping, but as Nashavety's entourage passed, they quickly turned to shoveling coal.

❧

Grigeni threw a blue splash of color into the air before him, swirling it into a turning wheel. The abandoned corner of the castle provided the privacy he needed to practice some sky painting.

The screech of an owl shattered the silence. Startled, Grigeni looked up at the window high on the wall of the shadowy chamber. He spied the hunkered form of an owl silhouetted against the moonlight.

Grigeni tried his manifesting skill again with bright blue but had barely formed a circle before the sparks vanished. Not normally a man who cursed, he whispered, *By all that is plain!* He tried a splash of gold, forming it into a petaled flower. When it exploded in a shower of golden drops, his annoyance grew. Exploding flowers would hardly be appropriate for the celebration.

Tonight, for the feast in honor of Numinat's soldiers, there would have to be more than fine words and good food. Sky paintings would bring a fair number to the plaza, and since they could not expect the best artists to participate, a few manifesters with merely crow power would have to put on a show. Like himself.

A motion in the deep shadows by the wall. Grigeni's heart leapt, thinking it was Sofiyana's men.

"Be at ease," came the voice.

It was Andrik, the dark tones of his face giving him cover in the darkness.

"You might announce yourself," Grigeni said, recovering.

"I just have. What news from the lower city?"

"People will be there. Pyvel has given out the purses for food and drink."

Andrik drew closer. Lord Valenty's chief spy had always made him nervous. Among other things, it was unsettling that the man's *sympat* was a fiery-eyed stormhawk.

"That would be well. The more crowded the better. Makes it hard for soldiers to pursue us."

Grigeni nodded, though Andrik could not see it in the murk. "But the officers are spreading the word to watch the sky paintings from the roof and save Tanner's Square for the wounded."

Andrik remained silent, considering this. He had a lot on his mind, running the whole escape plan. Sofiyana—by the Nine, *Princip* Sofiyana—had learned that Valenty's true alliance was with Anastyna. Now the only part that Valenty could safely play was as a distraught noble, gossiping in the halls and staring out at the courtyard as though he could bring the *fajatim* back to make a different decision. The impression he meant to give was that he was now helpless to dislodge Sofiyana's grip on power. Helpless to save Anastyna from a sure judgment at the coming trial. Andrik found himself smiling.

"Has the *harjat* decided to help?" Andrik asked.

From the narrow windows in the dark hall, more birds were flying in to roost, chittering and screeching.

"Rusadka is the one who spread the word of the feast in army quarters." Grigeni had not been sure about recruiting Rusadka; he did not know her, but Valenty had made the decision.

"Leave the sky painting," Andrik said. "You will not be in the plaza long enough to make a difference. Go down into the city and stir up interest." He drew closer and said in a low voice, "If the plan goes awry, fade into the crowd. No matter what you see, say and do nothing."

Grigeni felt his gut tighten. The thought of failure filled him with dread. He had been in Valenty's service for twelve years; had been close to Pyvel since the boy was a small lad. He still could not believe that the princip—the former princip—faced a charge of treason. Faced the Tower.

Andrik put his hand on Grigeni's arm. "We have decided this, so do not waste your life, do you understand?"

"I do." But he was not sure he wanted to live in the new Osta Kiya. To live in the great city-palace now infected by Nashavety's endarkened powers.

Chapter Nineteen

Rusadka rested her head against the stones of the tight passageway. Cold seeped into her forehead, refreshing her thoughts and her intention to perceive the aligns.

In front of her, Elivasa turned from her work. "How do you fare?"

"I am well." She placed herself in accordance with the align, facing along its length. "Straight ahead for a short span, then we turn."

For what seemed a long time, they had been at work forging a new path through the stone. They did not know how far the evening had progressed, nor could they signal Valenty when to do his part.

Elivasa took a drink of water from the skin and rested for a moment. Her work was harder than Rusadka's pathfinding. Using her power of elements, Valenty's spy had to forge a way through the rock, parting bare stone to create a tunnel. To the nethers. The mortar that had been used to set the stones had long ago crumbled to dust, but the foundations of Osta Kiya remained strong under the enormous weight of the castle.

As they proceeded, the stone was reforming behind them.

"We are not making a route," Rusadka said, worried. "We are making a small space as we walk, one that forms around us."

Elivasa refused to be daunted. "Then I will do the same when we take the princip. The five of us will pass through the space I am making." She, Rusadka, Andrik, Valenty, and Anastyna. Elivasa wiped the sweat off her forehead with her arm. "If it does not kill me."

"I hope the princip is not afraid of small spaces." Rusadka muttered.

Rusadka's job was to perceive the align they had chosen—since in their wisdom the First Ones had built the walls of the lower castle along aligns—and keep Elivasa working in the right direction. But their work was more difficult than they had expected.

After the brief rest, Elivasa faced forward again, raising her left hand and directed her control of elements into the rocks, gradually parting them to extend their route.

Rusadka put her hand on Elivasa's shoulder. "Stop. Here, we turn." She pointed in a direction at a tangent to their old course and in a downward slope.

Elivasa nodded, angling her left hand accordingly. "Be careful that we do not crash through some ceiling down there."

"I will bring us in at ground level. I hope."

"How far is it?" Elivasa was tiring.

"Not far. Close enough now that I am sensing a small room." Rusadka shook her head. "A storeroom, maybe. But it could also be the guards' privy."

"By the almighty Deep," Elivasa groused. "If one of them is taking a piss . . ."

"He will wish he had not."

Elivasa laughed. Rusadka liked that. She had courage, even in these wretched walls.

The floor began to ramp down. *Valenty*, Rusadka fiercely thought. *It is time for you to use your sword if you can manage that.*

The stones parted and reformed behind them.

IN TANNER'S SQUARE, THE AROMA OF ROAST PIG FILLED THE AIR. Wood tables crowded the edges of the space, bearing baskets of bread and plates of winter apples. People were gathering as night deepened. But only a few. Pyvel looked around, hoping to see masses of people approaching, but the hoped-for crowds were not arriving.

In a narrow alley off the square, Pyvel saw Grigeni waiting for him. They had only a moment as they passed each other.

Grigeni muttered, "Pyvel. Take one more pass through the nearest streets. Find the lads who are still hanging about, get them excited. Berry pies, free ale. Then get you gone. It is time."

Pyvel nodded. He walked by, not looking back. Around the corner he spied a group of boys conducting mock sword fights in the light of torches shining down from the ironmongers shed. He would go beyond berry pie. It would be cakes. Cakes aplenty. And ale, too.

After spending some time in the backways near the plaza, Pyvel started down the Long Valley staircase. With the need for secrecy, he could not bring manifesting to light his way. He hoped he would not slip. The stairs from this plaza were narrow, and he could easily trip and fall. He went slowly, all the while wanting to bound down the stairs.

Eventually, the paths from several staircases met the main staircase, and he had a wider pathway down, but it was still black as a cave with the moon's crescent shedding little light. *Hurry*, he told himself. What if Valenty and the princip were even now making their way through the crowd with soldiers pursuing them, but the horses were not saddled and ready? What if the night stabler had not been drugged, and confronted him when he came to the corral like a thief? He picked up his pace.

He had a lot to do. There would be seven of them, with any luck—if no one was captured or killed.

Down, down, and further down, until the noise from the plaza sounded like voices from a distant world.

❦

Valenty strolled up to the two guards at the door to the nethers. He carried a basket of fruit and a lantern.

"Good evening," he said to the guards.

They frowned to see anyone approaching the access to the nethers.

"I have a few delicacies for the Lady Anastyna. I hope that is no problem. I will not stay long."

"My lord," one of the guards said, the strong, burly one. "No one is to pass. Orders."

As Valenty's team had expected, Sofiyana had made sure no one could get to Anastyna. "Well, she is a friend," Valenty said. "I am distressed to think of her in that rat-infested place." He made a moue of distaste. "A few pieces of fruit cannot hurt."

"Orders, my lord," the guard repeated.

Valenty shook his head regretfully. "If no exception can be made?" A shake of the guard's head. "I will leave this for you, then." He bent down to leave the basket on the floor. As he did so, he slipped a knife from under the cloth covering the basket, and rose, bringing the knife to the guard's throat, hissing, "Do not move!"

At that moment, Andrik rushed from the shadows and met the other guard as he brought up his staff to fend off his attacker. Andrik landed a solid kick to the man's crotch, sending him to the floor. While Valenty held the first guard at knifepoint, Andrik landed a fist to the other guard's head, and he went limp.

Soon Andrik had dragged the unconscious guard down the stairs, while Valenty waited on the landing just inside the door.

Andrik made quick work of tying his man up and dragging him into the shadows.

Valenty's knife had started a trickle of blood on the first guard's neck. "Please," the man whispered.

"I give you your life," Valenty said. "Get on your knees." As the man did so, Andrik joined them and bound the prisoner's hand and feet.

When they had both men trussed and gagged, Andrik raced back up the stairs to erase any sign of the fight.

Their first task completed, Valenty lit the lantern, and they hurried down the narrow corridor toward the prisoner cells.

"How many jailers are on duty?" Valenty whispered.

"Four have entered since she was brought to her cell." Andrik had watchers posted ever since Anastyna had gone into the nethers. There would be at least two more, those on the regular watch schedule. *Six, then,* Valenty thought. *Easy, if they were only jailers. More difficult if they were trained soldiers.*

When they came to the first crossroads, Valenty asked, "Which way?" He raised the lantern. Andrik read the signs etched into the rock and led the way down one of the routes.

They came to a chamber with a narrow wall slit allowing fresh air to enter. Andrik went to it and put his left hand on the sill. He kept very still, summoning his creature power. He had been gathering flocks of birds since sunset. They were roosting everywhere: at windows; in the grove of trees in the courtyard; on the roof of the palace behind chimney stacks and ramparts; and the in the trees of the roof garden. Now they would find the small, narrow windows of the nethers, windows no person could get through, but which would form no barriers to sparrows, finches, doves, and ravens.

A crow swooped onto the sill by Andrik's hand. "Come!" Andrik whispered, stepping away from the gap. "Come," he repeated as he and Valenty ran into the corridor, followed by a fluttering of wings.

As Valenty and Andrik rushed to the dungeon cells, the clatter and squawking of birds came too, overtaking them. The two men still had to watch for the directions hewn on the walls at the intersections, and this slowed them down. But soon they came upon a guard caught in a swarm of birds, flapping his arms and swearing.

He saw Valenty. "Get them off of me!"

"Let me help," Valenty said. He strode forward and smacked the side of his sword against the man's head. The guard fell. Andrik bound his arms and soon the two of them were rushing onward again amid thick flocks of screaming birds, all seeking exit from the nethers.

Around the next turn in the corridor they found several guards battling the seeming attack of the birds. The men staggered and pulled their arms around their faces to protect themselves, a gesture that helped Valenty and Andrik to pick them off one at a time. Some fought. Those men died. With only one man left, and Andrik winning the fight, Valenty began to check the fallen guards for the cell keys.

He did not notice when a man slunk from the shadows and rushed him.

A shout. "Valenty! Behind you!" He rose from his knees, but too late. The burly guard from the nethers door, free of his restraints, slashed down with a staff.

A sword knocked the staff from the man's hand. Rusadka stood there. Bringing her sword arm back from that swipe, she sliced through the man's neck, all before Valenty had regained his stance.

Andrik called from the door of Anastyna's cell. "Valenty! By the Nine, where is the key?"

Birds circled around them, screaming, flapping, diving.

By now Elivasa had found a dungeon cell key attached to a jailer's belt. "Here!" She threw it to Andrik.

Valenty faced Rusadka, making a small bow. "My thanks."

She regarded him, unimpressed. "I thought you were going to handle the guards."

"Looks like I needed a *harjat*," he said, grinning. A twitch in her face that might have been a smile.

Andrik stood with the princip, now free of her cell. "If we are done with words, let us go."

Valenty strode forward to take Anastyna's arm. "Now we run."

"I do not run," she said, annoyed.

"Tonight you do, my lady." He firmly pulled her forward.

Rusadka pointed down the hall. "This way!"

Elivasa hurried them into a small room without an apparent escape route. She strode up to a solid rock wall, her left hand outstretched.

A shadowy niche started to form.

Chapter Twenty

They had broken through the far wall of the palace. Elivasa staggered to her knees. She had succeeded in freeing them, but it had taken all she had. Rusadka handed Elivasa a skin of water.

They were in the lower city, with the high wall of the castle at their backs.

Anastyna wiped the sweat from her brow, looking relieved to be in the fresh air. Valenty put his cape around her shoulders. "Hold this tight against you, my lady. Hide your fine dress."

Rusadka watched from only a few feet away, getting her first good look at the princip. Unusually pale among Numinasi, the woman had light brown hair, and a delicate, heart-shaped face. Rusadka was surprised she was not taller.

Valenty knelt next to Elivasa. "Say when you are ready."

"Now." She rose to her feet, shaking off Valenty's help.

Everyone except Anastyna knew their roles. Rusadka would go first to scout. Valenty nodded to her, and she made her way down the steep hillside to a clutch of houses arrayed along the rock outcropping. It would be hard to explain why she was on the hill late at night above the dwellings, but she quickly reached a path skirting the front of the houses. From there, she had no need of stealth. Many people were out this night.

Under her cloak she hid her short sword on a leather brace fitted on her back. She hardened her mind to the possibility that she might be fighting her fellow *harjat*. Treason, they would call it. But it was treason not to oppose sorcery.

Thought fell away as she approached the plaza, the air glowing above it from torches and sky painting. On the paths and narrow streets, people headed to the feast. The sounds of the crowd grew louder. Singing. The smell of roasted meats.

Coming around a leather-working shop she stopped to take in the crowd. People milled around the food tables, while others clustered in groups talking and laughing. No soldiers threaded through the crowd. Or none in uniform. Casualties from the great battle sat in chairs and on the steps leading to the castle. Anyone coming down those stairs would find them a barrier. If luck was with them, no one would come in pursuit. That depended upon how soon the dead guards in the nethers would be found.

After a slow pass around the perimeter, Rusadka disappeared into an alleyway, making her way to the iron forge, closed for the night, but with a useful crook in the wall where Grigeni and Anastyna were pretending—badly—to be in each other's arms. She walked by them, saying, "Now."

With Anastyna leaning on on Grigeni's arm, she now had a different look about her: a longer face and darker hair. In her tattered cloak, she was well disguised, if Grigeni could keep the manifestation going. The couple followed Rusadka not far behind.

In a few moments Andrik would enter the plaza, scanning for trouble. Valenty, the most recognizable of the group, would enter last, undisguised, and with Elivasa on his arm. Any of their group who encountered trouble were to give a sharp whistle, and then Grigeni would hurry Anastyna off and down to the stables, leaving the others behind to create mayhem and hold off pursuit. If necessary, they would take a stand and fight to block the stairway. Four of them would: besides Rusadka herself, there would be Valenty, Elivasa, and Andrik, all good fighters. Well. Except against *harjat*. She would take on any of those.

At the far edge of the plaza, Rusadka took a roasted chicken leg and watched as Grigeni and Anastyna strolled by in the direction of the stairway leading to the stables.

Shouts from the middle of the square. Fallen tankards of ale, and people exclaiming and laughing. Deeper into the plaza, some took notice, but seeing nothing of consequence, went back to enjoying themselves.

Andrik appeared from one of the side streets. He moved slowly enough to fade into the background of things, and when next Rusadka saw him, he was stopping at a brazier to warm his hands. He noted Rusadka's almost imperceptible nod and moved closer to the stairs, prepared.

A manifester in the middle of the plaza threw a shower of golden sparks into the air. This was met by shrieks and claps of appreciation, and soon the fellow was surrounded by families, with children racing and yelling happily.

Valenty now made his way into the throng, with Elivasa at his side, laughing. She looked besotted with him. Her part to play. She played it well, and for all Rusadka knew, also meant it. When Valenty caught Rusadka's eye, she nodded at him. The signal that it was safe to escape down the stairs.

He lingered to watch the sky painting longer than Rusadka would have liked. *Move along, man*, she silently urged. Eventually, he and Elivasa moved to the perimeter and disappeared.

🙠🙣

"Do you not go down to the feast, My Lady Princip?" the maid asked as she combed out Sofiyana's hair.

Sofiyana winced as the comb caught on a snarl. "We do not celebrate the disaster of the crossings." She would allow the simple folk to have their observation, but she would not honor it with her presence.

Again, the maid pulled on her hair, catching another curl. Sofiyana grabbed the comb. "If you cannot do it!"

She ordered the maid away and used the comb to tease out the tangled strands. Nashavety had told her to tame her hair. How could she be a princip with violet-colored ringlets? But, fingering the silver torc around her neck, she had the proof. By elemental workings, it never tarnished. She had schooled herself not to keep touching it, especially during court functions. In private, she often caressed it, reminding herself who she was. A princip after all.

In preparation for bed, she removed the amber ring from her pocket and put it on. The safest place for the ring was on her hand. But only at night. During the day, in her pocket. She had to safeguard it, but wondered if it brought bad dreams. Sometimes awful visions poisoned her rest, disturbing landscapes with groping, clawed hands. . . .

The ring warmed as it encircled her finger. Nashavety was nearby. And then her voice, faint but distinct, moaning, *No, no!*

She turned to the room, dreading to see the demon-shape of her mistress. But this time, only the voice: *Anastyna flees. She flees!*

In panic, Sofiyana sprang to her feet and ran from her chamber. "Guards! Guards!" she cried.

Send soldiers! Find them!

Anastyna was escaping? Sofiyana raced to the great doors of her parlor just as they flew open, crashing against the walls. Soldiers entered.

Turning to the captain of her guard, she grabbed him by the arm. "Anastyna is trying to escape!"

In alarm, he looked at his tunic sleeve. From where the princip's ring had touched him, a tendril of smoke arose.

"The nethers!" she shouted.

As he and his men raced away, Sofiyana shrieked after them, "By your very lives, find her!"

Valenty helped Anastyna onto the back of Rusadka's saddle. He was alert for sounds of pursuit, but so far, they had made a clean escape. In the stables, the sharp smell of manure and hay drifted in the darkness, with the only light a small halo from Pyvel, enough that they could mount in good order.

With all the activity, horses neighed and those still in stalls pawed at the slats. Pyvel had put out fresh oats and had done a good job in selecting and saddling the horses, but Valenty did not like the confines of the stables and was eager to be on the move.

Grigeni sat rigid on his mount, having never ridden before. He jerked at every unexpected motion of his horse, making the animal skittish. Valenty knew he would not do well at a gallop and had given his Keeper of Books as much verbal instruction as he could in the two days prior.

As the group left the stables, the cold night air filled Valenty's lungs, clearing his mind of the fight in the nethers and the transit through the rocks of Osta Kiya's foundation. He longed for the room to ride fast and hard but first came the long descent to the plains.

Andrik and Pyvel led the group down the slope to the woods, followed by Rusadka with Anastyna and then Grigeni. Elivasa and Valenty took up the rear, both armed with swords they had smuggled into a shed near the stable. This was the most dangerous time. They had to trust the horses to find their footing in the dark and, from above, anyone with a sharp eye might spy them in the long gap between the stables and woods.

No one spoke. The only sound came from the horses' hooves and the creak of the leather saddles and stirrups. Once on the plains they would move fast.

If it came to an all-out run, Valenty feared for Grigeni and Pyvel, with them having so little experience riding. Everyone in the group knew that the only one they would stop for was Anastyna.

They emerged from the stand of woods onto the broad plains. Andrik gave a low whistle. Then Valenty heard what Andrik had. Horses coming.

He gave the signal to run, and Rusadka raced away with Anastyna.

Grigeni held on as his mount sprang into a gallop. Valenty glanced behind to see mounted soldiers breaking from the woods and charging after them. Elivasa took a position at the rear of the fleeing company so that she could deploy a wind to kick up soil behind them.

They had a few minutes' lead and pushed the horses hard, but Valenty doubted the race could go in their favor. As he turned to see if any soldiers had emerged through the cloud of sand, he saw a group of riders come from around the other side of Osta Kiya's great hill, approaching fast. They were now being pursued from two angles.

Rusadka shouted, "The new ones are *harjat!*" She pointed to a rock formation ahead. "We fight there!" She urged her mount faster, carrying Anastyna to the outcropping.

Fight? There would be no fight with such odds. But Valenty trusted her judgment.

At the rocks, he helped Anastyna off Rusadka's mount and led her to an overhang where she could shelter. He saw Pyvel and told him to gather the horses and tether them.

Rusadka was shouting something. As he joined her, she said, "They are with us! There are twenty-some *harjat*. They fight with us!"

The first of the *harjat* arrived and slid easily from his horse.

"Urik," Valenty said, his mood instantly buoyed.

"My lord. You know how to make enemies." He glanced behind him.

"Anastyna is with us," Valenty said.

"We are here to fight for her," Urik said.

The two men traded looks of understanding as the enemy riders began to close the gap.

RUSADKA HAD FOUND AN ALIGN ON WHICH TO TAKE A STAND. IT would augment her strength and the accuracy of her sword work. A soldier came out of the wall of dust on foot and, spying her, made for her position.

She engaged with him, a strongly built soldier, but at a disadvantage on an align.

Seeing her smaller size, the soldier barked. "Ask for quarter!"

Her answer was a lethal stroke into his belly.

FROM BEHIND A ROCK PYVEL LOOKED IN TERROR AT THE overwhelming number of soldiers. He identified Urik among them, and saw that he was fighting on Anastyna's behalf. Urik fought like a madman, and Pyvel watched in awe as the *harjat* took down his adversaries in startlingly brief matches.

Valenty was in the thick of the fight, Elivasa at his side. He lost sight of them as he noted that Rusadka now had six bodies lying around her.

A hand on his shoulder, and someone covered in blood looked down on him like a demon.

"Bring two horses," he said. Andrik. "We can get Anastyna away while the fight wages on."

Pyvel ran for the horses he had managed to tether. Soon Andrik and Anastyna were in the saddle.

Andrik looked down. "Come with us."

Pyvel shook his head.

"They will kill you, boy."

When Pyvel did not move, Andrik sped away with the princip.

He made his way back to the fighting ground, but what he saw there made his heart clench in dismay. Valenty was in the middle of a group of mounted men, his hands bound behind his back.

Urik and three of his men raced to his aid.

Valenty saw them coming. "Go!" he shouted. "Go to the princip!"

Pyvel saw Urik slowing. Then he stopped, as did his men.

The soldiers were leading Valenty away. Pyvel's eyes grew hot. Why did Urik not rush into their midst?

Elivasa brought two horses forward. Grigeni was on one of them.

"Get in the saddle, Pyvel," she said. "Show Grigeni how to handle his horse."

He looked in panic at the soldiers leaving with Valenty. "But why does Urik not help him!"

"Because we are to save the princip." She gestured for him to mount. "Now, Pyvel."

Leaving his heart behind, Pyvel obeyed, even though Elivasa did not have rank. "What about you?"

"I will make sure Rusadka has a horse."

He led Grigeni onto the plains, his mood desolate. The sounds of the fight gradually receded. As they galloped, foam swept from his mount's mouth. Ahead on the plain, he could see Andrik with the princip.

Behind them he saw a group of *harjat* following at a brisk pace but not a gallop. No one pursued them.

He brought his horse to a gentle lope and then to a walk. Grigeni slowed, looking amazed that he still sat his horse.

They had saved the princip. He tried to feel proud, but all he could think of was Valenty tied and captured and saying, *Go*.

Chapter Twenty-One

Along with Urik, Pyvel found himself riding next to the princip as they crossed the high desert of the outlands. She hardly spoke, a grim mood upon her. But she did allow him to handle her horse when they made stops.

Among the sixty who had joined them, the highest ranking was army Captain Lysandry, who took leadership of their band. He rode not far behind, conscious that his experience might not match Urik's.

They had been riding all day, resting only for the horses. Around them the flats stretched as far as they could see.

"My land is vast," Anastyna murmured, still sitting erect in her saddle, as though it were the throne she had lost.

"It is, my lady," Urik answered, mounted at her side. His attention stayed on the plains, scanning the horizon. They would see anyone approaching long before they were a threat.

Behind them, among the soldiers, rode Rusadka, Grigeni, and Elivasa. Grigeni rode like a dead man, pale, without expression, his body in shock from being in the saddle all day.

"Where are we going, sir?" Pyvel had been wondering, and finally could hold back the question no longer.

"Canyon country, boy. The river."

The Yanuri. The longest river in Numinat. He wanted to ask if they were going somewhere in a boat but held back.

Nevertheless, Urik answered him. "We go into the canyon at Crescent Gap. We can make our way north on the shoreline from there. We will camp on the strand at White Rock Turn."

Anastyna looked at him. "Have you ever seen the river, Pyvel?"

"No, my lady. Have you?"

Urik squinted a frown at him.

"That is all right, Urik," Anastyna said. "We must have some conversation since we are safe for now. And Pyvel, yes, I have even had my barge upon it. It is glorious."

He tried to imagine a royal barge, and could not, having never seen even a simple barge. But the princip had spoken to him as though he belonged there. Then he remembered that Valenty was taken, and his mood plummeted again.

They had been passing through rolling hills and, after coming around the last of them, they began the descent to the Yanuri. The river was as wide as the city-palace and very fast flowing, deep blue with white-flashing wave tips under the high sun. Profound cliffs rose straight up on both sides, iron gray and massive. The feeling of enclosure reminded him of the crossings battle, sights that were pinned into his memory. He knew how close spaces could mean slaughter and wished that Urik had chosen a different place.

"Sit up straight," someone muttered at him. He jerked his head to see that Rusadka had come up beside him. The *harjat* who had taught him how to ride. He dug his feet into the stirrups and sat tall.

"My lady," Rusadka said, acknowledging Anastyna. She then spoke to Urik, asking if it was time for her to ride ahead and see what could be put together for Anastyna at the camp. Getting his nod, she signaled to Elivasa, and they went ahead with a half-dozen *harjat*.

WHEN RUSADKA AND HER CONTINGENT GOT TO WHITE ROCK TURN, they found Andrik already there, building a raft.

"Going fishing?" Rusadka asked, dismounting. Andrik was a life-long spy, and she doubted he could build a decent raft. Spying was not a respectable occupation. And yet Elivasa was one such, and her efforts had produced the intelligence that Sofiyana spoke with Nashavety using the amber ring. And by this piece of information, they knew that the empty-headed girl with whom she had once shared an arcana was now infected with sorcery.

"Might try fishing," he said, refusing to be goaded. Rusadka knew they had planned for a raft as a back-door escape for the princip.

Elivasa came over to inspect, her expression showing what she thought of his efforts. "Perhaps it could be a door for Anastyna's hovel," she suggested to Rusadka.

Rusadka smirked. "Since it will not float."

"You both getting on fairly well, then," Andrik threw back, looking at the two of them. He glanced at Rusadka. "I thought you had no liking for spies."

"I do if they can fight." She added, "That is why you and I never shared a bed."

He snorted a laugh.

Elivasa and Rusadka began the work of making as much of a camp as the rocky beach allowed. Rusadka liked Elivasa. She was easy around soldiers, good on a horse, and fast with a knife. And knew how to tunnel through rock.

❧

THAT EVENING ANASTYNA SAT ON A LOG WITH THE BARK SHAVED OFF. Around her, poles made from tree branches of various heights were dug in at the corners. Horse blankets formed the walls on three sides while behind the enclosure towered a wall of basalt.

They were discussing Valenty. Seated in front of Anastyna were Urik, Andrik, and Rusadka, torchlight flickering on their faces.

"Is the army loyal to Sofiyana?" Anastyna asked Urik.

"Most of them, yes."

"And the *harjat* order?"

"For now."

Except for the twenty-two that were camped outside, Rusadka thought.

"Well, but we must do *something* for Valenty," Anastyna said. "Now is the time to reveal to them that Sofiyana is under Nashavety's control."

"I do not think it is wise," Urik said.

Anastyna doubtless was unused to soldiers, and his short answers did not please her.

"Not wise? She is under *creature power.*"

Andrik joined in. "We are seen as traitors, my lady. And there is still a charge of corruption against you. Who could carry the tale and be believed?"

"The Lord High Steward would be believed," she said.

"But Lord Michai does not know," Andrik said.

Urik rested one hand on a thigh as he sat, keeping his own council. They were all exhausted.

With the day's labors over, Rusadka was struck by their almost inconceivable situation. Sitting in a hut on a riverbank with the princip. Valenty in Sofiyana's clutches.

"And so?" Anastyna snapped. "Are we to do nothing for him?"

Urik's face had as much expression as the rock wall. "We are doing what he wants. Keeping you safe."

Andrik added, "So his sacrifice will not be for nothing."

Anastyna grew quiet. Her delicate face lay in shadow, and how she remained so fiery—so princip-like—after the escape and flight across the plain, Rusadka did not know. They waited for her to dismiss them.

Instead, in the pause, she looked at each of them in turn. "I must thank each of you for all you have done for me and for Numinat. This scourge will not stand. We will root it out." She paused. "Urik, your leadership will not be forgotten. You have done me many services, and I know you have a friendship with Valenty. So I am sorry for that part of what has come to pass."

She turned to Andrik. "Your role in the escape from the nethers was crucial. I will never forget the birds you summoned and the riot of confusion they caused with perfect timing. Valenty always assured me that you were his best man. I thank you."

Andrik nodded soberly.

"And Rusadka," Anastyna said. "You fight with such fury, I think you are worth three of any other soldier."

"Perhaps five," Urik murmured.

Rusadka's heart lifted. His comment was the one that counted.

Chapter Twenty-Two

The day after her encounter with Kiya, Yevliesza and her teacher sat at the table in Isha's hut. A warm gruel settled in Yevliesza's stomach as she waited for the day's lesson to start. They hadn't spoken about the wraith wolf. Isha only nodded at her when she had come in the previous evening and honored her student's silence.

In those hours in the woods with her *sympat*, Yevliesza had forged a connection with Kiya, one that was shining and new and also ancient, as though they had always been together, and not just in this life. She gazed out the single glazed window as she replayed in her mind her moments with Kiya.

"Do not get drowsy," Isha said. "We have work to do."

"I am under a wolf-spell, I think."

"Call it an honor. I think that is good enough." She picked at her teeth with a fingernail. "And now, let us go on."

They did need to go on. Isha still hadn't explained what she was supposed to do with primal root power. Or not do.

"I sense your impatience," her teacher said. "I have promised you clarity if you are brave enough to receive it. But first we must clean some things out."

"I thought we were in a hurry."

"We are." She snapped a look at Yevliesza. It felt like a slap. "You have not exactly been a quick student."

Yevliesza didn't want to argue, but some things were begging to come out. "If I have to give up everything, why don't you say so? It's what you want, isn't it? Drop my personal hopes, be brave, get the job done?"

Isha shook her head. "Once I was like you. Impatient. Ignorant. Alone among strangers. I was coming into my strength but unsure where to spend it. When I went into the woods to be alone, I learned how to hunt and build a hut and chop wood. Then I found a door in the forest."

A door. A metaphor for what came next. Yevliesza waited, letting her find the words.

"I had four powers by then. By that I knew how people limit themselves. They make up stories and reify customs and traditions. Limitations. So I learned to wake up. As I said, I had found a door in the forest, and I had to decide whether to go in. Eventually, I went."

She paused. "But that is my story, and this is about you. You of the ninth power, you, with all that love of Valenty and all that hate of Nashavety. What a stew of things!" She put her hands flat on the table in a gesture of transition. "So let us consider the Mist Wall. Tell me what it is."

"The Mist Wall?" Yevliesza paused, not liking how little she knew about it. "It's the engine of the world. Of the worlds. Letting the worlds arise." She remembered what Father Ludving had told her in Volkia. "It *reveals* the world already formed. Because the Mythos is the alterworld of Earth."

"Hmm. Very well. If that is how people think of it."

"Well, isn't it? The mechanism, the entity that rebirths the geography of the origin world?"

"I suppose so. But that is not very helpful right now." Her teacher got up and nudged at the fire in the hearth with a stick. Charred wood collapsed, burning brighter.

"What things really are is not an easy question. You have seen an animal emerge from the otherworld. What is that animal? What is the otherworld? Where do the powers really come from? Reality is more complex than most people take the time to consider. But as for the Mist Wall, it is not an engine. Not for you. For you it is a repository of things."

"What things?" Yevliesza was listening hard, trying to keep up. A log snapped in the hearth like a gunshot.

And then she knew. The door in the forest. "You went in, didn't you. That was the door you found. The door in the Mist Wall. You went in."

"Hard to say. Perhaps I did." She shrugged. "Might have been Ishtov."

"Please stop *playing* with me!"

Isha stood and circled the table to Yevliesza's place. She grabbed her forearms, forcing her to look into her eyes. "I am not playing. I am vastly serious. We may all die. Am I playing about that?"

Yevliesza pulled away from her grip. "So those people with their favorite legend, looking for dead loved ones. If people can go into the wall, if *you* went in, then maybe spirits *are* there?"

Isha returned to her seat. "Wherever the dead go, it is not into the Mist Wall."

Yevliesza sat back, trying to follow all of this. "But you went inside."

"I did. And when you go in you will come out either wise or mad."

"Go in?" she said, startled. She was going inside?

"Yes, go in. You must go. Everything is at stake. Go in to find out what you want."

That wasn't an answer, that was a process. She needed answers. "Can't you just tell me what I have to do?"

At one level, she knew. Sabotage the Volkish in the crossings. Somehow. She could envision collapsed tunnels, chaos. But she was horribly uncertain of her primal root power. Its strength. Her own strength or ability to do it right. Afraid of the consequences if it went wrong.

Not only that. She feared that once she entered the fight, she would draw the resentment of her friends. Of Valenty. For choosing the wrong actions in the crossings. It couldn't be only about Numinat. She had to be for the Mythos. Why the First Ones picked a stranger.

"It would be useful to get a little confidence, Yevliesza."

"Oh, confidence." The big words she used. Perspective. Clarity. Confidence.

"Accept what you are."

"Eight hells, I *do* accept it!"

Isha stared at her.

"But the Mist Wall. It's going to show me some big truth, and then I'll finally bring the walls of the crossings down, and everyone will live in their own isolated place without any connections and Volkia will be finished."

"If you say so. Here, though, is the thing you must understand well: I cannot force you to know. I do not even know the answer. I am a guide, not a conjurer."

Yevliesza sighed. "But the Mist Wall. How do you even get in?"

"I suppose I will have to show you."

"No one really goes in, right? It's some kind of dream-state? I would drink something, and believe I'm in the wall?"

"What odd ideas you have. No, you go in. Walk through the door and there you are." She watched Yevliesza as though waiting for more questions and protests. But Yevliesza was empty of words.

Isha broke the silence, saying, "You called the wall an engine. But the real engines are those that drive us. Things we want, things we must have, things we want to be. You are driven by these things, and it is not going to work for you."

Not working. Right. It was tearing her apart.

Isha's face softened. "It will be hard. You will see confusing things. You will see all the things you want and see them in a new light. You may see a loved one who has died."

"But it's not real."

"It will seem to be. You will see things that cannot be true but seem to be."

"So that's how the legend started. Spirits in the Mist Wall."

"That is the main reason those seekers are here. Because they long to have things that are gone. And they think I can talk with the dead."

"Can you?"

"I did not see *their* dead. I saw mine. In a manner of speaking."

"Would I see the dead?"

"You will see what you desire. See all of it, but in a new light. That is the truth I promised you. Once you see in a new way . . ." She shrugged. "Then you decide your path."

Yevliesza began to understand. It was true that she'd been confused about what she should do, and who or what she should love. If she could see it all in a new light, it might help.

"Once you see clearly, it is easier. In fact, it is simple."

All you have to do is stick your head out of the fog.

Isha took Yevliesza's silence as a good thing, and relented, saying, "Here is a thing I can offer you. If you go in, and if you decide you do not want the larger task, I will take the ninth power from you."

She could do that? The idea shocked her. Then how simple it would be.

Isha nodded. "Consider this. What if, when it departed from you, it went to someone else? The First Ones meant *someone* to have it."

Someone else. It might be better if it were. But . . .

Isha went on. "When you leave the Mist Wall you will be changed, either way. However, hear me well. There is a danger that you may become unseated in your mind."

Yevliesza put her head in her hands and sank into the looming proposition. The challenge of the Mist Wall. It was not only vastly strange, it was dangerous. But Isha was talking about seeing in a new way. She thought she could bear anything if she could only see her way. Know her own heart.

Isha's voice. "Are you willing to go or not?"

Yevliesza lowered her hands from her face. "I am."

Of course she was. You didn't get offered the first clarity of your life and say *maybe later*. You didn't walk right up to the door and not go in.

"Can Kiya come with me?" It seemed very important to have her wolf at her side.

Isha shrugged. "That is for him to decide."

Chapter Twenty-Three

High gusts swept down the canyon, chilling the evening, but still, Anastyna walked the beach, restless. The wind came fresh, with the smell of ice and water-soaked logs.

Rusadka watched Anastyna in her court dress and dainty leather shoes, strolling as though she were in halls of Osta Kiya. The woman did not complain or put on airs, but she was useless in a military camp. She supposed Anastyna's part was to lead, but lead what? They had a fighting force of little more than sixty.

It was no army. Soldiers loyal to Anastyna, but few officers. They had a master of horse, a cook, and a *numiner*, a recordkeeper to tally the value of extra services derived from personal powers. Twenty-two *harjat*, the ones Urik had persuaded to leave. All these slept on the beach, the senior-most against the cliffs.

Their camp could not be seen from the river until passing the beach where they were dug in. Or by searchers riding dactyls. Lookouts on the cliffs watched the skies as well as the flats. At a signal, Anastyna's hut could be dismantled and the soldiers hidden from view by brush combed from the sides and shore of the canyon. Rusadka distrusted the position. It was hemmed in. The cliffs bunched overhead like gigantic shut doors.

Anastyna's walk on the beach brought her close to where Rusadka stood. She saw the princip signal to Captain Lysandry. And then to Urik.

When the two men joined her, Rusadka heard her say, "We would have someone go to Zolvina. As our representative."

The princip looked at Lysandry. "Send your most capable soldier to assess the situation there. Outside the *satvary*, Yevliesza of House Valenty is being watched by a group of seven men, and we wish to know what is transpiring."

"Yes, my lady," the captain said.

"Furthermore, have him speak with Yevliesza and discover from her what she knows of Volkish arms, the state of the Volkish capital, and all things that we sent her to discover."

Anastyna had sent her to spy? And sent her without even telling Yevliesza what her role would be? When Duke Tanfred had revealed the whole story to Rusadka, they both had assumed that Anastyna had done it for political reasons. To secure a *fajatim's* loyalty by trading Yevliesza's trip of apology for the life of that *fajatim*'s son. Now, *now*, Rusadka knew it had been a more buried purpose.

"Shall we have the band of armed men rousted out?" Captain Lysandry asked.

"He may show his presence, but we cannot spare him or others to fight."

Urik said, "If they are Sofiyana's men, they would follow him back here."

"He must take precautions not to be followed."

"To leave immediately?" Lysandry asked.

Rusadka walked toward the group. The three of them stared at her intrusion.

Lysandry snapped, "Stand back, *harjat*."

Rusadka did not move but looked directly at Anastyna. "Please, my lady, send *me.*" She added, "I could not help but hear."

"Leave us, Rusadka," Urik said.

She paused, daring to ignore the order. Her mind spun, trying to pluck an argument out of the air. She should go. She needed to go. "Yevliesza trusts me. I have that advantage."

The officer took firm hold of Rusadka's arm.

"A moment," Anastyna said. Rusadka faced the group again, the officer's hand still gripping her arm. "Yevliesza considers you a friend?"

"Yes. We have been close since the align arcana."

Anastyna looked at Urik, who gave a small nod.

"We will hear more of this." She nodded in the direction of her makeshift quarters.

Once inside the walls of blankets, the group remained standing. Anastyna looked at Rusadka. "You say you are close. How close?"

"We sided together in the arcana against Sofiyana. We watched for Sofiyana's intrigues."

Anastyna looked at Urik.

"Valenty told me the two of them are close," he said.

Anastyna regarded her for several long moments. "You will go then."

Rusadka managed not to show her pleasure. She would see Yevliesza. And get off the beach.

"Yevliesza feels ill-used by us," Anastyna said, straight-faced.

Because she almost died of your intrigues, Rusadka thought.

"But bring her to understand that we do not condone how Prince Albrecht refused to send her home. He has earned my displeasure. You may tell her that and assure her that we did not know he would treat her as a hostage."

"Yes, my lady," Rusadka said in flat voice.

Anastyna brightened. "However, if in Hapsigen she learned things of assistance to the realm, then in the end her trip did a great deal of good."

Rusadka felt heat rise from her chest into her neck and face. She thought of Albrecht's demand that Yevliesza remove her dress to bare her back to expose the tracery; Albrecht having tried to have her body with creature power, an act of Trespass against person; Albrecht striking her, and once so hard she had a consternation in her mind for days. And her constant danger as she instinctively used her detention to uncover the secret of their machines.

Anastyna looked content with herself. "In the end, it all worked out, did it not?"

Her casual assessment had Rusadka's guts in a coil. She bowed her head in as respectful a response as she was capable of.

Once out of the royal hovel, Rusadka took her leave of Urik, and strode down the beach to unkink her limbs and her heart. In the heavy dusk, the river was a rushing blackness, glinting now and again in the moonlight. She tried to let the river clear her thoughts, but she kept hearing Anastyna's voice saying how well it had all worked out.

A figure moved toward her down the beach. Elivasa. When she got close, she said, "There is only one thing that can soothe such anger."

Startled, Rusadka snapped a look at her. "Strong drink?"

Elivasa looked out at the river. "A strong woman."

"I thought you belonged to Valenty," Rusadka said.

"I do not belong to any man."

Rusadka gazed at her. She looked fragile standing there on the riverbank, taking this chance without really knowing her, and a *harjat*, at that.

Rusadka nodded toward the arm of White Rock Turn jutting onto the beach. "Let us walk, Elivasa." They strolled, and the sound of the river faded as Rusadka focused on this strong woman walking next to her.

They found some privacy on a small spit of sand, with a rock wall at their backs, and the river slipping by on the other.

❦

THE *SATVARY* COMPLEX CROUCHED ON A SHELF OF ROCK HALFWAY TO the spine of the Numins, a place so high that winter was accustomed to overstaying its allotted time. But in early spring the snows reluctantly and slowly released their grip.

The Devi Ilsat and her helper Yarna moved at a slow pace across the landscape, conserving their strength for the long journey to Osta Kiya. It was avalanche season, and they trod carefully down the great slope. At a lower elevation was a village that could provide horses.

She hated to leave the domicile, but it was needful. Things had gone all wrong. Anastyna deposed, and the *fajatim* enthralled, so reports claimed. *Wrong indeed.* Something would have to be done, and she was not sure that Valenty, for all his network of spies, could keep the realm from its endarkened future.

The seven men who had watched them from behind the ridge were gone. The *satvars'* terrible worry was that four of them had gone after Yevliesza, not fooled by her early morning departure. The day after Yevliesza departed for the Agarvesky Forest, three of the watchers left their hideaway, leading four riderless horses. The others were undoubtedly tracking her. A calamity if they found her. *May the First Ones protect you*, the Devi Ilsat intoned to herself.

But perhaps she was safely with Ishtov now. They had not come this far only to lose the girl of the lost power to murder or imprisonment. *May the Mythos keep you from harm,* she fervently thought. The survival of the Mythos was on her shoulders. Perhaps it should not be, but it was too late to change that now. It was so easy to sink into unawareness, to take each day as though it was guaranteed. But from what Kassalya had seen coming, the world might be at a tipping point. Tipping into darkness. So now was the time to leave the *satvary* and try to help, in however small a way.

The High Mother looked ahead, into the white wilderness, with the stark, blue sky making the vast territory look even colder than it was. She imagined Yevliesza mantled with power, and not just over the crossings, but over herself. The greatest power. She hoped the girl would not be too headstrong with her teacher. More than anything, she hoped that she had arrived.

Yarna focused her elemental intention on the route to the village. The snow parted, blowing nicely up the banks on either side, baring the ice beneath.

"Do not slip, my daughter."

"No, High Mother. Nor you."

She would soon be in the halls of power to assess the situation and perhaps help. Yet what could one old *satvar* do? She did not yet know but put her thoughts to it as the two of them trudged on.

Chapter Twenty-Four

Steady, thudding wind scoured across the primordial lands. Before Yevliesza lay dunes, dry ridges, and sand. The land was dry and spare, with a few scabrous patches of oat-colored grass. And though the landscape was mostly bare, some areas had patches of brave green, even trees.

Ahead, the wall, towering and rippling. A curtain constantly retreating.

The height of the wall made her uneasy, so she didn't look up. Still, the drumming and thudding were enough of a terror, though she and Isha had plugged their ears with wool.

They had been traveling for a day and a half, and had entered the barrens late that morning. Because no horse would approach the wall, they carried their supplies in packs over their shoulders. Yevliesza's left hand ached, swelling with powers. The smallest finger of her hand was either numb or hot and sometimes both. How must Isha feel, she of the eight powers?

"Do you feel it?" she half-shouted to Isha. "In your hand?"

Isha shook her head. "Try to stay calm!"

Yevliesza tripped over something. Regaining her footing, she saw that she had stumbled on a green sapling. Knocked out of the sand, it sprang free, a hands-breath tall. The land would rapidly green and change now that it had arrived, now that it had been manifested by the engine of the wall.

She kept watch for Kiya, but if he was with her, he was traveling in the otherworld.

This close to the Mist Wall, Yevliesza saw that it was not arrayed in a straight line. The wall's fabric contained enormous folds forming canyons that appeared to stretch for miles. Overall brownish in color, at this close approach she saw it was streaked with blue-green, and sometimes red or purple, as though it was carrying all the colors needed to paint the world.

"If only the wind would stop," Yevliesza said close to Isha's ear.

Isha gripped her hand. "It can do no harm." Now that they were on the journey, Isha had been unfailingly kind. She often urged her to eat, doling out their rations and making sure she drank from the water skins.

On they went, not heading directly toward the wall, but at an angle. To the door. Somewhere ahead, the door. Now and again a slice of lightning flickered in the storm. Yevliesza pointed at one particularly noticeable one. "Lightning," she called out to Isha.

"No. An align!"

Yevliesza was astonished. Aligns lived in the wall. Yes, she could discern that now. And she had not even guessed it. She didn't know whether her hand ached because she was supposed to use her dominant power, root power, and hadn't. Or if with only one person possessing the ninth power, it filled her up to painful overflowing.

In fact, she had little idea how her second power felt, or would operate. And because it was the ninth one, neither did Isha.

In the far distance, a green line of trees. Yevliesza pointed at it. Isha nodded. She had said they would meet the forest again. The eastern Agarvesky. They had to cross the primordial lands to get there.

They kept on. The dark line became trees and then a gentle well of green like a welcoming den. They walked into a patch of forest.

The trees were small, none more than about twenty feet high, but they grew thickly, and the smells of pitch and wet soil filled the air in a welcome reminder of growing things. Overhead the wall hovered, now screened by tree boughs.

Once in this refuge, they made camp. The door must be close by now. While Yevliesza collected deadfall for a fire, Isha unpacked a twine-wrapped package of dried venison, two winter apples, and a small round of bread.

As they ate their meal, Yevliesza asked, "Isn't there anything more you can tell me about what I'll experience?"

Isha remained quiet for a time, then responded. "Accept whatever comes. Do not be passive, but do not fight what you perceive. Trust that even impossible things can teach you your heart."

"But something concrete? Something to be watching for?"

"Well. There is always a chance that there is someone else in the wall. Another person who is traveling there." She noted Yevliesza's look of concern.

"You mean, it would not merely be someone I see. Someone who is actually there?"

"Yes. I call them travelers. It does not often happen."

"So one person at a time in there. Usually. How can I tell which is which?"

"You will be able to tell. Do not worry. No one will get in."

Yevliesza swallowed, thinking about *travelers*. "You waited until now to say."

"A little confidence, Yevliesza."

She wished she knew whether Kiya would be there. She felt brave in his presence, and bravery was beginning to leak away.

With supper over, Isha threw the paper and twine into the fire and handed a small packet of berries to her. "Dessert," she said.

"Can't you be here when I come out?"

"To be your guide?" Isha said, eyebrow raised.

Oh, right. She had to be her own guide. She munched on the berries. "Delicious."

Isha shrugged. "Red thorn berries from near my cabin." Her gaze turned soft as she looked at her student. "When you come back, I may be here, or I may not. But I will bring your horse. Around the long way, so he will not be frightened by the wall."

Yevliesza hoped that Mitri would be all right on such a trek. Handre, his former owner, had said that Mitri didn't know he was too old for strenuous exercise. She hoped he would be safe.

When the camp chores were done and they were lying snug in their cloaks, Yevliesza lay thinking about the beloved dead and travelers and madness. She listened to the crickets and an owl and the thudding of the Mist Wall.

After a time, Yevliesza heard Isha whisper, "Sleep, my daughter."

⚬⚬⚬

SHE DREAMED OF A GREAT SHINING FOREST, WHERE EVERYTHING THAT should be green was silver. The wind blew through dazzling branches and sparkling leaves. Wisps of hanging moss fluttered, catching the sun in glowing nets. A pack of wolves raced along a wooded ridge, vanishing into the fog.

She woke up, still thinking of the dream. The night air was drenched in the smells of fir, wood sap, and smoke. The smells of the great Agarvesky. The thudding of the Mist Wall, which she sometimes could forget, now came at her in force.

By the light of the embers, Yevliesza could see that Isha had chosen to appear as Ishtov while she slept. That feat of manifesting impressed her more than anything Isha had done so far. The woman could use her powers even in sleep.

Now fully awake, she sat up. A wolf stood a few feet away, nose into the wind, fur ruffling in the breeze.

Kiya.

He turned from her and trotted a few paces, then looked back at her. She knew that movement. It was how he had acted outside of the Volkish palace the night of her escape. He was trying to get her to follow him. She put on her boots and laced them up. As she passed Isha, she considered waking her up, but decided not to disturb her.

There was nothing to be afraid of in the Agarvesky when you had a wraith wolf to protect you.

Kiya slipped into the trees, Yevliesza following, with only faint moonlight to show their way. Her wolf led onward, moving faster than she wished he were, since deadfall littered the forest floor.

Her mind wandered in its own wilderness. It might have been an hour later that the trees stopped. She and Kiya moved into empty blackness.

Now totally blind, Yevliesza put her hand on Kiya's head. They moved slowly forward over ground as flat as a plaza. She knew he was leading her into the Mist Wall; the idea had been growing and she couldn't any longer deny it.

The certainty of their destination now claimed her. She should have wakened Isha. Although Kiya was a wraith wolf, that didn't mean he knew what he was doing. Maybe that was something you weren't supposed to say about a *sympat*. And Kiya wasn't an ordinary *sympat*. He lived partially in the otherworld. Lived with the dead. Maybe he was wise.

She gathered her confidence. She had already decided to go in, and Isha believed she was ready.

They walked forward with the Mist Wall thundering somewhere in front of them. Though she couldn't see it, its abysmal sounds terrified her. A million flecks of light starred the air. *They were in her eyes*, she thought. Tiny flecks arising in a field of vision untouched by light.

Kiya stopped and she felt his head turn to look behind. They were being followed. The wraith wolf moved faster, and she clutched the fur on the back of his neck, lest she lose him.

Kiya snapped his head to one side and growled, which she knew from the vibrations in his skull, because she could hear only the wall.

Caught between the wall and whatever was stalking them, Yevliesza began to see the wisdom of going through the door, any door.

A line appeared in front of her. A vertical strand of light no wider than a wire. Then four bright lines defining a rectangle. It was like a door in a darkened room with light furring the edges from behind. It appeared to sit at ground level but wasn't attached to anything.

"Kiya," she whispered. "Are you sure?"

He trotted to the door and looked back at her.

Oh God, he was sure.

She moved a little closer to it. With the light around the edges, she was able to see the material of the door. It was made of wood. Forming it, five worn, vertical planks, moss-green in color. At the top, a gentle arch. Somewhere, she had seen this door before.

An iron doorknob. With that, she recognized the front door of the house where she had lived on Earth.

OK, then. This is my door.

Her hand rested on the doorknob. Though it was too dark to see its design, she knew exactly what it looked like. She felt the hammered indentations that gave it a pebbly look. Then the matching oval back-plate, with a thin raised edge as a frame.

Kiya pawed at the door. With the thundering of the Mist Wall, she couldn't hear his nails scratching on the wood.

In her peripheral vision, she saw shapes moving in from behind.

She turned the knob and pushed, crashing through the opening.

PART III
THE CITY OF HOLDFAST

Chapter Twenty-Five

She was on a crowded dirt road with people trudging along carrying packs and bundles. A few horse-drawn wagons stuffed with tables, trunks, and crates. People were dressed simply and fine, some with retainers and servants, others with children or elders in family groupings. Yevliesza stood at the side of the road watching them pass by, trying to calm herself and adjust to the scene before her. On all sides lay a terrain of rolling hills softened by grasses and stands of cottonwood and ash. A low sky swirled with dust as though from a distant storm. It was the only aspect of the view that suggested the Mist Wall.

She scanned the road, the grassy fields, looking for Kiya. But he was nowhere in sight.

A slim young man came by eating a sausage. He had a good face, with a pointed nose and ready smile.

People traveling, eating sausages, wagons full of goods. All impossible. *Try to accept it,* Isha had told her. *Whatever you see.*

As she watched the man, a few children harried him, begging for coins and food. He reached into a leather bag and handed out apples, all the while laughing and spinning around as though it was a game. He caught her eye and made a mock bow in her direction.

At the sound of horses' hooves, she turned to see five men on horseback wearing brown uniforms and peaked helmets. The crowd parted for them. Soldiers were an unwelcome development, a sign of danger.

But a smile tugged at her lips. She could almost hear Isha say, *Maybe the danger is finding the truth.* The truth of what she wanted; what she owed the world. How to believe herself capable of caring for this world in so much peril.

The man handing out apples joined her on the side of the road. He frowned at the soldiers. "They should not be here." he said. "The road belongs to us. They are from Holdfast."

"Holdfast?"

He nodded at something up ahead. For a moment the dust-streaked clouds parted, and she could see a city on a hill crowned by a palace. "The city."

She surmised that everyone was headed there. But why? If *why* had any meaning in this place.

"Hey-o!" the young man called as a cart passed. He grabbed Yevliesza's hand and pulled her toward the cart. "They have oat cakes if you have the coin."

She patted her trouser pockets. Empty.

A coin appeared in his hand, and he flipped it toward a girl riding in the back of the cart. She caught it and handed down a small cake to Yevliesza.

She thanked him for the food, and they walked together.

"Why are you on the road today?" she asked between mouthfuls.

"To see the city, of course. To find my fortune, like everyone. If you want to accomplish things, Holdfast is the place. If you have luck, you can win." He shrugged. "I usually do." He wiped his hands on his dusty shirt and held out his hand. "Reynard."

She shook it. "I'm . . ." she paused, not wanting to say who she was, and a false name did not immediately come to mind.

"No, let me guess," he said, eyeing her in mock concentration. "Eloisa." He scrunched up his mouth. "Or Lisbetha. No, too long." He snapped his fingers. "Liza! Am I right?"

"I like it." She played along with his good humor while also wondering at the fact that he chose a name that was a variation of hers. "Liza it is," she responded. "Sorry I can't repay you for the meal."

"No need." He spread his arms to encompass the throngs of travelers. "We all help each other."

"Who do the soldiers belong to?"

"The queen, of course." He looked askance at her. Finding it strange that she didn't know.

The queen. It conjured images of power, the kind of power that made things go so wrong.

As she looked at the city in the distance, the obscuring dust descended again. She was going to the city of Holdfast along with everyone else. Maybe the clarity, the knowledge that Isha had promised her was there. Somehow.

"I saw a wolf," Reynard said. "Was it with you?"

"A dog," Yevliesza said, protective of Kiya. "But he ran off."

Reynard laughed. "If you say so."

She wished Kiya was at her side or at least within sight. But perhaps he *was*, invisibly. The thought cheered her. Turning her attention back to Reynard, she asked, "Are you a magician? You pulled a coin out of the air."

"A magician? Nothing so grand. I do some tricks for children. What about you?"

"I'm going to the city. To find my fortune." True in its way.

As the sun sank lower, people left the road to make camp. Reynard pointed to a family gathered around a small fire. "That is where I will find a welcome and maybe a good meal. The little ones like me." He took her by the arm, and they made their way toward the fire.

The family greeted them, and the children wanted to see him juggle, which he did with a few apples. That earned them both a hunk of bread and cheese. As they ate, he said, "Now you owe me a favor." He grinned impishly. "For the meals I have provided."

She looked at him warily. "What can I give you?"

"You have to tell me a dream. Not just any dream. A good one. One that has always stuck with you."

"Sorry, I don't remember dreams. They're like a fire that burns itself out." She didn't want to tell him a dream. It would be like letting him in, and she wasn't sure about him yet.

His smile retreated. "Ah, but you owe me." He gazed at her with eyes that were not Numinasi, but deep blue. He was trying to put a hook into her. Maybe he had identified her on the road as someone he could control.

"What happened to 'we all help one another'?"

"We do help. But it is only polite to return the favor."

She stood. "I think you tricked me."

He spread his hands in an open, innocent gesture.

Her good feeling about Reynard evaporated. Turning away from him, she went up to her hosts, thanking them for the food. Then she walked away from the campfire, hoping that he wouldn't follow her.

A few people still walked in the direction of the city. Surreptitiously, she looked back to see if Reynard was following her, and it seemed that he wasn't. But she saw a small wagon approaching.

It pulled up next to her. "Hop in if would like a ride," its elderly driver said, a woman. The wagon was full of hay, pulled by a stocky horse that, unlike Mitri, seemed to know that it was old, so plodding were its steps.

She thanked the woman and jumped onto the open tailboard. She faced the road in back as they jostled along, her legs dangling, and with the sweet and dusty smell of the hay strong in the air. She saw no sign of Reynard, the man who wanted dreams.

The old woman drove the wagon in silence. As they continued down the road, Yevliesza felt a shadow of unease. She hadn't known what the Mist Wall would be like—except that she would see impossible things. So far things seemed normal. If this whole experience could be considered normal. But if she was supposed to learn something, it was still to come. The pastoral surroundings seemed both gentle and, at the edges, troubling. One thing she did know: the city was the queen's city. She pressed her hand on her stomach, trying to quiet her nerves. She thought she knew who the queen might be.

Nashavety. The one who *held fast* onto things. Like the old ways. Like hatred.

She deeply hoped that if Nashavety was here in some form, she was not a *traveler*.

Chapter Twenty-Six

Having left the canyon country of the great river, Rusadka rode into a prairie region of gentle, folded hills. For as far as she could see, grasses covered the land. It was unsettled, inhabited only by burrowing creatures and the raptors that fed on them. She felt a vast relief to be out of the confines of the Yanuri River canyon.

But she was being followed.

Taking cover in a ravine, she hobbled her horse and returned on foot to the top of the ridge. Lying in the camouflage of the grass, she watched and waited, the smell of dry earth and grass strong in her nostrils. Presently, in the distance a group of riders came into view outlined against the sky as they topped a hill. She counted ten. The princip's men. No one else would be likely to ride in the territory, not in such numbers.

Collecting her mount, she took a route through the defiles of the low hills, leading the trackers in a different direction than Zolvina. She hoped they might take the bait even if they weren't looking for a single rider. They were searching for Anastyna's band, but they might send a few soldiers after her, to interrogate anyone traveling in the outland.

It galled her to leave her route to the *satvary*. She wanted to know if her friend was doing well, though Valenty had assured her that she was, at least for now. According to him, outside the *satvary* armed men lurked. No doubt sent by Sofiyana, waiting to grab her if she ventured out. A worse possibility was that their mutual enemy from the align arcana was willing to go against custom and raid the place. The more Rusadka thought about it, the faster she wanted to get to Yevliesza. And now this diversion.

She took a course away from the mountains, occasionally traversing the great aligns of the prairie that, in this land of far horizons, seemed to stretch forever. Once she spied a dactyl and rider soaring in the distance, watching. They would not come near to investigate one rider.

By midday she was far off course for Zolvina but thinking she had lost her pursuers. She made camp along a stream where sharp-smelling pines gave shade and camouflage.

It was good to be alone. The last tenday had been turbulent, first with decisions about loyalty and duty, and then the anxious hours of the escape and the battle on plains beneath Osta Kiya. It had been a good fight. But the blood and lives lost were not the joy of it. In combat she knew her purpose. To serve her kingdom with her whole body and will. Purpose and moment became one. She lived for those times.

But in the camp at the great turn in the river she had felt off-balance, unsettled by the former princip and her royal ways. Though she was sworn to Anastyna, it did not go well to be too close to her person. To the workings of it all. Anastyna was small in stature. But on her shoulders was the fate of Numinat, at least if she regained the torc. To face the Volkish would take a strong leader. Anastyna did not look like a leader who might save the realm, but maybe there was strength underneath the trappings. There had better be.

Rusadka shook off these dark thoughts. The company of a good horse and open country lifted her mood. Her black mare with the white blaze munched on the low grasses that bent into the brook as Rusadka sat with her own meal of dried venison and flat bread.

She sensed movement among the trees. A shadow too large for an animal. Drawing her short sword, she moved to an open space where she could fight. The setting sun sent flickers of gold through the tree branches and shards of light off the rock-filled stream.

There. A shadow moved, the upright form a person. She lowered her sword.

It was Elivasa.

"You led me a merry chase!" Elivasa sang out, coming into the clearing.

Rusadka felt a smile coming on, but also annoyance. "You lead those riders right to me?"

"No, I caught their attention this morning and lured them off your trail and into a woodland. I managed to lose them. Then I lost *you* for most of the day." She stood waiting, a tentative look replacing her usual bravado. "Glad I found you."

"Aye," Rusadka responded, unable to think what her arrival would mean.

Elivasa cast a hungry glance at the remains of Rusadka's meal.

"Sit. I have extra."

"*Sit, I have extra* is my welcome?"

"Welcome, Elivasa. But I am surprised."

Her sometime lover cocked her head. "If you must have a reason, I decided to help you." She nodded off to the prairie, grinning. "Seems you needed it."

Rusadka tried to be insulted, but now her smile broke out in earnest. "Let us have supper, then." While she went to her saddle pack to find more bread, Elivasa took her palfrey down to the brook for a drink and tethered it loosely so it could forage.

Elivasa contributed a skin of ale, and they ate as Rusadka tried to figure out whether Elivasa's appearance was a good thing or not. "Did Anastyna grant you leave to go?"

"I am not sworn to Anastyna," Elivasa said as she chewed the stale bread. "Not sworn to anyone."

That was true. If she had allegiance to anyone, it was Valenty, and that might be a short-lived pledge, if Sofiyana indulged her penchant for cruelty.

Elivasa wore a thick riding skirt and, over her smock, a belted tunic. Her boots were covered in dust, as was her hat, but the hard ride had brought color to her cheeks. Dimpled cheeks. The cheeks went better with court dresses than these plain clothes. But Rusadka liked looking at her just the same.

Still, she had to make clear her purpose. "I report to Urik."

"Yes," Elivasa cheerfully agreed. She handed Rusadka a sack of shelled chestnuts to share. "I will second you since you have a duty to fulfill. Presuming there is no rule precluding an extra fighter?"

Rusadka pressed on. "We can do nothing for Valenty. I am bound for Zolvina."

Elivasa's expression went serious. "Granted. We go to Zolvina." She turned to catch Rusadka's gaze. "If you will allow the company."

They eyed each other until Rusadka put her hand on Elivasa's knee. "Done, then."

"Excellent," Elivasa said, and just like that it was settled.

A simple agreement, and satisfying. Rusadka could not bear a companion who talked too much. Sometimes she could not bear people who talked at all.

They finished their humble meal without further conversation, and as the nearby stream clattered over stones and continued its journey, she felt content to keep silent and listen to the creek with her companion.

❦

Guards no longer kept lookout on the roof of Rothsvund Palace. To provide a place for the *strigoi*, they had been relegated to the windows of the building's upper story. These days it was only the *strigoi* and Nashavety on the roof, where she liked to pace, thinking and planning.

She detoured around the piles of resting *strigoi*, some twenty-five of them by now, forming a humped landscape of demons. With her creature power, she was not afraid of them. They had been attracted to her from the first, back in her house in the forest, so there was that bond.

She did wonder whether they had come to Rothsvund to be near Strigo, Albrecht's *sympat*. Whether they were all part of say, a single pack, and must stay together. It was at Drogeliv, her mansion in the forest, where she had first seen them, having never even heard of them before she took up residence in the Volkish woods. But now, in their presence every day, she began to think of how they might be put to use. Whether in battle. But how could they be controlled? Might they not as easily feed upon her own soldiers as the enemy's? And so many of them, if they must all be together, how could her creature power hold the entire pack in thrall?

She would meditate upon the question.

But tonight she came to the roof for inspiration on larger issues. To gather the power of the night, which ranged over her head and around the palace in lovely darkness.

As Nashavety stood next to the parapet, the nearest demon hump stirred, and a wing moved away from a wizened face. It looked at her, blinking, and with a sickening little smile. "Go back to sleep," she told it.

She felt the night filling her soul, and her left hand reached out to touch the darkness. With her elemental power she summoned a scrying fog and stared into it from the ramparts. Her heart was agitated, and she sought comfort and, most of all, knowledge.

Anastyna was not yet captured, nor even Yevliesza. How Sofiyana had botched things! Disgracefully, the child had allowed Anastyna escape. Nor had her band of men yet found Yevliesza as she fled through the mountains. She regretted anointing Sofiyana as her replacement, yet who else did she have? *Fajatim* Vajalyna, perhaps. But the girl was her niece, so a blood tie.

What her young apprentice needed were dark arts, but she had not the mettle to embrace them. For one thing, she would have to chop off the small finger of her left hand—and then grow it back, altered. Actions quite beyond the ringletted royal.

She brought her concentration to the mist that huddled around the roof.

There in its shadows she saw a woman's form. A woman in trousers, boots, and a cape. Short hair, cut straight around her head. At her side, a wolf. Nashavety leaned into the parapet, absorbed.

The woman and wolf seemed to walk through a heavy darkness. Around them, a profound thudding sound. The woman turned to look behind her, her face anxious. By the Nine, by the dark and lovely Nine, it was Yevliesza. Where was she?

The wolf turned its head from side to side, watchful. Protecting her. And then, instantly, they were walking down a road full of people. What was this? Some place in one of the polities?

But now, in her mist-vision, a castle appeared in the distance. There could be no such place, not in Numinat. Was it merely a dream? Some uncanny plane of being?

Above the figure of the mundat girl, the sky swirled with dust and lightning. It was indeed a distorted place. And the wolf, how could a woman without creature power be with a wolf? A *sympat*, perhaps.

She closed her eyes to let awareness come to her, so she could deeply know. Her left hand throbbed with power. Could she be looking into a dreamworld?

And then—her powers did not fail her—she knew. This was inside the Mist Wall. A place derived from a story. A memory came to her of a legend that one could enter the Mist Wall. And there find spirits, travelers, mysteries.

In the legend, what was the great secret of going there? Ah. That although entering the wall was impossible, you could do so if you believed you could.

Prince Albrecht joined her on the roof. In growing excitement, he and Marshal Reinhart listened as Nashavety described her vision. Gone now, vanished like a ripple in a lake.

Albrecht believed that Nashavety had seen Yevliesza. A woman with hair cut to chin length. But he said that she could not be in the Mist Wall, an impossible thing.

That was the wrong way for him to think. She would have to steer him into the correct perception. "Perhaps the leader of the *satvars* knows the secrets of access."

"If it is real, we must go in and take Yevliesza," Reinhart declared, ever stating the obvious.

"First we must know *why* she went," Nashavety said.

"But penetrating the wall?" Albrecht persisted. "A foolish story."

"No, my prince. Many things are possible through the dark arts." She raised her left hand like a claw, reminding him of impossible things that had come to pass. "I know it is possible. She is there. And I know why. She seeks power. What power of the Mythos is greater than the Mist Wall?"

The point struck home with him. You only had to know the right words to use, like power.

"If so . . ." He paused. "If so, we must find a way in and send a unit to apprehend her. Or kill her."

But the place, the plane they were discussing was not a place of life and death.

"Nothing dies in the wall," Nashavety said, remembering that part of the Mist Wall belief. "We bring her out. Then she is ours to control."

She saw Albrecht's doubt.

"My prince. Would it not be more satisfying to keep her and use her as we see fit? We must discover what she knows, how she can influence a solid material as she did with you in the crossings."

Her thoughts were already on the difficult questions of how to penetrate that other place, to be—what did they call it—a *traveler* in its precincts. Like Yevliesza was. And when they found her, they would have her living body and not just an apparition.

A shiver of pleasure spread across her skin. It was within her ability to do it. The very night air coated her with power.

"Then let us take the witch-girl in hand," Albrecht said.

How galling that he used the term *witch*. An insult to her race.

Oblivious, he went on. "If we can go in, let us take her."

"Sir," Reinhart said, "send me. I will bring her to kneel at your feet."

Albrecht was watching Nashavety. "Can it be done, madam?"

"Oh, yes. But it is fraught with danger. Dire things can happen, things worse than death. One would have to believe it was worth it."

"It is worth it," Albrecht murmured. He nodded at Reinhart. "Let it be done."

"No." Nashavety said. "We must consider well who to send. It takes a particular quality to enter the wall."

"Courage, madam?" Reinhart asked. "Arcane knowledge? What?"

"You must either love something beyond all bounds or hate something to the same degree." She smirked. "Which do you think is stronger?"

Albrecht snorted a laugh. "Hate," he said.

A good student, this prince. "Even so." She regarded him a long moment. "Are you willing, Albrecht?"

He tipped back his head, looking up at the moon-drenched sky, and she knew she had him.

"When?" he asked.

"Now."

Chapter Twenty-Seven

The setting sun was only a smear in the dust-laden sky as the wagon turned down a narrow, rutted road. In the distance, Yevliesza saw a cottage nestled in folded hills. Behind the house, a stream meandered by, its waters black in the growing dusk. Nearby, she heard a rhythmic clunking sound.

The woman who drove the wagon easily hopped down from her seat. Yevliesza jumped down to help her unhitch the horse and noted the woman's deeply lined face and the black strands threading through her white hair. As they led the horse to a small stable, the woman said, "You may spend the night here, if you wish." Yevliesza wondered if she meant in the stable. Inside, it smelled richly of dung and horse-flesh. The woman used a pitchfork to dig into a pile of hay and toss it into the trough.

Watching her, Yevliesza was alert for any clues as to what this chance meeting could teach her, if anything, and wondered if it had been a mistake to come here rather than keep following the road. Had the woman and cart arrived for a purpose, or had she mistakenly taken the ride to get away from Reynard the juggler, who might not have been a threat at all?

Once the horse had fodder, the woman put her hands in the small of her back, stretching in pleasure. She set out for the house, with Yevliesza following. When they neared the cottage, she saw a white-haired man chopping wood on the side of the house, raising an axe in the air, and bringing it expertly down on an upright section of wood, splitting it.

Their path led through a garden with bushes of tomatoes and rows of carrots and lettuce. Along a fence, peas climbed a net, fighting for space with grape vines growing rampant. A gentle roll of thunder growled from the direction of the city.

The woman led her into a simple parlor with a steeply sloping ceiling and tidy, if sparse, furnishings. Then into a kitchen. Red-tinged light from the sunset streamed through a mullioned window. Without conversation, the woman stoked an iron stove and used a hand pump to fill a kettle. Fetching two pottery cups from a shelf, she urged Yevliesza to take one of the two chairs at a small table. Her host took the other.

While they waited for the kettle to boil, Yevliesza thanked her for the ride and, with that, ran out of things to say that would make any sense to an old woman who lived inside an impossible wall.

"It is the least I can do," the woman answered, making Yevliesza wonder what she meant. Offering a ride must be an everyday gesture, even here.

The woman's eyes were black, tinged with violet, and she regarded Yevliesza with a kindly gaze. A long silence followed as Yevliesza wondered about this woman who was beginning to seem like someone she should know. Violet in the eyes. Numinasi.

The kettle whistled, and soon they each had a cup releasing steaming fragrances of herbs and honey. Through the window Yevliesza could see the old man carrying split wood toward the side of the house. As he did so, his face came into full view.

A snap of recognition. It was her father. She froze in surprise. Her father, dead these six months.

Her father. She had tried to prepare herself for this . . . but no, she was not prepared, how could she be? She wanted to run out to him. But at the same time she knew, she *knew* he was not really here. Isha had said she might see the beloved lost. Longing overcame her. The longing to be with him again.

She looked at the woman on the other side of the table. If her father was chopping wood outside, then this was her mother. It couldn't be. But never mind, never mind, it was her, impossibly her, though she had never even seen a picture of her.

"I never meant to leave you," the woman said. Her mother said. The shade of her mother, or the impression the Mist Wall had conjured of her. The words carved into her heart.

"I know," she whispered. Her eyes grew hot.

A wistful smile came to her mother's face. "I left you too soon. But I was always with you."

She couldn't speak. What do you say to an illusion, even a beloved one?

"Drink some tea. For this time when we are together, do not be sad."

I was always with you. Yevliesza believed her. All the years she had grown up with only her father for company, she was in the home full of things bequeathed by her mother. Things she had brought from Numinat, things she had sewn, or crocheted, things that had been handed down from her own mother. Maybe it was less than what most children had of their mothers. But it was enough. It had to be. *You will see all the things you want and see them in a new light.*

Isha had told her that people usually wanted those who were lost. But that was not a road that she would go down.

"I'm not sad," she told her mother. She took another sip of tea. "Well, maybe a little."

Her mother reached out to cover Yevliesza's hand. "Good."

She felt herself growing drowsy as the evening settled in and crickets began their songs. The silence in the kitchen deepened.

"I am so tired," she found herself saying.

Her mother shook her head. "You cannot sleep. In this realm, sleep means something different than you might think."

"It means you're giving up."

"Yes. But night is falling." Her mother rose to fetch a lantern and lit the wick. "We have work to do if you are going to Holdfast." A guess. But a correct one.

She went to a drawer near the stove and removed a small wooden box, and placed it on the table between them. As she opened it on its small hinges, Yevliesza could see that it contained jewelry.

"I did not have a chance to show you this before I was called away. But I would like you to choose a piece from it. A piece that will remind you of what you already have."

"What do I have?"

"Oh, everything. Everything you need."

Yevliesza smiled to hear that. It was so simple, and she desperately wanted it to be true.

From the box, Yevliesza picked up a ring that appeared to be made of ivory. She turned it in her hand, feeling its silky smoothness. She wanted to try it on for size but thought that would mean she was deciding. For now, she set the ring aside.

A bracelet drew her attention. Its narrow width formed a cuff of deeply polished jet black. She loved the piece, in its simplicity and elegance, but she placed it on the table next to the ring.

Next, she brought out from the box a small chain long enough to encircle a woman's neck. Nine dark green stones comprised the front of the piece, each spaced a finger's width apart. She held the necklace up to the light from the lantern, noting the peaceful emerald depths of the jewels. It was a simple, lovely piece, but there was one more.

Picking up a large amber pin framed in brass filigree, she noted that the stone bore deep swirls of red and brown as though it was impossibly deep. In back, a sturdy clasp to keep it in place.

"Which should I choose?"

"The one that speaks to you."

Yevliesza looked at the ring, bracelet, necklace, and pin. White, black, green, and yellow. She chose the necklace. "Green for verdure," she said. Her mother's power.

"I am honored, my Liesa."

The next time Yevliesza looked at the box, it was gone. Startled, she put her hand to her neck, and found that she wore the chain with its green stones.

Plates with the remains of a meal lay before her—though she didn't remember eating. Her mother stacked them and pushed them aside. "Now we must look ahead to your journey to Holdfast. It will not be easy, and I am afraid for you."

"I think my *sympat* will watch out for me."

"Yes, the wraith wolf. But he can only help you three times."

She didn't like hearing that. She was depending on Kiya. "Three times, like in a fairy tale?"

"Those were not tales, my daughter. They were the truth. They held the wisdom of the folk, and that one is about strength. To become strong you cannot have too much help. Be your own strength."

Yevliesza thought back to her experience so far with Kiya. If the rules of the Mist Wall were that she only had three assists from her *sympat*, then she knew she had already used up one: when Kiya found the door in the Mist Wall and led her through. Maybe that was why she hadn't seen much of her wraith wolf. He was waiting for times of need.

The kitchen window revealed a slow dawn filling the sky. Night had passed more swiftly than it should have. Time to go.

Her mother walked her to the door. She reached for Yevliesza's hand and clasped it. Only that. A way of leaving-taking without saying goodbye.

As Yevliesza turned from the porch, she saw her father working in the vegetable garden. He raised the spade he was using and waved at her. She wanted to go to him, had been fighting with herself whether she should seek him out in the yard. But she could not have him, nor her mother. They were gone from her life. *You will see all the things you want in a new light.*

They stood, thirty feet apart, gazing at one another. "I love you," she whispered. He nodded to her, smiling, fully himself. Fully gone.

She turned and made her way to the road.

Chapter Twenty-Eight

At Osta Kiya, the Devi Ilsat was allotted a small room with a very nice view of the valley that plunged down through the tight forest to the Kovna River. She had a bed in a carved frame, a trunk with supple leather straps, and a padded chair. It was all very nice indeed, and she thanked the chamberlain profusely, but what she did not want was the chair.

She had asked Yarna to put the chair in her own room, and now she sat on the bed waiting for the princip.

Yarna came back in. "You should eat something, High Mother." Yarna meant that *she* should have a meal. But there was no time to waste.

"Yarna, please have a meal yourself in the dining hall. You have done all the work, after all." Making camp, cooking. All the Devi Ilsat had done was ride a horse.

"But—"

"Go, Yarna. I must speak with the princip." Yarna still hovered. "And she is coming to this room."

Yarna's eyes went wide. She ducked a nod and fled.

The Devi Ilsat clasped her hands in her lap and considered what she had so far found at the city-palace. Soldiers in positions on the roof, the whole roof, as enormous as it was. Inside the palace, halls often deserted except for guards posted throughout.

She had known that Anastyna had been deposed and imprisoned, but today she had learned that Lord Valenty had helped Anastyna to break out and flee. And that he was in custody. Numinat had a new princip, and this new one had been enthusiastically throwing people out of the Tower door.

The first victim, Lord Michai. A decent man and, for two princips, the Lord High Steward. For the first time in years, the Devi Ilsat was angry.

Everything was amiss. How, *how*, could these things have happened?

A knock, and the door opened. A uniformed man stood in the opening, wearing the red and white livery of the princip's house guard. Sofiyana stood at his side. She wore a sober brown dress of fine velvet, perhaps meant to give the appearance of a warrior-queen. It was a cunning look. Her violet hair was pulled back so hard her eyes slanted.

"My Lady Princip," the Devi Ilsat said. She started to rise but made a show of it being difficult.

"Please remain seated, honored Mother." Sofiyana looked around for a chair.

Before she could have the guard fetch one, the Devi Ilsat said, "Do sit next to me, My Lady Princip. There is plenty of room." She wanted to be near Sofiyana to try and read what, by the grace of the Deep, was going on. She patted the bed. "Indulge an old woman. I cannot hear as well as I once did."

Sofiyana dismissed the guard and reluctantly sat next to her on the bed.

"So good of you to come to my room. I am afraid the journey has taken its toll, and I am a little unsteady. Forgive me."

"It is nothing, High Mother. Of course you must rest. But was it wise to undertake such a long trip? Is there something I can do for you?"

"It has been many years since I came here," the Devi Ilsat said, letting her voice drift into revery. "Oh, I used to come. Princip Lisbetha and I were old friends, very close. But it is not the *satvar* way to hold on. And now things are changing once again." She smiled as though to say, *what can one do?* "So I have come to welcome you to your high duties and to pledge my help for your well-being."

"My well-being?"

"Spiritual well-being."

Sofiyana fixed a look at her. "How did you know there was a new princip in need of greeting?"

"Oh!" The Devi Ilsat chuckled. "Word comes to us, even in the mountains." She shook her head. "Things have changed so fast it shook me down to my sandals." She looked down at her feet. "Or, boots, I suppose, now that I have been riding a horse."

Sofiyana gave a flat smile. "Is there something you need from me, honored Mother?"

"Well, yes, there is a small matter. We recently had a troubling situation at Zolvina. There were some men hiding in the hills near the compound, and I think they were bandits. Never in all my years has anyone threatened our home. I would like to know if you think they might come back."

"These are troubled times, High Mother. I am sorry that you have this worry, and I will send a troop to make sure they are not hiding in the hills. To threaten a such a place is a grave thing. I will see them taken care of."

Tellingly, she did not ask how many men there had been. Because she already knew. She had doubtless sent them.

The Devi Ilsat turned more directly toward Sofiyana and grasped her left hand—since that was the closest hand, as she had planned it. She brought some emotion into her voice. "My daughter, you bring me great comfort. How tender it is to hear that with all the concerns of war, you would spare Zolvina such a service." She gripped Sofiyana's hand a little harder.

It was all she could do not to cry out in alarm. The hand leaked such a mixture of diabolics and confusion that she did not know how the woman could remain upright.

She patted Sofiyana's hand in an old woman's gesture but then resumed her grip. "It is such a comfort to me to finally have met you. To convey the greetings of the *satvary* to you."

The Devi Ilsat looked carefully into Sofiyana's eyes. Small threads of violet surged and faded like ragged thoughts. Inimical thoughts. For a moment the Devi Ilsat thought there was someone else looking out at her. She softened her gaze so as not to stare.

Sofiyana abruptly pulled her hand away. "We have heard that Mistress Yevliesza is a guest at Zolvina. After the rigors of her misguided mission to Volkia, how does she fare?"

The Devi Ilsat was prepared for the trick question. Sofiyana might well have been told by now that Yevliesza had left Zolvina and gone into the mountains. If the watchers had found her tracks. The *satvars* had seen half the men leave their spy-post on the ridge. But where had the other watchers gone? Following Yevliesza, she feared.

"Well, I do not know how she fares. She is a willful girl and left us in the middle of the night." But at least if Sofiyana was asking about Yevliesza, then her soldiers had not captured her. "If I see young Yevliesza again, I will tell her you kindly asked after her." She patted Sofiyana's hand.

Sofiyana pulled her hand away again. "You do not touch a princip without permission. You do not grip my hand." Staring hard at her.

"Please forgive me. I grow sentimental these days."

Sofiyana stood. "I will leave you to your rest. I have assigned a serving woman to you. Let her know if there is anything you need, and you will have it."

"How kind, thank you. I would like to visit with Lord Valenty."

Sofiyana checked her motion to depart. "He is in prison."

"Yes, I did hear. Would today be all right?"

"No, High Mother. He will have no visitors."

The Devi Ilsat shook her head as though she had been told there would be no meat at supper. "Oh, that is hard."

"Yes."

"When will his trial be?"

"Judgment has already been passed. He does not deny that he conspired to free Anastyna from custody."

"But may I not see him for his spiritual comfort, my daughter?"

"Is that why you came here, High Mother? For him?"

The Devi Ilsat paused for a deep breath. "No, Sofiyana. I came for you. For your sake."

For a moment Sofiyana looked completely open, as though it had been a very long time since anyone had shown care for her.

"If anything weighs on your heart, I am here."

Then her face shut down. "Nothing weighs on my heart, High Mother."

The Devi Ilsat was quite sure that was not true. The girl held secrets that lashed at her from within. Sorcery leaked from her pores.

"Thank you for the visit, my daughter. It is so good to become acquainted with each other."

The Devi Ilsat had just become acquainted with a problem. Numinat was led by a princip full of demonic energy. She was hollow. Behind her eyes: Nashavety.

⁂

SOFIYANA HATED THE NETHERS. THEY STANK OF RATS AND DIRT, AND reminded her of Anastyna's escape and the betrayal of the army. Some of the army, anyway, including some of the elite *harjat*.

By the light of her guards' torches, she made her way through the corridors carved from stone, wary of ambush. Who knew what might happen next, after so much chaos? As she passed the holding cells, she thought she saw fleeting shadows, wraiths that sprang to life in the torchlight, then fled into cracks.

At last she and her men stopped before Valenty's prison cell.

Collapsed as he was against the wall, he looked to be no more than a heap of rags. The Devi Ilsat would not have liked to see this. And would not see it.

Sofiyana glanced at her captain, and the man growled, "Sit up, sir fop. The princip will speak with you."

The prisoner stirred. He saw Sofiyana. "Perhaps you could spare a cup of wine?"

"A cup could be arranged." Though she would happily see him poisoned, she had need of him. "But I hear you will not speak to my jailers."

"Your torturers."

"My jailers seek to know your conspirators. It will come to light, Lord Valenty."

"I think not, demon."

Her captain took a step closer to the door. "Say that again and I will stop your mouth with dung."

Valenty turned away from them, looking at the wall of his cell. "Easy words when iron doors stand between us."

"Lord Valenty," Sofiyana broke in. "Your insurrection is finished. Now punishment will be meted out. Anastyna faces the charge of treason, as do you. Thousands died because she misused the army for the sake of the prince of Nubiah. And we know the names of those who fled with you. You have lost. Now all that is left for you in this world is a few more names. You will tell us who else conspires against our laws and ways."

"Any man or woman with honor enough to oppose you has already gone. Now you are hunting for spies among the cooks and chamberlains?"

She pushed on. "Is Lord Michai one of hers?"

Valenty looked up at her again. His face was bloodied, his hair matted, his skin no longer that olive, shaded tone that had reinforced his commanding presence. He was pale, with a sheen of sweat on his brow.

His words were measured and clear when he spoke. "The Lord High Steward admires Anastyna, but he is not *hers*. Unlike you, most Numinasi do not belong to others."

Well, Michai had already walked out the Trespass door. Michai, and a few suspicious maids who were undoubtedly spies. She had mentioned Michai only to move the confession along.

She came to her main point, the thing she was keen to know from him. "Where has the fugitive gone?" A long silence met this. "Eventually you will tell us. Let it be now." Threats and beatings did not sway him. She did not want to torture him too far, lest he simply lie to her and then be beyond questioning. But she had to know. Anastyna could raise an army. Nashavety was rabid to know her hiding place.

"I do not know where she is," Valenty said. "We decided that there would be no destination."

"I do not believe—"

He interrupted. "It would have been foolish to decide in case any of us were apprehended. A few of us were to think of three places of possible refuge. But no one was to share their alternatives. At the right moment, they would make the best decision given the circumstances."

"Who would decide?"

"Second-rank *harjat* Urik. Unless we had a virtuous *fajatim* with us. We would have deferred to her, but none of them were inclined to help us since they are now under sorcerous control."

Sofiyana ignored this. "What were your own alternatives?"

"I was excused from the exercise. My job was to devise the plan to free the princip. It was quite complicated."

"I do not believe you." She gripped one of the iron bars with her hand. "You have lost everything, Valenty. You are no longer a courtier. You are no longer even a spy. In fact, you are already dead. Everyone is gone from you. Give me the last thing I want to know, and you will have your cup of wine."

"I decline. The company, after all. I am used to better."

She turned in anger and stalked to the other side of the corridor. Raising a fist, she struck the rock wall, bringing an eruption of pain in her hand. He was determined to die a hero. Bile crawled up her throat as she remembered Nashavety's fury at Anastyna's escape. Nashavety hardly let her sleep, haunting her nights, filling her mind with despair.

She swung around and went back to the cell, wanting to throw open the door and beat the information out him. Through the bars, she growled, "Tell me or I will take you apart one limb at a time and burn them in front of you. By all the hells watching, I will make you howl the truth!"

"If I were you, Sofiyana, I would be falling apart, too. If you cannot find the princip, Nashavety will take your throne and give it to someone else. I could give her a few ideas, but she only talks to you."

She turned to her captain. "Make him sorry he said that. But avoid his face."

When the thudding of fists started, she felt a little better. But nothing could compose her mind when she thought of Nashavety's disappointment. To fail Nashavety. The thought of it was a well of cold water rising in her chest. Nashavety's care for her—love of her—was slipping away. Her world was tipping, and she looked into a chasm.

When she thought that Valenty had been suitably disciplined, she ordered the guards to bind his hands and feet, and walk down the corridor to give her privacy with him. They left a torch in a holder on the wall.

Sofiyana entered the cell and crouched by Valenty, whose head was now slumped against his chest.

From her pocket she took out the amber ring, fitting it on the second finger of her left hand. No matter what it cost her, she had to use it now to bring Valenty under creature control. The ring's emanations had given her mastery over the five *fajatim*. But she did not know if she could take on one more creature and keep them all under her sway. She could barely keep her thoughts ordered under the constant trickle of dark magic, much less extend her control over yet more creatures. But she had to try. She could not permit Anastyna to ride free among the polities, turning loyalties, recruiting fighters. She had to know, Nashavety had to know, where the fugitive was hiding.

"Look at me," she whispered. Valenty raised his head and did so, mockingly. She placed her left hand on his forehead. The amber stone flared with the light from the torches, showing the juvenile dactyl claw within, slightly curved, seeming to beckon her. She concentrated, summoning Nashavety's will.

"Come to me, Valenty. By the Mythos, I conjure you."

He closed his eyes against this invasion. A tiny membrane between him and her. It could not matter.

"Come, Valenty," she whispered from deep in her throat. "Come."

Valenty's eyes flickered open, darting glances here and there as though seeking escape.

She spoke again, her voice cracking. "Valenty. Give yourself to me."

When he could hold out no longer and opened his eyes to look at her, she saw the last of his will trickle away.

Weakened by the effort, she went to her knees. Pressing a hand against the wall for support and leaning into him, she kissed him on the forehead.

Now he was hers.

Chapter Twenty-Nine

Yevliesza reached the road to the city and started down it while the sun was still rising behind the hills. Already it was warm, with the sweet smells of blackberries and drying mud staining the air. In the far distance, a few people who must have risen before her were disappearing around the shoulder of a hill. Otherwise Yevliesza was alone.

The storm clouds that had glowered overhead the day before persisted, reminding her again of the roiling view of the Mist Wall seen from up close.

During the encounter with her parents, a weight had pressed down on her heart. It was grief from their loss, but on this bright morning—or what passed for morning in this place—the burden had lifted, replaced by another sense of things, a larger sense than loss. She had possessed a family. Though they were gone, they would always be her parents. Her father and mother had once lived in Numinat—were Numinasi. She was a part of that history, and they had inevitably led her back to where she belonged.

Whether the ruler of that land was fair to her or even decent, it was still her home, something that during her isolation on Earth she had yearned for without even knowing it. A home with helpers, friends, and even a lover.

She was grounded in Numinat, in the Mythos. It gave her strength to know she belonged in this new life. *You have everything you need,* her mother had said. Maybe that was true.

When she made the turn in the road, the city of Holdfast lay before her across a shallow plain. Surrounding the town, a stone defensive wall with rounded turrets at the corners. Through wisps of brownish mist she glimpsed a central castle in Holdfast's midst. It rose step-like from the surrounding city in successive stories, reaching to a square keep with crenelated battlements.

The view gave her pause. It was both grand and unsettling. Whoever ruled there wished to convey power and permanence. That would be Nashavety's style. Perhaps Anastyna's as well. Maybe it was the way of all ambitious people, but the city was also for ordinary people. Everyone was going there to get something. But the city held the truth under the longings. Maybe the city would show her that she didn't want some of the things she used to. Or that she shouldn't want them. She wanted that lesson. Then she would have the certainty to act. That was the theory, anyway.

She was not surprised to find that the road was deserted now. Each person entered on their own. Though she looked carefully, the gate through the city wall was shrouded in the dust-soaked air.

Drawing closer, she saw that a parkland of green shrubs lay in front of the wall. As she drew closer, the greenery revealed itself as a tall hedge that stretched as far as she could see in both directions.

Walking along the side of the enormous hedge, she came to a gap in the thicket. Through the opening she saw a path that turned a corner. It was a maze.

Now would be a good time for Kiya to make an appearance. It wasn't by any means guaranteed. *You can't get too much help if you want to be strong,* she recited to herself.

As she entered the maze, she found herself on a long path tunneling into the green. Walking down it, she heard bird calls and the chattering of what might be squirrels. Signs of life and normalcy. She hoped that this thicket might be merely a simple garden. But farther in there was a branching in the path, and then she was certain it was a labyrinth.

Left or right. How to choose? She remembered her experience in the crossings, in the back ways that had seldom been used and had never grown beyond cramped and small. At the time her mind had gone wide, allowing her to see a map of the place.

That wasn't happening here. She had to guess. She went left.

At one end of the corridor that came into view, she saw someone waiting at the next split in the path.

As she approached, she saw it was a youngster standing like a sentry. A young boy.

"Lost already?" he asked in a voice as high as a girl's. He looked to be about ten years old, sandy-haired and stout. "It happens all the time, believe me. I can lead you through for a coin or two." He cocked his head in what might be the direction of the city. "Been there lots of times."

"I don't have any money."

He crumpled his lips, regarding her with disappointment. "You should have brought some."

"Thanks anyway," Yevliesza said, not relishing favors, remembering Reynard trying to collect on the ones he dispensed. She pushed past the boy, taking a turn to the left into another pathway.

"Come back if you change your mind!" the boy called over the hedge wall.

Hurrying on, she kept track of the turns, left, left, and right, right, right. . . .

She grew more worried about the maze and how difficult it was going to be. She patted the pockets of her trousers to see if perhaps some coins might be tucked in after all. The boy might have been a decent guide because there was no way to know which direction to go in, and the height of the hedgerows didn't allow her to see the city wall over the top of them. But the pockets, empty.

Sweat drenched her face and underarms from the stifling air of the walled paths. When she found a patch of shade, she sank onto the ground to rest. How big *was* this labyrinth? She looked up at the rectangle of the sky defined by the hedge. The sides were clipped and neat, and she thought of Duke Tanfred and how his verdure power had created the means of her escape from Albrecht's palace. If he could only be here with her now.

Placing her hand on her neck, she found the necklace of emerald beads and counted the jewels. Nine. Nine powers. Counting from the right side, she touched each stone in turn. Stopping at the sixth. Every Numinasi child knew the chant of the nine: foreknowing, healing, warding, manifesting, creatures, verdure, elements, aligns, primal roots.

She was in a maze of growing things. Verdure was her mother's power. She got to her feet, feeling a bit dizzy from the heat, but the stones of the necklace steadied her as she fingered them.

Walking on with more confidence, she kept finding the sixth stone. She remembered that Isha had claimed that as a *providez* she had every power except primal roots. Isha had said that to exceed the allotment of two powers involved a shift in perspective, of not blindly accepting limitations. And hadn't she, as a stranger in Numinat not so long ago, questioned the ways and customs that seemed to bind everyone to outmoded modes of thinking? But what power could overcome a maze?

Left and left. Then right. She was either choosing with more relia-bility—or she was fooling herself.

Nashavety had sent him into the Mist Wall, but Albrecht had not expected a maze. In the wall of high, shaped bushes that stood before him, only one way in. A gap in the thicket.

She also had told him that the place would be dream-like and that he must allow himself no distractions. *Whatever you see, deal with it. Keep ahold of yourself. Remember what you are there for. Find her and bring her to me.*

According to Nashavety's vision, Yevliesza was in a large formal-looking garden. This giant thicket must be what she meant.

Behind it lay a great city surrounded by a defensive wall. That was the place where Yevliesza must be trying to reach.

If he failed to find his prey here, he would continue on into the fortified city. Naturally, she wanted the castle in city's center. She would be attracted to its mastery and power, as she had been attracted to Volkia and, yes, even to himself. The pretense of victimhood and simplicity had been false from the beginning. She wanted control and influence, and the Mist Wall held out the hope for her to achieve that, or she would not have come. He must stop her before she came back to the Mythos realms with renewed power.

He strode through a squared-off gap in the thicket. The starting point. Inside, he saw how straight-sided, trimmed hedges created a network of paths, but the close, looming walls restricted his view. He could not judge the way to go. After a few turns he grew uneasy. The hedgerows all looked the same; anything might be waiting around the next turn. He drew his sword and advanced.

Coming to another junction of paths he paused, trying to guess the way.

A shadow overhead. He looked up and saw his *sympat* with its small humanoid body and leathery wings. Strigo. Albrecht silently urged the *strigoi* to show him the way, since the creature could see the route from above. His *sympat* could naturally perceive his wishes, but beyond that, with his creature power he could direct Strigo's specific actions.

In response, his *sympat* cleverly circled around and flew from right to left over Albrecht's path. Albrecht took a left turn down the next corridor.

He moved more rapidly now, taking direction from Strigo.

The maze was unaccountably large. His exertions down the stifling green tunnels left him sweating and disoriented. Stopping to drink from one of his two water skins, he worried about finding Yevliesza if she entered the city before he found her. It might be more difficult to find her there. For the first time he entertained the idea that he might fail. He had failed with the woman before, in Rothsvund Palace, when he allowed her some freedom instead of keeping her under lock and key.

He concentrated, forming his intention to communicate. *Find the witch-girl, Strigo. Descend on her and hold her for me.*

He felt Strigo's acknowledgment. Then he added: *Do not feed on her. I have your meal with me.*

He patted the second pouch strapped around his chest. It was important to remember which skin contained water and which blood. On the other hand, he would gladly drink blood, if he could just find his prey and bring her out.

Once the *strigoi* had found her and subdued her, and having seen the maze layout, it could guide Albrecht to its location. If it could not do that easily, then the *strigoi* would have to hurt her enough to keep her immobilized and fly into view to lead him properly.

Albrecht had often imagined the ways in which he would use her once he had her again. Keeping the woman alive had become a very attractive idea.

With his *sympat* no longer guiding him, he sat down to rest, leaning his back against the hedge wall. He looked up at the empty sky. Strigo was off on the hunt. It would not take the *strigoi* long.

Chapter Thirty

The light from the hallway windows hurt Valenty's eyes. People lined the route, some bowing or merely watching as he walked by. To Valenty, after long days in the nethers, it felt like a dream to be moving among courtiers, nobles, and servants. And with a beautiful woman.

She walked by his side, acknowledging the bows, drifting along in her fine gown, guards on either side and behind. He tried to remember what was happening. And why he was with Sofiyana and not Yevliesza.

"Smile, Valenty," Sofiyana murmured. "Smile."

He smiled. She was the sort of person one should obey. A part of him was not so sure, though, and his smile quickly faltered. This was not Anastyna. But this woman wore the torc. It must be a dream.

"Bow to the next noblewoman you see."

He remembered that it was polite to do so. He nodded his head to an elderly woman he had once known, but whose name he could not recall.

How could he be at the princip's side and wearing rags? But when he looked down at his clothes, he found himself in fine wovens and velvet. His crimes, erased. The thought entered his mind with a stabbing motion. His crimes. Something that he had been called to do.

Crimes now forgiven.

So he would not be put to death, and Yevliesza would not learn of his execution and feel sorrow. And she would not think that his loyalty had been to Anastyna and not her, and that he had died for Anastyna, and that this proved that he did not love her.

They approached the royal quarters. Its four stories rose before him in fine stonework dressed in intricate carvings. Arched windows glowed with light; balconies jutted with their ironwork balustrades. The royal quarters. But it was not a good place. He came to a halt as he remembered that this grandeur housed a demon.

Behind him, a guard pushed him forward.

His companion's voice came to him. "Do not worry, my lord. Come along."

"Anastyna used to preside here," Valenty said.

"Be at ease, my lord. There is only me now."

Anastyna was in the past, then. He must try to keep things straight. As he resumed his forward progress, he heard her voice again. The new princip.

"Smile, Valenty."

He did so, and they passed through to the royal apartments.

❧

From her vantage point in the hallway, the Devi Ilsat watched as Sofiyana disappeared through the palace doors with Valenty. The display of the redeemed traitor now over, the crowd in the hallway thinned. She turned to Vajalyna, whom she had purposely sought out. "It is a comfort to see past rivalries put to rest, is it not?"

Unlike the other *fajatim*, Vajalyna was able to deport herself without obvious enchantment. Her mahogany skin well covered the sickly cast which the others displayed. But it might also be true that she needed less sorcery to keep her in line. She was ever Nashavety's staunchest ally.

Vajalyna responded. "Well, but he must show contrition."

The Devi Ilsat looked up at Vajalyna, who towered over her. "Oh! Let us hope that he does, my lady. But surely, he has already begged forgiveness?"

"It may be your job to think well of people, High Mother. But the rest of us need to see proof."

"And quite right, too. Quite right."

A few women came up to them, bowing their heads and asking for the High Mother's blessing. She could hardly stir from her room without meeting people who asked for comfort and sometimes for news of loved ones at Zolvina. With each suppliant, she took their hands, giving a bow of acknowledgement, murmuring to one, "May you find stillness and joy." And to the other, "May you find ease, my daughter."

Vajalyna began to excuse herself to follow Sofiyana into her quarters, but the Devi Ilsat begged leave to accompany her. "It pleases the folk to see the warm reception Princip Sofiyana has given me. It helps to smooth the transition, does it not? Perhaps this would be a good time for us pay the princip a visit. With so many people here to witness our unity."

Vajalyna's eyes narrowed. Thinking, thinking.

Then she smiled. "We shall see if Princip Sofiyana will receive us, then." She gestured for the High Mother to precede her, and the guard opened the great door. He nodded in respect to the High Mother and, noticing the sharp look from Vajalyna, ducked a bow to the *fajatim* as well.

"My son, may you know peace," the High Mother intoned. She appended, in case it might help him along the right path, "and honor."

He made eye contact with her in a way that people under creature power did not. Thank the Mythos, not everyone was subverted.

THE DEVI ILSAT SAT THREE CHAIRS AWAY FROM SOFIYANA AS SHE presided over the feast table. Sofiyana had the beauty, but not the presence, of Anastyna. Someone should tell her not to finger the torc around her neck as she was doing. As though she was afraid it would fall off.

The *fajatim* were in attendance, along with representatives of noble houses and a goodly share of army officers, all enjoying a lavish meal of game birds, fish, and mutton, as well as platters mounded with roasted potatoes and corn. On a side table, sweet pies by the dozen. There was a new *fajatim*, too: Daraliska, apparently Sofiyana's former steward at Raven Fell. The one who replaced Sofiyana as *fajatim* of Raven Fell when she stole the torc.

Valenty was seated at the far end of the table, his presence a statement of support, though—it could not be ignored—a muted one. Music from pipes and a harp added a gracious element, needed because conversation was low and stilted. Anastyna had been known to dislike formal dinners, and Sofiyana might be trying for an open, more welcoming affair. By the looks on people's faces, this was failing.

The High Mother had learned over many years how to observe without seeming to watch people. She did not think herself devious but found subterfuge to be what was required in the new regime. She needed to speak with Valenty, but it would be difficult in these close quarters. The idea struck that she must make Valenty merely one of many that she spoke with.

As a platter of roast beef was carried in, she took the opportunity to leave her chair and make her way to greet Alya, the *fajatim* of Storm Hand. She had known Alya's mother and received a startled smile from the woman. She was under strict control. It was in her eyes. The High Mother made a point of resting her hands on the woman's shoulders.

On her way back to her seat, she quickly exchanged pleasantries with Ineska of Red Wind and also Oxanna of Iron River, who was particularly infected, unable even to pretend to engage with the emissary from Zolvina *satvary*. The High Mother fixed a delighted smile on her face and gave her a parting hug. It was very difficult to act in a good-humored mood. The longer the meal lasted, the more she worried that she would come under creature control, merely by sitting at the same table as Sofiyana. But, if her charade was going as well as she thought, Sofiyana considered her merely an old woman who supervised other old women, who unaccountably had chosen seclusion over the pleasures of Osta Kiya.

Resuming her seat, she received a portion of beef, and exclaimed over its perfection. Sofiyana seemed glad of the compliment. Poor girl, to be buoyed by such things. She noted that Sofiyana often put her hand in a pocket of her gown as though she had a talisman there to shore up her courage.

When the pies were brought forward, the High Mother made her move. Walking down the length of the main table, she approached Valenty, who appeared to be toying with the food on his plate rather than eating. She greeted him fondly and, receiving an almost-smile, pretended to be moved by the greeting. Placing her hands on his shoulders, she pressed her hands tightly against him and moved closer to speak in his ear.

"May you be healed; may you be free of sorcery." Stepping back from him, she saw some life come back into his dark eyes. She beamed at him, then hugged him again, speaking low: "Anastyna is hiding at Zolvina. You may tell Sofiyana that."

When she released him, he was frowning. "Hiding?"

She took his hand. "What a lovely feast! I am so glad to see you making amends!" She murmured low, "Anastyna is in Zolvina. Tell Sofiyana that."

"High Mother?" he asked, looking confused.

She laughed as though he had uttered something witty, but she was distressed to observe what Valenty had become. "Tell her Zolvina. I promise it will be well,"

Giving Valenty one last, long hug, she left him, hoping her message had gotten through.

Sofiyana watched her as she resumed her seat. A large slice of pie awaited her. "Ah, my favorite!" she exclaimed, digging into her portion with gusto.

She stole a glance at Valenty, who looked more vacant than ever.

Sorcery hovered over the feast and the diners, dampening hearts and courage. But the Devi Ilsat would not abandon Valenty.

She had plans for him.

Chapter Thirty-One

Rusadka watched as Elivasa crawled to the top of the rock outcropping, flattening herself against it to get a view down into the watchers' camp without being seen. In the growing dusk, the crisp smell of snow lay thick around them.

The rounded top of the rock was bare from facing the afternoon sun, but in this region the peaks and ridges still carried heavy cloaks of snow.

Elivasa crept down from her perch. "The camp is abandoned."

"Let us see," Rusadka said. They crept around the ridge and entered the camp, swords ready. The firepit was covered in snow. "They have not been here for days."

She and her companion shared a knowing glance. Perhaps the men —soldiers, Rusadka had to assume—were in the *satvary*. They could not guess what they would find at there, but it did not seem likely that the men had given up.

The day was almost gone, but they made their way toward the *satvary* by the last of the light. No lights shone from the windows, nor did the inhabitants give any sign that they had seen visitors approaching.

The stone wall of the *satvary* had a wide gate made of saplings stripped of branches. Outside it they dismounted, drawing their swords. Elivasa placed herself to the side of the gate. The woman was not a warrior, but she had good instincts.

Valenty said the camp had held seven men. Elivasa had no sword training, so it would be an uneven match if it came to a fight.

Rusadka kicked the fragile gate open with a strike of her heavy-booted foot and charged in, Elivasa following.

The courtyard was empty. The domicile on one side, guest quarters on the other. A high walk along one of the walls, empty. Rusadka stayed on alert, identifying the doors through which attackers could still come. But all remained quiet. No *satvars*. That worried her. She wondered—and hoped—that whatever the cause of the empty compound, Yevliesza had left before it occurred.

Elivasa and Rusadka combed the outer buildings and found them deserted. When they entered the domicile, they found it, too, was empty. To Rusadka's relief, no bodies.

"Strange," Rusadka muttered as they checked the last of the *satvar* cells.

Elivasa nodded. "Where could one hundred old women have gone?"

"And why?"

As they exited the domicile, Rusadka saw a small bowl on the ground. She knelt beside it, noting that it contained food scraps.

"What is it?" Elivasa asked.

"Cat bowl," Rusadka said. "But the food scraps are fresh."

"Someone remains here, and not just a cat."

Rusadka stood and looked around as though she might suddenly see the person come out in the open. If the *satvars* were feeding a pet, it gave her some hope for their safety. But for now, the empty compound remained a mystery.

Night had crept into place revealing the ranks of silent stars, adding that vast perspective to the quiet *satvary*. "There is firewood stacked over there," Rusadka said, pointing to the gate leading to the gardens and supply sheds. "Perhaps the sisters will forgive us if we make a campfire."

"Why cook over a campfire," Elivasa asked, "when they have a cookery inside?"

"Easier for us to keep watch. We will hear anyone coming."

After laying the fire, Elivasa lit it with ease, pointing her left hand, bringing a flame which rapidly took hold.

As night deepened, she and Elivasa hauled blankets out of the *satvary* against the promise of a frigid night. Even with Elivasa's considerable elemental power, she could not make the air around their exposed nest warm, at least not for long.

Rusadka went to the top of the compound wall to keep watch for half the night, and Elivasa relieved her as the moon set.

It seemed she had hardly slept when Elivasa shook Rusadka by the shoulder. "Someone is here."

Rusadka jerked awake.

"I should have said someone *friendly*." An older woman in a light-colored cloak stood a few paces a way.

"It is Dreiza," Elivasa said.

Rising from her nest of blankets, Rusadka knew at once that this was Valenty's former wife who had become a renunciate. The joke in the barracks had been that Dreiza preferred a *satvar's* bed to the lord's.

"Lady Dreiza, I am Rusadka, third-order *harjat*."

Dreiza came forward with a worried look. Pushing formalities aside, she said, "We are surprised to see you. What brings you here?"

"We have come from Anastyna, who sought to know if you fared well."

Dreiza relaxed some, hearing the princip's name, but she was still wary.

Rusadka went on. "And we are looking for Yevliesza, who is personally known to me. We were in arcana together."

A few people, *satvars* by their garb, peeked out through the open gate leading to the gardens.

"Where have you been?" Rusadka asked. "We feared the worst."

Dreiza turned to the arriving *satvars* and beckoned for them to enter. They did so, entering the domicile with sacks in their hands. Going for supplies.

"Let us get out of the wind," Dreiza said, "and I will tell you." She frowned at the firepit that the women had slept by. "By a proper hearth."

⚜

Dreiza's explanation of events had their complete attention. Over a tenday ago, Yevliesza had left to journey through the mountains to seek the counsel of a woman whom the High Mother thought could help her sort out some things. Rusadka could well imagine what needed sorting out, but none of that was for others to hear.

Yevliesza's having left was good news until Dreiza's face fell into worry. "We knew that the compound was being watched, and we thought that Yevliesza had slipped away unseen. But then, the next day, we saw three of the watchers leave their hiding place behind the ridge, heading down the mountain. They led four extra horses."

The four others had followed Yevliesza.

"The watchers might have seen her leave after all or found her tracks." Dreiza spread her hands. "There was nothing we could do."

"We will be on her trail now, too. In the morning." Elivasa nodded at Rusadka's look. "But where is everyone else?"

Dreiza pulled her chair closer to the hearth where a good fire crackled. She related how the High Mother had gone to the capital city, having heard that Anastyna had been deposed and fearing the rumors of sorcery.

Dreiza went on. "Then, early yesterday, the High Mother sent a message—using a mirror she had given me. She said that we should take refuge in the ice caves a short climb away. Soldiers were coming."

"Soldiers," Rusadka said. "Not those who were watching from the ridge?"

"Not the watchers, a large force of soldiers."

The *satvars* had spent a frigid day and night in a mountainside cave and Dreiza was still shivering.

"Why would soldiers come here?" Elivasa asked.

"Because . . ." Dreiza's mouth tightened. "Because Sofiyana was using torture on Valenty to force him to reveal where the princip had gone. The Devi Ilsat suggested he say Zolvina."

"But the danger to you," Rusadka said. "Sofiyana's men will come looking for her. And when they do not find her, they will not hold back."

"Why we are staying in the caves." At the mention of it, Dreiza pulled her cloak around her more tightly. "It buys Valenty a little time, until they get here and find it is not true. So for now, the ice caves. It is cozy enough. A few of us came down today to carry up more wood for our fires."

"And feed the cat," Rusadka said.

Dreiza's smiled. "Yes. Lord Woe, our mouse killer." She drew herself up, making ready to leave. "You were in arcana with Yevliesza. So you have aligns."

"I do."

"You will need aligns in the mountains. We can tell you the patterns to follow. But then, the snow and ice. It would help if you had elements as well."

Elivasa smiled. "That can be arranged."

Chapter Thirty-Two

Coming to another fork in the path, the decision came again. Right or left? Hoping for inspiration, Yevliesza placed her fingers on her necklace's sixth stone as she had been doing from time to time, the stone she thought of as the verdure stone, pressing it between two fingers.

Perhaps left, came the thought. But maybe right. She sighed in exasperation. The necklace wasn't magic, and she couldn't go on pretending that it was. Her directional choices might be leading her in circles, repeatedly bringing her to the same junctions. Her confidence, so bright in her mind earlier that morning, began to evaporate.

Because the size of the maze was hard to judge, she didn't know how far she had to go. In growing dread, Yevliesza wondered if the maze was expanding. From the outside it had not appeared so large.

She looked behind, hoping to see Kiya, even if his assistance would mean using up one of the three.

Though she wanted to rest, to rethink her options, at the same time she felt like rushing forward, making quick choices by intuition. That might be more successful. Hurrying on, she made a choice that brought her to a short length of hedge with a turn at the end. Something was standing a few feet away. A large bird about three feet high standing on two legs, its back to her. It turned around, revealing that it was a child with wings.

No, not a child.

A monster. It barred her way. Leathery wings draped to each side. The creature's body was pinkish, and looked like a naked human, without hair or clothing, its male equipment hanging between its legs.

Her heart was jumping as though trying to break free from her chest. The thing was looking directly at her. She backed up, but in a moment, it had unfurled its wings and half hopping, half flying, it landed directly in front of her.

Its mouth was round and full of teeth. Nostrils flaring, it paused.

You can't be killed in the wall, you can't be killed. "Leave me," she croaked. Then louder, "Get out of here!"

It spread its wings into a wider barrier.

If she ran, it would chase her. But she must get past it. Shaking hard, she took a step to the side. It turned with her, backing her toward the hedge.

In the next moment the creature screamed and jumped onto her chest, crashing her against the hedge where jagged stems imprisoned her. The monster grabbed her arms with its own scrawny ones and, opening its teeth-lined mouth, screamed at an insanely high pitch, hosing her with spittle and the breath of rot.

It clung to her, staring into her eyes. Its face was so close it became her whole perception, a total world of monstrosity. Digging in her feet and trying for a stable stance, she bent her arms to bring her fists up— even while the creature held her upper arms—and pummeled its chest until she sensed it relaxing its grip.

It jumped down and stepped back, craning its neck to look up at her with what looked like surprise.

She yanked herself free of the hedge and staggered away. Running toward the next turn, her back shivered in expectation of the thing jumping on her from behind. Screams surrounded her.

She was screaming.

When she came to the turn, she chose a direction and ran on, choosing paths at random. When she could go no further, she stopped and bent over, hands on her knees. The only sound was her gasping breaths.

Alone. So far, she was alone. If the thing had chased her, it would already be here. Had she escaped? As the moment passed, she let herself hope. The sun glinted off the path. Just a slice of light. But there was no source of sharp light because of the dust in the sky.

It was not the sun. It was an align. Though she didn't think she had any more strength in her legs, she ran once more. Following the align.

A MOVEMENT OVERHEAD, A SHADOW OF WINGS. STRIGO WAS BACK.

Albrecht's *sympat* landed on the path in front of him. It opened its mouth, and emitted an unusual sound, a high-pitched singing whine.

"You found the woman?"

Strigo smiled, in that way it had of stretching its round mouth sideways.

"Take me to her!"

The smile broadened. As Albrecht looked down on the creature, he felt a stab of annoyance for its mincing ways, its pathetic smiles. "Take me to her," he said again.

From the *strigoi*, a tiny moan starting at a low register and zooming up to a screech. It was not moving to obey him. A few staccato notes like bird chirps escaped its misshapen mouth.

As the two of them stared at each other, Strigo made a sound that sounded a lot like *gone*. "Gone," it whined with a screeching pitch.

The *strigoi* could talk.

"Where is she?" Albrecht demanded. Then he realized the implication of Strigo's word. "She is dead?" A fear grew in him that his *sympat* was not under as much control as he had thought. "Report! Is she dead?"

"Ran awaaay?" it sang.

Even worse. Albrecht felt his temper rise. "You let her go?"

The creature looked away, cringing. "She strong, pushing!"

It was ridiculous, ludicrous. She had escaped? He bent down and grabbed Strigo by the neck. "Tell me!" He could throttle the creature as it crouched before him, weak, timid, ashamed. "Tell me!"

"Wo-min smell!" Strigo's eyes bulged as Albrecht's grip tightened around his neck. "Smell power, yes!"

Albrecht shook his hands free of the *strigoi*. "What power? You smelled her power, is that it?"

"Smell, yes. Different!"

Albrecht looked up from the cringing beast, considering the next turn of the hedge path, eager to get on with his hunt. By God, he needed to get on with it before she disappeared into the city.

"Looost power?" the *strigoi* sang, nearly splitting Albrecht's ear drum.

"Lost? What in the name of God are you talking about?"

"Smell wo-min. Lovely blood. Strigo hungry." Strigo looked up at him beseechingly.

Albrecht slipped the pouch strap off his shoulder and removed the stopper, handing over the blood meal.

Strigo guzzled the contents. A red drool snaked down its neck as it coughed softly like a human who had drunk too fast. The stench of the blood, now warm from the hot slog through the maze, disgusting.

Strigo nodded gratefully. "Root. She with root!"

"Root?" Albrecht asked in increasing impatience.

"Yesss," Strigo sang, keeping the word going, nodding repeatedly. "Power of roooot. Wo-min have!"

Albrecht sank into the words, trying to understand. He jumped to a thought. Excitedly, he knelt in front of his *sympat* and looked it in the eyes. "Primal root power?"

"It smelling like."

It could not be. But, could it not? Root power, which no one had possessed for a thousand years. "Primal root power," Albrecht whispered wonderingly.

"Yes, roootsssss," Strigo hissed.

Some said it was the root of all powers, that it gave access to all the powers. But the mundat girl did not have all of them. If she had, she would have used them against him when she had been his prisoner in Volkia. What was primal root power, then?

The crossings. The walls moving to her command . . .

Because the crossings were like roots. The way they grew and branched. Like the picture on the damn woman's back. And that was the meaning of primal root power, the ancient power the First Ones used to cross into Volkia. The power that had not been seen since the beginning.

If that was true . . . Albrecht's mind raced. The incredible power to control the crossings. He stood unmoving, letting the idea wash over him. Nashavety was right, the witch-girl did have a secret. How surprised she was going to be. He savored the thought. Madam Nashavety did not know everything.

He snapped at Strigo, "Show me where you found her. Show me now."

Chapter Thirty-Three

Yevliesza followed the align. It was merely a crease of molten light, but in this strange world she believed that it could lead her to freedom. She followed the crack of light as it knifed down the path, disappearing around a corner of the hedgerow.

With growing trust, she rushed on, pursuing the trail of light. Above the hedge peeked the stone wall of the city. Certainty now replaced mere hope: the hedge was going to release her. Another intersection, another turning of the align. By now she staggered with exhaustion, but sheer will drove her on.

Bursting from the last row, she left the green tunnels behind. Outside in the diffused sunlight, she sank to her knees. The cool air. The smell of cut grass. The warm stones of the city wall, brown and mauve and gray, blending in solid rockiness.

Looking at her arms, she saw where the monster's talons had gripped her arms. A few dots of blood welled from tiny punctures where the tips of its claws had dug in.

Someone was walking toward her. She jerked in alarm, but it was only the boy with the sandy-colored hair from the maze.

When he reached her, he looked down at her. "I could have gotten you here quicker."

Quicker. Would have been good. She felt a hysterical laugh wanting to get out.

He handed her a flask. "It is water. Honest."

What the hell. Her intuition told her that he was one to trust. She took a long drink.

"Since you had no coin," he went on, "I was going to guide you for nothing."

She got to her feet. "I didn't need any help. But thank you." He raised an eyebrow, accepting the flask back from her.

"Does it cost to get through the city gate?"

"The guards are asleep right now. You can just walk in."

She nodded at him and set out before the bird-man thing could find her again. The align had vanished, but she saw her way to the gate.

I didn't need any help, she'd said. Amazingly, that was true. The secret of the maze had always been with her. It wasn't in the chain with the green stones that her mother had given her. That was a prompt, not a solution. *You already have everything you need.* All she had to do was remember to perceive the aligns, the first form lesson of the align arcana.

⚜

STRIGO WAS CHATTERING AT HIM, "HERE, HERE, HERE. WO-MIN HERE!"

"Yes. She was here," Albrecht said. "Now find her again." He pushed Strigo ahead of onward, and the creature walked jerkily down the path, wings lifted into the air to keep them from dragging behind.

Sweat streamed down Albrecht's face. He wiped a sleeve across his eyes and hurried on, surprised by how fast the *strigoi* could walk on taloned feet. Yevliesza could be around any of the turns. He pictured her standing at the end of this tunnel, could imagine the panic in her eyes when she saw him. The prince of her nightmares. "Hurry!" he urged his *sympat.*

In the present tunnel of green he could look ahead and see that it was a dead end. In a few more steps, however, he saw that the hedge was split to allow a gap. Strigo went through, Albrecht following, and they started down another path.

Ahead, a wolf came around a turn.

The wolf was a stone's throw away as its gaze met his. He drew his sword. "Kill it, Strigo. Attack!"

Strigo held up its wings even higher and raced toward the animal. The wolf lunged at the *strigoi*, growling so fiercely that it sounded like five wolves, not one. Albrecht's sword was drawn, and he rushed forward, looking for a chance to strike.

Strigo was riding the wolf's back, slashing its claws across the wolf's skull as the wolf spun wildly, trying to dislodge the thing. Blood flew.

Then another wolf appeared, emerging from the thicket of branches. Albrecht charged forward to intercept it. At that moment a third wolf appeared, leaping in the air and crashing into Strigo.

Albrecht paused as more wolves emerged. A pack of them. In short order, the *strigoi* lay struggling on the ground. Albrecht backed up. They would come for him next, and the wolves would win the match.

But. Nashavety had said you could not die in the Mist Wall. He advanced on the pack. The narrow width of the hedge path would prevent the wolves from surrounding him if he was careful not to let any get behind him. He stalked toward them.

The wolves were done with their attack on the *strigoi*. Now they looked in Albrecht's direction. There were six of them, and six pairs of eyes watched him hungrily. He tightened his determination and went to meet them. As he did so, his vision blurred. He could no longer see clearly. The hedge appeared in fine-grained detail, but the wolves were fading. First into a kind of thin fog, and then, as he stared in confusion, they were gone.

They had not retreated into the gap in the hedge. They had disappeared while standing in the middle of the corridor.

He waited a few moments before he convinced himself that they were indeed gone.

Keeping his sword in hand, he walked to Strigo and knelt beside him.

The *strigoi* was covered in blood, making its wounds difficult to discern. Gashes bled freely where the wolves had savaged the wings and the tough but unarmored skin.

As it lay on its back, its chest rose and fell spasmodically. Strigo tried one of its ugly smiles but gave up. Its eyes locked on Albrecht's gaze as it growled low in its throat. One could not die in the Mist Wall. But one could become useless.

Albrecht stood, cursing his luck. Still holding his sword, he scanned the path. All was silent except for the *strigoi's* labored breathing. Taking a drink from his water pouch, he knew that the route forward would be more difficult now. But go on he would. The city was next.

As he started down the path, the *strigoi* moaned, calling to him.

He turned to look down at the creature. Returning to its side, he unstrapped the pouch holding the blood and dropped it on the ground where Strigo could reach it. His *sympat* looked up, its features softening.

"You are no use to me now," Albrecht said. He walked down the path. Rounding the corner, he continued on his way.

Before long he spied the castle wall cresting the top of one of the hedge walls. At last. The heat of the day had turned oppressive, and Albrecht stopped to remove his belted jacket and redistribute his weapons and the canteen strapped around his chest. He moved on, waiting for the final break in the hedge.

But it did not come. Turn and turn, walk and turn, and choose again.

Repeat.

After a long time, and seeming no closer to the exit, Albrecht found he needed to hack out a small indentation in the hedge just for the shade. Inside, a breath of cool, green air flowed over him, bringing him some relief. From his pack he broke out a ration of cheese and dried meat, gulping the food. He wanted to eat and then sleep, but that would be a mistake. He needed to escape this place before nightfall.

The food did not sit well. He lurched out of his den and lost the meal onto the dusty path.

Setting out again, he found he had lost sight of the city wall.

For a moment he stood and looked down the path in one direction and then the other. Then he looked up. Everywhere looked the same.

At the next turn, the same.

Chapter Thirty-Four

At the city gate, Yevliesza walked by the sleeping guards, wondering if this was her reward for conquering the maze. A weird idea. Or maybe it wasn't.

Now in the city, she stared around her. She still needed to settle her mind after the attack of that thing in the maze. And now that she thought more about it, why hadn't Isha warned her about *monsters?*

Around her, the cobblestone street was full of people, chatting or hurrying on errands. Women in smocks and long skirts; men wearing cloaks, loose trousers, and boots. The street wound out of sight as it climbed.

So as not to spend longer and draw attention to her behavior, she walked up the hill. She climbed past the half-timbered and well-kept houses, some with pristine white walls, and a few with windows, the glass thick and wavy, hiding what lay within. Leading away from the main street, alleys drowned in shade and the further reaches lost in darkness. Up ahead, a young woman emerged from a house carrying a basket and hopped easily over the gutter trickling by, redolent of waste and rot.

At a curve in the street she had a good view of the pale stone castle, its square towers topped by battlements and pierced by narrow openings. Squat and strong, but not as daunting as Osta Kiya.

Down a side street coming toward her, two soldiers in blue cloaks, their hands resting on their sword pommels. She ducked into the doorway of the nearest building so as not to attract their attention. They crossed the street where she stood and disappeared into the next alley.

Blue was a new color for soldiers. The others she'd seen, the ones on the road, had been uniforms of brown trimmed in white. If, as Reynard said, the brown were the queen's men, who were the men in blue?

The sight of the soldiers reminded her that this would be a good time to have a plan, a plan for what she should do here. In the back of her mind: Enter the castle at the stop. Confront the queen . . . and what? Depose her, pass her tests, steal from her? The queen who was likely Nashavety. She whose hatred fueled the Mythos war as much as Albrecht's ambitions.

But she had no plan. All she could do was be open to what came next, and use her powers, not all of them magic. Some of them plain, like intuition and confidence. She was learning some things about this strange environment, this engine of the Mythos, or repository of things, or whatever it really was.

Though people didn't seem to notice her much, she had been feeling ill at ease for the last few minutes. Her chest tightened as an understanding came to her. She was being followed.

Seeing an alley, she made a quick turn into its shadows. Who would be following her? Maybe soldiers in brown or blue. Reynard. Even Albrecht? The idea of Isha's *travelers* kept circling.

The urge to hide drove her farther into the side street, until she stood before a building with a shingle proclaiming Iron River. *Iron River*. The name of her father's ancestral hall. The door opened and when a few men emerged, a draft hit her face, heavy with the fumes of pipe smoke and beer. An ale house.

Iron River seemed like a portent. She entered.

Inside, it was even darker than the alley. The only source of sunlight was a window, more an assemblage of heavy glass squares than panes. A cold fireplace occupied one wall. Behind a plank supported by barrels, youngsters and a harried-looking older woman filled tankards from casks. At a few of the small tables shadowy figures sat hunched over drinks.

When she took a place at a table near the dark fireplace, her legs almost sighed from the relief. She had been almost constantly on her feet since she had entered the Mist Wall, which seemed to be days ago. But she had no need of sleep, and every time she felt tired, eventually, dream-like, it passed. Time was different here. It might not even exist. But in its coherence and vividness, it was not like a dream. She gripped the edge of the rough tabletop so hard that her palms protested in pain. The table was here, wasn't it? Her hand went to the necklace of green stones. It lay around her neck. She counted the stones. One, two, three, four . . .

The outer door opened and a man in a blue cloak entered.

The man turned his face toward the window. Black hair curled half over his forehead, as though he had been on hard duty. He pushed it back, and she recognized him. Valenty. Her heart rose to meet him.

He stood tall and poised as he surveyed the room, his blue tunic and leather belt fitting him like the officer he obviously was. He spied her and approached, looking more casual than he should have, more relaxed than *she* felt.

At her table, he said, "Yevliesza. I have been searching for you."

"Have you?" she whispered, unsure what to say. He took a seat. Her eyes caressed his face, the planes of it, his familiar features, the high forehead, the slightly crooked nose, the keen eyes beneath the slashes of his brows.

She held her breath, waiting to see what he would say, how he would be.

"Did you know you are being followed?" he asked.

So, no greeting of separated lovers. But this was not really him. Somehow, a representation, as her parents had been. Not really him. And yet it was.

"I saw you enter the ale room," he said. "I am on duty." A serving boy came close, but Valenty waved him away.

It was hard to take in his practical words when all she wanted to say was, *I've missed you. I went through the mountains, and men followed me, and they died, and then I met a good teacher and found my* sympat *who comes from the otherworld. And then I came here. Are you well? Do you remember me, do you love me?*

He leaned in, saying more pointedly, "Men are looking for you. Holdfast men."

So there was to be no recognition of what they were to each other. It was a test. She kept looking at him, wondering if she would be allowed to choose him. If she would let herself choose him, over all the larger things. But it was to be all business. A hard thing to remember, when all she wanted was to be in his arms. Still, she needed to move through this.

"What do the Holdfast men want from me?"

He cocked his head as though wondering if she really didn't know. "They want to take you to her." He glanced in the direction of the castle.

Valenty looked back at the tavern door. Satisfied that they were still undiscovered, he said, "Come with me. I have a horse, and I and my men are enough to protect you."

So that was how it would play out. The question of her possible life with Valenty. Here was the choice point, in this tavern. Too sudden, but it was here.

He watched her struggle to answer and, seeing her indecision, he frowned. "Do not throw your life away for nothing."

"Not for nothing. For something." Had she already made the turn, or was she only testing the moment, seeing what she would do? Commit. Or not.

"Besides, my wraith wolf will protect me."

Valenty snorted. "Do not be so sure."

"He has two interventions left."

"No. He disabled the evil creature in the maze." He noted her surprised reaction. "Albrecht followed you in there, accompanied by a blood-drinking creature. Your wolf brought its pack and disabled the creature. You have only one assistance left."

Albrecht. Albrecht was here. He had been right behind her in the maze. The thought wormed into her, setting off alarms.

Valenty softened at last, murmuring gently, "Come with me, Yevliesza. Before it is too late."

The decision, now explicit. "A moment ago you said that you're on duty." He was a soldier. A soldier with a cause. He fought against the brown-clad soldiers—somehow, she knew this—but they each had their paths. She couldn't be subsumed by his, any more than he could be by hers.

Putting off the answer to his question, she murmured, "You haven't said you love me."

His dark eyes flashed in concern. "How can you doubt it? I love you as my wife, as I've loved you since first we met."

They were married? Well, somewhere, somewhen. "I love you, too," she said. "With all my heart. But not past everything, not past everything I am."

The tavern door opened, and a soldier in a blue cape entered, looking pointedly at them.

Slowly, Valenty rose to his feet. He held out his hand, half a demand, half a plea.

She didn't take it.

Valenty lowered his hand and gave her a hesitant smile, as though trying to be brave. It was that smile that almost undid her. It lit up his face and reminded her that he did care for her. She wanted to say something brilliant. But silence was all she had.

He left with the other soldier, the door closing, not re-opening. The silent ale house. Her stunned surprise at her own actions.

She stared at the wood tabletop with its scars and splinters and patina of age. On her arms, the claw punctures from the monster, hard dots of dried blood. Weariness fell over her. What could he have said or done that would have made the moment turn out differently? Maybe put off the blue that he wore and adopt civilian dress. And then come with her, not the other way around.

So she was on her own. She might have guessed that this was how it would turn out. *Not past everything I am.* It was easy to think. It was easy to say. But to *do* it.

The serving boy approached again, ready to offer the drink of forgetting. She didn't look at him, but left the tavern with slow, steady footsteps.

The alley, now empty. She made her way to the bustling avenue that led to the castle, everyone concentrating on accomplishing, winning, getting lucky, finding their fortune. She walked on through the city, trying to concentrate on what was right before her, for whatever wisdom it might impart. The perspective that Isha had urged on her. When she left the Mist Wall, she could still choose Valenty. But now she knew she wouldn't.

Perspective was overvalued, she thought darkly.

She entered a wide plaza where a great crowd gathered. People pressed closely on every side, cutting off the view of what was going on.

From a side street, soldiers in brown and white emerged, mounted on horses. The crowd parted, and she saw that they were coming in her direction.

"She is the one!" someone in the crowd shouted. The person who shouted was pushing toward her through the press of people. "She is right here!"

The closest soldier was now upon her. He dismounted and took her by the arm.

Someone emerged from the crowd. Reynard. The one who gave her an oat cake for nothing.

The soldier nodded at Reynard, tossing him a purse. He caught it, holding it out to judge its weight, smiling appreciatively.

He looked at Yevliesza and his good humor turned cold. "You owed me a dream."

Chapter Thirty-Five

Elivasa knelt by the frozen body. They found it sitting up against a stunted pine, where the drooping branches created a partial shelter. Snow covered the lower body like a comforting blanket.

A frigid wind bore down on them from the icy peaks of the Numins. Elivasa pulled her fur cape closer. "Throat ripped out."

"So I see."

They had found one of Yevliesza's pursuers. Rusadka stepped closer. "Strange that a bear or a wolf left without its meal." The body showed little sign of tearing.

"Maybe a *kulmki*," Elivasa suggested. People said that the monster lived in isolated mountains and forests. "A *kulmki* would have the jaws for it."

Rusadka smirked. "You have seen one, then."

"Yes. In a nightmare or two." Elivasa looked through the dead man's pockets, finding only a leather thong that pierced a coin-sized piece of ivory. It was a talisman of purity. She withdrew it and hung it from the branch sheltering the body.

Further down the trail they found the other three men that had been tracking Yevliesza. Killed in the same way. And one clear animal track, preserved in the lee of a rock. "Wolves," Rusadka said. She turned, looking around the site in case the pack was nearby. These men had not been killed for food. If they had met such a fate, Rusadka worried that Yevliesza had not escaped, either.

She and Elivasa exchanged looks, neither wanting to express the thought.

As they continued down the slope of the mountain, the twisted trees gave way to hardy junipers. The mountainside faced the sun where each day a few inches of snow melted, then refroze at night. Here, the snow still had a frozen crust that sometimes supported their steps and sometimes collapsed.

They went on. The weather was changing, coming in like a horde of riders, clouds bunching overhead. A storm on the way, and they were still hours from reaching snow-free forest.

"Maybe not wolves," Elivasa said after not having spoken since they left the bodies. She walked behind Rusadka, using her companion's footprints to ease her steps.

"No, it was," Rusadka said. "I have seen their predations before."

"But I am thinking, not the usual kind. Might have been wraith wolves."

Rusadka, walking in front, turned to give her a look.

Elivasa shrugged, acknowledging that it was a stretch. "But wraith wolves would have fed on them. Even those creatures must eat. So if they were merely killing, why?"

They trudged along, considering this.

Finally Elivasa said, still thinking of wraith wolves, "They were not hungry, but they killed four men. It is almost as though they were protecting her."

Protecting Yevliesza. A strange and excellent thought. Protecting her because she was the keeper of the ninth power. A thing she could not share with Elivasa since she had promised Yevliesza not to reveal it. It was heartening to think of wraith wolves—fierce and mysterious —looking out for Yevliesza.

"I like the way you think," she told her companion.

"It is my years of being a spy," Elivasa threw back mischievously.

Rusadka could not help but smile.

A GREEN SEA SURROUNDED HIM. THE WIND STIRRED THE WATER, THE hot, green water. Albrecht stumbled, almost falling. He looked up at the sky, longing for air, the world, anything other than this green hell. He had slept. He thought he remembered sleeping, and falling into it, even if he feared it was all a nightmare. Yes. He had slept. But waking! Waking and he was still in the prison of hedges, and he could not bear it. But he was bearing it. He was a soldier, a prince. He would command the world to lead him out. Sometimes it said it would.

It lied.

He remembered speaking to a rodent. He'd been on his hands and knees looking at the creature, its fur, its eyes with their knowing, their pitiless knowing. It ran away. He remembered shouting.

Now he sat against a green wall in a ribbon of shade. He would not go further, would not go to the next branching, to be led on the brutal walk that never ended. Long ago, decades ago, he had been a king. He had commanded thousands, had lived in a palace. He had marched into kingdoms and taken them, what were their names. Alfan Sih and . . . others.

Nashavety. Help me.

He lay down against the flat wall of bush. He gazed at the sky. That thin plank of sky that one could see from the grave. It was beautiful. But treacherous. It showed itself, but always out of reach. He did not want to look at it since it just promised what he could not have. The outside. Life itself.

Closing his eyes, he knew that he would sleep, welcomed it like a lover, welcomed it for peace and rest and not thinking.

WHEN HE WOKE, HE WAS STILL IN THE GRAVE. HE HEARD AN ANIMAL sound, guttural. Near, very near. It was coming from his throat. He was growling in horror.

He crawled toward the next turn in the hedge, but now he was whimpering.

❧

NASHAVETY HEARD ALBRECHT'S CRY. *HELP ME.* BUT SHE DID NOT know how to help. He was caught in what, a garden?

Reinhart was at her side. "What do you see?"

"Our prince."

He no longer looked like a prince. In the haze that captured her vision, he seemed to be crawling on hands and knees. If he was hurt, had his *sympat* not protected him? This was not the outcome they so desperately needed. What they *needed* was to take custody of the girl and yoke her to their purpose.

"Do you see him?" Reinhart asked. "What is he doing?" He peered into the fog that she had conjured on the rooftop, but the man could not see a vision if it pranced on a table in front of him.

She stared into the middle of the roof, watching the scene unfold in front of her. "Actually, he is crawling in a garden," she said with all the venom his behavior deserved. He was no longer capable of doing the job she had sent him to do. From the looks of him, no longer capable of anything. Time for him to come home. She summoned power from the palace below, stealing from its denizens the powers needed to extract the prince.

She stretched out a hand to Albrecht. The small finger on her left hand throbbed with the effort of bringing him home. Which power she was using, she could not tell. Once she had started siphoning power from her servants at the enchanted house of Drogeliv, it was all mixed up. In the back of her throat, she tasted the nectar of creature power. And then the robust flavor of elements but tinged with manifesting. And now, to bring Albrecht back, an overlay of warding, protecting.

She saw him running toward her. *Come, my prince, come.*

Albrecht ran, but hardly came any nearer. Then, in an instant, he slipped from the haze and lurched onto the roof with such force that it took Reinhart by surprise, sending him staggering backward.

Albrecht. He was shirtless and weaponless, his hair greasy and limp around his face.

He fell toward Nashavety, collapsing down to his knees, hugging her legs. Albrecht was shaking, quite undone. And he had not brought Yevliesza.

"My prince!" Reinhart tried to help him to his feet.

At Reinhart's touch, Albrecht screamed. "No one touches me!"

"My pardon," Reinhart said, looking at Nashavety in alarm.

"Get up," Nashavety hissed at him. "Stand up and be a man." She yanked at his arm, and he rose. Now eye to eye, the two of them stared at each other. "Where is Yevliesza?" Nashavety asked, keeping as neutral a voice as she could manage.

Albrecht smiled, bringing up his index finger to make a point, like a schoolmaster. "She has the gift, you know." The roof's flickering torchlight reflected from his eyes. Or there was fire *in* his eyes.

"The last gift!" he cried. "You see?"

"By the eight hells, what is your meaning!"

Albrecht turned away, covering his face with his hands. "Primal, do you not comprehend? Primal power. We saw it when we touched her."

"You touched her? And did not seize her?"

"No, Strigo! He touched her, found it inside her." His face folded into a grimace. "He . . . let her go. Stupid, stupid. But he knows her. He can find her now. By the smell."

Was he talking about the ninth power? That the *strigoi* saw in her?

Her expression must have revealed her doubts because Albrecht drew closer to her. "She . . . has . . . primal root power," he said slowly, making it easy for her to understand.

His mind. His mind had become unseated. "Albrecht—"

"*Molds* the crossings, I say! Molds them into any shape she wants."

She tried to absorb this—this preposterous idea, this hideous idea. "You are saying Yevliesza has the ninth power?"

Albrecht sneered. "Yes, you foul demon. She has it."

A vast understanding entered Nashavety's mind. What if it was true? *That* would change everything. They must have the girl. If it was true, then immediately. "But where is she?"

Impudently, Albrecht shrugged. He pointed behind him to the mist, now rapidly thinning.

"And you let her escape?" Nashavety crowed. "Again?"

"But *I* escaped!" he said smiling, as though it mattered, as though he had not just lost the prize, the incredible prize. Her chest felt like something boiled within.

"I escaped!" he exclaimed again. He stood, his eyes wild, words tumbling out of his mouth, "Out of the green, the green." His expression turned pitiful as he beseeched her. "Do you not see?"

"I see, Albrecht. I see clearly." His mind, gone. Found the prize. Lost the prize. She regarded him with loathing.

Through the last wisps of fog, a movement. Then another figure emerged, small and staggering. A *strigoi*. Albrecht's *sympat*. It rushed at the prince, jumping on his back, bringing its hands around Albrecht's throat.

Reinhart drew his sword and charged forward, but Nashavety held up her hand, stopping him. The *strigoi* knows her, she thought. By the smell. The *strigoi* knows her.

The creature raked its talons over Albrecht's face, gouging his eyes, bringing him to the floor. As Albrecht thrashed, it rode him, clamping its jaws into the side of his neck.

By the Mythos, Nashavety thought as she watched. The man's *sympat* was killing him.

For a moment the creature raised its head, growling at another *strigoi* who approached to share the meal. The newcomer backed away.

Reinhart raised his sword to slay the beast, but once again, Nashavety raised her hand. "Push it off him, but do not kill it."

Reinhart slapped at the *strigoi* with the flat of his sword, and it fell away. Reluctantly, it slunk away to join its fellow creatures which had gathered to watch.

Blood pumped from Albrecht's neck as Reinhart knelt next to him. He shed his jacket and pressed it against the wound.

"Leave him," Nashavety said.

Reinhart looked up at her in surprise but obeyed. In moments, all semblance of life stilled. Albrecht lay dead.

Nashavety shook her head. So much for having a *strigoi* as a *sympat*.

As she gazed at the body, her thoughts turned to Yevliesza. How could it be that she had come upon the ninth power? And oh, to think of the control. Control of the crossings. The girl could mold the crossings. The ninth power.

She would have to personally take charge of her capture. She shook her head in annoyance. "By the First Ones," she muttered, "must I do everything myself?"

Reinhart stood before her, sword in hand. "No, madam," he said. "You have me."

Chapter Thirty-Six

The soldiers marched Yevliesza up the cobbled street toward the castle. She resented Reynard's betrayal, feeling it churn in her stomach. A little anger could be useful for what lay ahead. She had done other hard things in this place and now felt ready to use her strength again. Powers. Intuition. A bit of courage. Was it enough?

She wanted to enter the castle—it was surely the final test—but she feared the dark queen. Nashavety, a lingering nightmare. The memory of her saying, *Jump! Jump!* when she forced her to stand in the Tower door. That memory, always with her.

Crowds parted for her and her escort. When her steps slowed, the lead soldier, the captain, as she thought of him, pushed her in the small of her back hard enough to make her stagger.

Someone looked directly at her, a young woman she thought she might know, who placed her hand on her heart in what she took for a gesture of sympathy. A few people cheered—a hopeful note—until Yevliesza realized that it was not support but a jeer.

It was the way of things, that along the way some people were glad of your misfortunes and others helped you, believed in you.

As they continued, she saw people who once had scorned her: short

Byasha, the woman who led her arcana and blamed her for the deaths at the Bridge of the Moon; Jeder, the old gardener at Raven Fell, who enjoyed watching her work to clear rocks from the garden beds; Daraliska, Nashavety's steward who had applied the implement of torture to her hand. Others too, all of them striving in their own way, for their own goals and often against hers.

And now here, Reinhart of Volkia, a man with a tiny mustache and large, gaudy medals on his chest. And there, watching from a balcony of a great house, a woman with violet hair, smiling down on her, well satisfied. Sofiyana.

But there were others. People who nodded to her, giving encouragement. The one a few steps back who had placed her hand on her heart, that had been Breta, she realized, her serving woman at Prince Albrecht's headquarters. Over there, in the depths of the crowd she thought she saw Duke Tanfred and Father Ludving trying to thread their way toward her, but too late, she was already past them. The memory of her friendship with them cheered her. A figure sitting astride a horse: Rusadka. She had emerged from one of the side streets. Soldiers crossed their swords in front of her, barring the way. *Rusadka,* she whispered, feeling a smile come to her face.

There were others: Grigeni and Pyvel, and down in front, Lieutenant Martel from Volkia, who dared to give her clues about elemental power feeding the machines of war. And paid dearly for it. Then a woman in *satvar* dress, the color of oatmeal, hair braided, her face creased in concern: Dreiza, who had been a friend even if most people would have turned against her if they had been in Dreiza's place. All these people she saw, and many more who were strangers. She wished them well.

Although she was a prisoner, she still had won things. To see clearly. To know what she wanted. It was not the past, with all that had been lost. It was not to follow a guide through the maze of the world. Not to find rescue from the man who loved her. Now, the last thing.

The castle wall looked ever more imposing as they neared it, its sheer sides without features or ornamentation, rising like the uplifted rock of the world. They passed through a gateway, entering a dusty yard that lay deserted.

The captain, who had not spoken a word to her, took her by the arm and led her through a massive iron door.

Inside, the vast entrance hall lay in colorful splendor. Rich red walls were topped with a band of glossy, carved wood. Overhead, a barrel-vaulted ceiling ornamented in gold. From a pair of arched windows ingots of sunlight pushed their way into the room, leaving the furthest corners cloaked in shadow.

It was a hall of giants. Amid all this glory, carved wood chairs, tables inlaid with tiles, and sets of full-body armor standing up like metal sentinels ready to stir into life.

Her footsteps and those of the captain echoed on the squares of the stone floor. The other soldiers had stayed in the yard or disappeared. Disappeared, she thought, because she could never decide whether people whom she saw continued to manifest once they were gone from her sight. It wouldn't do to think about it too much. This was the Mist Wall, and she had to take it as it came. Just the same, she pinched her forearm to be sure *she* was real. It hurt. So that, at least, was clear.

The queen wasn't waiting for her in the entry hall. Yevliesza took in a fresh lungful of air, letting it go, releasing some of the tension. Of course the queen wasn't waiting here for her. She'd meet Yevliesza in an even grander place. She touched the talisman at her neck. *I have what I need.*

All the rooms were enormous and, since the windows were on only one side, bathed in gloom. On top of the tables, hutches, and pedestals were displays of ornamental silver plates, decorative porcelain, marble figurines and busts, and other useless but elegant objects such as bouquets of glass flowers, jewelry on velvet boards, candelabras that had never held a candle and etched glassware refracting what light managed to reach them.

The soldier took a position at her side as they walked on.

A few functionaries in brown and black livery shuffled through the halls on their mysterious errands. As well, men in court dress, their fine velvets saturated in jewel colors, the women wearing headdresses with veils, a few of the men in elaborate cloth caps ornamented with feathers.

"Where are we going?" she asked the captain, not expecting an answer nor getting one.

They entered an immense gallery with paintings along one side and windows opposite. The ceiling was not only vaulted, but it was also cut out in sunken layers like a reverse wedding cake, the series of rectangles receding higher and higher into the ceiling, each one engraved and painted with gilt. Chairs lined the tapestry-hung walls, chairs that Yevliesza doubted anyone had ever sat in.

The overdone furnishings cloyed, making her wish for a small, tidy room with comfy furniture.

As she passed a window, she looked out to see a courtyard below, with people in court dress milling and talking. A small raised pool lay at its center in deep shade. On the edge of the pool wall, a cat, licking a paw.

She and her escort entered a lavish bedchamber with a four-poster bed swagged in brocade. This room was even darker than the great halls, and she stumbled over the edge of a fancy rug.

The guard reached down and pulled the rumpled rug flat. He led her on, saying, "One of these rooms will be yours. Say which one you would like."

"I won't be staying, though."

"Everyone stays." They passed out of the bedroom.

"Is that why you call it Holdfast?" she quipped.

No response. She had never seen a guard, even in the real world, laugh. They had it drummed out of them—God knew the world could do that to you—unless it was just against the rules.

"How much farther?" she asked as they entered a room like a feasting hall. Long tables, big fireplace, chairs. It was all starting to feel repetitive.

"Not far."

She had been planning to find her own way through the castle. The impulse had been growing in her and now became acute. *Ditch the captain,* she found herself thinking.

"I lost something when I tripped in that bedroom. I'm going back."

"What did you lose?"

The first thing that came to mind: "My cell phone."

"Meet me back here," he said. "And be quick about it."

She had chosen correctly. This was the palace of things. The rules allowed you to win things back. Or so she told herself. Her mood lifted as she realized how easy it might all be. If you sounded approximately correct, you could get by with not knowing what the hell you were doing.

She returned to the sleeping chamber with the four-poster bed, shutting the heavy door behind her. It closed with a satisfying whump. The captain wouldn't pursue her, she felt. She hoped. But whether or not she was free of him, she wanted to choose where to meet the queen.

Alone at last, and needing to collect her thoughts, she collapsed into a big wooden chair without any padding but with carving fit for a king. She listened to the creak of the palace as it settled its weight into the surrounding bedrock. She listened for her thoughts, skittering here and there like small, frightened mammals. Her eyes went unfocused as she stared at the brocaded bed covering. *You do not sleep in the Mist Wall.*

It is all a matter of perspective.

Just poke your head out of the fog.

She was in a fog now. What was she fighting for in Holdfast Castle? To defeat the queen. But that didn't sound right. She fought against the queen. But in this place, what was she fighting *for*?

Wasn't it to know her purpose? To find the thing that was honorable, or right in the larger view. And to gain confidence that she could follow through.

Footsteps approaching. She sprang up from the chair and rushed to a door to get away. The door she chose led to a back hallway with light pouring in from an archway. Through the archway was an armory full of wicked-looking weapons. Pikes and scimitars hung from the walls. Body armor stood rigid, held upright by poles.

Looking out the armory window, she saw a lavish garden enclosed by high walls. In the center of the wall, an iron-clad door.

The door opened, and a group of the queen's men came through, roughly pushing ahead of them a man in a blue uniform. It was Valenty. His arms were bound behind him, his hair hanging loose as the guards dragged him into the garden. When he regained his footing, he walked obediently as they led him out of sight. *Valenty.* She leaned into the windowsill to try to see where they had taken him, but they disappeared along the side of the castle. Seeing him as a prisoner worried her even if it wasn't real. Unless, in some way, it was.

She turned from the window and went on, each room or gallery or hall leading directly into the next great room or hall.

Now she was actively looking for the queen, hoping to find her in a place that could give her some advantage. Nashavety must be expecting her by now.

In the middle of another hall she stopped to look out the window. Beneath her was another view of the courtyard with the numin pool. A woman in a lavish midnight-blue dress sat on the edge of the raised pool. Gathered around her, a half-dozen people looking cowed, defeated. Next to the woman, a crown resting on a small pillow.

The woman had a long, quite striking face, with strong but attractive features. Her black hair lay in soft waves down her back. She was young, maybe no older than Yevliesza. And then she knew. This was Nashavety. A young Nashavety.

The young Nashavety pointed a finger at the window where Yevliesza stood. Taking their cue, two guards strode out of the courtyard, coming for her.

Yevliesza ran. She wasn't going to be hauled in front of the queen by guards. That wasn't how she was going to meet the queen. At random, she chose one of the doors lining the hall and yanked it open, slamming it shut behind her.

Chapter Thirty-Seven

Yevliesza needed to get down to the main floor. Somewhere
there would be access to the courtyard with the little pool and
the crown on the pillow.

When she saw the crown on the cushion, she had known what she
was supposed to do. Take the prize. Accept the power struggle as real.
Her part in it, an obligation, the thing that was happening whether she
wanted it or not. To fully accept it, acknowledging doubt, but taking
action beyond personal consequences. To know that she could do it.

I can take the ninth power away from you. Give it to someone else.

She was not going to give it up. The Devi Ilsat said that they
needed someone who didn't owe allegiance to any one realm. She was
it, and she was ready.

Ahead, the murmur of many voices. A hall lay before her with
people lined up on each side. The path down the middle led to a set of
tall double doors.

Heads turned toward her as she stood at the entrance to the great
hall. There had been a lot of great halls, but this was the final one. The
one she had been looking for.

She walked down the path through the crowd, not looking at faces,
finding her intention to do the right thing, the right thing by her own

standards. The line of people seemed to stretch longer than the hall itself.

When she reached the end, a young boy she recognized put his hand on the door latch, and as he did so, turned to her. "Shall I open the door?"

She had to decide whether to let the boy from the maze open it or do it herself. But it wasn't important who opened it. Only who walked through it.

"Thank you," she said. "Please do." She smiled at him. "And no fair charging me."

He put on a hurt expression. "I would never!" Then he shrugged. "Well, the queen does not charge for an audience in any case."

So the queen *was* on the other side.

A water flask on a strap hung from the boy's shoulder. He handed it to her. "You must be thirsty."

Yevliesza hesitated only a moment. She took it, thanking him, and pulled the strap over her shoulder. Sometimes a gift was just a gift.

Yevliesza nodded at him, and he pulled open the door.

She was in a courtyard. The afternoon brightness hurt Yevliesza's eyes as she took in her surroundings. The courtyard was enclosed by castle walls surmounted by a walkway along the battlements. Guards patrolled there. Nashavety—young, but no less imposing—sat on the tiled edge of the pool. A round pool. A numin pool. Beside the pool stood her guards and servants and five women who she suspected were Numinasi *fajatim*. Oh, and Valenty, there too. He sat at the malwitch's feet looking dejectedly at the ground.

"Welcome to my castle," Nashavety said in the same resonant voice Yevliesza remembered so well. "It was well that you came, or I would have had to drag you here." She put a hand on Valenty's shoulder. "As I did with this one."

"Let him go."

"I would, girl of the mundat, but he is mine now. He cannot even bear the sight of you."

Yevliesza glanced at the crown. Then her gaze shifted to the pool.

"You cannot have it," Nashavety said.

But which? Which could she not have? She thought that Nashavety meant the pool. Not the crown. The pool.

Perhaps . . . perhaps the numin pool was what she had to wrest from Nashavety. The crown was the lure. It was just a thing, whereas the numin pool was the real point. The clarity and the knowing. Across her skin, an uncanny shiver. The numin pool was the goal. In the Mist Wall, it was the prize. A way of being with the world. And she had almost blindly failed the whole test.

Nashavety eyes narrowed. "Do not be greedy. The pool is mine. You will take nothing, but instead you will become one of my creatures." She cocked her head at Yevliesza in mock concern. "It will be so much easier. You will not have all this *confusion* in your life. You will always know what you should do because I will make it clear."

Yevliesza looked around at the contented servants in the garden. Even the *fajatim* were her servants. Unnatural servants. Letting Nashavety define the world.

"They are under creature power," Yevliesza said.

Nashavety brightened, color coming into her cheeks. "Oh yes, it is most gratifying." She smiled, and it was no better a smile than she had as an older woman. Too stiff. Too many teeth.

Nashavety's intense look almost ensnared her, and she brought her gaze back to the pool. The prize. But how to lay claim to it? Looking at Valenty, she saw that he was finally meeting her eyes. Almost imperceptibly, he shook his head.

What was he trying to tell her?

"My dear," Nashavety said, "you must give me that water flask."

"Why?"

"Because you cannot carry anything with you into my dungeons."

Valenty whispered, "You must drink from the flask."

Yevliesza knew a clue when one came along. This place was jumping with clues, and you had to be alert lest one smack you in the forehead. She pulled the stopper from the flask and took a long swig. At the same time, Nashavety scrambled up from her seat and lunged, grabbing the flask's strap, jerking it away.

In the commotion, the flask fell on the ground. A silvery liquid poured from it. The mercurial contents seeped into the ground. That was all right. Yevliesza didn't need to drink again.

She already had it within her. The numin pool. The clarity. You could carry it within you if you knew how to see. She stepped back from Nashavety, darting a look at Valenty. "Come with me," she said.

"I cannot. But as for you—it is time to run."

"You cannot leave!" Nashavety cried, jerking a look at her guards.

"You can always leave," Yevliesza said, knowing it for the first time.

The guards advanced, a dozen of them if she included the ones on the battlements. These men were now clattering down the steps toward her.

But there was something else on the battlements. A flash of gray and grace. Kiya bounded down the steps, pushing past—or was it through—the soldiers.

Here was the one favor she had left. Saved for last.

With Kiya at her side, Yevliesza rushed toward the corner where an open-sided turret anchored one corner of the courtyard. Soldiers closed in on her, but seeing the wraith wolf, they drew up short. Kiya growled, a low vibrating rumble that could have scared Yevliesza witless had she not already been scared witless.

Dashing into the turret, she found a stairway leading downward. She made for it, clambering down the stairs, emerging onto the outside of the castle where the stairs continued. She and Kiya descended fast, their feet barely touching the stairs, down, down past the bedrock foundation, toward the city of Holdfast. Then down the cobbled streets, Kiya at her side, her lungs straining, people staring.

Kiya pulled ahead and made a scrambling turn into an alley. Yevliesza followed, heart pumping hard. There, embedded in the frontage of a medieval house was the scarred, planked door they had entered a lifetime ago.

Yevliesza took hold of the doorknob. Turning to look behind her, she saw that the alley was still empty. But the soldiers could appear at any moment. Her hand went to the necklace. It was gone. Lost? She didn't know.

At her side, Kiya whined, urging her to open the door. But it was locked.

A voice right behind her whispered, *There is no door.* A flicker of dark evergreen trees entered her peripheral vision. Kiya sprang through the closed door, the one the voice said wasn't there, and disappeared.

"How do I get out?" Yevliesza said, her voice breaking at the edges. Behind her she heard the soldiers enter the alley.

You are already out.

"Kiya," she said, having troubling saying the word.

He is well. Around here somewhere.

She was lying on the ground staring up at a bright river. No, it was the sky, narrowed by trees, trees everywhere. A face bent over her.

Isha.

It was cold amid the trees. A chill gripped her face like a mask, but the rest of her was warm. A fur cape lay over her. Under her, a nest of evergreen boughs, by the scent of them. She stared at the treetops, waiting for the next turning point in her list of wants, must haves, and should have beens. "Is this a test?" she heard herself whisper.

"No."

A simple answer. Isha was usually not one for getting right to the point.

"Are the soldiers coming?"

"No, my dear. The soldiers cannot find you here." Isha helped her sit up. She had been lying next to a rock outcropping, and now leaned against it as Isha rearranged the fur cape around her shoulders. She brought a cup of water to her lips and urged her to drink. Yevliesza drained it and drank another.

Isha settled in beside her, against the rock. For a time all Yevliesza heard was the rumble of the Mist Wall, a never-arriving storm.

"So. Do you want me to take the ninth power from you?"

She had never considered letting it go. Well, maybe for a few seconds she had thought how simple her life would be, how according to her ingrained hopes it would be to have done with it. "I'm keeping it."

"Ah. Keeping. Well, then."

Yevliesza pulled the fur cape closer as the wind picked up, bringing its icy forest fingers around her face and hands. "You never could have given it to someone else, could you."

"Probably not."

"Isha. Where have I *been*?"

"Where do you think you were?"

She thought back to that night when Kiya had led her to the door. Isha had been sleeping. The fire, burned to embers. She and the wraith wolf had walked for a long time through the trees, the roar of the wall growing ever louder. But before that . . .

"The thorn berries," Yevliesza murmured. Their last meal together. "It wasn't dessert."

"Sometimes things are not what they seem."

Annoyed, Yevliesza blurted, "Is it 'Sometimes a swim is just a swim,' or is it, 'Sometimes things are not what they seem?'"

Isha huffed a laugh at her indignation. "Wisdom is knowing which is which."

"Did I go *anywhere*?" Had it all been a trick?

"You went inside, deep inside."

Of course she had. Where else would all those things have come from? "Inside where the numin pool is."

"Is that what you found?" Isha cocked her head, considering. "The numin pool inside. I like it. But then, what good is it?"

"Well, you can think of it that way. That it reflects reality, the thing you may not like, but that you have to deal with. How things are."

"Or," Isha said, "you could just look around and see the same thing."

She knew what Isha meant, but she had returned only a few minutes ago, and so far, she was damn well keeping the numin pool. "Isha," she patiently said. "I'm ready for what's coming."

A small, knowing smile. "Good. It is good to be ready. It is all anyone can do, but most people cannot manage it."

"But still. Where *was* I, really?"

"Inside yourself. But also in a plane of the spirit."

"Not in the wall," Yevliesza mused. She reached up to touch the necklace her mother had given her, forgetting that it had disappeared along with Holdfast.

"And everything I learned is true?"

"I imagine so. But I was not there, so how could I know?"

"Kiya was there?"

"I would not be surprised. He moves between the worlds."

Isha's eyes narrowed as she saw Yevliesza absently touching her arms. "Roll up your sleeves."

Startled, Yevliesza remembered the demon-creature and its claws. She pulled up her sleeves, exposing her bare arms. Isha leaned in for a close look.

"These scratches." Isha's expression hardened. "Tell me."

The puncture wounds were gone, but faint, red marks remained. "A child-sized monster with wings. It jumped on me when I went into a maze."

"There were travelers?"

It was the first time that Yevliesza had seen her teacher truly surprised. "At least one."

"I misjudged. So there was a creature with wings. Anything else?"

"I don't know. Maybe Albrecht."

Isha clasped her hands over Yevliesza's upper arms. She closed her eyes, to concentrate, to heal. The treetops swayed in the wind, and the Mist Wall faintly boomed.

When Isha sat back, Yevliesza asked, "It was dangerous?"

"Someone has powers I have not seen before."

Yevliesza nodded. "Nashavety."

"She can reach further than I guessed. How did you escape the winged creature?"

"It let me go." It had jumped off her, as though revolted. Or surprised.

"You escaped," Isha said, gazing at her as though seeing her anew. "By the Mythos, you overcame them all." She got to her feet. "Now we must go. They are coming."

"Who's coming?" Yevliesza started to rise, letting the fur cape fall to the ground, but a cloud of dizziness forced her to sit back down.

Isha was looking around her, alert, like a prey animal sensing movement. She lifted a satchel from the ground and slung it over her shoulder, securing it with a strap.

"Those who follow me." Isha sighed. "So difficult anymore to have peace and quiet. Now they will follow you, too. Remember when you went through the door in the Mist Wall—when you thought you did—there was someone following you?" When Yevliesza nodded, she said, "The pilgrims. They think they can get in just by wanting to."

"But how did they think I was going into the Mist Wall if I didn't go through a real door?"

"Because they thought they knew, when I took to you close to the Mist Wall, that is what would happen. They saw what they expected to see." She sighed. "No end of delusion, is there?"

"Am *I* deluded?"

Isha crouched down and cupped Yevliesza's face in her hands. "Never doubt it. Where you went, that was true. Do not call it a delusion."

"Why encourage the idea that you can go inside the wall? Why did you tell *me* that?"

"Because you had to take it seriously. Believe it. If you had not, you would not have learned anything. When I bring someone to that place, they should be prepared to go on a journey, a deep one."

"The power of suggestion," Yevliesza sighed.

Looking impressed, her teacher said, "An excellent way to put it."

Isha helped her to her feet.

"So I'm not the only one you've brought inside the wall." It deflated her to think so.

Isha gave her a stare.

"Unworthy," Yevliesza admitted.

"Everyone wants to be special. However, in your case, I must admit it is true." She cocked her head as though something had just come to mind. "I like the numin pool within. Keep that clarity. Seeing clearly is the greatest power. Being willing to."

Isha hitched her satchel more firmly over her shoulder. "I have to leave. If they see me here, I will be saddled with them all the way home."

When the teaching was over, it was over. But she wanted Isha to stay.

Seeing Yevliesza's reluctance, Isha said, "Remember not to rely on guides. Be your own." Isha dropped her facade of the no-nonsense teacher for a moment and gazed at her with bright eyes. "Farewell, Yevliesza. May you be safe, by the grace of the Deep."

She walked away, heading into the trees.

"Did you bring my horse?" Yevliesza called after her.

Isha didn't turn around but waved her hand behind her in Yevliesza's general direction.

PART IV
THE BLOSSOM MOON

Chapter Thirty-Eight

From the royal balcony, Sofiyana looked down on the great courtyard. A cold spring wind swept across it, tugging at her lined cape, and lifting the cloaks and skirts of the populace gathered below. The people of Osta Kiya had been told to come, but they did not look happy about it.

Two of the *fajatim* joined her on the balcony, as well as the army commander and, as a representative of the nobility, Valenty. It was not the full display of loyalty that she wanted—either at her side or in the yard below, but it would have to do.

A cheer went up from those standing at the periphery of the crowd, the soldiers who had been ordered to show enthusiasm.

Out of the corner of her eye, Sofiyana noted that Valenty had moved closer to the balustrade. Perhaps the cheer was for him. Disturbingly, he was popular, but for which attributes, she could not fathom. He was a womanizer, a lackey of the former princip, and had lately and conveniently renounced his treasonous actions. Now that he had been captured.

Sofiyana waved at the soldiers who had cheered and smiled at her subjects, some of whom had the temerity to glare back. Others were thrilled to see her, approving Anastyna's removal, the woman who had brought soldiers into battle for the sake of Nubiah and her lover. A great many supported her. Nashavety had assured her of it.

Moving closer to Valenty, she leaned in to whisper, "Smile at them, Valenty." He resisted for a few moments. Clutching the ring in her pocket, Sofiyana bore down on him, willing him to obey. At last he did smile. A slash in his face.

"Now, turn and smile at me," she murmured. He turned to her but did not obey. She clenched the ring so hard its sharp edges dug into her skin. *Do it, you wreck of a man! Smile.* He did so, but without enthusiasm. The balcony display was not giving the impression she wished for, of solidarity, unity.

"We will go in," she said to her retinue, itching to get Valenty in private where she could deliver the slaps he had earned.

For the past two days she had been concentrating on Valenty alone in order to extract Anastyna's hiding place. In vain. She had even loosened her hold on the *fajatim* to direct her intention solely to him but still he defied her.

Once inside the palace, Daraliska nodded a bow and took her leave. Nashavety's former steward, now *fajatim* of Raven Fell. She had stood with Sofiyana on the balcony, along with Vajalyna. But the other *fajatim* had stayed away, a troubling slight that showed how quickly her control wore off when she diverted her attention.

The household guard escorted Valenty to his room. She would join him presently and attempt to bring him under firm control. The endeavor was exhausting, even if Nashavety was doing most of the work. Whenever she thought of her mistress—which was most of the time—she felt small and helpless. She had failed to accomplish simple but urgent things. Apprehend Anastyna. Find Yevliesza before she got to wherever she was going after fleeing the *satvary*. The men who had been tracking her had not reported back and should have by now.

A voice from behind her. "My Lady Princip?"

She jumped at the sudden interruption. It was her secretary. "Yes? What is it?"

"*Fajatim* Ineska requests an audience, my lady."

"Tell her I will see her tomorrow." But Ineska barged in, past the secretary.

She could hardly turn away from the woman now. "Lady Ineska. I have duties at the moment, but is it something that will take only a moment?"

"Yes, if a moment is all we have," Ineska said, displaying an annoyance she would not have dared to a few days ago.

Sofiyana gestured her to speak.

"I come on behalf of Lord Valenty." She blinked, waiting. "Am I invited to sit?"

Ineska, no longer young, her face sagging in the usual places, but still managing to look haughty. "Do sit, of course." Sofiyana took a seat on a chair and watched as Ineska sat on the divan, spreading her skirts and arranging herself like a princip.

"I understand that Valenty has repudiated Anastyna," Ineska said. "It surprises me, but it is well, is it not? The former princip should have had the courage to stand trial."

Cautiously, Sofiyana answered. "Yes, he has finally realized his error."

"It lends validity to the actions we have taken." Ineska paused. "That *you* have taken."

Sofiyana felt a spike of worry that the woman chose to assert herself like this. Sternly, she responded, "The actions which the *fajatim* have supported."

"Yes. We seem to have done so. Still, his repentance does not look sincere when he remains here in the royal quarters. If he took back his holdings, his household, it would do better for us."

"How could it do better?"

"It would not look as though he had been forced. Whereas, if he is in detention, it has the opposite effect."

That Ineska was taking the initiative to advise her raised an ugly doubt about her control of the *fajatim*. At least this one. There would be time later to consider the fearsome thing she suddenly glimpsed humping toward her in the distance: a rebellion of the *fajatim*.

"I do see the logic," Sofiyana said, trying to maintain her poise. "I will consider it." Though she had no intention of doing so.

The woman nodded, regarding her impudently. As though challenging her. How could this have happened so quickly when Ineska had been her creature for almost a month? Did Storm Hand and Iron River share her support of Valenty? Had the *fajatim* begun to question their choice of princip?

Sofiyana rose. "Thank you for coming to speak with me, Lady Ineska." She crossed to where she was sitting and sat next her. "I consider you my wisest advisor." She took Ineska's hand in her own. Ineska's gaze flickered with doubt, but under compunction, quieted. "Truly, I do."

From her skirt pocket, she felt the heat rising. She squeezed Ineska's hand a little tighter, holding her gaze.

⁂

SOFIYANA HAD FINALLY BROKEN THE MAN, NOT BY FORCE BUT BY softness.

Up until now, Valenty had been stubborn, used to having his way with people and politics. In the last tenday, she had managed to subdue him, but the harder she pressed her will on him, the more obdurate he became. It was exhausting to control things. She had thought it would be the opposite, but the truth was, the more you controlled, the more you incurred resistance.

But today she had learned something. Sometimes you give a little to achieve much. Rather than focus her will upon him, she withdrew some of her control. "Let us be reasonable," she had told him, trying to adopt the right tone. "I do not ask much. The woman must stand trial. It is fair that she does so, like any other citizen."

He turned his attention to her with a close regard. When he really looked at her, she thought him handsome, even appealing. He was still wary, but now, open. She liked him better when he was not weak.

And then he told her where Anastyna was. The simple truth when he had undergone so much to hide it from her. He whispered it—whispering, as though that made it less of a betrayal!—that Anastyna had planned to take refuge at Zolvina.

Zolvina. Did the Devi Ilsat know of this? Valenty had said no. Anastyna planned to simply go there and ask for shelter, trusting she would not be denied. It was just possibly true. Although the old *satvar* had been in residence there as recently as eight or nine days ago, it was possible that Anastyna would not have set out for Zolvina yet. Licking her wounds. Taking stock.

Anastyna might well choose the *satvary* as a refuge, with its remote and difficult terrain. She had only sixty followers, a number that could be accommodated there.

If a force could be brought against the place, superior numbers could quickly overwhelm the defenses and extract her. If Yevliesza had not slipped away, it could have been two fish with one spear. But despite Nashavety's harping, Yevliesza was the lesser catch.

Sofiyana took in a few slow cooling breaths. With each exhalation, she felt her anxieties flap away like vultures that had been feeding upon her. In a few days Anastyna would stand before her, bound and defeated.

Bound and defeated. Do you hear me, my lady? I will have accomplished so much of what you have asked of me. Depose Anastyna. Take her place. See her walk out of the Tower Door.

But not Yevliesza.

And what, by the eight hells, was her mistress's purpose for Yevliesza? Perhaps simply to extract justice for how she had ruined Nashavety. A form of justice that was suitably degrading. She was eager to see it.

Chapter Thirty-Nine

Yevliesza stood among towering fir trees. The wind streaming through them was pungent with the sharp smells of sap and decomposing wood. Wind. Trees. A low sun. She leaned against the rugged bark of the nearest tree and tried to figure out what to do next.

Kiya was sitting beside her. She went to her knees and buried her face in his fur, allowing herself to just be with him. But even he couldn't wipe away her concerns. So much to do. Most of which was not completely clear to her. But whatever good things she could do, she would.

Still, it was no excuse to hug a wraith wolf. Kiya shrugged her off and walked a distance away. The forest stretched as far as she could see in every direction. Of course it did. This was the Agarvesky. Isha had left her a skin of water, and she picked it up.

As Kiya set out, she followed him until he disappeared, as was his habit. She had let Isha get away before she had learned where she should go. And where to find her horse.

A man was standing not far off.

Seeing her, he approached, weaving through the trees. He was dressed in furs, and was older, with a wisp of a white beard. "You are the pilgrim?" he asked.

She didn't like that he had driven Kiya away. "What do you want?"

He chuckled. "That is an interesting question. Sounds like one Isha would ask."

"You know her?"

"No, I cannot claim to. But you know her." He turned, gesturing at someone Yevliesza couldn't see. "She took you into the wall."

"Who are you signaling to?" She didn't like how this encounter was going.

"My friends. Do not worry."

Soon three others, two women and a man, threaded their way into view from different directions. They had been looking for her.

One of the women came within a couple of yards of her. She wore her long hair in a braid down her back. Plain of face, she wore better furs than the old man did. "Welcome back," she said. "We have been waiting for you." The woman gazed at her rather too intensely.

"What's your business with me," Yevliesza threw out. "Or do you expect me to guess?"

"My apology if I am being rude. My name is Riyura. I am—we all are—seekers. You passed us by when you came through camp not long ago with the *providez*. We seek the wisdom of the Mist Wall. And we think you have been there."

"You followed us through the primordial lands."

Riyura smiled ruefully. "I admit that we did."

The woman was not yet of middle age. She had a rounded, peasant's face, and shrewd eyes. "We saw you and your dog enter through a door. But when we got close to it, it was gone. *You* were gone."

The sun was sinking rapidly. "I'm looking for my horse. It's dappled gray with a black main and tail."

"Oh, yes," Riyura said. "The *providez* brought it to the village." She pointed behind her. "Your horse is waiting for you."

"Can you take me to it?" Yevliesza asked.

"Whatever you want," the older man said, waving his companions

to start walking. "I am Bandry. We will take you there, only we wonder
. . ."

"Bandry!" one of the woman hissed. "Let Riyura ask her."

These people were starting to annoy her. She had been lost in
Holdfast Castle for hours and then almost captured by the dark queen
and skewered by her guards. "You'll take me to my horse, except for
what?"

They climbed over an enormous fallen tree, with a new tree
springing from its fertile belly.

"What Bandry was about to say," Riyura explained, "was that we
would like to know where the door is."

As though the Mist Wall was an amusement park. "I'm afraid you
can't. It only opens when it's ready to. If you don't see it, it's not
ready." This was not exactly the truth, but it was all she could come up
with that she thought they might accept.

The seekers looked downhearted to hear this, and they proceeded in
silence. *And he isn't a dog*, Yevliesza said to herself. She recognized
that she was so tired she could hardly stand up and had not thought
through what she was going to say to anyone about where she had
been. She hadn't realized she would *have* to say something.

Riyura spoke up. "We have been here for days waiting to see you
come out, and then we recognized you and your dog."

He's not a dog.

"We should ask her," the younger woman said.

"No," Bandry said. "Too soon."

Riyura saw Yevliesza's questioning expression. "They want to ask
if you have seen anyone . . . anyone special. Inside. Who may have
asked after us." She glanced at the other two women and Bandry.
"After Ekka, Asry, or Bandry. Or me."

"No, I didn't." She had to put *that* question to rest.

"Are you sure?" the youngest woman, the one named Ekka, asked.

"Yes. I'm sure." They walked on, not pressing her.

Bandry looked at her slyly. "That is not a dog you have there. It is a
wolf."

"What makes you think I have him?"

He shrugged. "Seen a few of 'em, I have. Wolves."

Yevliesza ignored him. "Where is my horse, exactly?"

"At the village. Branova. Just past that hill," he said, pointing.

The hill was a very great distance away, so it seemed to her. She had started to worry that since she had refused them information, they might turn on her.

"You have friends waiting for you," Riyura said.

Instantly, Yevliesza was on her guard. "Who?"

"They did not give their names."

Bandry guffawed. "Not to the likes of us. Just seekers, looking for truth, so you can figure we are of no account. They were women dressed as fighters."

"But it wasn't Isha? Or Ishtov?"

Bandry grinned. "So you know about that, do you? How she is sometimes a man?"

She wasn't going to turn into these people's new best friend and didn't answer.

After they rounded the shoulder of the hill, she saw a cluster of houses about a mile away. A layer of smoke hovering from chimneys. The village. She felt weak from lack of food and had to urge her legs to go the distance.

As they walked down a muddy road toward the hamlet, she saw thatch-roofed houses and outbuildings. Around the village, farmsteads with small barns, doors ajar as people finished the day's chores.

Riyura pointed to one of the houses. "Janov's house. He is the village master who is stabling your horse."

As they entered the village outskirts, Yevliesza stopped and turned to the group. "Would you all please sit down? I'd like to talk to you for a moment." She pointed to the side of the road where an enormous oak commanded the edge of the village. They left the road and her escort sat under the tree, forming a semi-circle before her.

She needed to say something to them, but she wasn't sure what. She was grateful that they had helped her to find the village. But the way they had latched on to her had to stop. Obviously, they hoped to hear things from her. She sat down facing them, crossing her legs and rubbing them, already dreading having to get up again.

Looking at their eager faces, she tried to think of what to say. She decided on the truth.

"If you've been waiting at Isha's camp for some time, it means she won't meet with you. That's just how she is. You won't be able to enter the wall." They would never partake of the red thorn berries. They needed to hear the reality of it so they didn't waste their lives looking for the door. "If you have lost people that you love, I'm sorry. Try to remember that this happens to everyone. Everything we have will be lost, eventually. We all know this, but we have to think about it more, so we really know it."

The four of them looked at her with blank expressions.

What else did she know? She plowed on. "Try to figure out what you value the most. Then work to get the qualities you'll need to act on them. Once you have some skill, stop doubting yourself all the time. Think of your present life as a fog. Then stick your head out of it and finally know your heart."

More blank looks. Well, she certainly hadn't said it very well. Maybe she should have waited until she had better words. She stood up, slapping the pine needles off her trousers. "That's it. That's all I learned. It may not be much, but maybe it's enough."

Ekka raised her hand.

"I don't take questions. I'm not smart enough. But I'll tell you this: Isha won't answer your questions, either. Go home. If time allows, swim in a lake. Spend time alone. Don't look for a teacher. The good ones spend most of their time avoiding students."

She started to turn away, then remembered that they had helped her. "Thank you for bringing me to the village." Wishing she had a better exit line, she added, "Good luck."

Maybe they wouldn't follow her. She really had nothing to give them, much less what they hoped for.

The village master's house was a modest log cabin, its only pretensions a peaked roof and a fancy chimney. In the side yard was a paddock. She recognized one of the horses. Mitri. She also recognized someone leaning against the paddock rail, even from behind. It couldn't be, but unmistakably, it was. Rusadka. Tears sprang into her eyes, and she stopped in her tracks.

Rusadka turned. A smile crept across her face until it became a grin. "Yevliesza."

"Rusadka," Yevliesza croaked.

"You do not look very happy to see me," she said with obvious enjoyment.

"I am happy." Tears snuck down her cheeks.

"Good." She turned to a woman with light brown hair who stood next to her. "This is Elivasa. A friend of Valenty. And . . . of me."

Yevliesza nodded at the woman. She wanted to hug Rusadka, but figured that her friend wouldn't like it any more than Kiya had.

"What are you doing here?" she asked.

"Business of the princip."

There didn't seem to be anything more to say. Well, there was everything to say, but she was so tired she couldn't think of anything. In another moment, Rusadka had her by the arm and was leading her up the porch stairs to the cabin. A robust-looking man with a paunch covered by a work apron emerged from the front door.

He wiped his hands on his apron and looked them over, his face friendly but guarded. "I am Janov, master of Branova." He looked from Rusadka to Yevliesza to the woman called Elivasa. "I have met two of you, but this newcomer?"

"This is—" Rusadka began but stopped as Yevliesza put a hand on her arm.

"I am the horse's owner," Yevliesza said. "The horse with the black mane and tail." It might not do much good to withhold her name, but no sense advertising it, either.

His face brightened. "Ah! Owning the horse. The *providez* called you Keeper. You are welcome to our village."

Keeper? It was the first she'd heard of that.

The village master took in her dusty clothes, her ratty fur cape, her hair just long enough for a thong to tie it at the back of her neck. "You have had a far journey," Janov said. "Would you like to share the pottage of my hearth? Or," he added, looking more closely at her face, "rest first?"

"Rest, please," Yevliesza said, almost asleep on her feet. How long *had* she been in the Mist Wall? She called it that even though it actually hadn't been the Mist Wall. She was vaguely embarrassed that she ever thought it *was*.

Rusadka led her into the cabin and through a door off the great room. Here was a tiny bedroom that held a pallet raised from the floor by sturdy posts. Rusadka sat her on the bed and kneeled to remove her boots.

"Valenty," Yevliesza said. "How is Valenty? And Isha. Is she here?"

Yevliesza lay back on the straw mattress, her eyes closing before she was entirely flat. *Valenty,* she said again, or thought she did.

"We will talk tomorrow," Rusadka said, covering her with a blanket.

Chapter Forty

She woke the next morning as dawn leaked through the window shutters. Her hand traced the skin on her neck, looking for her mother's gift. Gone, she remembered. Her mind was sluggish with sleep, but gradually the world came back to her.

The farmhouse was cold, the hearth, dark. In the main room, all lay in shadow. Before someone could engage her in conversation, she donned her cloak and slipped out the back door.

A frigid low fog covered the ground of the paddock where a half dozen horses huddled together. The sun still lay behind the forest, sending shafts of green light past the tree trunks like spears. From among the group of horses, Mitri came forward. He greeted her at the split-rail fence, thrusting his head through. Around his muzzle, white hairs had crept in more than she had noticed before. The sway in his back was noticeable, but being a large horse, he still looked strong. And had an appetite. He nuzzled her hand, but she had nothing to give him.

"My loyal Mitri," she murmured. He had undertaken a long journey, and it heartened her to see him again.

Isha had brought him, but she would not have lingered. She had nothing left to teach Yevliesza. The rest she had to come to by herself.

But it intrigued her that Isha had bestowed the name Keeper on her. It was a parting gift, and she liked it. She was the Keeper because she had decided not to give away her second power. She realized that since Isha had brought Mitri here days ago, she must have known she would want to keep it.

Today would bring news of Osta Kiya and the war, and she was glad she had a good night's sleep to prepare for it. Her larger duty was entwined with all of that. Yesterday Rusadka had said she and Elivasa were on the princip's business. Whatever that business was, it didn't mean that Yevliesza had to make it her own. She was eager to hear Rusadka's news. Eager to find out what her friend had been doing since they had last been together—even before Yevliesza had gone to Volkia.

The sound of frozen mud crunching underfoot. She turned to see Master Janov coming to join her at the fence. His face was well-lined by his years in the harsh climate of the Agarvesky. In the freezing dawn he wore only simple clothes, with a leather jerkin over a wool shirt and trousers. He was a big man, and his bulk either kept him warm, or he was used to cold mornings.

He nodded to her and handed over two apples wrinkled from winter storage. She offered one to Mitri and then the other, both disappearing into the horse's mobile lips.

"I do not know your friends very well," Janov said. "One is a *harjat*, of course. But we all know of the *providez* Isha. Many of us have seen her in the woods. When she came here a few days ago, she told me that you have passed all her tests."

He had been watching the horses as he said this and now looked directly at her. "For a long time I had a knowing that you would come here."

A foreknowing. He had expected her to come out of the forest.

"Whatever you need, you have only to ask."

"Thank you, Master Janov." It seemed strange to think he had been expecting her, and not just because of Isha bringing her horse. The sky at the top of the distant trees was turning the color of butter, while stars still owned the sky overhead. "I may need to ask something of you."

"You may ask. But now, people have begun to gather," Janov said. He cocked his head toward the road.

Now she noticed there were figures in the darkness moving toward the master's front porch.

"Oh," she said dispiritedly, suspecting what the gathering was about.

"I can send them away."

She looked at him, taking his measure and deciding right then to confide in him. "Do you have something for breakfast? I could eat a horse." Mitri jerked his head away as though he had heard. "Sorry, my friend, I didn't mean it," she said, stroking him between the ears.

"I do," Janov answered. "My nephew and his wife will be coming to build the fire and prepare something. This holding will be theirs someday, and meanwhile they help with the chores and cooking." As they walked toward the house, Rusadka and her companion emerged from the barn where they must have slept and stood for a moment, talking.

Janov went on. "I have no children. Nor wife, since my Grida died."

Yevliesza had wondered where the rest of his family was. "What has Isha told you about me?"

"Only your name."

"Keeper?"

"Well. She said Wolf Keeper." He nodded at a shadow moving across the field of stunted grass.

Kiya.

"I saw the wolf patrolling last evening. He will not be welcome to help himself to my cows."

"I'll make sure he knows."

He looked askance at her. She should be more careful about what she said. It was bad enough that people thought she went into the Mist Wall, much less accompanied by a wraith wolf—or any wolf.

A figure walked toward the paddock from the road. Riyura.

She greeted Janov in a familiar way, and he ducked a nod at her. "Riyura."

"Can I speak with the visitor, Janov?" Her pleasant expression was meant to look innocent, but Yevliesza didn't like her determination to meddle.

"That is as she chooses," Janov said, glancing at Yevliesza.

"It's all right. I'll speak with her." Janov left them alone, heading to the barn.

"I have been thinking about what you said to us yesterday," Riyura began. "You never answered how you got to Isha's attention. She singled you out. We would like to know how."

She wasn't going to leave it alone. These people might not just be seekers. More like committed devotees.

"Did she see you in a dream? Did you bring her a special gift?" She spread her hands in a reasonable gesture. "It is just that we had been waiting to see her for over a month. And then you came riding in."

This had to stop. "Isha took me in because I lived with *satvars* for a time. They assured her that I didn't want to see dead loved ones or gain special powers."

Riyura frowned at that. "And we *do,* I suppose." She snorted a laugh. "So that is how it is."

"I'm afraid so."

They both noticed at the same time a movement near the barn. Kiya was walking toward them.

Riyura backed up. "You are not afraid of it."

Yevliesza wished that Kiya had not come right at that moment. She hoped he would not suddenly vanish. There would be no end of rumors and meddling if they saw that.

Kiya stopped about twenty feet away and sat. He regarded them, his fur ruffling in the wind.

"I think that wolf is your *sympat,*" Riyura slyly said.

Yevliesza gave her a blank look, making clear that she wouldn't answer. Was she going to be able to shake this woman off?

"Now you are prying." Yevliesza started for the farmhouse. She turned back to face the woman. "I have nothing to hide, Riyura. But I don't owe you my life story, either. I would like you to leave me in peace." She nodded at Kiya. "Me and my wolf."

"So he is your *sympat!*" Riyura said.

"He doesn't like people coming up to me unless I know them. So I think you should leave."

Riyura smirked and left to join a knot of people standing in the road.

⁂

AROUND THE PLANKED TABLE, YEVLIESZA SAT WITH JANOV, RUSADKA, and the woman named Elivasa. Janov's nephew and his wife served bowls of porridge while Janov cut hunks of bread and cheese. A platter held toasted chestnuts and a few good winter apples.

Rusadka related her own news first, of the massacre in the crossings, the deposing of Anastyna and her escape ahead of a trial on false charges of going to war to court favor with Chenua of Nubiah. And that Sofiyana had been elected to replace her.

Sofiyana as princip! It was absurd. It was sickening. As much as Yevliesza disliked Anastyna, her fall from power was ugly news. As was her loathsome replacement. At a time when they needed wisdom to deal with the Volkish, now they had Sofiyana.

"Sofiyana is not the only bad news," Rusadka said.

Seeing Rusadka hesitate, Yevliesza felt a crimp in her chest.

"You know that Valenty planned Anastyna's escape. Elivasa and I carried it out, along with others loyal to the princip, including Grigeni and Pyvel. They all had their part." She paused. "But Valenty was captured on the plains before Osta Kiya. They pursued us, and we were outnumbered."

Yevliesza had known he was a captive. God, she had *known* it, but didn't want to believe it. In the Mist Wall, she had seen him in custody. Hoping it wasn't real. But the unforgiving truth was that Sofiyana had him as a prisoner. The vivid image of the Trespass Door. *Oh, Valenty.*

Rusadka held her gaze, giving her time to absorb this.

"Could Anastyna do nothing?" Yevliesza whispered.

"She wanted to. But there were too few of us. Sixty-three, including the boy Pyvel and Grigeni, untrained to arms." Rusadka watched as Janov's nephew and his wife departed, leaving them to their meal. "Sofiyana has become vicious. She ordered several people to fall from the Tower, including High Steward Michai."

The news shocked her. Lord Michai dying. And that way. That terrible plunge. Sofiyana used the Tower, like her mistress before her, when Nashavety had urged Yevliesza to throw herself into that headlong fall. *Jump! Jump!*

And now Valenty was likely to stand in that awful place. As her stomach churned, she wished she had not eaten.

Rusadka went on. "We know that while still a *fajatim* at Raven Fell, Sofiyana spoke at night with the demon Nashavety." She glanced at Janov. "The former Numinasi noblewoman who now has gone over to Volkia."

"Spoke with her how?" he asked.

"An amber ring she gave to Sofiyana."

Janov frowned deeply. "This Nashavety uses unnatural arts? And the new princip does as well?"

"She does," Elivasa said. "I oversaw Valenty's spies in Raven Fell Hall. Sofiyana's personal maid was one of mine. Many nights she heard Sofiyana—and sometimes saw her—speak to the ring. A voice answered her."

"By the Nine," Janov muttered. "Using sorcerous means . . ."

Yevliesza stared at her. Nashavety had control over Sofiyana. So Numinat had already fallen. Nashavety had always had creature power, but now she funneled that power—or some darker power—through the amber ring. She didn't want to believe it, but Valenty had told her about the haunted Volkish mansion of Drogeliv—which had almost ensnared him with its twisted power. So the malwitch could enliven even stone and timbers, could bring hallways to consciousness. Magic gone mad.

It was all part of the tapestry of events, and she knew of one more thread: "The Volkish harness one of the powers to their machines of battle," she said, pushing aside her plate. "Elements."

"We know," Rusadka said. "I have fought those machines."

"They brought them to the fight in the crossings?" It was coming, it was all coming, just as Kassalya had said.

"They did. We were not prepared, though you brought word out of Volkia."

The table went silent then, each of them with their own unsettling thoughts.

"This darkness, this war," Yevliesza finally said. "That's why the Devi Ilsat sent me to the *providez*. And why the *providez* accepted me as a student. Because of the war."

"That is the piece we do not know," Elivasa said.

They had come to the next part. Yevliesza's part. She looked at each of them in turn. "Not everything should be told yet. But here is some of it.

"I was with the *satvars* at Zolvina for a couple of months. Among them is a foreknower who sees with an almost unbearable clarity. The sisters took her in to protect her. This foreknower said that the Volkish would bring terrible things, disastrous things, to the realms. Using machines powered by elemental power, power bled from soldiers who have that birthright gift. She foresaw the Mythos being ripped apart.

"The *satvars* asked for help from the First Ones. And that's when I —for some reason, it was me they chose—received some strengths to help. So I could work against the Volkish."

An almost imperceptible nod from Rusadka. She had been with Yevliesza that night when she guessed the meaning of the patterns on her skin. Now her friend knew how the First Ones were involved with that gift.

"You received strengths?" Janov asked. "You mean powers?" He made a warding gesture with his left hand, bringing it to his chest.

"Nothing that's a trespass," Yevliesza hastened to say. "But there is a bad side to it. What the First Ones gave me, that strength can be dangerous for the Mythos all by itself. They gave it to me because I was a stranger, I guess. They thought I could look at things in a way that's measured, that protects all the realms, not just this one."

She noted the expressions. Elivasa and Janov, appraising. Watching her.

"You learned to use that power, then." Rusadka said, nodding.

"Not exactly. I learned to know my heart. I learned to accept the things I'll come to lose. I learned that I am a servant."

Maybe not the more forceful things that Rusadka wanted to hear. "But I'm going to fight. In the ways I can."

"What ways?" Elivasa asked.

"I can be disruptive." She was going to add *in the crossings,* but though she did trust the three of them, she couldn't bring herself to say something that the Volkish might get wind of.

"People will say I went into the Mist Wall. Some people out there right now believe that."

"The Mist Wall." Janov shrugged. "That old story."

"Some people believe it's more than a story. Some of those people out there think I went in. They're mistaken, and I don't want to draw attention to myself."

"Only a few are so misguided," Janov said. "In the villages, just a few. People will lose interest once they hear from you."

She looked at him hopefully. His steadiness, a comfort. Rusadka's as well. And this Elivasa seemed to have a good head on her shoulders.

"Volkish agents might already be looking for me. So, if you talk about me to others, it's better not to call me Yevliesza. Call me Keeper, maybe. Wolf Keeper." She feared that Nashavety, having seen the writing on her back, might figure out what it meant. Yevliesza still had to hide.

But not the Keeper.

❦

RUSADKA AND YEVLIESZA SAT ALONE IN THE CABIN'S MAIN ROOM AS Janov went out to care for the horses and with Elivasa having decided that it was time she learned how to milk a cow. Yevliesza was avoiding going out to meet with the group outside, which had grown to at least forty people.

"What did you mean that Elivasa is a *friend* of Valenty's?" Yevliesza asked. Going to give him up. But this thread of jealousy.

Her friend gave her a pointed look, meaning in Rusadka-speak, *You are deluded about the man.* "Elivasa is one of his trusted spies."

"How do you know her?"

"I have fought at her side." Rusadka looked at the embers in the hearth. "Without her we would not have saved Anastyna. She can part stone walls." She nodded to herself. "Useful."

"And? Do you . . . like her?"

"Well enough."

Well enough for what? Yevliesza wondered but did not want to intrude.

Rusadka went on without a prod. "I admire the woman."

Ah. A romance. "And she admires you?"

"Well enough." Revealing nothing in her expression.

Yevliesza wouldn't push her. Eventually she would know more.

Rusadka filled her in on the escape from Osta Kiya and the pursuit by the soldiers. Anastyna and her troops were taking refuge in a sequestered place in the Yanuri canyon. And now Anastyna "begged to know" what she learned in Hapsigen of Volkish war preparations.

Yevliesza responded, "Duke Tanfred escaped Volkia with me. I asked him to tell her what I learned. And to tell you, as well."

"And he did. But she wants to know if there is anything further."

Yevliesza had been thinking about this since breakfast. "Maybe there is."

"*Maybe* is no answer for a princip."

"She is not a princip, though."

"Yes, she is." Anastyna was princip, unjustly deposed, and therefore still the princip.

They sat in silence while Yevliesza struggled to compose a better response to Anastyna's request. Any meeting with her would be complicated. It seemed like everything that lay ahead was complicated. Even the rest of the day was. The people waiting outside.

"I think I'm ready to be more honest with her."

A raised eyebrow.

"Well, you always wanted me to be. Maybe you were right. I think I should listen to you more often."

A flicker of irony in Rusadka's face.

"So I'm going to tell her about the ninth power."

"At last," her friend murmured.

"But she'll have to trade me for it."

Rusadka stared at her. "That is bold."

"I've become bold."

"What tests did you pass, Yevliesza? What happened in the forest?"

What happened. She had gone into herself and come back again, better. Simple.

Sort of simple. "The test was to know what you have to do. And then to believe that you can do it. With all the things that you want to hold onto, which is the one you must do? That you *will* do. I was in a state that was like sleep but wasn't sleep. I saw my life clearly." Her voice cracked, remembering it all. Remembering Valenty in the blue uniform, a rebel against the brown uniforms. A hero, a lover. "And I chose."

"You chose the Mythos," Rusadka said. Understanding her. She of so few words, knowing so much. Her heart softened, looking at her friend.

"I always knew," Yevliesza murmured, "even before the tests. But now I trust what I know." At the numin pool in Holdfast Castle, she took a drink of the water. And then it was inside of her. Where it always had been.

"So then," Rusadka said, "Anastyna."

She did need the princip's help. "Is there anyone among her soldiers who has a noble manifesting power? Any woman?"

"Manifesting?" Rusadka asked, puzzled. Yevliesza waited for her to answer. "Yes. The one who has taken charge of the meals. And an army *numiner*. Both of them with noble gifts."

Great. A cook and an accountant. "Either of them good in a fight?"

Rusadka shrugged. "They are both army, foot soldiers. Able to ride." Her face held questions.

"Because I need them to help me bring Valenty out. I'm going to Osta Kiya. You can decide if you want to come with me after you hear my plan. If Anastyna gives me the cook and the *numiner*."

A smirk was Rusadka's answer. Miss a fight?

"But," Rusadka said, "you chose your power, not your lover."

Yevliesza rose, glancing at the crowd that she could see out the front window, filled with crude glass, showing only a fractured view of the gathering. Rusadka had a fair point, but still, she found herself saying, "She can't have him."

She knew she couldn't have him, either. But things were not going to end this way.

Chapter Forty-One

Janov stood in the great room in front of the door leading to the porch. "Riyura has been telling tales in the square."

"About me?"

"She has. Riyura means well, but she cooks up these stories, always looking for answers, mystical things. She is saying you went in. That she saw you do it."

"It didn't happen, Master Janov. They followed me out of the forest and asked if I'd seen people they know. People that have died."

"Riyura, aye. She is one who believes things like that. The stranger the better. But there are reasons why. We have a hard life here. My neighbor Viyur lost his son last year when the river flooded. A lot of people lost friends and relatives. They want to hear about them."

He saw that she was looking at the window. "If I tell them to leave you alone, they will."

He had an authority about him and a comfortable-in-his-own-skin attitude that people no doubt responded to. "Thank you, Master Janov, but let me speak to them."

"The *providez* would never do that," he said.

"Isha has more to lose than I do. I'll be leaving, and she's staying in the woods."

"When you leave . . ." he began. She had told him she was going to speak with Anastyna. "When you leave, I could go with you. Another in your party in case soldiers find you. And I know the forest. And this side of the plain, where the watering holes are."

He would be a good man to have on the journey, however far he accompanied them. "I would like that. If you are sure?"

"Settled, then."

She glanced at the door, and he opened it for her, following her onto the porch.

"Here, now," he said to the group. "The Keeper is my guest and is good enough to say a few words to us. But only a few. That will have to be enough."

About fifty people stood in the yard and spilled onto the road. High clouds stacked overhead in the surprisingly warm afternoon. The air was humid and silent. She saw Riyura in the back of the gathering, surrounded by people chatting with her. She looked like she was in charge of things, and enjoying it. Yevliesza spotted Ekka and old Bandry, who had found spots inside the front yard.

"Sorry to keep you waiting here," Yevliesza began. "I don't have much to say. I think you're here because there are rumors about the Mist Wall. Some of you may believe them, but I don't. Here's all I know. I came to the *providez* because I was confused about my life. She told me I had been going about everything wrong and that I needed to work harder at seeing who I really was." Her words sounded unconvincing, even to her. She was no Isha.

"The reason she doesn't usually give advice is that she tells people things that are unpleasant to hear, like 'You have been mucking everything up and you need to get smarter.' I think she can tell just by looking at you whether you might have to work hard at being more thoughtful.

"And she's not interested in helping people contact loved ones who are no longer with us. Mostly, the way you contact them is through your memories. That's all." She wondered if that was the truth. She felt she had really met her mother, that she really looked like that, would have said those things. And her father. A plane of the spirit, Isha had said. But nobody here was going to make that journey, so this was the best thing to say to them.

She looked at Master Janov, who gave her an encouraging nod.

Rusadka stood in the back, leaning on the split-rail fence in a stance that seemed to convey disgust, though her face was impassive. Yevliesza knew the woman. A lot got said just in the eyes.

"Did you see my Fiodor?" a young woman holding a baby asked hopefully.

"No, I didn't. I'm sorry. I didn't go into the Mist Wall. I got very near it, and it looked like I went in. But when you think about it, how would anyone enter a place like that?"

Riyura was smiling knowingly, shaking her head.

"Riyura," Yevliesza called out to her. "You saw what you wanted to see. You didn't see the truth."

Someone shouted, "Did you see Evard? He is taller than most men, with a reddish beard."

"Mila?" came a voice.

"Anna? Or her twin brother, Oleg?"

Yevliesza could only shake her head, over and over. *No. I did not see him. No, I did not see her.*

From the front of the crowd a gruff-looking man said, "The dead are always close to us." With his long beard and rumbling voice, he seemed like one who would have strong opinions.

"Maybe they are," Yevliesza said. "But it's not my job to find them."

Janov came to her side. "I told you what they are like. I will send them home."

It seemed harsh to leave them without hope. But worse would be to encourage them to live in the past. In the back of the crowd, Riyura was already interpreting her comments for those around her. People were looking to Riyura for advice and teaching. Yevliesza saw how this kind of thing could happen so easily, that you ended up leading when you knew so little.

"Who are you?" asked the woman holding the baby.

It was the hardest question in the world. But, to get it over with: "I'm no one."

"That is not true!" Riyura called out.

Yevliesza looked at Rusadka, and instead of cynicism, she glimpsed a kinder expression. She, of all people, knew that Yevliesza had power to alter the crossings. The crossings that now were occupied by the Volkish army and were used to pass through for conquest. Yevliesza was someone to these people or could be. But what could she admit to?

"I'm . . . I'm the servant of a power that has been lost. I'll bring it back. If I can."

"Keeper," someone said.

Not to be outdone, Riyura called out, "Wolf Keeper."

Overhead, the clouds had stacked up, curdled on top, flat and blue-gray on the bottom. A fat drop of rain fell on Yevliesza's hand. "I'll do what I can to help you with what's coming. The dark times. Be watchful. Be prepared to hear of war."

"Volkia," someone said. "They brought war to Alfan Sih. And Norslad."

"And I'm afraid they mean to come here."

The bearded man frowned, looking to Janov for some comment.

But a silence opened in the gathering. The mood was different than when she had first come onto the porch. They were reminded of events far from here, events that might draw close.

"Don't believe everything you hear about me," Yevliesza said. "I'm going to do my best, but it will be hard."

Someone asked, "What power was lost?"

Another voice asked, "Do you have the power, or are you servant to it?"

"Both." She had waded in further than she had intended to. She wasn't sure if she had deflected people from thinking that she was a teacher, but she felt that they deserved something of her, something more than Isha's *leave me in peace*.

"I'll come back," she said, not knowing how, but thinking she would. She had learned in the Mist Wall how small decisions could mean large things. "But my companions and I are leaving. And if you can spare him, Master Janov will travel with me for a time."

The woman with the baby said, "Aye, Janov. Does not even milk his own cows. We can do fine without him, and bein' none the worse."

A laugh went through the group, and Janov accepted the gibe gracefully.

Elivasa appeared in the side yard with the horses saddled, leading a couple of them by the reins.

It was time to go. Thankfully, Janov would come along. She hoped he would go all the way to meet with Anastyna. She thought that Anastyna would allow her to leave again, but the woman was hard to predict. Janov's presence, and Yevliesza having at least some good will in the village of Branova, might make her think twice about issuing orders.

More drops splashed in the yard, raising the smell of wet ground and the nectar of spring flowering shrubs. If it rained in earnest, they would have to ride through it.

Yevliesza was in a hurry.

☙❧

It did rain hard as they set out. By nightfall they were still in the Agarvesky Forest and camped there for the night. The next day, the route was precarious, over hill after wooded hill, the ridges sometimes creased by streams running high from snow melt. Janov knew the way out of the forest if not the further route to the Yanuri. For that, they possessed a crude borrowed map from the village that had been drawn a hundred years ago.

They kept a sharp watch for Sofiyana's soldiers who would be searching for Anastyna. Yevliesza was dressed in what a peasant woman might wear on the road, with a tunic slit up the sides over a smock and a skirt tucked into her belt when mounted. To draw attention away from her short hair, she wore a loose leather cap with panels covered the sides of her face, coming to points at the bottom. Maybe a man's head-covering, but something a farmwife might adopt.

Elivasa and Rusadka would draw the most attention. Women dressed as fighters, but Rusadka refused to travel in disguise or without her short sword attached to her saddle and her knife at her belt.

As they rode, sometimes Rusadka and sometimes the merry Elivasa regaled them with further details about Anastyna's rescue from Osta Kiya. Valenty had masterminded the whole thing, a plan that he had quickly devised when Anastyna ended up in the dungeon of the nethers. Little did he ever think that he would be saving Anastyna from her own people.

Strangest of all was the tale of elemental power being used to pass through castle walls, with Elivasa parting stone, but blindly, and Rusadka sensing the path with her affinity for aligns along which so much of the castle had been built.

Over a miserable, spitting fire that first wet night, Elivasa teased Rusadka about saving Valenty's life.

"She did *what?*" Yevliesza blurted.

Rusadka shrugged. "He forgot to watch his back."

"Aye," Elivasa said gleefully. "And the man who nearly took his head off was one of the guards he had tied up and left to wiggle free." She poked at the dispirited fire with a stick, doing little to revive it. "Should have slit his throat when he had the chance."

Rusadka failed to hide her smile at the woman.

Yevliesza liked watching them together. They were well-suited. One taciturn and steady, the other with quick opinions and a ready laugh. But she had learned they were both fighters, each in their way —Elivasa, trained as a spy, and often posing as Valenty's lover while feeding intelligence to him gleaned in the palace.

All this, from a time that seemed lost in the distant past. Life in the city-palace. Ugly at times, but also the place where she had loved Valenty, and he had loved her.

Things were different now. Sometimes almost unrecognizable.

Such as going to see Anastyna and telling her everything.

Chapter Forty-Two

Sofiyana stared at the small mirror she held in her hand. It showed a courtyard surrounded by stone walls. Squatting in the middle, a numin pool. In the distance, icy mountain tops peeked through shredded clouds. Zolvina. It was empty. By agreed-upon signal, the image told her that the rebel forces were not there.

Carefully, she set the mirror down so as not to break it. Then she cried out, a groaning scream that filled the room. They were not there. By the eight dark hells, not there.

Her maid rushed into the room. She waved the creature out, barking, "Get out! Get out!" The woman departed, eyes wide.

A cold bitterness seized her. Nothing was working out. And now, this. She imagined Nashavety's reaction, and the thought of the woman was unbearable. Yanking the amber ring off her finger, she flung it away, sending it under an ornate chair against the wall.

A deep breath. And another. She must control herself. Her army patrols would find Anastyna. They would. If the rebels were in the polities looking for support, then more people knew where the former princip was. A force of sixty needed food, supplies. Their horses did. They would emerge from hiding, eventually.

A glow from beneath the chair caught her attention. The amber stone glimmered with its strange, hot light, like the eye of a predator.

Nashavety, nearby. Nashavety in her very skin. Crawling toward the chair she reached for the ring, gripping it in her fist.

The glow, insistent. She whispered into the ring, "Empty. Zolvina is empty."

The familiar voice: "Empty?"

"One of my patrols is in Zolvina. It is empty."

"Anastyna may be hiding there. Without her troops."

"No one is there." Delicious, to contradict her.

"They must put a *satvar* to the question of where she is. One or two. Until they know."

"Everyone is gone, even the *satvars*."

"How can they be? There is nowhere to go. Make an example of one of the old women. In full sight of the others."

The idea stirred her. But the *satvars* had abandoned the place. There was no one to torture.

"By all the hells watching," Nashavety growled. "Use the power of your office. Valenty told you she would be there. If she is not, make an end of him. And then find the woman you have replaced before she comes back and throws *you* from the Tower."

"Yes, my lady." The expected response. An empty response. Panic surging. From the start of her reign, she had been afraid to the point of panic. Almost fifteen days of wearing the torc, each of them a special torment. "If you were here, you would know what to do."

"I am here. I am always watching you."

Watching her like a pet in a cage. The idea made her sick. She had begun to hate Nashavety, and how could that be? She would be nothing without Nashavety. She was already nothing. Hollow.

Walking hollow.

She ran her fingers behind the torc, pulling it away from her throat, trying to free herself of it. But the collar stayed. Of course it did. She was the princip.

Standing up, she wiped the damp from her face, pressing on her hot eyes to empty them of their slickness. Time to be strong. It was that or give up.

Composing her features, she began to make plans.

The first thing was to punish Valenty. His lies about Zolvina. The door in the Tower would do for him. There would be a second new moon this month. A Black Moon, it was called. A good time for a walk out the Trespass Door.

She had witnessed several people walk out—or be pushed out—the Tower door. An impressive end, with the screams lasting so long. She recognized that she was stimulated by it, even the horror of it. She did not want to look, but she did. Each time she was riven with an acute awareness that she was alive. How easy it was these days to forget the sweetness of life. It had been so long since it had tasted sweet. In the Tower, a special awareness of it.

Maybe this time she would step forward and push the prisoner. Imagining it, she shivered.

❧

THE ROOF OF OSTA KIYA STILL HAD A FINE GARDEN, THE DEVI ILSAT was happy to see. It was here in the Verdant that she made a show of enjoying the sunny afternoons, all the while sowing tales among those strolling here. As she sat at the fountain overlooking the courtyard, people came by to pay respects, and Sofiyana's obvious spies hesitated to stop them.

She could well imagine that Sofiyana did not like her popularity, so she always tried to talk about a smooth transition in times of change. This appeared to mollify the household guard who were everywhere these days.

A servant woman came up to her. "High Mother, a blessing?"

"Yes, my child." She took the woman's hands in her own. "May you be safe and healthy until your far-off allotted years."

The woman whispered her thanks.

She had begun second phase of her plan to help Valenty. She did not know when Sofiyana's detachment of troops would reach Zolvina, but when they did, they would not find the princip. The ruse had prevented Sofiyana from executing Valenty as quickly as she might otherwise have done. Now, on the Verdant, in the halls of Osta Kiya, the Devi Ilsat had begun saying how Valenty had agreed to relinquish his holdings and take the vows of a renunciate, a *satvayan,* for men taking vows. How she would accompany him to the *satvaya* at Koluri, where the High Father was known to her. With Valenty under Sofiyana's control, she would know the renunciation story for a lie. The important thing was for the people to believe it. To make it dangerous for Sofiyana to execute him. The *fajatim* Ineska had also been spreading the word of Valenty's new vocation. Ineska was shrewd, knowing the man's popularity.

The Devi Ilsat was not afraid of Sofiyana. The woman had a ruthless streak but would not dare to touch the High Mother of Zolvina. She might send her away, though. The very reason she made a show of loyalty.

By the gentle Mythos, there were so many good reasons for seclusion, for remaining aloof from high doings. But the days of remaining aloof had been over since she and her inner circle had intervened in the matter of primal root power. Seeing how that had turned out had been a hard lesson in humility. Still, as Osta Kiya grew dark, she had to try to do some good.

A frail young man knelt before her. "A healing, Mother?"

She placed a hand on his shoulder, perceiving an unnaturally laboring heart. "May you grow truly strong and live with ease. May you be whole and filled with health."

He thanked her and met her eyes with gratitude.

"Get you to a healer's care, my son."

"Aye, Mother. I will."

With no one else needing her at the moment, it was time to make a circuit of the garden and speak with people about Valenty's vow of renunciation. But Ineska was approaching. With her, a few noblewomen.

The *fajatim* turned toward the Devi Ilsat where she sat by the fountain, but a guard appeared at her side, preventing her from making contact.

Ineska's handsome older face grew indignant, but the guard was clearly in no mood for argument. That Ineska did not put him in his place was a bad sign. The Devi Ilsat worried that Sofiyana was casting her dark net more closely over the *fajatim*. If sometimes she softened her control, she might well apply it again if she saw unsuitable behavior.

Ineska passed by without acknowledging her.

The Devi Ilsat had never felt more impotent. Numinat was at risk. Not immediately from invading kingdoms, but from within. The torc had passed to an empty young woman, now tainted with sorcery. A decent and brave man was in chains. The threads of diabolic power were spreading over Osta Kiya.

In that sobering moment, she resolved to take a further step. There was one thing that she had not yet tried. She glanced at Ineska and her party as they disappeared into the depths of the garden.

❧

"SHE SAID SHE WOULD TRY TO COME," YARNA REPORTED TO THE DEVI Ilsat.

"Try?"

"Yes, Mother. She did not seem to be paying strict attention."

Yarna was not the brightest of the *satvar* sisters. But she had a fine elemental power, so useful for traveling through heavy snow. Not so useful for sensitive diplomatic missions.

"The *fajatim* Ineska is not paying strict attention, my daughter, because she is under diabolic creature control."

"Yes, it was apparent."

"Did she say when she *might* arrive?"

"No, Mother."

"Then—"

She was interrupted by a knock on the door. At the High Mother's nod, Yarna opened the door and turned to announce the visitor. "Lady Ineska, High Mother."

Yarna admitted her, leaving the two of them alone. But Lady Ineska stayed near the door. "What is this night-time summons, High Mother? You might have come to me."

"Forgive me for asking that you visit, but I was not sure I would be allowed to come to you."

"Not allowed?"

"My lady, I fear for our princip. I fear for her indeed." At Ineska's frown, she plunged on. "She is not the vivacious young woman I had been led to expect. My people told me that she had an exceptionally spirited nature."

"She is the princip now."

"Yes. But I fear that she is ill in her heart." She pressed on, seeing Ineska's face beginning to close. "And is making others ill. Perhaps you have noticed this among the *fajatim?* A general feeling of insensible, spiritless behavior?"

Ineska's eyes narrowed. "Spiritless, you say? What can you mean?"

The Devi Ilsat took a deep breath. "I mean involuntary."

Ineska pursed her lips, barely letting the word slip through. "Involuntary."

"Yes, involuntary. Unfortunately."

They stared at each other for time. At any moment Ineska might turn and leave. Her only hope then would be that Ineska would not disclose this conversation to Sofiyana.

"I hope I have not overstated what I have observed. But as you may know, I am a healer. My noble gift. Might there be times when you feel that . . . insensibility of which I speak?"

Ineska looked perplexed. She swallowed as though trying to express something, but she hesitated.

The Devi Ilsat held out her hand. "The healing touch. It is my gift. If there is any ease I can bring to you, pray allow me to bring it."

Emotions flickered across Ineska's face, none staying for more than a moment. A hand came up to her breast.

All she had to do was reach out.

Chapter Forty-Three

Leaving the forest behind at last, Yevliesza, Rusadka, Elivasa and Janov came out onto a prairie that seemed to extend to the edge of the world. Tufts of low clouds moved over the land like ghost ships.

As they rode on, they saw buttes dotting the landscape. "The Plain of Monuments," Janov told them. "This is the start of them."

Yevliesza's thoughts circled around the coming meeting with Anastyna. Her hope was to borrow a few soldiers. Anastyna might not be in a mood to give them to her, but she wasn't exactly powerless. She had the advantage of primal root power. Let Anastyna consider *that*, and she might make concessions.

Soon the formations took on distinct shapes, some tall and narrow, others like mesas with sentinel spires at one or more edges. Pointing, Janov gave their names: Gray Fort. First Ones Pillar. Castle Rock. The largest butte was some seven hundred feet high, Yevliesza estimated, edged with pinnacles, and rising to a small, flat top.

"The Citadel," Janov said as they approached. A long spine linked two halves of the formation like a fairyland causeway.

As they left the monuments behind, Mitri was in the mood for a run, and Yevliesza leaned forward, urging him to go. As they galloped, she had a harder time than she had expected. Mitri sensed her fragile grip and slowed.

That was when Rusadka's horsemanship lessons began. Yevliesza learned how to gently hug her mount with her thighs, the better to notice the distinctive movements involved when Mitri was trotting or loping. She practiced holding on to the saddle to feel these different gaits and let her whole body move with, not against them.

Abruptly, Rusadka stopped, turning her mount to face something in the distance. Riders approached. Four of them. Both Rusadka and Elivasa moved forward, putting Yevliesza behind them.

"They are known to me," Janov said. "The Lord Warden."

Janov had sent word to Eiger Polity's warden about the visitor from the forest and the journey they would make across the plains. Now it appeared that informing him had not been enough. He would see the visitor for himself.

"Lord Kirady," Janov said, when the horsemen drew up before them.

The Lord Warden was a small man, slim and wiry, of an age to have white hair and beard. But he did not look weak. He sat astride his horse with ease, nodding at Janov and then casting a shrewd look at the three women.

Rusadka noted this. "We are on the princip's business, my lord."

Kirady nodded imperceptibly. "But which princip?"

"The true princip, Anastyna," Rusadka shot back.

With the air of someone used to command, the Lord Warden tossed what might be an ironic look to his men. Janov had said that for hundreds of years Kirady's family had been invested with stewardship over one of the Numinat regions called polities. The polity they were riding through.

"Which of you is named the Keeper?" the Lord Warden asked.

"I am," Yevliesza said.

He considered her. "Call yourself a *providez*, do you? Bringing tales of the Mist Wall, we hear."

"You heard wrong," Yevliesza said. Janov gently coughed behind her. A warning.

"I'm no seer, my lord. I know less than you do about the Mist Wall. But I've spent some time with the *providez* named Isha. My time with her was at the request of the High Mother of Zolvina." She added, "I'm told I was not a very good student."

Kirady exchanged indulgent looks with his men once more.

Janov saw it and spoke up. "People followed her out of the forest, claiming they saw miraculous things, but she has denied it all."

Kirady dismounted, at which signal they all did, except for the lord's men. He approached her. "I would hear your story, if you have time to tell it." Looking back at the distance they had covered, he added, "You have ridden hard."

She was willing to tell some of her story, and it looked like she would have to. But first, a little trust.

"My lord, I spent time as a Volkish prisoner this winter. Anastyna sent me on a mission, but Prince Albrecht reneged on his promise of safe passage. They may come here looking for me, so I want to use the name Keeper. My other name is a secret I need to keep."

"To do Anastyna's work?" He looked around the vast plain. "Recruiting troops, are you?"

"No. She wouldn't send me on a task like that. But as to the Volkish, I'm likely to go back to their kingdom. And they're going to wish I didn't."

Now Kirady's smile was genuine. "Brave words. And maybe not for the likes of me to know?"

"I would tell you, sir. If you keep my intentions secret." She glanced at the three mounted men.

"Do you say Anastyna approves you?"

"Anastyna does not command me. The *providez* taught me to be free of that. I do better for the Mythos if I'm not governed."

Kirady let his gaze veer off into the prairie. "You claim much. But you are a young woman with a small escort and little riding skill. I doubt you are a fighter." He looked at Janov.

"Hear her tale, my lord."

"Ride with us, and I'll tell you," Yevliesza said. "But we're in a hurry. We'll spend the night in the city of Tanaya. Janov told us we can reach Anastyna's camp by second quarter day tomorrow."

"Anastyna, is it?" Kirady looked at Janov, wondering why he hadn't been informed. He rubbed his chin under his beard, considering her. "I will hear your story."

"All right. But I need your word that you won't share the parts that would put me in danger."

"Are they treasonous parts? I am Anastyna's subject, as you should be."

The subject was tricky. When she did not immediately answer, he raised an eyebrow.

She asked him, "Is it treasonous to disobey Anastyna? I'm confused about what I owe her."

"It is not treason if you do not help the enemy. Still, you are Numinasi, and in my view owe her obedience. But if I like your story, I will not prevent you from going your own way."

Janov obviously trusted the Lord Warden. But she didn't, not yet. If Kirady couldn't look beyond Numinat, he wouldn't approve of her vow to serve the Mythos first.

"I would like you to say that you won't prevent me in any case."

His eyes narrowed. "The price for your story is to prevent me from acting upon what I learn. Then why tell me?"

"I hope you will approve of me."

He took his time before answering. "We will see. But that is not to say I will help you."

It was as much of an agreement as she was likely to get. When they mounted their horses again, Yevliesza and Kirady rode in front, and she told him who she was. The primal root power, and its significance. It was a risk, but it was time for risks. Time to gather a supporter or two, and she thought that the Lord Warden could be an important one.

He listened, watching her carefully as she made her claims. Frowning often, but withholding judgment for now.

THEIR GROUP OF EIGHT RIDERS CAME TO THE OUTSKIRTS OF TANAYA, A sprawling city laid out along a river. In the early dusk, lanterns cast light from a few doors, and smells of cooking met them in the narrow dirt streets.

Yevliesza ached from the ride and suspected that Mitri felt the same way. Kirady was still not engaging in conversation. She felt more exposed, having added another name to the list of people who knew about the lost power coming to rest with her. Not only friends and supporters, but now the people of Branova, Janov's village, who had at least heard of her new *strengths*.

Kirady had sent one of his men ahead to find accommodations and, at Yevliesza's request, to ferret out the services of a seamstress. By the time they entered the courtyard of the inn, rooms and a meal waited for them.

Rusadka took Mitri's reins and led their two horses to the stables.

"You don't have to do things for me," Yevliesza said, following her.

"Do you know what your mount needs and how to get it from the lazy stable boys?"

"Well, we don't know they're lazy."

Rusadka's half-lidded stare was eloquent.

"But thank you."

Rusadka muttered. "I'm going to stand out in your group of disguised *satvars*." She held her hands out, palms up. Her skin was dark as iron, and she wore her hair in the *harjat* way, gathered in a bun at the back of her head. "Someone will recognize me."

"Not without your sword," Yevliesza said to get a smile from her. Unsuccessful. "If you're seen in the halls, yes. But you can stay hidden until we attack."

"It is not our way to go in disguise." The *harjat* way.

Yevliesza nodded. "You don't have to come. I don't need a bodyguard."

"Yes, you do."

The stable boy finally arrived, and Rusadka turned to instruct him about their mounts.

Later than night, Yevliesza, Rusadka and Elivasa sat before the fire in their shared room. Elivasa had a tankard of ale, but Rusadka and Yevliesza drank water. Rusadka, because she considered herself on duty and Yevliesza, because she seldom did. Sometimes, when she and Valenty were courting, they had shared a glass, and after a few sips it had taken all her resolve not to end up naked with him. The time came when they no longer kept apart from each other. But that time was over. It struck her hard to think of it, here at the end of the day before the snapping fire, her boots pulled off and her thoughts conjuring him as a lover.

Elivasa went over the plan for when they got to Osta Kiya. She was keen for it. Valenty's fellow spy. Yevliesza was glad to see her devotion to him, ready to yank Valenty from Sofiyana's grip.

"We risk you falling under Sofiyana's control," Rusadka said, looking at Yevliesza.

Yevliesza wasn't going to say how she would handle becoming a captive. It hadn't changed from the time she had contemplated Prince Albrecht discovering her secret. To sever the little finger from her left hand. She had thought about it so many times, it no longer held dread. It didn't solve everything, but if Sofiyana handed her over to Nashavety at least the enemy wouldn't be able to force her to use her abilities.

Rusadka went on. "Are you sure you want to take that risk?"

"I won't leave him enslaved."

Elivasa looked at her approvingly.

"Servant of the lost power," Rusadka murmured, gazing into the fire.

It was as much of a rebuke as Rusadka had ever used with her. But she was right.

Still, out of everything she had to lose—might easily lose—one thing she would keep for herself: an attempt to gain Valenty's freedom. There was nothing particularly logical about it or wise. But the bitch couldn't have him. Whoever was coming with her was welcome, but she was going to Osta Kiya.

THE TOWN WAS WELL PAST THEM, BUT THEY STILL MET PEOPLE, MOST with wagons, but some in carriages and on horseback. No well-defined roads, but a crisscrossing of routes, the terrain flat enough for easy passage.

By the time they spied the mounted soldiers they were too close to evade them. Rusadka squinted into the distance. "Ten riders."

Kirady said, "I will ride forward to speak with them."

Rusadka exchanged glances with Yevliesza. Neither wanted to trust Kirady that far.

Rusadka rode closer to Kirady. "Let them come if they will, my lord, or we raise suspicions."

Three of the riders peeled off from the larger group and quickly approached.

The foremost of them met Kirady as he brought his horse a few steps forward, his men just behind him. The soldier took in Kirady's quality horse and gear, and his well-dressed escort. "Sir, Durgai of the Royal Guard."

"I am Kirady, Lord Warden of Eiger Polity. What is your business here?"

"On royal business, my lord. If we may speak with your party, we will not detain you further."

"What business? I know my polity and its doings." The two men regarded each other, appraising.

Yevliesza saw them looking at her, but mostly they regarded Rusadka. In an instant she knew that they had identified Rusadka. Now Kirady would either fight or hand them over. It was ten of Sofiyana's men to six fighters on her side—if Kirady's men were on her side.

Elivasa's hand was on the pommel of her short sword. Rusadka had said she could fight, a little.

"The princip's business," Durgai said. "I will speak with your people."

One of Kirady's men slowly drew his sword. Kirady turned a little, hearing the weapon slide from its scabbard. "Let us first hear who you are looking for. We may have word of them."

"One is Yevliesza of house Valenty, my lord."

"This is a name we have not heard. Is she someone we should be watchful for?"

"Aye, my lord. She could be in disguise. Using some other name." His gaze traveled again over the women in the group. Yevliesza could see Rusadka shift her weight forward, feet deeper into the stirrups. The silence opened wider, sucking the day into it. Mitri moved his feet nervously, his nostrils flaring. Yevliesza patted his neck, drawing the attention of the lead soldier.

Durgai cut his horse out and around the group, approaching her. Rusadka remained still as a stone.

"Your name and business, mistress," he said.

"My Lord Kirady speaks for me."

Before Durgai could respond, two of Kirady's men brought their horses closer.

Durgai turned back to Kirady. "Princip Sofiyana will hear of this, if you interfere."

"She will hear from *me* if you do not move away."

Someone drew a sword. Yevliesza heard it slide free. A blade flashed in the sun. No clang of metal, but weapons drawn, Kirady and his three, Durgai's two men. A short distance away, the other guardsmen now galloping toward them.

"Take them!" Kirady cried.

In the next moment Durgai fell from his saddle, getting a chopping blow from one of Kirady's men. Mitri backed up, whinnying, and Yevliesza struggled to keep him from bolting. Elivasa plunged forward on her mount, taking on one of soldiers. Janov jabbed his knife at a man whose mount was too close for him to wield a sword. Another of Kirady's men swept by Janov, felling Janov's opponent from his horse.

Rusadka and one of Kirady's men were already rushing onto the plain to meet the horsemen bearing down on them. Behind them, two more of Kirady's men, catching up. They met the newcomers some fifty yards away. Yevliesza saw Rusadka swinging back her sword to strike at one horseman, her own horse expertly sweeping by at just the right distance for the blow to land. Coming up fast, another soldier on her off-hand side. Her arm was at the end of its swing, and she hauled it back across her body, taking the second rider down with a chopping blow.

Kirady, having taken out his man, raced to join the fray. Through the dust, Yevliesza could no longer see the fight. Janov and Elivasa had stayed behind with her, but now he said to Elivasa, "I'll go. They need help."

"They do not need help. But I might." She cocked her head at Yevliesza. Janov debated taking orders from a woman but remained at Yevliesza's side.

"Don't risk your life for me," Yevliesza told her. "They will not kill me."

Elivasa barely looked at her. "I have my orders." She glanced at Janov. "You decide for yourself." She dismounted and, using her knife, slit the throat of Durgai, who lay badly wounded in the dust.

Yevliesza turned from this, shocked to see her kill him where he lay helpless.

Elivasa said, for Yevliesza's benefit, and maybe Janov's, "No one is spared today. We are too near Anastyna's camp."

Riders emerged from the fray. Kirady, his three men. Rusadka. No one else.

They left the dead soldiers where they lay as their mounts loped back to the group. It had been short, brutal work. Yevliesza tried to believe it was for Anastyna's sake. They had recognized the traitor Rusadka; they were near the Yanuri canyon where Anastyna hid. Now, no one left to carry the tale. But it was for herself as well. Her life and Anastyna's intertwined. Who will be princip. Who will control the ninth power.

Kirady rode with grim concentration. He had stepped into the course of events now. There could be no turning back.

NASHAVETY MADE HER WAY DOWN THE DIRT ROAD, CARRYING A satchel. It was highly annoying, but the carriage horses refused to come near Drogeliv. Her coachman had to stop some distance away and would have to carry her bags to the house. Dusk was falling, cloaking the road in murk. On either side of her, the thick woods had already fallen into night.

She emerged at last into the clearing before the mansion, a dwelling like no other. Its motley collection of features looked like an edifice built by an insane child, with its turrets, gables, jumbled roofs, and haphazard stonework, and carved wood beams. Two upper windows caught a slash of sunlight, like fiery eyes.

Drogeliv was not just a house, but a being. After her maiming in the Tower of Osta Kiya, it had taken her in, loved her. Perhaps it was no great honor to be someone the thing adored, but she owed it a great debt. Drogeliv had succored her when she was weak and inspired her to discard convention and abandon herself to sweet, dark urges. She did appreciate the place. But it was the only thing in her life that she had ever been afraid of.

She tramped up the steps of the porch, put down her portmanteau, and placed her hand on the doorknob. "I'm home," she whispered. The door's padlocks fell open with a clatter, and she entered.

❦

AFTER HER ACTING COOK, HER COACHMAN, TOOK AWAY THE REMAINS of her plate of boiled pigeon, Nashavety went to the solarium where a bank of windows overlooked the depthless woods. A waxing moon lent the trees a brocade of silver, and she sat in an overstuffed chair, feeling at peace after her sojourn in Hapsigen. She would go back in a few days, but for now, she would take a well-deserved rest.

"Drogeliv," she murmured, "I have missed you."

The curtains twitched, and from deep inside the house she heard something crash.

"I know I have ignored you, but keep your temper, my dear. I am here now, and we shall explore the depths once more."

She idly tapped the fingers of her left hand on the chair's armrest, stirring up dust from the upholstery. Well, not dust, actually—a small cloud of mold. From her regrown finger, reminding her of the price she paid for her diabolic habits. She sighed. Worth it.

As she gazed at the woods, she let her mind touch on the tasks to come. Anastyna was still at large and must be disposed of. Albrecht was dead. Marshal Reinhart would soon consolidate his support and become Lord Commandant of not only the army but the realm. She needed Reinhart because Volkia would never accept a woman as leader. Reinhart would follow her dictates. He knew another ruthless soul when he met one and had correctly guessed that he was no match for her.

Their army would soon march on Numinat. Once the realm was brought to heel, she would take the torc for herself. That had always been her goal. Princip of Numinat. And, given her dark arts, it would be in perpetuity.

Albrecht had seen himself as King of the Mythos, or some such grand ambition. She had a more modest goal. Empress of the many kingdoms, each with their own ruler. She had never trusted foreign elements. Once she claimed the torc of Numinat, she planned never to leave the realm again.

The ways and customs of her own land had always been enough for her, and she longed to return to them. Of course, some customs might have to be tweaked a little. She looked down at her gloved left hand with its small finger shaped permanently as a claw. Sometimes emitting small wisps of mold.

She would handle these matters in due course. But amid all this, one thing reigned supreme: the ninth power, nestling in her thoughts like a bright jewel in a velvet box. And coupled with that power, the girl of the mundat. Although Albrecht had failed to apprehend her in the Mist Wall, he had come back with staggering news. She possessed a controlling power over the crossings.

She remembered that day in the Raven Fell communal bath, how the girl had tried to hide her nakedness, not wanting to reveal the tracery on her back. And she had never guessed! Alarming that

Numinat had her, but she was vulnerable to capture. Anastyna did not protect her. She must not know of the girl's power, and Yevliesza seemed to have no allegiance to her, much less to Sofiyana. That was the ugly thing about the girl. No allegiance.

Nashavety must lay hands on her. Let Anastyna huddle in exile. She had been effectively nullified. But this girl of the lost power, that one, she must track down. Before her unusual power could be used against Volkia.

But how, how to find her.

Drogeliv! she whispered. *Where is she?* But the house, even empowered as it was, could not speak. Rather, it changed shape, altered corridors, felt incursions, and laid traps for those it found disagreeable. Brought visions.

Show me, she fervently demanded. How, how to find her.

The chair began to grow softer and then to bloat, tightening around her. The arms, plumping, the back swelling behind her, until her body was held in a brocaded, dusty embrace. In alarm she snapped, *Enough, Drogeliv!*

The beastly house did not respond. When she tried to move, she could not.

At that moment, almost enfolded in the chair, forced to remain in that sitting position, she caught sight out the windows of something in the line of trees. A hump in the ground moved, like a bear turning over in its sleep. As she watched, the mass separated and became five or six figures. *Strigoi*. One of them lifted its wings for a stretch. She had often observed their lumping behavior.

Why was Drogeliv forcing her to look in this direction, at the winged demons? Were they somehow the answer to her question? Then she knew. They *were* the answer. Drogeliv's message: The *strigoi* will find her.

But, *strigoi*? It did not seem possible. Until she remembered Albrecht's words, what he had said about Strigo a few moments before the beast killed him. *Strigo knows her. He can find her now. By the smell.*

Strigo had touched her. And remembered her pattern, her scent. Well enough to find her, so Albrecht claimed.

The chair relaxed its grip. The group of blood demons faded, only a vision.

Ah, Drogeliv, she thought. *My dark guide.*

The house had pointed the way, and now her mind raced to imagine how it would all unfold.

It would take careful planning, but within a few moments she knew the first steps. The delicious first steps for her favorite *strigoi* . . . and all its delightful friends.

Chapter Forty-Four

The *harjat* warriors parried and thrust with long staves. Not real weapons, Pyvel thought, until he saw a man go down, lying stunned. It was as Urik had told him: *Use anything as a weapon. You are armed even with hands and feet alone. With staves, an escalation.*

Pyvel liked to watch the exercises. He had his role: helper to the weapons master, with cleaning and stacking of weapons and laying them out just so in the rock alcove. Begrudgingly, the weapons master sometimes showed him a few things about weapon-making, but even that was considered a *harjat* privilege and not for the likes of him.

He saw how the sparring pairs did not look each other in the eye. They watched the shoulders to know the next direction, or sensed it, or even forced it, because these fighters could draw an opponent into a move. *How do they react so fast?* he had wanted to know. Urik had said, *Your body knows. No thinking. Only doing.*

It would be a long apprenticeship if ever he was accepted for *harjat* training, his new goal. And not before he was sixteen, which was still in the far distant future—two years.

He jumped when someone came up behind him. Urik.

"Sir!"

Urik gazed at him as though he was a piece of driftwood. "You did not see me approaching."

"No, sir."

"You are carefully watching the *harjat* sparring."

"You can learn a lot by watching," Pyvel said, remembering that Urik had told him that when he asked when he could start practicing with a sword.

Still, the flat gaze. "The men saw I was coming. Even those with their backs turned. They saw the men opposite take note. They knew without looking."

His mood plummeted as he realized that Urik was finding fault with him.

"A warrior must know the wider circle. Not just his opponent. That man behind you is your next opponent."

Pyvel nodded. He knew Urik well, from their trek out of Volkia, but he would never consider speaking informally to him.

"Everything is practice," Urik said. "Use everything." Despite his attempts at self-control, Pyvel's expression must have exposed his dismay, because Urik said, "If you want to be a fighter, the army will teach you to use weapons. If you want to be a *harjat*, you must use everything."

The men were watching them, faces serious. They had noticed over the days at the river that Urik sometimes talked with him. That gave him a small measure of status. Sometimes one of the *harjat* would deign to notice him, or nod. Otherwise he was of no account.

"Thank you, sir," Pyvel said.

But Urik was looking down the strand.

One could not see beyond the shoulders of rock that enclosed either end of the beach where they camped, but something caught Urik's attention. In another moment, the call of a bird—from one of the look-outs. Movement on the beach stopped, as soldiers looked down river.

Anastyna had come out from her residence made of driftwood and blankets.

No one had approached their encampment since they had arrived. Though they knew that whoever was coming must be a friend, soldiers rose from their cook fires, and *harjat* stood along the line of the water, waiting.

Pyvel's heart sped. It would be Rusadka returning. And Yevliesza with her? And then the hope thrust up inside him that it would be Valenty. What a welcome he would have!

It was a long wait. There were lookouts on the cliffs spread out far up and down the river. The signal passed along. In case of treachery, the raft waiting, the men selected who would take the princip to safety, or what safety the river could offer. The *harjat* would give everything, dying to the last warrior.

Grigeni came forward to stand next to Pyvel, putting a hand on his shoulder. Grigeni was no longer the tutor, the Keeper of Books. His skin had darkened from the sun, his hair turned greasy, and his clothes already needing patching. But he held himself tall. They did not speak, not wanting to be disappointed that it was only Rusadka returning with nothing to show for her travels.

The first horse to come around the headland was a soldier, one of the lookouts. Behind him, Elivasa, their horses splashing along the shoreline. Rusadka came next, and directly behind her, by the Nine, Yevliesza.

She saw him immediately, and gave him a welcoming smile, then nodded sweetly at Grigeni, who bowed, lower than was proper.

Among the newcomers, four people Pyvel didn't recognize, important people by the look of them, sitting tall in their saddles and armed. Urik approached to receive the lookout's quick report, and soon the group was dismounting as the camp watched silently, waiting for the news, the reasons new soldiers had come amongst them. Pyvel wanted to go forward to greet Yevliesza, but more important things would come first.

Anastyna's steward spoke with Urik, and soon Yevliesza was brought up the beach to where the princip stood outside her makeshift quarters with the wind snatching at her skirts, and her face, neutral.

Anastyna looked paler than ever, her dress soiled at the cuffs and hem. Without the torc, she looked strangely vulnerable. Yevliesza made a bow, perhaps not as low as she should have made.

Anastyna's face lost the temporary pleasantness she had marshalled.

"My Lady Princip," Yevliesza said in greeting, making clear she believed that Anastyna still held that title.

"Yevliesza. We are happy to see you." All formality, even in front of a driftwood hut. "You will want refreshment after your journey, but first we would hear your report, so long awaited."

"Yes, my lady. And I have other things to tell you. Things besides the Volkish task you sent me on." Seeing the slight rise of an eyebrow, Yevliesza pushed on. "Regarding the war and . . . Valenty."

"Of the war and Lord Valenty," Anastyna mused. Turning to a man standing next to her, she told him to summon Urik and her army commander.

Yevliesza quickly said, "I can't speak in front of the army commander, my lady. But I will accept Urik."

Anastyna's face did not show anger, but her eyes were as cold as the Yanuri. "You do not say who comes to our counsels. We will have Captain Lysandry here."

It was a roadblock. She would not speak to the military, except for Urik. "Then my report is going to be brief. There are some things that only you should hear."

Anastyna paused, perhaps considering how Yevliesza was going to pay for the insolence. Yevliesza knew how it sounded: presumptuous, threatening. There was no help for it.

"May I ask that Lord Warden of Eiger Polity join us?"

Anastyna looked past her to where Kirady was standing a short distance away.

"Very well." She murmured to her assistant, who looked to be an army officer, and he left to arrange things.

A woman stood at the door of the hut. She held back the blanket that covered the opening, and Anastyna went through. Her attendant kept the blanket drawn aside, and Yevliesza and Kirady followed. She wished that she had asked for Rusadka. She wished there was someone who could be at her side during the coming minutes: Isha, perhaps, or the High Mother of Zolvina. It was a bad time to begin shaking. She pinched her arm, hard, to get a grip on herself.

Once she was seated on the driftwood log in front of Anastyna, Yevliesza felt on firmer ground. Anastyna was not surrounded by magnificence and finery now. She had no household guard, no Lord High Steward of the court, no imposing nobles standing in attendance. In fact, she sat on a driftwood log herself.

The Lord Warden received a greeting from Anastyna, and stood to one side, there being few places to sit. Also standing to one side, the *harjat* they called Urik. Valenty's guide and aide on his own mission to Volkia. Yevliesza trusted Urik because Valenty did. Still, it had been a compromise to allow anyone in the meeting from Anastyna's side, other than the princip herself.

Anastyna asked her to first relate why she had taken residence at the *satvary* and had kept away from court.

It was a question that was better put off for later, but Yevliesza answered that in Volkia it had been driven home to her how far Prince Albrecht's ambitions went for conquest. She felt she had a role to play but needed time to figure out what role it might be.

"A role? Was it not your role to report to us?"

"I told everything I learned to Valenty, asking him to inform you. Also, I asked Duke Tanfred to tell what we learned, and any other things of military value that a noble of that realm could reveal. He said that he would."

"And he did. Duke Tanfred was also helpful, the few days he stayed at court." She paused. "It has been made known to us that Duke Tanfred has returned to Volkia. He has an intention to foster—and lead—the resistance against Albrecht's reign."

"There is a resistance?"

"So he believes."

But to go back to the kingdom that called him a traitor . . . It was horribly dangerous. And in keeping with the man she knew so well, to sacrifice himself for his country.

Anastyna went on. "Now, however, we would also like to hear more of your mission to Volkia. Especially what sort of man Prince

Albrecht is. One hears reports, but you had time to discover more about him."

What could she say about the man that would not make her feel degraded? "He is a vile man and poor leader," she managed to say. "But I hurt him in a fight."

Kirady reacted in surprise. Urik gave no reaction, but she felt his eyes on her.

"We have been informed that you wounded him. During your escape."

"I meant to kill him, but he was strong."

Anastyna glanced at Urik, her face showing incredulity. "Kill him? When you were running away?"

"I waited for him. And hoped to kill him." It was rude not to give more details, but this wasn't the time to admit how she had hoped to trap him. And she had let some bitterness into her voice, also shockingly rude. "Please excuse me," she said, her eyes downcast. Wanting to say, *You sent me to a man who used me. I told you what these people were like, and you didn't care. So yes, I damn well hoped to kill him.*

After a prolonged silence, the princip said, "Well, we have not heard that he is dead."

"News can be slow from Volkia."

The air had turned poisonous. Not what Yevliesza had intended. Without success, she searched for a transition to a better topic.

Anastyna said with an even temper, "We must ask your pardon for the mistake of sending you to Volkia. We erred in judgment." She looked perfectly comfortable with herself when a little shame would have gone a long way. "We would not have wished you to be unfairly held or disrespected."

She didn't know. Anastyna didn't know how Albrecht had used her. Maybe not all the ways he might have, but enough. No one was going to know, but with the tenor of the discussion, she thought that Anastyna had begun to realize the extent of her *error in judgment.*

The real subject had to come soon, or she might miss her chance. "I'm here to ask for your help, My Lady Princip. A request."

"You may speak." She cocked her head. "This has to do with Valenty?"

"Yes."

"Yevliesza. We have not the troops to break him free of Osta Kiya's dungeons. Had we the power, it would have already been done."

"But I would like to try. If you could assign me some people to help."

"We can spare no troops for this. We are weak at the present, though one's heart would wish to do otherwise." She spread her hands. "And so." End of discussion.

"But I'm only asking for four soldiers," Yevliesza said. "One is Carlaty, a *numiner*, Rusadka tells me. And Mura. They're capable manifesters, and I need help with disguise. Also Elivasa and Rusadka if you'll grant them leave. Then I'll bring Valenty back to you."

Urik glanced at Anastyna and received her nod to speak.

"He would not ask it of you," Urik said. Then pointedly, "Nor want it."

She regarded this seasoned *harjat*, a man who had saved Valenty's life several times. "I know. But I need to do this thing. This last thing."

"Last thing?" Anastyna asked.

Yevliesza hadn't put it to herself that way before. It might be true, though, that her enemies would find her. Before or after she wreaked havoc on their plans.

"I think in a little while I'll be given over to a larger task. But this smaller task—I need to do it." When no one responded, she went on. "I know what it's like to be under an evil power, to have your personal choice removed, to be helpless and preyed on. We know that Sofiyana is under Nashavety's control. It's diabolic power. I can't serve the Mythos until he's free of her."

It was a longer speech than she had meant to give. It didn't sound convincing, or noble in any way, but it was the truth, and she thought everyone in the room might feel the same if they didn't have obligations that prevented them from acting.

And she was damn well settled on acting. Sofiyana was a mewling, weak, and despicable woman. That she was princip of Numinat was horror enough. That she had Valenty was somehow so much worse.

"Serve the Mythos?" Anastyna was asking. "What can you mean?"

"My Lady Princip. We'll get to that next. I'll tell you everything I know."

Anastyna drew herself up. "We cannot send four good soldiers on such a mission." She paused. "However, if they volunteer, we will permit it."

Yevliesza was so surprised she could not speak. Then: "Thank you." Rusadka and Elivasa, she already had. It was a start.

"And so." Sitting on the royal log, Anastyna rearranged her skirts. "What is this thing you have promised to share?" She added, sarcastic, "The thing that you refused to say in front of our commander."

It was time to tell her of the second power. It was time that Anastyna learned that she did not own Yevliesza, and why. Time that she heard how Yevliesza was a weapon, but not a subtle weapon. A world-altering weapon. One that the *satvadeya* did not entrust to any one realm, only to an outsider.

It would be a hard thing for Anastyna to accept, but once she knew —if she even believed her—she would never again be able to use her in a royal way. Yevliesza wanted her to know that she would work against the Volkish. It would give her standing. And allow her to work with Anastyna while being free of her.

If the princip reacted badly, if she tried to claim Yevliesza as her own, then the Lord Warden of Eiger Polity would speak up for her. Anastyna hadn't yet gone to the polities to ask for men at arms. When she did, it wouldn't go well if Kirady was hostile to the princip. He'd heard how the First Ones had made their choice. And it seemed to Yevliesza that he wasn't going to argue with it.

Anastyna might not forgive Valenty that he had kept this from her. But that was for them to work out. Of course, Anastyna could still try to restrain her, but she would see in the end how it was pointless. Yevliesza could, and would, refuse. Anastyna could at least be glad that the power hadn't gone to someone of dark intent even if it had gone to one of rebellious intent.

"Well?" Anastyna demanded. "Speak."

"My lady, you know that the Devi Ilsat in Zolvina has a close circle of *satvars* called the *satvadeya?*"

Anastyna waved her hand. Everyone knew. "You said this pertains to the war?" she asked, impatient.

"Yes, it pertains entirely to the war."

Again, the lift of Anastyna's hand.

Yevliesza took a slow, calming breath. Her tale was a long one. She might have started with the markings on her skin that gradually altered from the burns she had suffered from the lightning strike. Instead, she began with Kassalya, and what she knew of the coming catastrophe of Volkia. And how the *satvars* had asked the First Ones to send a power to repel invasions of conquest.

How the power was one that could disrupt the access of armies to other realms, but that could also put the fragile Mythos in danger.

What power, Anastyna wanted to know.

When told it was the Ninth Power, and what that power was, Anastyna rose from her seat. She could not believe it. She paced back and forth in the confines of the hut, tossing out questions and refuting the answers she received. Urik and Kirady watched her warily, Urik probably sharing her incredulity, and Kirady waiting for a more worthy reaction from a princip that he hoped to support.

It was a remarkable outburst of emotion. And Anastyna hadn't even heard the worst yet.

"May I go on, my lady?" Yevliesza finally asked.

"Does the story grow more strange?" she asked in exasperation as she took her seat again. "If you have come here with wild tales, if you plan to sow rumors of *satvar* deeds of trespass . . ." She stopped, eyes blazing.

"You can ask the Devi Ilsat if it's true. And don't say trespass. It wasn't trespass. They were trying to save the Mythos."

"Save the Mythos," Anastyna snapped. "If this is what goes on at Zolvina—to summon spirits, imagining the end of us! And you, Yevliesza. A part of this how? How?"

"The power is written on my back." She waited for another eruption.

Anastyna's eyes flashed in anger. "A message from the First Ones, perhaps?"

"If you know what it is, My Lady Princip, I would like you to tell me."

"Do not pull us into this elaborate story. Do not insult my lords Urik and Kirady if you do not respect your princip."

"The power came into *me*. The power of primal roots, the roots being the crossings. And I used that power to create a new path into Alfan Sih for Prince Tirhan. So when you ever see him again, you can ask him."

Yevliesza turned her back on everyone and untied the string that held her shirt closed at the neck.

She turned her head toward the princip. "I think you need to see what's on my back. I hope it's still there. I only ever saw it once for myself, and that was in Volkia where they have mirrors the size of windows." She yanked her shirt over her head, exposing her back.

"Bring a torch and look closely," she suggested, waiting for another burst of Anastyna's temper for the offense of disrobing during an audience.

She had planned to ask permission to bare her back, but what would she have done if Anastyna had refused? The patterns on her skin might not prove anything, but if nothing else they tended to match up with the rest of the tale, that of a young woman being invested with a power beyond anything that an individual should ever have.

"These grew from burns?" Urik said from close behind her.

"Yes. Because lightning was the . . . delivery mechanism, for bringing my second power after I was too old to have a natural development."

When her back had been thoroughly viewed, she put her shirt back on, and turned to face the princip.

As she looked at Anastyna, she thought how difficult it was for people to give up their cherished ideas, their opinions, and the stories they told themselves about their past actions, and future ones. She could almost see her ideas dropping away like dead leaves, some of them still clinging to the tree, but doomed to fall. She was nothing they could have predicted, nothing they could control without killing her. The silence in the hut was crushing as they came to terms with what they had seen and heard.

She thought of Isha, and what she would think of this moment. *There is no end of delusion. Of the stories people tell themselves about how things have to be. Just poke your head out of the fog.*

Anastyna's voice was almost a whisper. "You can create or destroy paths in the crossings?"

"To some degree. I'm not sure how much."

"What do you plan to do?"

That was a decent question. The princip had phrased it in a good way. Not, *What shall I have you do?*

"I don't know yet. I thought I would go into the crossings and disrupt things. It's as far as my thinking has gone. Large actions would draw Volkish attention. A tunnel might collapse more extensively than I had planned. Maybe catastrophically. My biggest fear is that it would hurt the Mythos in some structural way."

Anastyna had been standing since she took a closer look at Yevliesza's back. Now she sat down, looking a bit dazed.

"I can't be a part of your military plans," Yevliesza went on. "I'm not even sure what my powers are capable of. Add to that, we have no effective way to communicate. If I make things worse, I'm going to stop. It will be my decision because it has to be. The power is in my bones, and I can't give it to anyone else."

Kirady spoke up. "If the common folk knew what you were, it could be a rallying point. They would be more committed fighters, and more numerous, when the invasion comes."

"But my lord," Yevliesza said, "no one can know. Prince Albrecht may suspect what I have. Nashavety may suspect. If they knew for sure, they'd hunt me down. They'd bind me to their purpose. The danger of me going into the crossings is that I end up being used against Numinat."

Anastyna's voice cut into the discussion. "No one is to know." Her gaze lingered on Yevliesza, maybe trying to square up what she used to think with what she knew now. "Urik, would you please summon our steward?"

As he left the hut, she turned to Yevliesza. "We will have a meal prepared for you. And a good place to sleep."

"I don't need anything special, my lady."

One of Anastyna's eyebrows rose a fraction. "We will say how to receive you. And that will include a good bed."

The steward came through the flap, looking around, sensing the sober mood.

Receiving Anastyna's orders, he left to make preparations, including discovering whether the desired volunteers were willing to go on the mission.

Chapter Forty-Five

Yevliesza's two new volunteers made an unlikely addition to the team assaulting the great city-palace of Osta Kiya.

Mura, a big woman with thick braids threaded with white, ruled the main cook fires of the rebels. She was a talented manifester, often the butt of jokes about how she made the food look better than it ever was.

Carlaty was the smaller of the two additions but trained as a soldier and with a reputation as a scrappy fighter. She was also a *numiner* who loved details and numbers. Reluctantly, she handed over the book of *numin* credits to another soldier, giving many instructions for proper accounting of extra services provided by those whose deep affinities proved useful beyond a soldier's duty.

Yevliesza finally had to cut her off. "Carlaty, it's a long ride to Osta Kiya. We need you to leave as soon as you change." Carlaty and Mura would travel as *satvars* using the disguises that had been hastily assembled in Tanaya the night before. They would arrive at Osta Kiya four days in advance of the rest of the group.

Yevliesza and Rusadka had worked out the details of Valenty's extraction, with Elivasa contributing suggestions based on years of spying in the city-palace. First, Carlaty and Mura would arrive unexpectedly to see the High Mother. Their story, a death at the *satvary*. They counted on the High Mother playing along in public until she discovered the strangers' real purpose. Which was to enlist her in holding a vigil in the palace courtyard for the next full moon of the month, the month that Yevliesza would always think of as May. The full moon—called the Blossom Moon—was in six days.

They hoped that Valenty would be allowed to attend. They had learned from Anastyna's spies that Valenty was being represented as having given his allegiance to Sofiyana, so maybe his presence would not only be allowed, but required. If he didn't attend, they would have to penetrate the royal quarters, a much harder operation, but one which Elivasa thought was possible.

Once they had Valenty, they would escape down the thousand stairs to the plain, the steep and sometimes treacherous access to the agricultural fields and the flats where the army held maneuvers. Where no one would expect them to go, because it took so long to descend and there would be no cover from the arrows of the sentries on the roof.

If, during the attack, the High Mother was exposed as helping, she would be removed as well, although she was not an expert horsewoman, nor presumably was the attendant she had brought with her. One goal of the mission was to preserve the Devi Ilsat's innocence in the affair, or enough of a veneer of innocence that she could not reasonably be accused.

The longest discussion centered around whether, if an opportunity arose, they would kill Sofiyana. For days Rusadka and Elivasa had deferred to Yevliesza, letting her make the decisions. But now they found themselves at odds, Yevliesza saying no because the *fajatim* had chosen the new princip, and the use of sorcery could not be proven to people. Rusadka argued that Sofiyana had committed trespass against persons by binding their will to her own—or to Nashavety's—and that she might deliver Numinat to the Volkish.

In the end, Anastyna made the decision. Sofiyana would not be killed. A strictly political decision. The army was loyal to Sofiyana, as were many, if not most, of the populace. Sofiyana's murder could not be explained. "The murder," Anastyna said, "would cast a shadow on my righteous cause."

Elivasa was the only one who, by her expression, dared reveal what she thought of that decision. For once, though, Yevliesza agreed with Anastyna. It was a strange feeling.

Carlaty and Mura were given the best horses that could be sparred, and they set out, riding hard.

⚜

THAT NIGHT, YEVLIESZA SAT AT A FIRE PIT WITH GRIGENI AND PYVEL, happily catching up. Joining in were Rusadka and Elivasa, as well as Elivasa's fellow spy, Andrik, who had helped Yevliesza in her trial for treason, when he had sought out and found the courier who had ridden with her on the dactyl the night of the lightning strike. That courier had seen Nashavety's amber ring when her hand appeared in the sky; it was proof of Nashavety's murderous intent against Yevliesza, which ended up sending her into exile.

Grigeni sat next to Yevliesza. He was glad of the decision to go after Valenty and wanted to go along but knew that he would only be a liability on such a mission. He could barely sit on a horse, much less ride one. "I wish I could help you take him out."

"Don't worry, Grigeni. We'll get him. We won't leave him with Sofiyana."

He looked at her, taking her in, maybe seeing that she was different than before. She wished she could tell him more of what had happened to her. So much of her new life was about withholding: from Grigeni and Pyvel, from Anastyna. Withholding from Valenty and a life with him. The life she could not have with him unless he left Anastyna's service.

She put her hand on Grigeni's for a moment. She looked to the river, listening to it, the rush of its waters combing past the high rock walls of the canyon. Earlier, she had noted how the soldiers on the beach looked up to the cliff tops, alert for the appearance of soldiers.

Sofiyana's men were combing the flats, looking for Anastyna. How strange it was to think that things had come to this.

Pyvel was talking. The group encouraged him as he repeated the tale of Anastyna's escape from the nethers, including Pyvel's last view of Valenty as he'd been led away by the soldiers. Rusadka watched Pyvel recite the details of the escape, embellishing Valenty's role with enthusiasm. If Yevliesza was not mistaken, Rusadka showed some indulgence as the fourteen-year-old described an essentially military maneuver in which his only role had been to saddle the horses. It was certainly not all that he had done, but that was undoubtedly Rusadka's soldierly judgment.

⟡

IN THE MOONLIGHT, YEVLIESZA WALKED DOWN THE GENTLE SLOPE TO the river, swift-flowing and black. It reminded her of the great Volkish river, the Danstree, which she had watched flowing by so many days at Albrecht's palace. Longing to ride on it. Dreaming of an escape. Barges, ships, canoes. Lifeboats. To take back her life.

Which she *had* taken back.

A voice from up the beach a little. "The Yanuri is in full flood."

Anastyna. "Snow melt off the Numins," she said, musing.

It was dark, and Yevliesza dispensed with the bow that couldn't be seen. "I had never seen a great river until the Danstree."

"Thinking about the bad days in Volkia."

"Sometimes."

Anastyna came down the beach to stand next to Yevliesza, looking out at the river, or at the sound of it. "I have been thinking about past things, too."

So not saying *we* when referring to herself. She would be more regular, a real person. It was hard to think of her that way.

"The way things started out with you. Back when you first came here."

Yevliesza waited to hear how things were back then. How Anastyna thought they were.

"It was a time dominated by Nashavety. She always distrusted the outside world. And now, look, she lives with the Volkish. But in the old days, unthinkable. She never approved how Princip Lisbetha dealt with the mundat. About their new ways with . . . small machines?"

"Nanotechnology."

"The unpronounceable word. She would have had us barricade the crossing to the mundat. Cut off all contact. Not that we ever had real contact. Envoys, only. But we did not barricade the crossing to the origin world. Maybe the small machines could have leaked through in any case. But think what did come through. The, what did you call them, the people with the evil myths?"

"Nazis."

"Yes. They came. So Nashavety was not completely wrong. But wrong about the other realms. To her, they were all foreigners. A threat, one way or the other. Their ideas. The way they looked and did things. And then you."

She looked at the river as she spoke. A way of keeping her distance even though she stood next to Yevliesza. The princip and the commoner. But on the beach, more equal.

"At first, I blamed the courier for bringing you to Numinat. He should have left Ansyl and you alone, under the circumstances. You were happy there."

Puzzling, how Anastyna thought she knew this. Except she was right. She had been happy. Wishing her father was not slipping away, but her small life suited her, connected by TV, the internet. Trips to town. The local boy. Maybe she had been content. But it had been lonely, lonely in ways she realized only after coming to Numinat.

Anastyna continued. "But then, when it looked like you would recover from your burns, I thought perhaps you could be a good thing for us. Teach Nashavety that the outside world was not a threat. You were young. Brave in the face of our harshness. I arranged for Valenty and Dreiza to take you in. How that worked out, you saw. Nashavety hated you more than ever. Not you. What you represented.

"I wanted contact with our sister realms. Trade, certainly. But culture, learning. I invited envoys. Tirhan, Chinua. I suppose I moved too fast.

"So she hated me. She meant to bring me down. For the good of Numinat, you understand. That is how she saw it. The outside leaking in. Soon you are the outside. Everything that was particular to Numinat would become general. The old ways lost.

"She meant to remake you as Numinasi, since you should have been, if Natia had come home to birth you. But you resisted Nashavety. And you had won over Valenty, Dreiza. Even Prince Tirhan favored you. The world was shifting under her feet. It drove her to desperation.

"But I want you to know that I always hoped for your success. People think that a princip may do as she pleases, but that is far from the case. Sometimes you were rash. The Bridge of the Moon collapsed. You were not responsible, but it looked that way. People died. Nashavety undermined you at every chance. Soon people doubted you. But I never did.

"People thought that Valenty just wanted you as a lover. But when you first arrived, he only wanted you to succeed. Sometimes a new thing is just what is needed. You were the test. Is there not a saying in the mundat? A bird underground?"

"Bird? Oh. The canary in the coal mine."

"Yes. The test of the outside in Numinat."

"Then the insult to Prince Albrecht when you met him in the crossings. And he falsely claimed he wanted an apology. The Volkish cherish honor above all things, what they are known for. Oddly, with so little honor."

Yevliesza knew about Volkish honor. Albrecht's sexual predation, but then withholding somewhat. For honor.

"I did not know it was a ruse. I could not have foreseen they would hold you hostage. We were not at war. I held back from marching to save Alfan Sih. He would not provoke me for nothing. But he did. Still, it was too dangerous to send you. I should not have. But I was afraid of angering him when an apology was simple." She paused. "I have asked you to pardon me."

She wasn't going to repeat the request.

"The pardon is given, My Lady Princip."

Anastyna glanced at her. "It is well, then."

It was well. Well enough, anyway. Anastyna had her nice story of how she was good and true. All she had done for Yevliesza. The bad things, not her fault. Afraid of angering him when an apology was simple. Even Nashavety could be, if not forgiven, at least understood. The politics of it. The politics of not killing Sofiyana. Casting a shadow on her righteous cause.

And here, standing next to Yevliesza, was the woman, the ruler, who Valenty would come home to. The royal hut on the Yanuri. The righteous cause. Saying goodbye. Each going their own way.

Do I have it right, Isha? Is this how I do it?

The river flowed on. You decide. Things that are lost, you let go of. Because it's your duty, maybe. Larger than you, same as for Valenty. You don't grow by wishing things were different. Everything is moving onward, with or without you. With or without your full care and understanding.

The river flowed on.

Chapter Forty-Six

Sofiyana had a list. Things she was supposed to do. All written down, to help her remember each day's tasks. She sat at her desk near the great windows of her parlor, watching the light drain from the sky.

The list was long: Meet with the military commander to hear plans for defense. Invite the *fajatim* to attend. Hear the requests of the noble houses. The petitions of the guilds. Spend time with each of the *fajatim* to stir the embers of their devotion. Prepare to execute Valenty, as Nashavety was now almost daily demanding. As she had demanded the deaths of the boy Pyvel and the *harjat* Urik, for misdeeds in Volkia. Misdeeds that were unclear to Sofiyana. She would be happy to throw them both from the Tower since they had joined in Valenty's treason, but they were with Anastyna's fugitive group and could not be found.

She stared at her hand. Her thin, bony hand with the veins branching in blue tributaries. Losing weight. Becoming a wraith, like Nashavety. Consuming herself to accomplish the list.

A knock at the door. She hid the list in the folds of her skirt as her steward interrupted her ruminations. Would she speak with the High Mother of Zolvina?

It was not on the list. But the High Mother kept asking to see her, and she could not always say no.

Wearily, she lifted a hand in agreement.

The old woman came before her, bristling with energy and happy good will. Dinner was well past, and still she was at work, though always saying how age was taking its toll, as though at any moment she might collapse. She could only hope that the High Mother did not fall dead in front of her, lest Lady Ineska worry that people would find blame in it.

"High Mother," Sofiyana said in restrained greeting.

"My Lady Princip." The Devi Ilsat looked around for a place to sit, but Sofiyana thought that the woman might make the audience a short one if kept standing.

"Thank you for seeing me so late in the day, but I was hoping for permission to attend the Blossom Moon vigil."

"Permission is needed?" Everyone would be there.

"As a courtesy since I am not a citizen of Osta Kiya. I would like your permission to join the Great Circle."

"There will not be a Great Circle. It is a festival, not a vigil."

"Oh! But it is always a vigil. Or, my goodness, is my memory fooling me? The fifth month, the Blossom Moon . . . no, I think there is a circle. Traditionally." When Sofiyana made no response, she rambled on. "And it would be fitting for the Blossom Moon. For the flowering of your reign, which has just begun." She paused, waiting. "I hoped to join the circle. But I could also be outside the circle and observe. Such an honor."

It was not a bad idea. The flowering of her reign. People would like the symbolism.

"And a few of my *satvars* if you deem it appropriate. To strengthen the ties between *satvary* and palace."

The old woman had received a visit of *satvars* yesterday. "Were you expecting the *satvars,* High Mother?"

"Oh my, no." Her face lost its good humor. "In fact, sad news. One of my *satvadeyas* has died."

"I am sorry. Lost to old age?"

"Oh, not at all. She was not old, only ninety-two. Fell into an ice crevasse. Everyone is quite upset about it."

"A crevasse? Her duties took her outside?" Sofiyana had assumed that the *satvars* seldom left the compound.

"She had business with the Irusen *satvary* and was journeying there."

"I am sorry. You will be leaving for the burial?"

"No burial is needed. She is buried in ice and snow." The High Mother's mouth crumpled as she contemplated this. "But as to the circle, my lady?"

How quickly she sprang back from sadness. Perhaps the Devi Ilsat was having some trouble with her concentration. She did seem unduly happy for a supposed renunciate. For a moment, hearing the news about the death, Sofiyana had hoped that the old woman would finally leave, but apparently, she was enjoying her stay. Banquets, high affairs, vigils.

"I will convene a Great Circle," Sofiyana conceded. "It could have an uplifting effect. As you say, for the flowering of my reign."

"Excellent, my lady! Might my *satvars* and I join in, then?"

"Of course."

"And I think it would be well for Valenty to join hands in the circle. If his intended avocation is approved, sacred festivals will be an important part of his life."

There was simply no end to the meddling. "I will consider it."

"Excellent, my lady! I am sure people will be relieved by such a gesture."

"Relieved?"

"That the new reign will be a flowering, and not—"

Sofiyana looked up at her sharply.

"And not, well, one would not want to say, a *wilting*. That would not do at all. Let us say *flowering*. As befits the Blossom Moon."

At last she went away, leaving Sofiyana staring after her. The High Mother had been an annoyance from the moment she arrived. Always claiming that she was here to provide reassurance and stability during the political transition, and yet intruding in ways large and small. But she had to admit that she quite liked the idea of the Blossom Moon as a symbol of the new reign. Perhaps the old woman was not so bad after all.

Slowly, she brought out the task list, laying it on the desk. She reached for a quill, adding *vigil*.

⚜

For the next three days, Yevliesza was often in consultations with Anastyna, usually in the company of Captain Lysandry, Urik, and now, Kirady, out of consideration of his position. Lord Warden of one of the largest polities in the outland.

Anastyna was hunted and at some point, would have to fight. But she needed an army, and it would have to come from the polities, each under the rule of hereditary princes or appointed wardens. Now, hearing about the fight between Kirady's men and the soldiers, Anastyna was inspired to begin sending out her people, testing which of the polities would join her, or whether their allegiance was to Sofiyana. When Elivasa returned from the mission to free Valenty, she would accompany the recruiters, testifying to the sorcery of the princip: the amber ring and its ties to Nashavety who was in the camp of the Volkish.

Anastyna would not seek a battle with Sofiyana anytime soon. She must build her strength. And build the support of the polities to establish herself as the princip in exile. The true princip, ready to lead again, no matter who sat in the royal apartments.

No one except Elivasa was happy about Yevliesza's mission to Osta Kiya. Women only in the group, and only five of them. Sometimes she thought she saw Anastyna looking at her strangely. *Was not this person once my subject?* Once. But no longer. She would have to get used to it.

"If Sofiyana knew who you have become," Urik had said, "she would keep you, ensorcell you."

She was too valuable to risk. But her enemies didn't know what she was. That was her protection, as thin as it might be.

Lord Warden Kirady remained silent when the subject turned in the direction of the mission's risk. He had seen the pattern on her skin, and he thought it meant something. Something beyond her second power. A bestowal, perhaps, of the Mythos itself. A sign that Volkia could not bring the arisen worlds under its control. He believed in her, past what he should. Even though the thing she was doing seemed reckless. Entering the great city-palace and fortress of Osta Kiya.

But she had told him on the journey from the polity, "If we succeed in bringing Valenty out, if a few women dressed as *satvars* could do such a thing, it strikes a blow. It tells the Numinasi people that there are those who don't accept the false princip."

He had nodded, liking this. "One slash on the bear's face is a victory, if you are a fox."

She heard him repeat the saying to Janov. It circulated in the encampment. The soldiers and the *harjat* liked Yevliesza's plan, the daring of it. It lifted her spirits to see the camp behind her.

As she had expected, Pyvel begged to go. Her answer, a perfect one. "But Pyvel, you are not a woman."

That got a smile out of him. A small one, but it was good to see.

Two nights later they left the camp in darkness, the three of them, Yevliesza, Rusadka, and Elivasa. Three horses on leads, in case Mura and Carlaty and the High Mother were exposed and had to run. The wind tore down the canyon, pushing at their backs; spume from the river hit their legs, making for a cold ride.

They rode single file down the strand, Rusadka in the lead, then out of the gorge through Crescent Gap, and up into the rolling hills beyond the river canyon. The weather was unsettled. And rain, especially, could interfere with the rites in the palace courtyard. They counted on the vigil but had a backup plan.

They rode on under the nearly full moon, the rumpled hills they passed through giving them cover from army scouts. Yevliesza knew Mitri's ways by now, his gait, from walking to gallop, and his calmness. If one of the horses spooked at a grouse or a rabbit, Mitri stayed firm. She kept her heels down in the stirrups and stopped thinking so much about riding, letting Mitri show her the way.

Elivasa came to ride beside her. "We do not want wind tomorrow. Not wind like this."

Yevliesza knew it. Elivasa was a powerful elementalist. But the wind could dispel any fog she conjured, and for an elementalist, wind was harder to control.

When Yevliesza asked Rusadka about the wind, she said, "By the middle of tomorrow night, maybe it stops. But if not, the Devi Ilsat's attendant, Yarna, will keep a haze around you. And Elivasa will help her."

If she had time. Elivasa would be stalking soldiers.

Still, Rusadka's assurance settled her. Her friend was not worried— did not *seem* worried—about the wind. About capture. All the things that could happen now that they were walking into Sofiyana's den.

The hours passed as they made their way through a terrain of low hills dotted with sagebrush and stunted trees. Their only sightings were of hawks and the occasional deer. At midday, when Osta Kiya was almost in view, they made camp in a narrow defile with a few shrubs and willow trees. They brought out grain for the horses, dried meat and bread for themselves.

Yevliesza climbed the slope to keep the first watch as the others caught up on sleep. In the bright sky, clouds flattened and streamed, riding the wind. Tomorrow they would quietly enter the great fortress of Osta Kiya. Her hand touched her neck. No talisman of the nine stones, left behind in the Mist Wall. She loved the memory of that gift. She remembered her mother's voice: *You cannot sleep here.* Stay awake. Awake to it all.

She went over the plans for the next night. They would be dressed in the oat-colored tunics and trousers of *satvars*. All except for Rusadka, who would not go in. She could not, being too recognizable: her dark skin, her *harjat's* build. Her role would be on the outside. Approaching the fortress at just the right time of night was critical; Carlaty meeting them to confirm that a Great Circle would be a part of the Blossom Moon observance; bringing Valenty out, with Rusadka taking him on her mount.

She imagined being with him again. He would be distant, confused. Urik had prepared her for how ensorcellment looked, having seen Pyvel infected. But still, she would be with Valenty again, however he was.

Before sunset, they would break camp and move into the steppe lands toward their destination. How strange it was to be returning to Osta Kiya this way. But it had all been strange, every day of her life here since she first flew on a dactyl and saw the alter-earth unfolding below her. And becoming wounded—in body and heart—and falling in love with everything, even the hard things.

She looked down the slope to see that her companions had lain down to rest in each other's arms. Rusadka loved Elivasa, this unlikely woman who looked like a noblewoman—who *was* one—but who could fight like a badger and knew how hide in the shadows. A spy. Like Valenty.

They seemed well-suited for each other, but Yevliesza found herself just a little put out that she was no longer Rusadka's closest friend. Or maybe it wasn't that. Maybe it reminded her what normal people could have. But that was wrong, too. People chose. She had chosen.

She turned back to her watch, thinking of what was to come. The right time frame to approach the castle in the dark was short. At heavy dusk they would be impossible to see from a great distance. That advantage would improve as true night took over the flats. Until moonrise. The full moon. So for a little while they had cover to get to the foot of the great outcropping on which Osta Kiya was perched. Once in that relative shelter, they would be hard to make out.

Just the two of them, she and Elivasa, dressed as *satvars*, climbing the thousand stairs.

Chapter Forty-Seven

"**B**ut I have never brought forth a storm before!" Yarna whispered, her face twisted with anxiety as she walked the roof garden with the High Mother.

"No one is talking about a storm. A fog, my dear. Only a fog."

"Or a fog!"

Yarna had dispelled snow from wintertime paths, melted barriers of ice, and now she could not create a mist? "Go into the courtyard grove and give it a wee try."

"What if they catch me?"

"It is a cloudy day. No one will arrest you for a little fog."

"Yes, Mother," Yarna said, mouse-like. She was not one for plots and intrigues. She would never make it to *satvadeya* rank.

Yarna left to practice her fog. Below in the palace, Mura and Carlaty remained in their shared room except for meals, and even at those occasions it would be highly unlikely that they would encounter any soldiers, much less any they once knew. As for appearing at the Blossom Moon rite, a few people knew that the Devi Ilsat had received a few visitors from the *satvary*, but there might well be confusion about just how many *satvar* visitors there were. If anyone was counting.

For her own part, the vigil would be difficult to manage in exactly the right way. She would come out at sunset, as agreed upon with Sofiyana, and be the first to take a position, seated on the east side of the Great Circle. Of course the moon would not be visible over the ramparts until later. That early in the evening people might join her in the silent vigil, either in the circle or near it. Eventually Yevliesza and Carlaty would take positions on the circle on the north side to discourage Sofiyana and Valenty from using that point on the circle, so that they might choose to stand on, or near, the south side nearest the grove of trees. Then they had cooked up a way to sow confusion so that Valenty could be snatched from his guards. And what a confusion it would be!

She had been told not to help. Only one assignment, to greet Valenty, gripping him hard, sending at least a little healing into him. Then to act terrified and confused. Such behavior on her part would not be dignified nor set a good example for handling a crisis. But this was not Zolvina. It was the den of monsters.

She had let Lady Ineska know that she hoped Valenty would be allowed to join the vigil. Because of his decision to become a *satvar*. A show of unity and reconciliation, she had suggested to the *fajatim*. Ineska likely did not believe the *satvar* vow idea, but she still had enough wits about her to want such a show for Valenty's sake, to protect him from the usual sentence for treason.

The plan seemed good. Or at least adequate. Now all she had to do was wait.

And worry.

❦

Hugging the side of the castle, Yevliesza and Elivasa looked down at the plains, down the steep side of the granite perch. At their backs were the ancient stones of Osta Kiya melded into the still more ancient rock outcropping. A narrow footpath circled it like a torc. The night had settled into calm except for errant gusts that yanked at their tunics and trousers. Not strong enough to push them over the edge, the edge that didn't bear thinking about, dropping to the far distant plains.

Carlaty met them at the opening of the stormwater outfall. Above them, the Tower loomed, its mass blended into the dark vault of the sky. Below them, the rest of the fall. The plunge down from the Trespass Door. Yevliesza could not help but think of Lord Michai, once Anastyna's chamberlain. Accused of treason. His punishment a horror.

"Do not fall," Yevliesza whispered to Elivasa as the woman edged past her to help move the gate aside. Elivasa squeezed Yevliesza's arm in reply. It was Elivasa who knew of the drainage channel. That a gate covered it, one that was heavily barred on the inside. It was the escape route that Valenty had planned for Anastyna, a route that connected with the royal apartments, and one that Anastyna might have used to escape had she not refused to run.

Carlaty slid the bar from its heavy slot, and the three of them managed to open the gate, releasing a scream of metal that almost stopped Yevliesza's heart.

Once inside, they huddled in the channel, dry now, lined up along the length as Carlaty relayed all that she knew about the ritual, now underway. As planned, the Devi Ilsat was already sitting vigil there, and before long the princip and the *fajatim* would join her. Once key locations on the circle were taken, people would fill in the circle so that hands might join. More people than expected had come early to join the High Mother, about one hundred so far. Most did not presume to take a place on the circle but took up places nearby. Perhaps the growing numbers in the courtyard showed how unsettled people felt, with the former princip fled; the deaths at the Tower; the coming invasion, the one the Volkish were surely planning.

Whether Valenty would be in the circle was the one thing they didn't know. Sofiyana had not promised but was considering it. The Devi Ilsat said that *fajatim* Ineska hoped that he would be allowed to come and might be cajoling Sofiyana into doing it. It was not clear to the Devi Ilsat how much sorcerous control Ineska was under, and whether she believed that Valenty would give himself over to the life of a *satvar,* as the High Mother's rumor had it.

In the semi-dark, Yevliesza heard Elivasa mutter, "Renunciation is not his strongest gift."

Yevliesza found herself smiling. She tried to imagine Valenty living that life, and failed, utterly.

"There is news of Volkia," Carlaty said. "The palace has heard that Prince Albrecht is dead."

Dead? "Is he?" Yevliesza whispered.

"Killed fighting in Alfan Sih. He was part of an action on the front lines. So they say."

"Good, the bastard," Elivasa said.

Died in Alfan Sih? A soldier's death, but they might claim that, not wanting to say that he had died of her knife wound. In the crossings.

Hard to believe he was gone, even if she had hoped for it. But if he was dead, how had he been a traveler in the Mist Wall? Her conversation with Valenty in the ale house. How Kiya had attacked Albrecht. Attacked him but couldn't kill him. A mystery. It all depended on when he died. If weeks ago from the knifing, then he had been no more real than the young Nashavety. But if he died only a few days ago, then at the time she had the Mist Wall experience, he had still been alive to be a traveler.

Carlaty was now manifesting a glow to light their way. Time to go.

They made their way through the tunnel, following Carlaty and her light. Albrecht's death seemed unreal. A menacing presence, often in her thoughts. Now gone. She was glad of it, but what would come next for Volkia? Was it a chance for Volkia to come back to the light? Maybe Duke Tanfred succeeding him? But that was a foolish dream. Tanfred would by now be a hunted traitor.

Carlaty's voice in the darkness. "They say that a Volkish noble named Count Reinhart has stepped up to the role of commandant." A matter-of-fact tone of voice for such ugly news.

Reinhart. Even worse than the man he replaced.

They continued beneath the palace's great halls, a place of vast silences and stoic calm. Carlaty had entered the drainage tunnel from one of the abandoned rooms under the ground floor. The three of them couldn't take that route, because at some point they would emerge into a major palace corridor and be seen. Even though they were disguised as *satvars*, it would look odd for them to emerge from the basement rooms.

Elivasa knew the way to an offshoot tunnel leading to one of Valenty's household chambers. It was the route that continued all the way to a small room in the royal apartments, a path he had taken many times for secret meetings with Anastyna. She said that the room they needed was the scriptorium, a room Yevliesza remembered for its books and scrolls.

They took this route. At times the tunnel narrowed so much that they had to turn sideways, but eventually the three of them entered the scriptorium, where a thick tapestry hid a gap in the wall.

They peered out the window to see the courtyard and the Great Circle slowly filling with people. They could just make out the Devi Ilsat's pale uniform as she sat by herself on the east side of the circle. Hard to see, because manifesting globes were not enlivened, the better to view the full moon. Carlaty said that when the moon was at its highest point, the song of the Blossom Moon would fill the courtyard. By Yevliesza's gauge, that would be in about two hours.

The three of them sat on the floor to rest.

"What are you thinking about?" Yevliesza asked Elivasa. She wondered if the experienced spy was as calm as she looked.

"I am not sure who to worry about more. Valenty or Rusadka."

Yevliesza was glad she wasn't the only anxious one. "I'm nervous, all of a sudden."

"When you escaped Volkia," Elivasa said, "you fooled Prince Albrecht and the Volkish officers in the crossings. Maybe harder than grabbing a prisoner from a yard."

Elivasa was trying to bolster her confidence. And what she said was true. When desperate enough, you could do more than you ever thought.

Yevliesza turned to Carlaty. "Mura has the hardest role. Is she ready?"

"She has practiced. Her manifestation will be very convincing."

It would need to be.

"Mura knows that when we have him she must get to Valenty's residence ahead of us? To tell the household staff we will be coming?"

"She knows."

"I think your role will be the hardest," Carlaty said. "You must get Valenty to come with us."

How strange it would be if he refused.

Chapter Forty-Eight

The High Mother sat cross-legged on the circle. As the gathering in the courtyard multiplied, most people were standing, but the Devi Ilsat's vigil had already been long, and no one could complain if an old renunciate sat.

The moon was high now, approaching the zenith. She wanted to appear deep in concentration, but she kept her eyes half-lidded, watching and scheming instead of dwelling in respectful calm. To subvert the ritual in this way was troubling, but now was no time for niceties.

She occupied the point on the Great Circle directly across from the west point, upon which Yarna now stood. Usually a person of consequence took the east position, but she hoped that a few odd behaviors would be tolerated from guests.

A gentle mist rose from the ground near Yarna, hardly noticeable as it spread on the breeze. But Yarna would have help from another elementalist who would be secretly entering the palace tonight.

She noted two women in *satvar* dress now making their way around the circle to the north point, the one closest to the Tower. In the darkness, she dared open her eyes to make sure one of them was

Yevliesza. But then she remembered that Yevliesza's features would appear altered. Disguised. Yevliesza, who had risked everything to come for Valenty. Risked far more than she should have. *You foolish girl, may the Mythos protect you.*

From far across the courtyard, someone began to sing, the lovely melody of this full moon. Time to stand. She managed to get up without toppling over, not as easy as people might think.

She watched for the *fajatim*. They would precede Sofiyana, who would hopefully take the circle's south point near the trees. Ideally, Valenty would be positioned near her on that side. Once separated from his guard, he would be near a door, or nearer a door than at other segments of the circle. If circumstances warranted, they could take him into the trees and thence into a door on the opposite arm of the castle.

Presumably the fog brought by the elementalists would provide some cover. But by the looks of the courtyard, they should work faster.

⚜

THE GREAT CIRCLE OF THE MOON CAST A GENTLE SILVER LIGHT OVER the yard. Hundreds of people had now arrived, standing silent. Many more stood at castle windows and on balconies. Repeatedly, the song of the Blossom Moon spontaneously began and faded.

Yevliesza felt exposed, standing on the circle. She wished she had a mirror to convince herself that she didn't look like herself. Carlaty's changed features were reassuring: her chin, too square, forehead too high.

To Yevliesza, the six *satvars* in the courtyard were painfully obvious. She had seen Mura standing on the edge of the crowd near the Tower, and Elivasa on the other side of the courtyard, near the grove. Yarna was on the circle, across the way. People might wonder how many *satvars* had come to visit the High Mother. Where had *six* come from?

At times the wind gusted, dispelling the fog. When Rusadka set a fire in the stables it would contribute to the murk. That diversion had to come at exactly the right time. And Mura's manifestation. Could she make it convincing? Would anyone notice that it was a *satvar* who provided the voice? Mura was, after all, standing in the open. But by then, chaos.

No one will notice, she murmured.

"Stop fidgeting," Carlaty muttered.

"Am I?"

"By the great almighty Deep, yes."

The mist was growing thicker. Now a light fog. But the higher the mist rose from the ground, the more the breeze lofted it away. Why weren't Yarna and Elivasa working faster?

"Here they come," Carlaty said in a low voice.

From the main palace door, the *fajatim* approached as a group. Right behind them, Sofiyana. Two guards accompanied her. In back, Valenty, walking with his own guard. In the crowd, more soldiers.

As hoped, Sofiyana took a position on the south point. Between her and Valenty, two guards. Always one to ignore the court's custom of women wearing dark or dull colors, she wore a bright green gown. A statement. Green for the Blossom Moon. Her reign of verdure.

Unexpectedly, the *fajatim* separated into two groups, flanking Sofiyana and Valenty. Another layer of protection. Sofiyana growing paranoid.

Yevliesza strained to see Valenty. "Is it him?" she whispered.

"Someone dressed as a nobleman . . . Ah yes, it is Valenty."

THE DEVI ILSAT HAD LEFT HER PLACE ON THE CIRCLE AND WAS walking toward Sofiyana and Valenty, only a few yards away. The spontaneous singing grew louder, now swelling with hundreds of voices.

The Devi Ilsat bowed to Sofiyana and murmured, "In your great journey, may you find freedom." An ambiguous blessing, but it was all she could bring herself to say.

Turning to Valenty, she approached him with her arms outstretched. One of the guards moved to stop her, but she was already murmuring blessings and quickly took Valenty into an embrace.

"Wake and be healed," she whispered into his neck, expecting at any moment to be yanked away by the guards. She felt the dark bestial magic swirling under his skin. "I banish all sorcery from you, now and forever." The sorcery shied from her—she felt it recede—but it still bound him. There was more to give, and she had only a moment to decide. Her own life energy held potent healing, but it would put her at peril. Without another thought, she gripped his upper arms, holding on for a moment longer, sending her utmost healing into him. When she pulled away, she staggered, but kept her feet.

Forcing a vacant smile onto her face, she turned away and managed to walk back to her place on the circle.

A hearty-looking woman who stood next to her, took her hand to complete the circle once more, but looked worried. "High Mother, do you fare well?"

"Yes, my daughter. But perhaps you could hold on a little tighter."

Soon she would be able to sit down on the grass. Once people started yelling and running, no one would notice an old woman collapsing.

❧

It would be anytime now. Yevliesza stood, senses acute, waiting for a tremor in the crowd, a stirring from something gone wrong. Carlaty, next to her, waiting in stillness as though before a battle.

And then it came, a murmur growing around her. Not in the circle, but outside it in the surrounding courtyard. Someone pointed at the Tower. And then a few more. Now, instead of gazing at the moon as it occupied its highest point in the sky, people were staring at the Tower.

Yevliesza managed to keep hold of Carlaty's hand as she twisted around to look where people were pointing. "It's there," she whispered. Mura had begun her manifestation.

One of the three doors at the top of the Tower was on the courtyard side. A woman wearing a silver gown stood in the doorway. Exclamations rose from the gathering. Was she going to jump? Though it was beyond Mura's power to make it look like Anastyna, people would recall how the former princip had often worn a silver gown.

Then came the voice: "Free us from sorcery! Free our land!"

The figure in the Tower door pleadingly reached out a hand. "Nashavety controls Sofiyana! Let Anastyna protect you!"

Gasps rose from the crowd as several guards ran from the yard into the castle.

Sofiyana recoiled, releasing the hands of the guards on each side of her. She pointed to the Tower, giving orders.

Again, the loud call: "Sofiyana is full of sorcery!"

As more people surged toward the Tower, Mura stopped calling out but maintained the image in the doorway with her strong affinity. The effect of the image jolted the courtyard from peace to mayhem. People shouted and milled in agitation, some of them surging toward the Tower for a closer look, others fleeing the yard in panic.

The first wisps of smoke came in on the breeze. Soldiers from the barracks were running across the far end of the courtyard toward the steps leading down to the stables.

In the confusion, Yevliesza and Carlaty rushed across the circle toward Valenty. Yarna had already broken ranks and moved close to him, bringing up a cloaking fog.

Elivasa, who had been lurking in the crowd, was busy in the murk using her knife to take down soldiers. Yevliesza ran into the melee, grabbing Valenty. He resisted her, but not with his whole strength. Carlaty was there a moment later, taking Valenty's other arm. "The trees," Carlaty told her, judging their best route.

They half-walked, half-dragged Valenty toward the grove just as a gust of wind suddenly cleared the area of fog. They were starkly exposed, twenty yards from the shelter of the trees.

One of the *fajatim*—Ineska, Yevliesza saw—pointed to the roof. "More of them up there!" she screamed, and the few soldiers around them looked to the ramparts.

Fog still swirled in places, adding to the confusion. As time slowed to a crawl, Yevliesza glimpsed Yarna standing in the middle of things, eyes closed, working on fog.

By this renewed cover Yevliesza and Carlaty entered the grove of trees. There, by the bench in a clearing, the cloak they would use to disguise Valenty. And a sword in case of need. The soldiers in the courtyard all had swords; the imitation *satvars*, only knives strapped to their ankles. Carlaty grabbed the cloak.

Thick smoke surged through the trees. The wind, earlier their enemy, was blowing the smoke into the courtyard from the stables below.

Yevliesza took hold of Valenty's shoulders. "Valenty, it's me!"

He looked directly into her eyes. "Reckless as ever," he fiercely said. "By the eight hells, give me a weapon."

Carlaty threw the cloak around Valenty's shoulders, and he fastened the ties.

Yevliesza was so startled by his clear headedness that she didn't immediately notice the sound of someone approaching the small clearing where they stood.

A soldier came into the clearing, followed by two more.

"Thank goodness!" Carlaty said, running to them. "That way!" She pointed in the direction opposite of the one they planned to take.

But she had forgotten to disguise herself.

The foremost soldier raised his sword. "You are no *satvar*. Carlaty the traitor." He advanced as the other two soldiers stalked toward Valenty, swords drawn. Valenty dove for the sword, for a moment putting the bench between him and his attackers.

They approached him on two sides, and he spun around, slicing his sword in a vicious circle. They stepped away, then advanced again.

Carlaty had snatched a knife from its sheath at her ankle and backed into the woods, using trees to deflect the sword swipes from the first soldier. Her knife, no match for the longer blade.

One soldier came in close to Valenty, holding his sword above and behind his head, ready to strike, but Valenty lunged forward, kicking him hard. Then he pivoted to face the second soldier, an agile fighter, the man's blade already descending. He met it with the flat of his blade, deflecting the blow. As the man swayed from the jarring contact, Valenty moved in and punched him in the face with the cross guard of his sword.

Already the other soldier was advancing, leading with his sword. Valenty swung his own blade down to meet the advance, and their weapons clanged. They separated, as the soldier that Valenty had kicked found his feet again. They came at him from two directions.

Yevliesza drew her knife and started forward to somehow distract one of the attackers.

"Get back!" Elivasa had finally joined them and swiftly advanced, having found a sword somewhere in the mayhem. She swung her arm against Yevliesza, sending her staggering, and without pausing, engaged one of Valenty's men with her sword.

He gave Elivasa a lopsided grin. "A *satvar* with a sword? You might hurt yourself with that."

"I had other ideas," she threw back, raising her weapon and waiting for his move.

Yevliesza watched, frozen in place, as swords cracked against each other with murderous blows. Elivasa was overmatched, desperately dancing out of the soldier's way, using the close trees to hamper his sword swings.

Valenty was grappling closely with his now lone attacker, their swords useless, but held in their hands. At close quarters, the soldier jammed an elbow into Valenty's neck with such force that Valenty fell on his back. As the soldier rushed forward to finish him, Valenty brought his weapon up and gutted the man with an upward thrust.

On his feet again, Valenty swept past Yevliesza to help Elivasa, coming upon her attacker from behind, and brought his sword in a slice across the back of his neck. The man fell.

They looked for Carlaty. There was no sign of her.

Elivasa snapped at Valenty, "Drop the sword and come with me. Hood up!"

Valenty held out his hand for Yevliesza.

"No, go!" she said, sticking to their plan. Not too many people walking together. When he came to grab her arm, she hissed, "My plan. My rules. Go!"

His hand came around her upper arm. "How has your plan worked so far?"

"My goddamn plan, Valenty," Yevliesza spat at him.

Elivasa hissed, "Now!"

"I will meet you," Yevliesza said, trying a brave smile. "Go."

Valenty paused, looking at her fiercely. Then, with Elivasa practically dragging him away, he disappeared into the trees.

She and Carlaty were to leave together, two *satvars* walking in a dignified manner, hopefully not streaked with blood.

Yevliesza glimpsed shapes in the smoke-shrouded trees. Carlaty and her opponent. She picked up one of the cast-off swords and crept deeper into the grove.

A flutter of green silk. And then the whole shape. Sofiyana.

She had a knife. Their eyes met, and Sofiyana lunged, leading with her knife, missing, but ramming hard enough into Yevliesza to send her sprawling, jarring the sword from her hand. Sofiyana rounded on her, rushing forward, but her knife hand was caught by her skirts. From her position on the ground, Yevliesza slammed her foot into Sofiyana's stomach, knocking her over.

Grabbing her fallen sword, she swung it back, low to the ground, and hit Sofiyana in the side of the head with the flat of the blade. Sofiyana screamed and tried to scramble to her feet but Yevliesza jumped on her, pounding her face with a fist. Once, twice, again.

At last Sofiyana lay gasping, unable to rally.

Yevliesza was still on top of her. She bent close to her. "Get clear of sorcery, Sofiyana, or we will kill you." She paused, out of breath. "But," she hissed, "not tonight."

She looked at the torc, and for a moment considered how to get it off Sofiyana's neck, but there was no time.

Carlaty had come. She helped Yevliesza to her feet.

"Where is the soldier?" Yevliesza asked, breathing hard.

"Lying dead."

They left Sofiyana on the ground where she lay and walked out of the trees. Around them figures moved through the smoke. Soldiers and citizens, the soldiers now scouring for Sofiyana. It would not be long before they found her.

Carlaty threw a disguise on Yevliesza as they hurried through the palace toward the scriptorium. When they arrived at Valenty's apartments, they found Mura waiting inside the entryway with four of the household staff. All of them looked up as Yevliesza and Carlaty entered.

"Valenty?" Yevliesza asked. The house steward said, "He has already come through, but hurry, lest someone check here."

Yevliesza murmured low to Mura, "How is the High Mother?"

"Sitting in the Great Circle. A bout of dizziness."

"And Yarna?"

"Crying and whimpering. Perhaps sincerely."

Safe then. An old woman and her assistant undone by chaos in the courtyard.

Carlaty nodded to Yevliesza and left the room with Mura, to go back into the castle halls. The two of them would stay behind. The High Mother's companions, acting dazed and frightened. Soon to be dressed in new, bloodless tunics.

A few moments later, loud banging on the hall door.

The steward looked at Yevliesza, waiting for her to disappear. Yevliesza raced toward the scriptorium.

Standing in the room, holding a richly embellished sword, Valenty.

"It was a good plan," he said, taking her into his arms. A brief embrace, and then he held her at arms' length. "But you know there are archers on the roof."

"Unavoidable," Yevliesza said, unwilling to show her vast relief when they had so much yet to do.

Their escape down to the plains of Osta Kiya passed like a slow-motion dance.

The close passageway through the stone walls, the drainage channel where Elivasa waited for them, then outside, the high, narrow path to the stairs. Outside, the air too bright, with the moon turning against them, gilding every move with silver.

Shouts from the ramparts. Elivasa had brought swirling fog, but it was not enough. As arrows pierced the air around them, Valenty raised his left hand and drew a warding over them. As they clambered down the stairs, the shower of arrows continued to fall. Soldiers had now arrived on the stairs above, rushing down, but Yevliesza, Valenty, and Elivasa reached their horses first.

Rusadka was there, noticing before anyone else that Valenty had taken an arrow. She shouted to Elivasa. "Valenty is wounded. Help him up!"

Quickly, Elivasa boosted him up behind Rusadka.

Yevliesza, her heart sinking at the news that Valenty was hurt, jammed a boot in Mitri's stirrup and threw herself ungracefully into the saddle.

"Hold on for your life!" Rusadka cried at Valenty. She set off at a gallop.

Elivasa slapped the extra horses on the rumps, shouting at them to send them out of reach, and then she and Yevliesza left Osta Kiya just as the soldiers reached the bottom of the stairs.

From around the other side of the towering hill, mounted soldiers were spilling onto the flats. Rusadka had scattered the horses from the stable, but they had not gone far, and dozens of soldiers were now in pursuit.

Their only chance was to outrun them. They could do it. Yevliesza thought they had just enough lead time as they charged onto the plain. Mitri ran like the devil was chasing them, not far from the truth, his gallop sturdy and thunderous.

If they could make it into the folded hills near the river, a tributary of the Yanuri, they might lose their pursuers.

But Yevliesza was falling behind.

Ahead, she saw Elivasa pointing in front of her, as though they needed to know what direction to go in.

But Elivasa wasn't pointing in the right direction.

She was pointing at a line of riders that Yevliesza could just make out in the distance.

Was it her imagination, this army on the horizon? But as they raced onward, the mirage became reality. It was an army, Anastyna's army, she dared to hope, but larger than before. Yevliesza shouted in joy and let Mitri carry her onward.

As they drew close, the ranks opened to receive them. Soldiers on horses, soldiers on foot. Urik, amid the mounted ones, watching the enemy approach.

Kirady at his side, having brought his troops. Down from Eiger Polity, it must have been. Three, four hundred of them.

Rusadka was helping Valenty down from the saddle, as out from the ranks came Grigeni. Yevliesza started to dismount to go with him, but Rusadka said, "A healer, first. Let them do their work."

Grigeni ran to Valenty and, seeing that he was able to walk, guided him on foot to the rear of the troops.

Yevliesza turned her horse to ride up the small slope to the ridge where Urik sat his horse among dozens of *harjat*.

He glanced at her, his eyebrow raised, perhaps for her having brought a horde of Sofiyana's soldiers onto the plains. "So you are back."

"Someone had to get him."

"A good fight, was it?" he asked. "Your *satvar* Elivasa is covered in blood."

"I almost killed a princip." It sounded bizarre. But it was mostly true.

Urik raised an eyebrow at that, but his attention went back to the plains.

Sofiyana's horde was stopping. They had seen the fighting force waiting for them. The approaching soldiers were milling as they took stock of the odds. They began turning away. They would not come to the fight, not this night.

Urik glanced at her. "Anastyna had doubts. Do not tell her if it was a close thing."

Anastyna had not liked the plan. Now that Yevliesza had value, she did not want to have her at risk.

Dazed, exhausted, almost giddy, Yevliesza turned her mount down the slope. Mitri flattened his ears, as though she was depriving him of another good run. She slowly walked him into the mass of soldiers and went to find Valenty.

Chapter Forty-Nine

He was lying on the ground, eyes closed, his head propped up on a saddle padded with a blanket. A healer sat beside him, his hand resting on the side of Valenty's face. Nearby, soldiers had dismounted and were resting. No battle this time.

A bandage wrapped around Valenty's middle held in place the covering over his injury. "How is the wound?" she asked the healer.

"Which one?" The arrow or the sorcery.

"Both."

"He will heal."

She sat by Valenty's side, watching him sleep.

She thought it a miracle, seeing him there, safe, if not whole. Brought out of the darkness by seven women including the Devi Ilsat, a *harjat*, a *satvar*, a spy, and two soldiers who had an affinity for manifesting. She didn't want to disturb him. But it was not enough to see his face. She wanted more of him, always more. But it had to be less. At least for now, and maybe for always.

Coming awake, he whispered, "Yevliesza?"

She took his hand. "My love."

"Not too long," the healer said, then left them in privacy.

Valenty gazed at her, holding tight to her hand. "I've been . . . in prison. Osta Kiya. It is a prison, now."

"Yes, sadly."

"How is my wound?"

"You took an arrow in your side. It will heal."

"There were *satvars* in the courtyard," he said. "In disguise?"

"Yes. Some of them were army. The High Mother helped. *You* helped."

He started to laugh, then winced. "As much as you would let me." He reached for her hand. "I have been dreaming about you. Every day. I feared for you."

"And I have been crazy with worry for you." She brushed a strand of hair off his forehead, her fingers lingering there.

"How long have I been in prison? Some of the days are lost to me."

She could well imagine. "Seventeen days. Sofiyana had you, and she used her ring. You know what ring I mean."

"Demon power. Because she could not break me any other way."

"You did not break."

They stayed silent awhile, the Blossom Moon finally setting as dawn reclaimed the sky.

"Anastyna," he eventually said. "She is still free."

"She is. In fact, we have . . . reconciled. I told her everything, Valenty."

Now, in fact, Anastyna was standing some thirty yards away, waiting her turn, attendants and advisers around her. And this time, her falcon on her wrist. Her *sympat* had found her, and it made her look more noble, even in her soiled dress and without the torc.

She hadn't reported to Anastyna about the mission. Rusadka would do that. Soon she would learn about Albrecht's death. And add that to her calculations of how the war would go. So much was changing.

She waited another moment to say what she had come to say. Anastyna was waiting. They wouldn't have much more time.

"I'm leaving, Valenty. To do the things I have to do."

"Do you know what you have to do?" He still gripped her hand, stroking her palm with his thumb. Attraction pulled at her.

"I do. But I had to go into the Agarvesky. I met myself in the forest."

A flicker of a smile across his face. "Did you like what you saw?"

And did she? Maybe she didn't like it, what she was, what she had to be, but at least she was sure.

"Yes," she answered. "Because it's all I have." There was an extra blanket lying across the saddle, and she lifted it up, draping it over Valenty's legs and chest. "It's getting cold."

"Where are you going?"

"Here and there. I'll be on the move." She took a chance. "You could come with me. When you recover, you could meet me."

He didn't answer. She had known he wouldn't come, but her heart took a long, bleak fall.

"It's all right," she murmured.

"Do not go," he said, his face now troubled, but whether from the arrow or her leaving, she didn't know.

"Always know that I love you," she whispered.

"Stay with me, Yevliesza. We can fight them together."

But they couldn't, not if he was staying here, with Anastyna. As she knew he would. His duty. His father before him, serving the princip.

She bent down and lightly kissed him.

His hand came up to the back of her neck, cupping it. "I will find you again."

The words pierced her, and her eyes blurred.

A movement behind her. Anastyna. Yevliesza stood up, nodding in respect. She paused, looking down at Valenty, and managing to smile. A barely perceptible smile crossed his face. How you say goodbye.

As she walked away, the consoling thought came that she would at least be far away from Anastyna and her politics.

And the sweeter thought: *I will find you again.*

She went in search of Janov and Kirady, to tell them that she would set out that night. She had to leave quickly, or she would be tied to Valenty. His recovery. To endlessly discuss the ninth power, what it could do, what she should do. There was no place to go with that. And she had already given him up once, in the Mist Wall. Better to leave in the night, find her own camp, if Mitri could go some distance, as tired as he might be. They needed rest. But not here.

A few cookfires flared. Not cold rations for the troops, not for the officers. She found Kirady at one.

The Lord Warden walked with her to the edge of the camp, explaining that he would stay with the princip, as he called her, his troops augmenting Anastyna's few. But not at the river. She needed a stronghold.

Janov would go with Yevliesza, if she would have him, Kirady said. He would appoint another village master for Branova. If she would have him.

"Gladly," she said.

Kirady nodded, then pointed out into the plains. "Your wolf is waiting for you."

She squinted into the dawn light to catch a glimpse, but she didn't see Kiya.

"Janov told me." He shrugged. "Wolf Keeper." He gave her a knowing look. "Not an ordinary wolf."

"He comes and goes," she said. Then she wondered. "You have creature power?"

"I do, but I like to think this wolf allowed me to see it. Not a mistake. An honor, perhaps."

He turned as he noted someone approaching. Rusadka. "I will get back to my troops. And I will tell Janov to find you."

"Thank you, Lord Warden. For all you've done."

He nodded. "We both serve." He looked out to the flats, hoping to see the wolf again, and then took his leave.

Rusadka approached, leading her mount.

"Anastyna released me," she said. "Do we overnight here, or move on?"

Always one to get to the point. "What about Elivasa?"

"She will join us in due course. Anastyna wants her to help with recruitment."

All squared away, then, Yevliesza thought, suddenly happier than she had felt in a long time. "So I have two who will follow me?" Rusadka and Janov.

Rusadka looked behind her, noting five soldiers leading their horses toward them. By their colors, Kirady's men.

"Seven," Rusadka said, grinning. "More than enough."

~*~

Follow Yevliesza, Valenty, and Rusadka to the story's conclusion in book four, *Keeper of the Mythos Gate*. Coming soon!

Acknowledgments

Each time I write a novel, I go through a stage when I wonder if I can carry it off. It is at times like these that I especially appreciate the encouragement of others, including family, friends, devoted readers, and fellow authors.

For standing by me and my novelistic endeavors, I want first of all to thank my husband, Thomas Overcast, for assuring me that I know exactly what I'm doing (and for believing this in the first place!) and for his steadfast support in all things, writerly and the rest of life.

My deep thanks to fellow writers Sharon Shinn, Louise Marley, Theresa Monsey, and Melody Kreimes for assistance and support. My appreciation to Jim Thomsen for his skillful copyediting throughout this series.

The Arisen Worlds series would never have seen the light of day without the advice and enthusiasm of Anthea Sharp, a superb guide in the paths of independent publishing as well as staying the course in the complex new world of publishing. To her, I owe a special debt of gratitude.

Thank you to my advance readers who helped me to refine the story and tell it smoothly: Michele L. Casteel, Charles Hirst, Marilyn Holt, Morgan Mead, Marisa Miller, Lisa Montoya, Eric Morris, Veronica Rood, Janet Smith, and Leeann Smith.